Praise for

RORY CLEMENTS

'Dramatic . . . pacy and assured . . . Well crafted, it has all the pleasures of an intriguing lead character, intricate plot and fascinating historical context'

DAILY MAIL

'Rory Clements's timely spy thriller set in the 1930s evokes a period of political polarisation, mistrust and simmering violence. *Corpus* is fast-paced and there are plenty of red herrings to keep you guessing'

THE TIMES

'This clever novel, rich in deceptions and intrigue . . . *Corpus* is a standout historical novel and spy thriller by an author who can turn his hand to any historical period he chooses'

DAILY EXPRESS

'Clements juggles his story's disparate ingredients very skillfully'

LITERARY REVIEW

'A dynamic, fast-moving murder mystery brimming with menace, violence and intrigue . . . This fascinating pre-war era comes breathtakingly and insidiously to life . . . Clements is undoubtedly on to another winner'

LANCASHIRE EVENING POST

'*Corpus* is a compelling novel, the writing is subtle . . . the research makes the plot utterly convincing. Clements kept this reader guessing right up to the last page – and beyond'

HISTORIA MAGAZINE

NUCLEUS

Rory Clements was born on the edge of England in Dover. He was an associate editor at *Today* newspaper, followed by stints at the *Daily Mail* and *Evening Standard*.

Since 2007, Rory has been writing full time in a quiet corner of Norfolk, England, where he lives with his wife, the artist Naomi Clements Wright, and their family. He won the CWA Ellis Peters Historical Award in 2010 for his second novel, *Revenger*; and three of his other novels – *Martyr*, *Prince* and *The Heretics* – have been shortlisted for awards. *Nucleus* is the second of his thriller series featuring Professor Tom Wilde. The first, *Corpus*, is available in paperback from Bonnier Zaffre.

To receive exclusive news about Rory's writing, join Rory Clements's Readers' Club at www.bit.ly/RoryClementsClub and to find out more go to www.roryclements.co.uk.

RORY CLEMENTS
NUCLEUS

ZAFFRE

First published in Great Britain in 2018 by
ZAFFRE PUBLISHING
80–81 Wimpole St, London W1G 9RE
www.zaffrebooks.co.uk

A CIP catalogue record for this book is available from the British Library.

Hardback ISBN: 978–1–78576–371–7
Trade Paperback ISBN: 978–1–78576–372–4

Also available as an ebook

1 3 5 7 9 10 8 6 4 2

Typeset by IDSUK (Data Connection) Ltd
Printed and bound by Clays Ltd, St Ives Plc

Zaffre Publishing is an imprint of Bonnier Zaffre,
a Bonnier Publishing company
www.bonnierzaffre.co.uk
www.bonnierpublishing.co.uk

For Geoff,
A true friend

APRIL 1939

CHAPTER 1

The room was square, airless and its single window was closed. Located on the third floor of the vast IG Farben building, it had been chosen for its bland anonymity and its thick, deadening walls. As a precaution it had been swept for listening devices that morning, but no one expected to find any. Why would anyone bug such a room?

Five men sat at a plain elm-wood table. A sixth, Reinhard Heydrich, paced behind them in his immaculate SS uniform, his profile pale and predatory, his short fair hair oiled away from his smooth, bloodless forehead; his hands clasped behind his back.

At the head of the table sat General Erich Schumann, a man equally at home in the military and scientific worlds. Today he wore a brown civilian suit, with a party badge at the collar. As a scientist, he was known for his work with explosives and acoustics. As a soldier, he was head of research at the *Heereswaffenamt*, the Army Ordnance Office. As a man of culture and the grandson of the composer Robert Schumann, he liked to think of himself as something of a musical genius in his own right.

Next to him, and less prepossessing, was his younger and cleverer subordinate Kurt Diebner, a nuclear physicist. His thinning hair was swept back, his eyes encased in round tortoiseshell spectacles.

Sitting opposite Diebner was Otto Ambros, an untidy man with a sandy, greying moustache. For five years he had worked for the chemicals giant IG Farben, developing weapons here in Frankfurt and at various other plants.

The last two men round the table were using aliases, at the insistence of Heydrich. If you had chanced upon them together in a Munich *Bierkeller*, you might have thought them brothers, but they were in fact unrelated. 'Herr Grün' was an agent with the *Abwehr* – military intelligence. His shirt front, bulging across his large frame, was damp with sweat. The other – known to this day only as 'Herr Schwarz' – was an officer in the *Sicherheitdienst* or SD, Heydrich's internal intelligence agency. His eyes followed his master's every move and word.

'Well, gentlemen,' Heydrich said. 'You have been given time to gather your thoughts, and so you will now bring them together. No minutes will be taken at this meeting, and no one will make notes either now or later. Herr Professor Schumann, straight to the point if you please . . .'

Schumann nodded. 'Four days ago, Paul Harteck, who is closely associated with the *Heereswaffenamt*, advised us that a fission weapon – an atomic bomb if you prefer – is no longer the stuff of fiction, but an immediate possibility. This follows recent advances made by Otto Hahn in Berlin and the Joliot-Curies in Paris. In the past twenty-four hours I have spoken with Carl von Weizsäcker, one of the finest of our younger physicists, and he says making such a bomb might be remarkably easy.'

Heydrich stopped pacing. 'Should he not be here?'

Schumann raised a doubtful eyebrow. He respected Weizsäcker's scientific opinions and was impressed that he enjoyed the confidence of his peers, especially Niels Bohr and Werner Heisenberg, but Schumann did not trust him; his loyalty to the party was uncertain. Perhaps as the son of Hitler's second-highest Foreign Office official, he believed himself untouchable. Such men needed to be watched.

'No,' Heydrich agreed. 'Perhaps not.' He resumed his pacing. 'Herr Dr Diebner?'

Diebner's shoulders stiffened and he gave a brisk dip of his head. 'We are pursuing this technology as a matter of urgency. Tomorrow, advanced and targeted research will begin under the auspices of the *Arbeitsgemeinschaft für Kernphysik*. We are gathering together the best men. Unfortunately, the *best* does not necessarily mean the most reliable politically. I will be watching them closely and reporting directly to General Schumann regularly.'

'That alone may not be enough,' Heydrich said.

'Indeed not, Herr *Obergruppenführer*. This is now a race.'

'And you believe the British, French and Americans understand the implications of this, Herr Dr Diebner?'

'Yes, sir. The Paris laboratory has repeated Hahn's experiment and has discovered that secondary neutrons are released in fission, meaning that a runaway chain reaction is possible.'

'A runaway chain reaction?'

'In other words, a bomb. An atomic bomb. Powerful enough to destroy a town, perhaps. The most destructive weapon ever conceived. Everyone in the close-knit world of particle physics knows what it means. I believe there is much excitement in Britain and America.'

'Then it is, indeed, a race,' Heydrich said. 'But this is not the Olympic games. There is no room for sportsmanship here. This is a matter of survival and conquest. Even as we strive for this weapon, we must prevent our enemies acquiring it.'

None of the others spoke.

'As I understand it,' Heydrich continued, 'the pre-eminent laboratory outside Germany is in Cambridge, England.'

'Yes, sir,' Diebner said. 'The Cavendish Laboratory. The atom was first split there.'

'I want to know what they know, and I want to know what they can achieve.'

'Of course, sir.'

'And when we have *all* their knowledge, we will cut the tendons at their heels so that they cannot run, so they cannot even *enter* the race. To which end, I have brought you gentlemen here today.'

The men gazed at each other around the table. There was a shuffling of hands and feet.

Heydrich nodded towards the chemist. 'This is Herr Dr Ambros. He has been doing important work for IG Farben, work which will be at your disposal.' Heydrich's narrow eyes widened a fraction and he nodded to Ambros.

'Thank you, Herr *Obergruppenführer*.' Ambros paused until he was sure he had everyone's full attention. 'We have a new chemical compound – one that we hope will have major implications in the course of any future military campaigns. Full-scale production is planned in the months ahead. We believe – *I* believe – it will perform the task you require in this present operation. It is subtle and transportable. And as far as I am concerned, its use in this operation will have the bonus of being an invaluable test of its effectiveness.'

The room fell silent.

Heydrich turned towards Grün and Schwarz. 'So it is up to you – and to our friends abroad. Herr Ambros is giving you the tool, the Scavenger will give you the means. You will make it work.' He walked over to the door and turned the handle. 'I will return this afternoon, by which time every piece will be in place, every possibility accounted for. Clear heads, gentlemen. Find out what they know, and then destroy them.'

MAY 1939

CHAPTER 2

Geoffrey Lancing felt sick. Above him, the little green biplane circled against a clear sky and prepared to land. He had longed to see his sister again; yet now the moment had come, he was riven with apprehension. The world adored her, but he knew the truth.

Boldbourne was a private airfield. A small, unremarkable place a few miles south of Cambridge, one of many such aerodromes dotted around the English countryside. It had no runway, as such, just a broad, flat expanse of grass. It was of limited use when the rains came and churned the turf to mud, but the land drained well here, so it was fine for its purpose most of the year. Now, in late May, the ground was parched after a dry spring.

There were three buildings: a large corrugated-iron barn that served as a hangar for a couple of light aircraft, and two squat, flat-roofed brick constructions. One of them contained chutes and flying suits and there were some armchairs and a table where fliers and their companions could relax with a flask of tea or a bottle of spirits. The other building was a workshop, where spares, fuel, oil, coolant and the mechanics' tools were stored.

The green biplane was on its final approach now. Clarissa had always been a superb aviatrix and today she was at her best; she came into land with barely a bump. Lancing, standing alone on the concrete apron in front of the buildings, watched nervously. As she taxied towards him, he could see her exquisite face through the screen. She brought the little aeroplane to a halt and killed the engine.

Her telegram two days earlier had sent a shiver through his veins. His sister, the great movie star, was coming home for the summer. She would be staying at Hawksmere Old Hall with the Hardimans, she announced. There would be champagne, jazz, dancing and tennis.

In the past eight years, Geoff Lancing had only seen Clarissa on the silver screen. But now here she was, in the flesh, stepping from the cockpit, more slender and gorgeous than ever, even in her boy's flying jacket, goggles perched on her forehead. Glamour personified. The elder sister he adored and feared in equal measure. What would she demand of him this time? Of all the men in the world who loved her from afar, who genuflected at her very name, only he knew her secrets, and even then not all of them. And yet he could say nothing, for he was in thrall to her.

She was smiling; arms wide for his embrace. A perfunctory kiss on the cheek; then the hug and her exquisite scent enveloping him like a Parisian boudoir.

'Welcome home,' he said. The words seemed hopelessly inadequate.

'Geoffrey, darling, you're so fresh-faced! You're still my baby brother. You don't look a day older.'

Nor did she. She was thirty-two now – two years his senior – but looked younger than ever. The magic of Hollywood, perhaps.

'How was my landing?'

'Oh, you know, not bad for a beginner.'

She laughed and jabbed him in the ribs.

'All right,' he conceded. 'It was perfect, as always.'

'Lovely little thing – Hornet Moth. She was waiting for me when the boat docked at Southampton. But come on, you've got a car for me, yes?'

'Powder-blue Hispano. Devil's own job to get hold of it at such short notice.'

'You're a miracle worker. Let's go. Can't keep the champagne waiting. I want dancing and picnics, cocktails and croquet, and I want to meet all your friends, Geoffrey. Especially the handsome ones.'

'Oh, my friends are all far too dull for you. Swots to a man, just like me.'

'I don't believe that,' she said, grabbing him by the elbow and pulling him along with her. 'What about Tom Wilde? He sounds like fun. You've told me so much about him in your letters, so I must meet him. Just consider yourself my social secretary. So much to talk about, darling. Come on, I'll drive.'

Tom Wilde was ushered into the Oval Office by the president's private secretary, Missy LeHand. Roosevelt was already standing at the side of his enormous desk, his hands gripping the edge, but he made no move towards his guest. Wilde waited by the door, his eyes acclimatising to the light that streamed in through the three high windows behind the president.

'This is Professor Wilde, Mr President,' the secretary said.

'Wilde,' Roosevelt thrust out his right hand, holding firm to the desk with the left. He nodded to his grey-haired secretary and she bowed out, closing the door behind her.

Wilde approached across the oval carpet, then dipped his head in salute. 'Mr President.'

They shook hands.

'It's a pleasure to meet you, Professor Wilde.' He waved towards the leather sofa against the wall. 'Take a seat. I'm sorry to have kept you waiting. Please take a seat. Don't worry about me.'

'Thank you, sir.' Wilde sat down and found himself at a disadvantage; FDR remained standing.

The President noticed his guest's discomfort and smiled. 'I hope you're not put out. It's the devil's own job for me to get myself standing, and I wanted to be on my feet when the German chargé d'affaires arrived. Didn't want that damned Nazi looking down on me. The bastard's gone now. Actually, as Nazis go, Thomsen is a fair enough guy.'

The room was cool and pleasant – an aroma of clean air and polished wood – but the president was sweating and Wilde guessed he was in pain. Paralysed by polio eighteen years earlier at the age of thirty-nine, he fought like a demon to make the world see him as able-bodied and capable of standing at the lectern for speeches or at important events; Wilde was well aware that it was all show. He began to rise. 'I could assist you to your chair if you like, sir.'

'Would you? That would be swell.'

Wilde lent him an arm and guided him to his desk chair.

'Ah, that's a sight better. Now then, Professor Wilde, sit back down again and let me start by saying that I have admired your work from afar for some years.' Roosevelt flipped open a silver box, took out a long cigarette and lit it. As an after thought he proffered the case to Wilde, who shook his head. 'I was most impressed by your book on Sir Francis Walsingham and his destruction of the Queen of Scots.'

'Thank you, sir.'

'Power raw in tooth and claw.' The president grinned, acknowledging kinship with Walsingham across three hundred and fifty years. He drew deep on his cigarette, and then flicked the tip at an ashtray, though there was, as yet, no ash to dislodge. 'But we're not here to discuss the lethal machinations of a spymaster, nor your own literary attributes. What interests me is that you live in England. I am, of course, disappointed that a man of your talents and accomplishments should choose to live out-side America, but let's make use of it. America needs men like you. As a Cambridge don, I guess you meet a lot of well-connected, knowledgeable people, so I ask you this: is there going to be war?'

'Yes, Mr President. And sooner rather than later.'

Roosevelt nodded. 'Did you read my Chicago speech?'

'Yes, sir. And I agreed with every word. The world is about to explode and America will not be protected by the oceans alone.'

There was a knock on the door and a servant appeared with coffee. Roosevelt waved his hand towards the desk and the man put down his tray. 'How do you take it, Wilde?'

'Black. No sugar.'

The servant poured the coffee and backed out of the room with a bow. As the door was about to close, another face appeared round it.

Roosevelt cupped his hand and signalled the newcomer to step for-ward. A man of about fifty emerged from the shadows. His gingery red hair was razored sharp at the sides and back, leaving a thick shock on top. His face was narrow and freckled, and he wore a military uniform, minus cap or jacket.

'Do you know Dexter Flood, Professor?'

Wilde rose to his feet once more. 'We haven't met, sir, but of course I know of him.'

'Colonel Flood is presently seconded to the War Department, on the Army General Staff, though like you he has a background in academia.'

Flood crossed the room and shook Wilde's hand. 'Good to meet you, Professor. I've heard a lot about you.'

Had he? What had he heard? Wilde certainly knew something of Flood. In the early thirties, he had attended a lecture he gave: *Friends and Enemies: Fascism and Bolshevism in the Old World.* Flood had taken a hawkish line against the Soviet Union; less so against the fascist movements in Europe. Perhaps that had been understandable before the full threat of Hitler and Mussolini became clear.

'Colonel Flood is central to the reason I asked you here, Tom. If you agree to help us, he'll be your point of contact.'

Why *had* he been summoned here? The question had troubled and intrigued Wilde since the invitation arrived by courier at his mother's Boston home two days ago.

'Oh, you have to go, Tom!' his mother had insisted. 'An invitation from the president? Of course you have to accept!'

Wilde had shrugged. Of course he'd go, but he was more than a little surprised; he had no idea Roosevelt had even heard of him.

Flood poured himself a coffee and cream and spooned in sugar, then took a hard-back chair to the right of Wilde. He had a pad of lined paper and he unscrewed a large red fountain pen. He scribbled a heading at the top of the pad, and then underlined it.

'OK then, here's a straight question, Professor Wilde,' Roosevelt said, 'and I want a yes/no answer, one that hasn't been filtered through embassies and the State Department. Where does England stand in all this? Are they expecting to be part of this coming war?'

Once again, Wilde did not hesitate in replying. 'Yes.'

'They won't just roll over? They're not going to sign up to some kind of dishonourable fudge with the Hun?'

'No. That won't happen, not after Czechoslovakia, though there are some who would wish it so.'

Roosevelt nodded slowly, as though Wilde were confirming something he already suspected. 'Now tell me about morale. Do the British think they can win? Because Joe Kennedy and plenty of others sure don't think they can.'

'I don't think it ever occurs to the British that they could possibly lose. The last time they lost a war was against us a couple of centuries back.'

Roosevelt laughed out loud as he stubbed his cigarette in the ashtray, immediately fishing in his silver box for a fresh one. 'The history man speaks.'

'But people aren't happy about the prospect of war. Many fought in the trenches and they don't want it to happen again.'

'That's understandable.'

Wilde had always liked what he read about Franklin Delano Roosevelt. He was a man of intellect and high education who managed to communicate with the working man and woman and make them believe he was on their side. The evidence seemed to prove their faith was justified. But you could never be sure, not with politicians. Any history man would tell you that.

'How long have you been home, Wilde?'

'Ten weeks, Mr President, much of it visiting my mother in Boston. I've given some lectures at the east coast universities, tried to sell a few copies of my new biography of Sir Robert Cecil and I've listened to some blues and jazz.' He had also spent hours at the graveside of his late wife, Charlotte, and their child, talking to her about Lydia, asking her thoughts and advice. But that wasn't something he needed to share.

'And you're going back when?'

'The ship sails tomorrow.'

'Did you get to hear Billie Holiday?'

'Caught up with her at Café Society in the Village, sir. Worth the trip over just for that.'

Roosevelt adjusted his rimless pince-nez on the bridge of his patrician nose and stared for a moment at Wilde. It was unlikely the President had the freedom to go to jazz clubs in New York.

'Lucky you,' Roosevelt said. 'Anyway, down to business.' He nodded in Flood's direction. 'Over to you, Dexter.'

'Thank you, Mr President.'

Wilde met the colonel's serious gaze. He wondered why Flood hadn't made general; he surely had the qualifications: hero of the Great War having led an assault that captured a German command post in September 1918, military historian with a professorship from Princeton, something of an expert on European politics in the twentieth century. Had he fallen foul of someone somewhere – surely something or somebody had halted his advance?

'Have you heard of fission, Professor Wilde? The new science papers coming out of Germany?'

'Sure, I've heard of it, even tried to understand it. Why?'

His old friend Geoff Lancing had attempted, briefly, to explain it to him; it was a difficult concept for the layman.

'Because there are physics men here in America who believe it means that a superbomb might be possible. What some people like to call an atomic bomb. Even Einstein believes it's no longer merely the stuff of H. G. Wells. The War Department has to take such warnings seriously.'

Fission. Lancing, a brilliant young physics professor back in Cambridge, had bubbled over with enthusiasm – and not a little trepidation – as he'd tried to interest Wilde in the subject. Much of the technical detail had gone over Wilde's head, but he had got the gist. This wasn't just splitting the atom; this, as he understood it, was bursting them apart with explosive force.

'I have a good friend who tried to explain it,' said Wilde, 'but I couldn't claim to understand the fine detail.'

'Nor me, Professor, nor me,' Roosevelt said. 'How could a tiny thing like an atom cause an explosion? Gas, that's the thing that scares me. The Italians have dropped it from the air in Abyssinia, so you have to think about it coming from the sky onto a crowded Western city. Hell on earth. But this atom thing, well, that beats me . . .'

'It really isn't my field, Mr President.'

'Of course not. Back to you, Dexter.'

'OK, Wilde, you're not a scientist. But you have eyes and ears. And you're going home to Cambridge, which is the place where it all began. The Cavendish Laboratory.'

The Cavendish, in the heart of Cambridge, was where men had first split the atom. The lab had long been at the very heart of experimental particle physics and Geoff Lancing was one of its leading lights.

Wilde studied Flood. What he saw was a career man who hadn't quite made it to the top, but still managed to wield influence. Perhaps he had spent too long on campus, not enough time on the parade ground.

'We need to know what's going on there,' Flood continued. 'The world of atomic physics is a small place. There are questions to which we would like answers. For instance, do Britain's top men believe this superbomb is possible? How difficult is it to make? Who are the real brains – the leaders in the field? We'd like to hear what you can find out. And we'd like to hear it in layman's terms. Simple as that.'

'Then I'll keep my eyes and ears open.'

'Come on, Wilde,' Flood said. 'We know your background. You may not call yourself a spy, you may not be part of any agency, but goddamn it, Professor, you're in the thick of it already! You take briefings from Vanderberg at the US embassy, you watch your contemporaries like a bird of prey . . .'

'Take briefings from Jim Vanderberg? He's a friend, that's all, an old college friend. We just talk, shoot the breeze like friends do.'

Flood held up a defensive hand and grinned. 'No one's accusing you of anything, Professor. You do good work. We've got a pretty good idea what you did at the back end of '36. You're just the sort of guy we need.'

Did Flood really know Wilde's role in those events? The foiling of the conspiracy to prevent the abdication of Edward VIII had been a closely guarded secret. Wilde shrugged. 'I suppose I should be flattered.'

Roosevelt clapped his hands. 'Good man. We don't want to be caught off guard. If anyone looks like they're going to get a superbomb, I want to know about it.' He glanced at his watch and Wilde began to rise, as did Colonel Flood. The interview was over. Ten short minutes in which they had covered the likelihood of war, the possibility of an atomic super-bomb and the pleasures of jazz. All that and good White House coffee. The President put the dying butt of his second cigarette in the ashtray groove, then leant across and shook Wilde's hand warmly. 'Good to meet you, Professor. Keep in touch. I need a clear, unbiased voice over there in the dark days that lie ahead of us. Missy LeHand is my gatekeeper and she will tell you exactly how to contact me. I'd value your view over those of a dozen diplomats. Just keep everything short and to the point. On the science matter, communicate with Dexter.'

'Certainly, Mr President.'

'And perhaps you'd send me a signed copy of your new book.'

'It would be my pleasure, sir. I think you'll find that Sir Robert Cecil was every bit as ruthless in his own way as Walsingham.'

'Power politics! Nothing changes down the ages.'

Flood walked towards the door. 'I'll show the professor out, Mr President.'

'Thank you, Dexter.'

As the door closed behind them, Dexter Flood clapped his hand on Wilde's shoulder. 'Glad to have you on board, Wilde. You keep me in the loop, OK.'

'Of course.'

'This friend of yours inside the Cavendish, that would be Dr Lancing, right? Augustin G. Lancing?'

Wilde moved away from Flood's chummy hand. 'What makes you think that?'

Flood shrugged and grinned through his mass of freckles. 'A hunch, Wilde, just a hunch.'

'Well, you should know that Lancing has wisely dropped the Augustin. He's Geoffrey Lancing. But why mention him particularly? I know two or three people inside the Cavendish. There's a Cavendish man in my own college.'

'That would be Paul Birbach, right?'

'You know a lot, Colonel.'

'Who else?'

'What?'

'Who else do you know in the Cavendish?'

'Only passing acquaintances, I'm afraid.'

'Torsten Hellquist, yes?'

'Yes, I do know him slightly. Why?'

'Because Hellquist and Birbach are the ones that worry us. They have dubious sympathies. We don't believe they're on our side.'

So that was why he had been called here. Somehow they knew about his acquaintance with Lancing and Birbach and Hellquist. If they knew so much already, why did they need him?

Flood lowered his voice. 'I want to know what goes on in that Cambridge laboratory. I want to know about those two goddamned foreigners, what they're doing – when they screw and when they fart. Got it?'

'I won't see them that much, I'm afraid. Our paths don't cross that often.'

'Then find a way in. Use Lancing. Ask him who's best – who among his researchers has a brain the size of Texas? Those are the guys we need to worry about – the clever fellers, not the also-rans. No one gets a super-bomb before the USA. *Comprende?*'

Wilde did not reply.

'There's one other thing. Have you heard of Milt Hardiman?'

'No, should I have?'

'Only if you read the society columns. But he's a good man, for all his wealth. A patriot. He's over there and he'll be making contact with you. He's on our side and he'll be working with us on this. Confide in him – work together. He can get messages to me.'

'Milt Hardiman.'

'Milt. Short for Milton. Everyone calls him Milt. Just don't play poker with him – he'll rob you blind.' Dexter Flood grinned and put out his hand, gripping Wilde's in a warm, friendly handshake. 'You'll be OK, feller. Serve your country.'

A few minutes later, walking out into the fresh air on Pennsylvania Avenue, Wilde tried to make sense of the whirlwind meeting. One thing was clear – the invitation to the Oval Office had been nothing more than an attempt to schmooze him, so that Dexter Flood could use him. *Schmoozed and used.*

Roosevelt's role had been peripheral. He had been there to flatter Wilde. Devious bastard. For all his down-home, folksy appearance, Roosevelt was as wily and unscrupulous as Queen Elizabeth I's spymaster, Walsingham.

In which case, who exactly was Colonel Dexter Flood?

JUNE 1939

CHAPTER 3

Eva Haas and the man she knew only as Baumgarten drew up outside the barbed wire of Dachau concentration camp near Munich in a large, closed-top Opel car. In the vehicle's trunk, there were two sets of hiking clothes, one for her, one for Arnold Lindberg.

Baumgarten was dressed in the full, menacing black uniform of an SS captain – a *Hauptsturmführer*. Eva wore a dark, sexless jacket and skirt, with a party badge at her breast, a face scrubbed clean of make-up, with her hair hidden beneath a braided wig, in the tight style favoured by Wagnerian singers at Bayreuth. She looked at herself in the mirror and the face that stared back at her was horribly similar to that of the sinister Gertrud Scholtz-Klink, leader of the *NS-Frauenschaft*. Eva was shaking and tried to bring her body under control. She must show no fear.

'Hell on earth,' Baumgarten said, looking through the electrified wire at the regimented rows of prisoner huts. On both sides were watchtowers manned by guards with sub-machine guns.

'First the telephone,' Frau Haas said. 'We do nothing until I know for certain.'

'Of course.' He smiled reassuringly, put the Opel into gear, then drove at a steady speed into the nearest village. They scanned the dull, empty streets for a telephone kiosk, but were out of luck. 'Perhaps the railway station,' he said.

The station had no public phone, but Baumgarten approached one of the platform guards, a small, timid man whose eyes bulged in terror at the sight of an approaching SS officer. The little man's body stiffened and he snapped a sharp salute. 'Heil Hitler!'

'I need a telephone.'

'Yes, sir. In the signal box. Let me take you, sir. Wesselmann will help you, sir.'

The signal box was a hundred metres away at the point where the road crossed the track. The signalman, Wesselmann, was less deferential than his colleague but had no option but to allow the call. No one could refuse an SS officer.

'Please leave us,' Baumgarten said.

Reluctantly, the signalman abandoned his post and climbed down the steps. From the window Eva could see him light up a cigarette.

'Now call her,' Baumgarten said.

Her hands wet with sweat, Eva called a number in Berlin. It was answered after less than a minute. 'Miss Forster?'

'Frau Dr Haas?'

'Yes, is –'

'All is well, dear, he's on the train. No fuss at all, and he's in a carriage with some nice children. I heard just an hour ago that the train has now crossed into Holland. All is well, my dear.'

'Thank you, thank you, Miss Forster.'

Eva's terror ebbed away. Her hands and body stopped shaking. Now, there was no doubt in her mind. She had to get out of Germany – and if Baumgarten had an idea that might work, she had to try it.

Together, they drove back towards Dachau, but they stopped on the way and parked in a lay-by in the shade of thick woodland. Baumgarten climbed out of the car and removed the bags with their hiking gear, placing them carefully in a bramble thicket. 'They may search the car,' he explained.

At the concentration camp, they were confronted once again by barbed wire, watchtowers and by an endless line of shuffling prisoners on the other side of the wire. Eva felt enveloped by a profound fear and darkness. *Arbeit Macht Frei*, the entrance sign said, *work makes you free*. No freedom behind this wire. They pulled in at the main gate and climbed from the vehicle, presenting themselves at the guardhouse with sharp, straight-arm salutes. Baumgarten did the talking. Even in uniform, women were nothing but helpmeets and breeding machines in the new Germany.

Baumgarten slapped a signed and stamped paper down on the counter in a high-handed manner. 'Transfer to Sachsenhausen. Inmate Lindberg, Arnold,' he said, and rattled off Lindberg's official prison number.

The chief guard, like Baumgarten an SS officer complete with death's head insignia on his cap, laughed. 'Doesn't he like the food here?'

'He is needed for questioning in Berlin. Prinz-Albrecht-Strasse.'

The guard stiffened. 'Ah, yes, well, that makes sense, of course, Herr *Hauptsturmführer.*' Prinz-Albrecht-Strasse was the headquarters of the SS, the Gestapo and the SD, the domain of Heinrich Himmler and Reinhard Heydrich. If the orders came from there, then there could be no argument; Sachsenhausen was only a short drive from Berlin.

The guard looked at the transfer paper supplied by Baumgarten, then shuffled through his own record of the day's orders. 'He is not on the list, Herr *Hauptsturmführer.*'

'Nor will he be. This is top secret.'

The guard looked uneasily from Baumgarten to Eva.

'This is Frau Haas, my secretary. She will take notes on the journey.' The implication being that time was of the essence: the interrogation would start immediately.

'I must put a call through to the commandant.'

'Do that, but be quick. We have a long drive. Here' – he handed over a swastika-embossed card – 'tell him to ring that number. Tell him my name is Baumgarten.'

The guard's eyes widened as he looked at the name on the card. He clicked his heels and saluted. 'Yes, sir, straightaway, sir.'

An hour later, they had Arnold Lindberg in the car. The camp commandant had asked them to stay for lunch in the officers' mess, but Baumgarten had tapped his watch and declined.

There had been no time for greetings or explanations. They drove back to the woodland and collected their new outfits from the thicket. In the event, the car had not been searched, but better safe than sorry. Eva changed quickly and then, with great difficulty, persuaded her uncle to do the same. She had to help the shaking man to do up the buttons on his shirt. Then Baumgarten drove them to the station at Munich, handed them tickets to Innsbruck – and bade them farewell.

Lydia Morris clutched the grainy photograph, stared at it for a few moments, then raised her eyes and peered across the concourse of the railway station. There were so many children, all in coats and hats, despite the June warmth. Each carried a small box or case and each had a number and a name on a tag hanging by a string around their necks. Like so many parcels.

Which one was Albert? She looked again at the photograph that the child's mother, Eva, had sent her. It really wasn't very good. One or two of the boys might fit the bill, but she wasn't at all sure. A photograph is a dead, static thing, and these children were alive and moving.

It was difficult to think with all the noise. The hiss of steam, the railway men's whistles, the background murmur of men and women here to collect their new wards, the yelling of the newspaper sellers and the porters trying to outdo each other, the greetings and farewells of passengers, the common daily discourse of the railway workers and the echoing clatter of metalled boots on concrete. All this and the stench of oil and smoke and sweat.

Lydia wove through the crowd of waiting adults towards the children. She felt very small beneath the soaring vaulted roof, all glass and steel. The children were silent and scared. Their journey from Germany by train and boat had been long and full of emotion. For some it had been an adventure with cheerful bouts of singing and gratitude for the gifts of food from the kind mothers of Holland when they crossed the border. For others it had been unutterable misery, nothing but tears, unable to eat. But now at Liverpool Street Station, they were all as one – exhausted and homesick, their faces drawn and wide-eyed yet trying to smile, anxious to please. Few of them had any real idea where they were. They were strangers in a strange land. Was this the end of their journey? Who would be meeting them? They all yearned for their mothers and fathers. When would they be joining them?

She made a beeline for the most likely of the two boys she had spotted. Close up, however, he didn't really resemble the boy in the picture. The only thing he had in common with the photographic image was the pair of round, metal-framed spectacles perched on his little nose. She glanced at his name tag: Blaustein, Isaac. Moving on, she approached the second boy. The child tried to smile, but his tears were very close to the surface. She smiled back and put a comforting arm on his shoulder. It wasn't Albert.

There were more girls than boys, which narrowed her search. She studied each of their faces in turn, took their labels between her fingers and examined them quickly. She smiled at each of the boys and said '*Wie heissen Sie?*' – what is your name? Each of them pointed to their name tag and answered most correctly, with stiff shoulders, meeting her gaze as they had been taught to do by their loving parents and their strict schoolteachers.

Lydia did not feel confident enough to engage them in conversation; her German was rusty from lack of use. She said the boy's name in the form of a question: 'Albert Haas? Do you know him?'

They all shook their heads. The name clearly meant nothing to them.

Bertha Bracey appeared at her side, large and comforting like a mother duck. 'Not found him yet, my dear?'

She shook her head. 'There are so many of them.'

'No more than usual.'

No, of course not. Lydia had met several of these trainloads of children over the past three months and there had sometimes been twice as many as today's quota, but this was the first time she was supposed to meet one specific child.

'This is very different, Bertha.'

'I know, my dear. But don't worry, they'll begin to thin out soon and then we'll find the little chap. Whatever you do, keep that smile fixed to your face – let them know you're friendly.'

'Bertha, I have changed the habit of a lifetime and dressed up for this and done my hair, or perhaps you hadn't noticed. Of course, I'll smile.'

The older woman laughed. 'Yes, I had noticed the hair. Very nice.'

Lydia raised an eyebrow. She rather thought that Bertha wasn't at all impressed by her efforts: neatly brushed hair and a rather frumpy summer dress which she hoped would make her look more like a homely German Jewish *Hausfrau* than the slightly tattered bohemian English-woman which was closer to the truth.

'Perhaps he's still on the train. He might have fallen asleep and been forgotten, Bertha. I'm sure that's happened before. I'll just hop aboard and look.'

'Do that – and don't worry. We'll find him. We haven't mislaid one yet.'

Albert Haas wasn't on the train. He wasn't on the concourse of Liverpool Street Station. Something was clearly amiss. The two leaders who accompanied the children from Germany were already on the ferry home and had been replaced by English leaders at Harwich, neither of whom had any recollection of the boy.

'He can't have got on the train,' Bertha Bracey said. She put an arm around Lydia's shoulders. 'Come on, my dear, let's get back to Bloomsbury and call Berlin.'

'But that's not what the cable said.' Lydia had seen the telegram from Miss Forster. It said quite clearly that Albert had boarded the Hook of Holland train with the other children at Berlin's Zoo Station, in the Charlottenburg district.

'There must have been some sort of mix-up. Those affairs can be pretty grim when they separate the children from their parents. We'll sort it out.'

Lydia looked at the small photograph of Albert once more. Behind the spectacles, she thought she detected intelligent, sensitive eyes. He wore a formal jacket over a white shirt with a white, lacy collar. Rather girlish and a little too serious, Lydia thought. Albert Haas looked as if he needed to get stuck in with some rugger boys. Toughen up. She tucked the picture into her jacket pocket, but she was reluctant to leave. How could Miss Forster have made such a fundamental mistake? He was either on the train or he wasn't.

Shafts of sunlight angled down from the cathedral heights of the station. The parallel beams cut through the glass and girders, the smoke and the vapour, and lit the heads of the children like so many angels.

'Lydia?'

'You're right, something must have happened. Perhaps he was taken ill at the last moment.'

'More than possible.'

The terminus was almost clear of children now. Apart from two boys of about twelve and a girl of seven or so, they had all been paired off and most of them were beginning their onward journey, by train, bus or motor car, to their new lives in far-flung corners of England.

Lydia had watched each of them go with their new guardians and felt a pang of envy; she should have been taking her own ward home today. Eight-year-old Albert was the only son of her old friend from Girton, Eva Haas, or Eva Grad as she had been then. Although they had never lived in each other's pockets at college, Lydia had been very fond of Eva, and the two women had kept in close touch. When Eva married her fellow scientist Klaus Haas back in 1930, Lydia had been a guest of honour at the wedding in Munich. That had been the last time they had seen each other, but the letters never ceased.

And now she wanted to take Eva's little boy into her home in Cambridge and lavish love and comfort on him until Eva could get to England, or until the situation improved for Jews inside Germany.

Her eyes were fixed on the last three children. They had, at last, linked up with their guardians and were being bustled away. Lydia's eyes followed them, all hope of meeting Albert vanishing with their receding figures.

Bertha Bracey's dedicated band of Quaker volunteers, the German Emergency Committee, had moved from Friends House to Bloomsbury House four months earlier to coordinate their refugee work with all the other organisations trying to help Jews escape persecution in Germany, Austria and Czechoslovakia.

Bertha's main task was to find pledges of £50 from sponsors willing to give a home to a Jewish child. Without the pledge of money and a home, it was almost impossible for the children to get a visa. The British government was willing to help, but insisted the refugee children should not be a burden on the public purse.

As secretary of the Inter-Church Council for German Refugees, Bertha had a staff of a hundred people and was based on the third floor of the former Palace Hotel. They all knew what they were trying to do, and why, but no one would admit the whole truth. No one voiced the obvious point that if parents were willing to put small children on a train and send them to an unknown future in a strange land, they must have a powerful – and terrible – belief that the alternative of staying put would be a great deal worse.

As soon as she reached her desk, Bertha picked up the telephone and put a call through to Berlin. Lydia watched her intently. She spoke quickly, in English, explaining the situation to Miss Forster, one of her Quaker contacts in the city. Bertha grimaced and shook her head grimly at Lydia.

'And you're certain he was put on the train?'

Lydia could hear the response. 'Yes, he was on the train.'

'Well, something must have happened between Berlin and Harwich. Perhaps he wandered off when they stopped in Holland, or at the port while they were boarding the ferry.'

They talked for another minute, and then Bertha said, 'Well, thank you, my dear. As soon as your leaders return, do talk to them. And I'll call you if I hear anything.' She put the receiver down.

'This is madness,' Lydia said. 'It doesn't make any sense.'

'There must be some sort of simple explanation. Go and get some food and rest, my dear, I'll deal with it.'

Lydia felt drained. 'No. We need to talk to the other children on the train. One of them must know something.'

Bertha picked up a square packet from her desk and handed it to Lydia. 'Sandwiches. Corned beef. You've got to eat something.'

She couldn't help laughing. 'Thank you, Bertha.'

'And here's the list of telephone numbers. Can you call them all yourself, Lydia? I must get on with other things.'

'Of course.'

Bertha looked at the younger woman for a few moments. 'You know, my dear, it is not my business or my way to push religion down people's throats, but I can't help feeling that it would do you no harm to come along to the meeting house once or twice. Just for some quiet reflection.'

Lydia shook her head. 'I can't, Bertha.'

'Of course. I understand. But if ever . . . well, you were brought up in a Friends' household, so you know the drill.' Bertha turned back to her work.

Lydia's father had been a Quaker and she loved the Quakers and all they stood for, but she simply didn't believe in a deity. Without enthusiasm, she began to eat the sandwich. Just half, then she reached for the handset of the black Bakelite telephone and began to call the numbers listed. After a fruitless hour, she leaned back in her chair and stretched out her arms. Poor little Albert Haas. Where was he? And poor Eva – how would she cope if something had happened to her boy?

CHAPTER 4

They had been walking for many hours, always uphill, into the mountains. Their journey had passed largely without incident, although once a rattle of gunfire had echoed across from the slopes of Madrisa on the border between the province of Ostmark – formerly known as Austria – and the freedom of Switzerland, halting them in their tracks. Eva Haas and Arnold Lindberg had stopped, scouring the peaks and paths ahead of them, before their breathing subsided and they moved on, closer to the high pass.

Eva had a map in her head, a picture of this place from when she and her late husband Klaus had walked this route back in 1930. They had been on honeymoon and made love in the guest house and in the open air. They had laughed and splashed, naked, in a blue glacial lake.

The Alps had been her joy in those far-off days. The smell of the grass, the heat of summer, the gasping cold of the streams, the touch of Klaus's body. All within the soaring coliseum of the mountain peaks, in the lee of the Madrisa. Even the men and boys in the valley, sweaty in their leather shorts with their sickles, slashing at the long grass, had a sort of romance.

But the romance was long gone. Now there was only fear.

Eva pulled Lindberg up the last few feet onto the St Antönierjoch ridge. 'Take one step forward, uncle,' she whispered. 'And you will be in Switzerland. This is the border. We are safe.'

He did not even squeeze her hand in acknowledgement.

'If only we had some champagne.'

'Ach, I would prefer a beer,' he said. 'A cold stein of weissbier.'

'Then soon you shall have it. We are free, uncle. *You* are free. You will sleep in a featherbed this night.'

And soon, she thought, I shall be with Albert again. But first they must watch for Swiss frontier guards. If they were seen, they would be bundled back over the border without ceremony.

The last kilometres were harder than she had expected. The paths down-hill were slippery and very hard on the knees. Once they spotted a Swiss border patrol a few hundred metres away and Eva forced her uncle to duck down behind a boulder. But the two uniformed frontier guards, guns slung across their backs like hunters, moved on.

Her uncle stopped again. He returned to the same question he had been asking ever since he had left Dachau. 'I don't understand. How did you get me out of the camp, Eva? Who was that man, that Nazi with you?'

She was losing patience. 'That was no Nazi, uncle. He wore the uniform, but he was a Jew, like you and me.'

Eva had been living in a modest apartment block in the working-class Prenzlauer Berg district of Berlin, having been dismissed from her research job at the Kaiser Wilhelm Institute in Munich. When he first approached her outside her rundown block, he was wearing a black SS uniform that was obscenely tight across his Oktoberfest beer belly. She had thought she would die of fright.

He introduced himself as *Hauptsturmführer* Baumgarten and she said nothing, merely trembled and waited to do what she was told. But then he laughed and confessed that he was no Nazi and that he wished to help her. 'May I?' he inquired, stepping forward towards her door.

'Of course.' She didn't know what to think, but she didn't seem to have much option.

He made himself comfortable inside her apartment, pacing about as though he owned the place. He explained that he was a member of an 'underground railway', helping Jews escape the Reich. He had flaxen hair, Aryan features and spoke of Jewish friends who were talented forgers.

He said the British wanted Arnold Lindberg out of Germany. They did not want a man with such a brain and so much scientific knowledge to be at the Nazis' disposal. The same applied to her.

Eva had already applied for exit visas for herself and Albert, but without success. This man Baumgarten was offering her a way out.

'And this includes my son?'

'You will go separately. He will be put on a *Kindertransport*. Have you heard of them? Trains full of children being shipped across to England each week. Their parents cannot go with them. You will have to join him another way.'

She was not wholly convinced. 'I will have to have proof that my son is safe first. I will not leave Germany without him.'

'Then it will be arranged.' Before he left, he had apologised for his SS regalia, but he had wanted her to understand that he had the means to do what was necessary.

Two days later, Baumgarten arrived in civilian clothes and together they travelled with Albert by U-Bahn to the western suburbs, clutching his small box of belongings. In a grand house, close to the southern bank of Schlactensee, they met a Miss Forster, a Quaker, half-English, half-German, who promised that she, personally, would put little Albert on the train. There was a place available in three days' time, she said. With great reluctance, Eva had entrusted her son to Miss Forster. She hugged him, but could not kiss his face for fear he would see that her own was awash with tears, and then she had turned away and left him in the Englishwoman's care.

Albert had been brave. He had not cried out or called to her, and she had not turned round to him as she went out through the high doors.

And now, at last, they were in Switzerland, although even here they were still not yet safe. It was not until they were a couple of kilometres further on from the border and they found themselves in summer pasture again, with cows grazing the lush grass, their bells clanging, that she began to relax. Oh for some bread and some fresh butter from these beasts! The very thought made Eva salivate. No one has really tasted butter who has not had it straight from the churn, high in the alps.

Late in the afternoon, they came to the village she remembered, St Antönien.

She put an arm around her uncle's shoulder. He was so thin, she felt he would break. Not yet forty years old, but he had the demeanour of an old man. She pointed downhill into the village. Ahead of them was a small chalet hotel. Outside, a man sat alone at a table, engrossed in a beer and a newspaper. Something made him glance up and he gave them a cheery wave.

His name was Philip Eaton and he was a member of the British secret services.

Lydia's head was on her folded arms, eyes closed. Anyone walking into the room would have thought she was asleep, but when the telephone rang she was instantly alert.

'Hello? Miss Bracey's office.' She blinked rapidly, trying to clear her vision.

'Is that Miss Morris?'

'Yes, yes it is. Who's calling, please?'

'I'm Mrs Weeks from Bury St Edmunds. My maid told me you called earlier this evening. Something about a missing boy. Is that right?'

'Yes. A boy named Albert Haas. Do you know something?'

'It's possible. I picked up a girl of twelve – Anna Rosenheim – who is to stay with us until she can be reunited with her parents. She told me something happened at the German–Dutch border.'

Lydia's heart pounded. 'Can I speak to her?'

'She has no English at all, I'm afraid. But I'm fluent in German. She said they were stopped for ages at the border before they were allowed to cross into Holland. The German officials tipped out all their bags and confiscated anything of value, and generally made themselves unpleasant. They paid special attention to one little boy and made him go with them. When the train eventually moved, he hadn't returned, so she thought he must have been put in another carriage. But perhaps not . . .'

'Who were these officials? Does she know?'

'Hang on, I'll ask.'

Down the telephone, she heard Mrs Weeks speaking German, then a girl's voice, also German. Mrs Weeks came back on. 'She's not entirely sure. She doesn't think they were regular customs men. One was in uniform, one in civvies. Uniforms don't mean a great deal to children, do they?'

'Could you ask her to describe the boy?'

There was another rapid German conversation on the other end of the line. 'It seems the boy wore metal framed glasses,' Mrs Weeks reported. 'She remembers he kept pushing them back on the bridge of his nose.

He was dark-haired and very quiet. Didn't say a word to anyone. *Zaghaft* is the word she used – timid. But that's hardly surprising. I should have thought all the children were pretty fearful.'

'You said she thought he was six or seven. Albert is eight.'

'Well, of course, Anna can't be certain. The boy was small . . .'

'So from what Anna says, if this was Albert, it's possible he never left Germany.'

There was a deep sigh at the other end of the line. 'They're utter beasts, aren't they? To treat little children in such a way. I'll call you if Anna remembers anything else.'

CHAPTER 5

Tom Wilde arrived back in Cambridge in the early afternoon of a warm day in early June, a week before the end of term. Back in March when he left, he had leant into a blustering squall of rain as he struggled into the station. Now, as he stepped out of the train, the sky spoke of a proper English summer. But for all that, he was dismayed by the view from the taxi window, so great were the changes wrought on the town by impending war. Sandbags were being piled high on the pavement around several public buildings, including the police station on St Andrew's Street and the magistrates' court.

A band of about thirty boy scouts was marching down the road just before Jesus Lane. The taxi and other vehicles had to stop to let them past. Several cyclists rang their bells in frustration. The Scouts, shoulders back, knees bare beneath khaki shorts, carried a banner that said defiantly: WE'RE READY, ARE YOU? Wilde smiled. The optimism and certainty of youth.

'Looks like everyone's getting set for war,' he muttered.

The driver picked up his remark. 'Sad but true, sir. I've found myself an allotment out Cherry Hinton way – no more'n hundred foot by thirty – and planted spuds, spuds and more spuds. That'll see the family through a few months if worse comes to worst.' He turned briefly to look at his passenger. 'Is this your first time in Cambridge, may I ask?'

Wilde laughed. 'Lived and worked here about five years now.'

'You sound like an American gentleman, sir.'

'Something like that.' The traffic was moving again. Wilde wound down the window. The cab was stuffy and thick with stale cigarette smoke and he was impatient to get home. He wondered what awaited him. One of the books he had read during his time at sea was Priestley's *English Journey*; he had been amused by his brief but excoriating description of Cambridge as being primly pleased with itself. Wilde could not but agree – but Priestley had also commented that it was 'a lovely old place, far lovelier now than Oxford'. And Wilde had agreed with that, too.

At last the taxi pulled up outside his modest Georgian house.

While the driver struggled with his bags, Wilde opened the front door and was confronted by spotless cleanliness and the floral whiff of potent household products. Doris, the charlady he shared with Lydia Morris, had been busy preparing the place for his homecoming. It was certainly an improvement on the smoke pollution he had endured in the cab and on the train from Southampton. Even in the dining car, the food had a faint flavour of soot.

Scores of letters and packages – two and a half months of mail – were piled up on the table in the kitchen. Most of them would be bills and missed invitations, he guessed. He would look at them all later. He removed his jacket and hung it on the back of a chair, then took off his tie and rolled up his sleeves. He was sweaty and smoky and he needed a shower, but first he wanted a whisky. He found a half-full bottle in the sitting room cabinet where he had left it back in March, and poured himself a good measure. Neat.

Glass in hand, he wandered around the house. The three bedrooms, the bathroom, his study. Everything was clean and tidy, but there was a silent, unlived-in feeling to the place. Unloved and unoccupied. Was that how it always felt, he wondered, or was it simply because he'd been away?

He looked out from his study window, over the small back garden, which had been well-tended and mowed. The beds were bursting with flowers and the apple tree was in leaf, just losing the last of its blossom. He looked across to Lydia's back garden next door. It too, looked in pretty good shape. Was she in? He had wired ahead to let her know when he was arriving and had rather hoped she might meet him off the boat at Southampton, but that was probably expecting too much.

He unstrapped one of his bags and pulled it open. On the top was a new Billie Holiday disc. He had been captivated by her rendering of a dark and devastating song about a lynching, but he hadn't been able to find it on record, so he had bought everything else he could find by her in a local store. He located the record player, on a low table beside the wireless, and put on 'These Foolish Things'. He turned up the volume. The sweet sounds brought new life to the house.

When the song had finished, he showered, then dressed in clean white shirt and flannels and stepped out from the front door. His eye caught the red pillar box on the pavement at the far end of Lydia's house. The words *An Phoblacht abú!* had been hurriedly painted in dripping black. Wilde grimaced. He knew well enough the meaning of the words: *the Republic forever*. He knew, too, the implication: IRA sympathisers were in town. Word had reached the American newspapers of their activities in England these past few months – over a hundred explosions around the country since the beginning of the year.

He turned away and walked up to Lydia's house and rang the bell. Doris answered the door.

'Hello Doris, no Lydia?'

Doris shook her head, but managed a broad smile. 'Welcome home, Professor Wilde. No, Miss Morris is still in London, I'm afraid. She asked me to tell you that she would call you on the telephone in the next day or two. I'm sorry, Professor.'

'Not your fault, Doris. And I have to thank you for caring for my place so well. It all looks fine and smells good, too.'

'That's very kind of you to say so, sir. I've aired it every day, except when it was bucketing down. You'll see I've switched on your new refrigerator and I've put some groceries in there and in your larder. Mr Raymond has done a good job with the garden.'

'Indeed, he has. You'll have to tell me how much I owe you. Shall we settle up at the end of the week?'

'That will suit me very well, thank you, sir. Oh – one more thing, Professor. There was a telephone call for you while I was dusting this morning. Mr Philip Eaton from *The Times*. He asked if you could give him a call. I left his number on the pad by the telephone.'

Eaton? They hadn't spoken in over two years. Wilde had rather hoped their paths would never cross again. 'Thank you, Doris,' he said. 'I'll call him.'

Wilde happily accepted that he would never measure up as an English gentleman, but Harrow had taught him about good and bad form. And it would be bad form not to call Eaton back.

Even so, he hesitated. Philip Eaton may have been on the staff of *The Times*, but his true calling was secret intelligence, ostensibly for MI6, though Wilde harboured doubts about his true loyalties. 'We're ready, are you?' the Scouts had chanted. But Wilde didn't feel he was ready for Philip Eaton. What the hell did the smooth bastard want?

Only one way to find out. His finger went to the dial.

The call went through to a secretary, then a minute later, Eaton came on the line.

'Professor Wilde?'

'Speaking.'

'Good of you to call back, old boy. I know you've only just returned. Hope your journey wasn't too exhausting.'

Doris must have told Eaton he'd been away. Or perhaps not. Eaton made it his business to know everything, one way or another.

'What can I do for you, Eaton?'

A pause. 'I've got a favour to ask. But first, can I ask a rather personal question: what exactly are your living arrangements with Lydia Morris these days?'

Wilde almost laughed out loud at the gall of the man. 'None of your business, Eaton! But I'm sure you have a vague idea of your own. You tell me how *you* think things are.' He took a hefty mouthful of whisky. He was beginning to think he'd need another shower after this call.

'Well, I know you've kept both houses, and I also know you haven't married, so, well, it all seems a bit unconventional.'

'And why is that any business of yours?'

'Normally it wouldn't be, but as I said I have a favour to ask you – both of you, actually. I want you to take in a pair of refugees from Nazi Germany. You'd have the man, a displaced physics professor, and Miss Morris, meanwhile, would look out for his niece, who also happens to be a scientist and an old friend of hers from Girton. They're important people. You'd be doing your bit.'

'Have you put this to Lydia yet?'

'Yes, and she's agreed to play her part.'

Did he have any option? Wasn't every right-thinking person obliged to help refugees at this critical time? 'I suppose you'd better tell me more.'

'The man's name is Arnold Lindberg. You probably remember the name.'

Wilde went cold. How could he forget the name Arnold Lindberg? The deadly events of 1936 had started with a bungled effort by a friend of Lydia to get Arnold Lindberg out of Germany. It had all ended tragically, with the friend dead and Lindberg in Dachau. The greatest surprise was that he was still alive. Wilde said nothing.

'Are you still there, old boy? What do you think?'

'What's this about, Eaton? Why me? Why split them up?'

'I was planning to come up to Cambridge later today. Perhaps we could talk then.'

'As I recall, Dr Lindberg was a friend of Horace Dill. Wouldn't he be a better host? For one thing, my German's pretty basic.'

Eaton's voice softened. 'Yes, Dr Dill would have been a good bet as he and Lindberg are old friends, but what you probably don't know is that Horace is very ill. He wouldn't be able to take in a guest at the moment.'

Horace ill? He had a lot to catch up on after ten weeks away. Wilde sighed. 'All right, Eaton. Come up – and you can tell me everything.'

'Shall we say six o'clock at the Bull?'

'No, I have matters to attend to in college, and then I'm coming back home.'

He wanted to be on his own turf for this meeting.

'Then that's where I shall see you.'

Wilde had never been entirely comfortable with some of the more arcane traditions of Cambridge, yet he experienced a warm feeling as he crossed the Old Court with his gown flapping behind him: this was a little acre of English heaven.

The lawn was green and lush, the ivy on the walls in full summer leaf. At his side, one of the porters toiled under the weight of a large box of his books and papers, which had been in storage during his absence. Wilde, clutching the neck of a bottle in his fist, went ahead up the stairs to his rooms. At the top, he saw the welcoming face of his gyp, Bobby, one of the men who served the needs of Fellows and undergraduates alike, keeping fires stoked and kettles filled.

'Good to have you back, Professor. You've been missed.'

'By whom, Bobby, your bookie friends?'

The porter below was struggling to make headway. 'I'll help you with them in a mo, Mr Fenton,' Bobby called down to him, before turning his attention back to the professor. 'I'm sure I've tipped you a winner or two, haven't I?'

'Are you suggesting I'm in profit?'

Bobby grinned, revealing gums almost devoid of teeth. 'I don't think I'd go that far, Professor Wilde.'

'Well, all is forgiven if you have a bottle of Scotch on the premises.'

'As always, sir, as always. Fresh from the Buttery this morning.' He noted the bottle his master was carrying. 'Looks like you're well prepared for disappointment, though, Professor.'

Wilde held out the bottle. 'This is for you, Bobby. Bourbon.'

Bobby had been the gyp on these stairs ever since Wilde's arrival at Cambridge five years earlier, and long before that. Small and wiry, he had at one time been apprenticed to a Newmarket trainer and had entertained hopes of being a top jockey, but a bad fall had done for his dreams. Not that he had lost his love of racing or horses. He looked at the American whiskey bottle with raised eyebrows. 'Never heard of it, sir, but thank you. You're a gentleman.'

'I'd be interested to know what you think of it. Personally I prefer the Scotch variety, but there are plenty in the States who swear by this.'

'I'll share it with the lads and let you know the verdict, sir. It'll be a rare treat. And now, how about a pot of good English tea, Professor? You'll have missed that in America.'

Wilde did not reply. He was staring at a picture on his wall – his *only* picture, a Winslow Homer painting of an American scene that had been left to him by his father; it showed a farm boy looking out across an endless prairie. He shook himself back to the present. 'Thank you, Bobby. A cup of tea would be fine in a while. And perhaps you'd see if Hall can make me some sort of late lunch?'

'Of course, sir.'

'Before you go, what is the news of Professor Dill? I've heard his health's not been too good.'

Bobby grimaced. 'It's not looking hopeful. People say he's got—'
He mouthed a word that Wilde took to be *cancer*.

'Is he in his rooms?'

'Most likely, sir. He doesn't get about much.'

'I'll go and call on him now. Leave lunch half an hour.'

Horace Dill's rooms stank of stale cigar smoke, sweat and sickness. Wilde
rather felt he could do with a gas mask, but he managed to smile as he
stood at his fellow history man's bedside. Dill was propped up on a bank
of pillows.

Wilde took Dill's hand. The skin was parchment thin and mottled, and
his face was gaunt and more angular than he had known it. 'You look a
sight, Horace.'

'And welcome back to you, too, you filthy Yankee capitalist.' Dill leant
forward, retching and gasping for breath.

Wilde reached for the tumbler of water on the bedside table and held
it to Horace Dill's mouth. Dill pushed it away. After a few seconds the
coughing fit subsided and Dill slumped back into his pillows, taking
short, difficult breaths. Wilde proffered the glass of water once more.

'I don't need fucking water, I need a fucking cigar.'

'Is that wise?'

'Wise?' Dill hacked out a laugh and began coughing again. Clutching
his mouth with one hand he pointed towards a table at the far end of the
room with the other. Wilde shrugged and went to fetch the half-smoked
object from the ashtray where it had been deposited. If Dill had cancer, his chances looked pretty bleak anyway. Why deny a dying man his
one pleasure?

When Dill had recovered from his coughing, Wilde saw that he
had specks of coughed-up blood on his fingers where he had cupped
his mouth. Wilde offered him a clean handkerchief and smiled as Dill
brushed it aside. 'Here you are, then.' He handed him the remains of
the cigar.

'Light,' Dill said.

Wilde found a box of matches on the floor near the hearth. He
struck a match. For a few moments he held the flame at arm's length

from Dill, who now had the stub of cigar wedged firmly between his cracked and mottled lips. Shrugging, Wilde moved the flame forward and lit the ash-blackened tip.

Dill drew as deeply as his corrupt lungs would allow, coughed furiously, then rasped, 'Thank you, Wilde. I confess it's good to have you back.'

'Do you need anything, Horace? Grapes, for instance?'

Dill tried to laugh, but immediately clutched his chest, wheezing. Wilde gently removed the cigar and stubbed it out in the bedside ashtray. 'Grapes in fucking June?' Dill managed to croak.

'Perhaps not. Anyway, I'm at your service, whatever you need, and I come bearing news which you might think to be good. You recall Arnold Lindberg and the way he fell into the Gestapo's hands in '36?'

Dill's rheumy eyes lit up at the name.

'Well, it seems he's managed to slip out and is presently hiding up somewhere in Britain under the protection of your old student Philip Eaton.'

'Arnold's really out?'

'So I'm told.'

'Well, that's a fucking miracle! I want to see him.'

'It could happen. Eaton's coming to see me later today. He wants me to give Lindberg a room in my house.'

'He should be here, with me.'

'That's what I said, but apparently word's got out that your hypochondria was playing up.'

'You know, Tom, you can make light of it, but it's true. I'm not at all fucking well this time.' Dill's voice was faint and strained, his breathing shallow and rasping.

Wilde took the ailing professor's hand again. It was clear the old Bolshevik really didn't have long, might not even survive the summer. Even his anger seemed to have dissipated. 'Well, in the absence of grapes, I'll promise to bring Arnold Lindberg along. You can discuss the Communist revolution and the downfall of fascism to your hearts' content.'

Dill's eyes were closed. Not quite sure whether he had fallen asleep, Wilde continued to hold his pathetic parchment-skin hand for a few minutes, then slowly slid away.

Back in his own rooms, lunch was waiting for him on a tray, two plates of food kept warm beneath silver cloches. Also waiting for him, lounging back in his desk chair, with his feet up as though he owned the place, was his friend Geoffrey Lancing, a young man with the secrets of the universe at his elegant fingertips and a set of flying goggles perched on his forehead.

Lancing, a small slender man, leapt to his feet, grinning. 'Good to see you back, Tom.'

'And I'd like to say it's good to be back, Geoff, but if I'm honest, I haven't quite made up my mind yet. The jury's still out.' On the voyage across the Atlantic, it had all come back to him – the pettiness of college life, the jealousies, intolerance and spite of so many men in the gowns and squares of academe. He had not been at all sure that his mother wasn't right when she had exhorted him to stay in America and join the diplomatic service. So what *had* brought him back? The English summer was a big draw, of course, but most of all, there was Lydia . . .

'Worried about the prospect of war?' Lancing said. 'Don't be. We've got the Spits. Been up in one with 19 Squadron out of Duxford this very morning. Tom, she's sleeker than Garbo with more firepower than Mae West . . .'

'Don't you have to be in the RAF to fly one of those things?'

Lancing laughed. 'I slip in with the University Air Squadron. And I have a friend or two in 19. Highly irregular, of course, Tom, but they know I'm already very experienced.'

'I imagine your father could pull a few strings for you?'

'Good Lord, what a suggestion! Heaven forfend.' He winked mischievously. Lancing's father, as everyone knew, had been an ace in the last war when the RAF was still the Royal Flying Corps.

'Are you going to enlist?'

'I'm halfway there already, to tell the truth. When the war comes, wild horses won't hold me back. I'll be in the air and you can slum it in the trenches, Wilde.'

Wilde's thoughts briefly went back to Washington DC. Dexter Flood had been interested in Lancing. Was he expecting Wilde to spy on a friend? What did he think Lancing could reveal?

'Are you up for a drink, Tom? Eat your lunch, and then I'll stand you one at the Eagle. I want to hear all about the US of A. And I have some big news to impart'

Wilde laughed. 'Now that sounds like an offer I can't refuse.'

CHAPTER 6

For a moment, Lydia didn't recognise Eva Haas. Her dark hair was longer than she remembered, but the rest of her was somehow diminished. Her once plump, almost voluptuous figure was now slender and athletic. And she was visibly shaking, her eyes darting and fearful.

'Eva,' Lydia said, crossing the chaotic room on the third storey of Bloomsbury House. The floor was littered with the results of their work, thousands of files packed in hundreds of boxes; the table piled high with papers, in use or awaiting filing. Normally, this room would be occupied by up to a dozen of Bertha's army of volunteers, but they had vacated the room so as not to intrude on the crisis surrounding the missing boy. 'You have heard the bad news, yes?'

Eva nodded, her jaw tight, her dark eyes wide.

'I'm so, so sorry,' Lydia said. She hesitated a moment, then took her in her arms. There was no resistance, nor did Eva respond. After a few seconds Lydia stepped back awkwardly from the embrace. 'No one seems to have any idea where he is.'

'Mr Eaton has told me everything.'

'We are continuing to do everything we can. Our people in Berlin are making inquiries, so is the Embassy. Unfortunately the convoy leaders know nothing. They did not see Albert leave the train. We have also contacted all the other children from that carriage and they pretty much agree with what Anna Rosenheim has told us. From their descriptions of the men, it seems likely that one was a uniformed border guard and one was plain-clothes Gestapo. There was also a woman on the platform who may have been with the men.'

'They want me to go back there. That is their clear message to me. They are holding him hostage to force my return.'

Lydia was silent for a few moments. Of course, it seemed probable that Eva's conclusion was correct. Why else would Albert have been taken from the train other than to put pressure on his mother? A mother would do anything to save her child, but surely Eva could not go back to

Germany. From all that Lydia knew of the regime, they would keep her from the boy anyway, and probably consign her to a concentration camp.

'Mr Eaton says he will be lobbying the German embassy in London and talking to some of his own people in Berlin. He is also contacting the authorities in the Netherlands, in case he crossed the border. Mr Eaton assures me it must be some terrible mix-up.' Eva shook her head helplessly. 'Oh, Lydia, I can't bear it. Albert means everything to me.'

'I'm sure Mr Eaton is right,' Lydia said, taking Eva's hands in hers. At least she had stopped shaking. 'Someone obviously knows where he is – and even the Nazis wouldn't stoop to harming a child.'

'Wouldn't they?' Eva gave a hollow laugh. 'I fear you do not know the new Germany, Lydia.'

Eva had come here in a taxi, leaving her uncle in their modest hotel in South Kensington. Eaton, who had driven them all the way from Switzerland, had called Lydia to say he would be going to Cambridge later in the day to ask Tom Wilde about lodgings for Lindberg. If Wilde was unwilling to help, Eaton would seek out another host. 'I'm afraid it's not entirely straightforward, Miss Morris. Herr Dr Lindberg's presence might cause difficulties with some people.' He did not elaborate further.

Eaton had warned Lydia that her old friend, though stoical, was in a very fragile state after receiving the news of her son's disappearance. It was arranged that Eva would stay at a small London hotel while Lydia was working with the Quakers to find Albert; they would return together to Cambridge in due course.

'Do you know the worst thing, Lydia?' Eva said. 'It is the casual everyday cruelty Albert has endured these past few years. The other children at school shunned him. I had no idea how bad it was until his sixth birthday when I organised a party for him – and no one came. Not a single child. And then the Nazis excluded Jewish children from their schools altogether. Albert says nothing about this, but what must he be thinking? What must this do to a gentle young mind?'

Lydia did not know what to say.

Eva sighed. 'I would so like to believe Mr Eaton that it is all a mix-up, but I don't. Nor do you, not in your heart.' She tried to smile. 'And so I suppose I have no option, I must go back to Berlin and suffer the consequences. Perhaps if I do, they will send Albert to freedom. Last month they opened a new concentration camp especially for women at Ravensbrück not far from Berlin. I can die there while Albert lives.'

The telephone rang. Eva and Lydia stared at each other. Lydia stumbled across the boxes in her haste to pick up the receiver. She grabbed a pen and a pad and began making notes.

Eva stared at her, straining to hear the conversation. Lydia avoided her gaze, fearing more negative news. Eva turned away and walked to the window. She stared out across Bloomsbury Square, her eyes fixed on the street below as though her son might somehow appear among the passers-by. Suddenly she stepped back from the window and hurried to the door.

Lydia put her hand over the mouthpiece. 'Eva?'

'I have to get some air, please. Five minutes.' And she was gone.

A rector in Wolverhampton was on the telephone. The child he had taken into his care believed he remembered Albert, although he had not been in the same carriage.

'He says he looked out of the window and saw the boy being led away by two or three men and a woman, both in uniform and plain clothes. From his description, it sounds as though it might be the boy you are looking for.'

Lydia thanked the clergyman and replaced the receiver. The call added nothing other than confirming what little they already knew. She went to the window. Eva was standing in the street, almost directly below, talking to a man. From above, all Lydia could see was his hat and the black tips of his shoes. He was large, almost twice Eva's size. Who was he? Lydia watched, for a moment, trying to make sense of the encounter, and then made for the door, taking the stairs down two at a time.

Outside, Lydia stopped at the top of the stone steps leading down to the pavement. The man Eva had been talking to was already a hundred yards away, hurrying northwards in the direction of Great Russell Street. He had a rolling gait, like a sailor returned to land after months at sea. Eva's eyes were fixed on his retreating back.

'Eva?'

Eva turned abruptly, eyes wide.

'Who was that man?'

'Which man?'

'The one you were talking to. You were deep in conversation with him.'

'Oh, that man.' Eva shrugged. 'It was nothing, Lydia. He was asking the way to the Marylebone Road. I was trying to recall my knowledge of London, but I wasn't doing very well.'

She forced a smile, scrabbled for a cigarette from a pack she was clutching.

'From the way you were talking, I got the impression you knew him.'

'No, no. He was a stranger.' Eva put a cigarette to her lips and struck a match to light it. As an afterthought, she offered the pack to Lydia, who shook her head.

'What are we going to do?' Lydia said, half to herself, half to Eva Haas.

Eva drew nervously on her cigarette and said nothing.

'Promise me you won't do anything rash, Eva.'

'No, I will not do anything rash.' Eva put the back of her cigarette hand to her cheek and wiped away a tear. 'Goddamn these things, I hate them. I have never wept for anything or anyone.' She drew at the cigarette again, aggressively. 'Lydia, I thank you for all your help and concern in this matter. I think there is nothing to be done, and so I must put myself to work. I must do something. Perhaps Eaton will take me up to Cambridge today.'

Lydia took her into her arms again, and this time Eva succumbed to the embrace, racked with ungovernable sobbing. *No,* Lydia thought, looking round at the beautiful summer day, at the trees in full leaf in this lovely part of London, at the men in shirt sleeves and the women in their summer dresses, *this is not good enough. There may be nothing to be done by you, but what about me? I might be able to go where it would be suicidal for you to tread.* She felt responsible for Eva, but more than that, she felt a duty to Albert. He had, after all, been entrusted to her care.

The Eagle was heady with alcohol and smoke and loud voices. Tom Wilde and Geoffrey Lancing bought pints at the bar and tried to find a quiet corner of the ancient pub, but there was no such thing, not today, at least. They wedged themselves close to a window in the smoke room and clinked glasses.

'So what's the big news, Geoff?' Wilde took a deep draught of the beer: his first English bitter in months. He looked around at the other drinkers and was surprised to see how many of them carried gas-mask boxes; he supposed he should do something about acquiring one.

The young physicist took a deep breath. 'You'll never guess who's over for the summer, Tom.'

Wilde raised an eyebrow. 'You're right. I won't. Who?'

'Clarissa.'

'Clarissa?'

'You know – my sister!'

'I'm teasing you, Geoff – of course I know who you meant! I was merely registering surprise. We don't often get movie stars in Cambridge.'

'She's staying with American friends at a rather grand house and estate near here. Milt Hardiman – have you heard of him? Lots of wild parties and tennis planned.'

Milt Hardiman. The man who would be contacting him, according to Dexter Flood. Interesting. A spy might wonder about the coincidence. A good spy might think there was no such thing as coincidence. 'Well, well, that *is* big news. Hasn't she got any films on? To what does Cambridge owe the honour?'

Lancing shook his head. 'Don't try talking to her about films. She's fuming. Had a huge bust-up with Selznick when they picked some bloody little unknown – her words – for this year's big picture. It was a part she was desperate to get. Anyway, I rather think she stormed off in a fury . . .'

'Hollywood's loss is our gain then.'

'Don't worry; she'll go back – and demand even more for her services. Clarissa has never had doubts about her worth.'

'Put me in the line, would you, Geoff?'

'You're already at the front of the queue. Actually she's rather keen to meet you. Perhaps when I mentioned you in my letters I should have been a little less flattering.'

'I very much doubt the glamorous Clarissa Lancing will have the slightest interest in a dull-as-dishwater academic.'

'You wait! Anyway, tell me – what did you do in the States? Sell millions of your new book, I hope.'

Wilde went over most of the ground: his ailing mother, the campuses he visited, jazz nights at Café Society. He mentioned his invitation to meet the President, which impressed Lancing.

'Remarkable, Tom – what did you talk about?'

'This and that. My books, Billie Holiday.'

'And that's it?'

'No, he was fishing. Wanted to know whether I thought there would be a war. Would Britain fight? He talked about gas bombs. Even got onto this new thing out of Germany that you mentioned – fission?'

'Really? Was he concerned?'

'Interested.'

'So he should be. The implications are obvious to any particle physicist. Well, well, so the politicians are waking up at last. About time, too.'

'Won't you tell me about it again? I confess I feel rather ignorant about a subject that is clearly of some importance.'

Lancing's eyes were bright. This was *his* subject. 'The new research means the immense power of the atom can be harnessed. In essence, it's pretty simple, but the details are complex. Everything ever devised by man – from the knife to the steam engine – has had the potential for great good or great harm. You know all this because you're a historian. The thing is, fission once harnessed will likely be the same – a life-giver and destroyer – but a millionfold on both sides. Hahn and Meitner have potentially unleashed a monster.'

'I'd love to know a bit more.'

Lancing shook his head. 'Not here, and not against this din. We'll share a quiet supper soon and I'll explain it all very carefully.'

Wilde looked at his watch; there were matters to attend to at college before Eaton arrived. Mail to be checked, a courtesy call on the master, progress reports on the undergraduates under his supervision who had been looked after by a professor from Peterhouse during his leave of absence. He also wanted to talk with Jim Vanderberg at the US embassy in Grosvenor Square, get the lowdown on Dexter Flood.

'Can I call in on you at the Cavendish tomorrow, Geoff?'

Lancing finished his drink. 'Eleven o'clock sharp. I'll show you around.'

Henty O'Gara gripped the handles of the bag with dry fingers and palm. His brow and top lip, likewise, were dry. These were the places those in the know – customs men, police officers – always looked. Sweat on the top lip, damp palms: these were the giveaways that suggested you had something to hide.

But this man, whatever he felt inside, didn't betray such nerves, even though the bag was heavy and contained gelignite and detonators, among other things.

'Name?' the landlady demanded.

'Declan Burns,' he said. It was the first lie. 'Here's my travel document.'

She was a thin woman with a pinched, cheerless face. She looked at the document closely and saw the word Ireland. 'You're Irish then?'

He grinned. 'Was it the accent that gave it away?'

She didn't get the joke. 'No, but it says so here. Ireland, it says.' She looked up and studied his face, then glanced at the bag. 'That's a heavy suitcase you have there.'

'I'm doing a great deal of travelling. I'm a salesman.'

'You're not one of those bombers are you, Mr Burns?'

'Would you like to look in my bag, missus?'

'Why, what's in it?'

'Shirts, pants, socks, books and bombs.' He was still grinning. 'Don't worry about the bombs, they're only small ones.'

Her lips pursed sourly. 'I assume that's your idea of humour, Mr Burns.'

'Sorry, missus. You know, I've got this and that. A few unmentionables. Will I open it for you?'

'No, thank you.' There were certain things ladies never did, and one of them was inspecting gentlemen's undergarments. The very thought of it . . .

'But you've got a room I can have for the week?'

She hesitated, weighing up the pros and cons. Filling an otherwise empty room and making a couple of pounds against the disgrace of having a vulgar and impertinent Irishman under her roof at a time when they were setting off bombs all over England. Mercenary interests won the day. 'Very well, Mr Burns,' she said. 'But I'll have no funny business in my house. No women callers, no alcohol, no whistling. Is that understood?'

'But I can build my bombs, can I?' he said, so quietly that she didn't hear.

'What was that?'

'I was just agreeing to your terms. No women, whistling or whisky.'

'Money in advance.' She held out her right hand.

'Two pounds, was it?'

'Two pounds ten shillings.'

It was daylight robbery. This place stank of unwashed bodies and over-boiled cabbage. Slowly, he counted out the money then deposited it in her hand.

Her fingers curled around the cash, then she reached to a rack behind her and removed a key. 'Follow me. It's here on the ground floor. If you're not in by ten o'clock the front door's locked and no amount of banging will get you in. Breakfast is at six-thirty. Porridge, two rashers of bacon, two eggs, two slices of toast and you'll share a pot of tea with the other three men on your table.'

'Will there be marmalade with the toast?'

'This isn't the Ritz, you know. Supper's at six. Soup, meat with spuds and two veg, pudding with custard.'

'Well, it all sounds just grand, missus.'

The room was at the back, looking out over the garden. It had a single bed and a window of rotting wood that appeared stuck fast. Well, sod that, he'd be opening it all right. The landlady nodded to the bed. 'Sheets are clean on. I expect the bed to be made every day. Hospital corners, mind. The lav and bathroom are one floor up, but there's a chamberpot under the bed. You'll empty it before you go out in the morning. Are you looking for work, Mr Burns?'

'As I said, I'm a travelling salesman.'

She looked at him as though she didn't believe for a moment that he had work, but handed over the key and left the room, with a last backward glance of disgust in his direction. He couldn't resist a laugh. After she had gone he locked the door and opened his valise. He pulled out his shirts and spare trousers. There beneath them were three dozen sticks of gelignite and half a dozen electric detonators.

O'Gara glanced at his wristwatch. Four o'clock. He'd have to call Hyde soon. The bastard hadn't answered the last three times. The phone just rang and rang. It was unnerving. An operative without a controller was like a ship without a rudder. So he'd call him first, then go to the library. Please God, Hyde would answer this time.

He guessed the public library would probably close in an hour. From the depths of his bag, he pulled out a padlock and secured the grips together in such a way to make it impossible to open. It would be enough to deter the landlady, but would easily be bypassed if she got worried and called the police. It was a risk he would just have to take.

He found the book in the rather magnificent reading room of the Free Library in Wheeler Street. It occupied the high-domed space at the rear of the Guildhall, an altogether too grand salon for the somewhat down-at-heel men and women who were reading the newspapers at lecterns or whiling away their days at the long benches, heads bowed low over books and magazines.

O'Gara smiled at a young woman and took a seat at her side. She turned her shoulder to him, as though he were intruding on her space and privacy. He put the book down on the table in front of him. It was an old, slim volume – at least two centuries old – but it looked in pristine condition, as though it had never been much in favour. He opened its leather cover. The title page revealed it to be *Grace Abounding to the Chief of Sinners,* by John Bunyan, dated 1666.

He flicked through the leaves until he came to page twenty-four. There it was, the small slip of paper he had come for, exactly where it was supposed to be. He glanced around the room. Everyone was engrossed in their own reading. No one was looking at him.

His right hand covered the slip of paper and closed around it. For five minutes he read the words in the book, the spiritual tract of an imprisoned

Puritan gentleman, perhaps as much of a rebel in his own way as Henty O'Gara had been brought up to be.

Surreptitiously he removed his hand and slid the paper into the breast pocket of his jacket. Finally he closed the book and returned it to the shelf where he had found it.

At the desk, he thanked the librarian who had pointed him in the right direction.

'Did you find what you were looking for?'

'Indeed, sir, thank you,' O'Gara said. 'A brief moment of spiritual guidance. It's all we can ask for, isn't it?'

'We don't get much call for *Grace Abounding*. Personally, I find it a comfort on the rare occasions I delve inside.'

'Well, good day to you.'

He tried calling Hyde again. Still no answer. This was alarming. He returned to his lodgings, where he studied the slip of paper from the book in the library. It was encrypted, of course. A few minutes later, he had decoded the message and memorised it. He struck a match and burnt the paper in the grate, then returned to the joyless single bed. It was harder than a prison mattress. He glanced at his watch. Still four hours until dusk. Time for a nap, but sleep would not come easily.

And then to business. And, all being well, contact with the Scavenger.

On the west coast of Ireland, Dorian Hyde hesitated a few moments on the far side of the road from the pub. There was no sign outside, nothing to say that this was a boozer, but anyone would know what it was: the reek of beer and smoke told the story, even across the street. It was a low, single-storey building that looked as though it had been constructed of mud, then dried out and whitewashed. Not untypical of the commonplace houses in these northern reaches of Galway, outside the town itself and a little way to the east of the Corrib River.

At last he gathered his courage, crossed the road and ducked inside. The doorway would have made a man of five and a half feet dip his head, and Hyde was a six-footer plus another couple of inches besides, so he was almost bent double. Once inside, he straightened up, feeling enormous and out of place. Eyes turned to look at him and kept looking at him.

Hyde touched his flat cap, which was not far from the ceiling, and nodded to the dozen or so drinkers. He was dressed as a working man, loose trousers held up with knotted string, shirt sleeves rolled up tight, cloth pack with meagre contents slung over his left shoulder.

The other drinkers did not acknowledge him further, but turned back to their pints.

Even as he entered he had spotted Connell's sallow cheeks and his grey, grizzled head, but his eyes did not linger there. Instead he tilted his chin to the barman. 'A pint of stout, if you will.'

The barman said nothing, but began pulling the pint.

'I was told there might be work in the town,' Hyde said.

The barkeep, a bull of a man with bulging biceps and a navy beard, snorted. 'Who ever told you that's a liar, mister. Where you from?'

'Kildare.'

'Jesus now, that's a distance.'

'Walked the whole way.'

'Should have turned east instead of west, swum to England. That's where the work is. Look at these fellers,' – he swept the taproom with his eyes – 'barely an honest day's work between them these past six months.'

'What of the fishermen? Would there be work on the boats now?'

'Not a hope in hell. You might get a place on a passing freighter if you don't mind going to the ends of the earth, but that'll be your lot.'

'Well, I'll maybe try the harbour anyway.' He spoke just loud enough that Connell, a couple of places along the bar, could hear him.

The barman shrugged and turned away. Hyde downed his pint, wiped his sleeve across his mouth, nodded to nobody in particular and ducked back out into the cool Galway dusk. He strolled down to the harbour and sat on the dock, swinging his legs. Connell appeared an hour later, just after dark. He didn't sit down, merely stood with his hands deep in his pockets looking out across the lights of the teeming boats.

'Do you want to get me killed, Captain Hyde?' he said from the corner of his mouth. 'Coming in there like that. Is that what they teach you in the British secret service?'

'I need to know about O'Gara. I don't trust him. I need to know the truth about him.'

'I can't talk here. You're as obvious as a wolf in a sheep pen.'

'I'm as Irish as any man in this town, Connell.'

'Ah, well, that was always the Anglo-Irish mistake now, wasn't it? Thinking youse was one of us.'

'You watch the way you address me, Connell. Remember who's the chief around here.'

'My apologies, captain.'

'Where then?'

Connell lit a cigarette, then crumpled the pack and dropped it. 'I'll be there at midnight.'

A little while after Connell had gone, Hyde picked up the cigarette packet. Inside he found a slip of paper with a map and the name of a house two miles along the coast to the west.

CHAPTER 7

When Tom Wilde arrived home, Philip Eaton was already there, waiting in his car. Wilde felt a mixture of emotions as he looked at him: curiosity over his request for assistance with the German refugees, but also distaste. Three years after their last encounter, it was never going to be an easy meeting. Not for Wilde, at least.

In the winter of 1936 they had worked together to foil a conspiracy by enemies of the British state. Wilde, the amateur, had joined forces with Eaton, the professional spy, to prevent a blood-soaked atrocity on British soil, but the operation had left Wilde with a profound sense of unease about the true motives and loyalties of the MI6 officer.

Eaton climbed out of the car as soon as Wilde reached his front gate. He afforded Wilde a friendly smile and put out his hand. Wilde hesitated for no more than a heartbeat before shaking it, but it would have been long enough for Eaton to note the slight hesitation.

'Good to see you after all this time,' Eaton said.

'Quite a surprise, Eaton. Quite a surprise.'

'Oh, I'm sure you didn't think you could avoid me forever. Anyway, you look well. And you're clearly prospering. The new book's selling like hot cakes, I believe.'

'Come indoors. I've got tea or whisky.'

'Hmm. No contest.'

They settled in the kitchen over tumblers of Scotch. Wilde got straight to the point. 'You'd better tell me everything.'

Eaton was in no hurry. He warmed the whisky glass in his hands and reclined back on the wooden chair. 'As I said, we've got Lindberg out of Germany.'

'And how exactly did you extract him from the concentration camp?'

'England has friends. Friends who despise the Heydrichs and the Streichers. It was important for us to get him to safety. A war's coming and the fewer men with Lindberg's intellect left in Germany, the better it will be for the world. And now that he's out he needs to come here to Cambridge. He needs access to a lab – and the Cavendish is the place.'

'Don't avoid the subject. If I'm to help, I should be given the courtesy of a little straight talking. I want to know how he escaped.'

'The Jewish underground.'

'And they can get prisoners out of Dachau, can they?'

'You'll see the evidence with your own eyes. Hear it from Lindberg's own lips.'

'And then how did he escape Germany?'

'He and his niece walked through the mountains if you must know. I was waiting for them in Switzerland.'

'Posing as a *Times* journalist, of course.'

'Not *posing*, Wilde. I *am* a *Times* correspondent, as you know very well.'

Among other things, thought Wilde.

'Look, I'm telling you the truth. Lindberg is here in England with Frau Haas and they need somewhere a little more permanent than a London hotel. That's the size of it. I suppose they could both stay next door with Miss Morris, but it seemed to me that with you here, it might be more comfortable if you had one each. Miss Morris with her friend, Lindberg with you. Share the burden.'

'How long would you intend him to be here with me?'

Eaton gave a non-committal shrug. 'Hard to say. Hopefully things will settle down and we'll find him lodgings of his own – perhaps rooms in one of the colleges.' He sighed. 'I have to come clean with you. His disappearance from Dachau has caused ructions in Berlin. Himmler is beside himself with rage. You may recall that Lindberg insulted the little creep? Well, Heinrich Himmler doesn't forgive easily. He wants Lindberg dead.'

Wilde's stomach tightened. So it wasn't lodgings that Lindberg needed, but a safe house. 'You're expecting an attempt on his life?'

'Not *expecting*. But it's possible. Germany has agents here. That's why I'm bringing Lindberg to someone I trust. You know all about keeping your mouth shut.'

Wilde did not feel flattered. Nor did he feel at all reassured that Cambridge was the correct place to keep an enemy of the Third Reich safe from harm. The town was full of people of all races and political creeds, including Nazis, Mosley's Blackshirts and their sympathisers. As for the Cavendish Laboratory, how would Lindberg's presence in that crucible of cutting-edge science be kept a secret?

'As I understand it then, you'll be asking me to put *my* life on the line? And what of Lydia if she's looking after the woman – will she be in danger, too?'

'I said I wouldn't lie to you and I meant it. Yes, if word gets out that Lindberg's here, you could be at risk. But I also know from my own experience that you and Miss Morris do not lack for courage and resourcefulness.'

Wilde ignored the soft soap. 'Have you spoken to Lydia yet?'

'Yes, of course. She has been a party to this all along.'

This was a bad idea. A very bad idea. 'Why not keep them on an army base somewhere?'

Eaton poured himself another shot. 'Herr Dr Lindberg has just spent the last three years of his life in the barrack-room hell of Dachau. I think he deserves rather better than another dose of barracks, don't you? Isn't that the difference between our civilisation and Hitler's barbarism?'

Wilde had been backed into a corner. 'I'll do it. But he'll need to fend for himself, because I have work at college – and I had intended going down to London to help Lydia when the long vacation starts next week.' Not only to help her, of course, but to try to plaster over the lesions in their long-distance relationship. He knew she resented him for not accompanying her to London to help with the refugees; likewise, he had desperately wanted her to accompany him to America to meet his mother. Who could know whether it might be her last chance?

He and Lydia had not parted on the best of terms but he had missed her – and he rather feared that she had not missed him. These were not matters for Eaton, however. 'When are you going to bring Lindberg up?'

'Soon enough. My colleagues at the ministry have been chatting to him, trying to find out what they can. He's providing some good intelligence – extraordinary the people he lived with in Dachau. Some of Germany's finest minds reduced to scrubbing the latrines.'

'What about Frau Haas?'

'Well, she *was* going to stay in London, but she insisted she wanted to come up to Cambridge right away, with me. She's got a room at the Bull. I'm not happy about it, though, Wilde. Not happy at all. I really would have liked the chance for a longer, more intensive interview with her. But it was her decision to come up; she was adamant.'

'Is she safe?'

Eaton hesitated a moment too long. 'I can't discuss our security arrangements.'

'Should I be armed?'

'That's up to you, Wilde. I can provide a weapon if you wish.'

Wilde sighed. 'I'm not sure I'll forgive you for this, Eaton. I certainly won't if any harm comes to Lydia.' What in God's name were they letting themselves in for?

'Come on, nothing's going to happen in sleepy old Cambridge!'

'And you can say that with a straight face? Do you intend the woman to stay at the Bull until Lydia gets home?'

'Why not? I wouldn't think it would be for long. Perhaps you could look in on her, make her feel at home.'

'If you think that would help.'

'More than anything, I would like to find them both space at the Cavendish. They've both done work there in the past. I believe Frau Haas was one of the first female student researchers there. My office has spoken with the lab's director, Lawrence Bragg, but he seems a little uncertain. He said they would happily have taken in a hundred German physicists if they had space – but they don't. America seems the better option. Personally, I would rather keep Herr Lindberg to ourselves. We'll need minds like his when the balloon goes up. See what you can do, Wilde. You have charm. Use it on your chum Lancing.'

Wilde stiffened. How did Eaton know of his friendship with Geoff Lancing? Perhaps he shared sources with Colonel Dexter Flood in the White House. He breathed out. 'I don't suppose I should be surprised.'

'That I know about you and Lancing? Well, the Cavendish and science in general has taken on a new significance in recent months on various fronts, and for various reasons I am not at liberty to discuss. The upshot is, men like Lancing have come under close scrutiny.'

'Under scrutiny?'

'Not just Geoff Lancing. They all have – all the clever scientists. With war probably no more than a year or two away, we have to take precautions. You're a Walsingham man. You understand such things.'

Of course he did. But he didn't always like them to be so close to home.

Eaton raised his glass. 'You're a good man, Wilde. We could do with people like you in the service.'

'Very funny. I've turned you down on that score already, if you recall. I'm American by birth. Very happy to work with the British, but not for them.'

'Indeed. I took your point when I first broached the subject. Talking of America, I believe you've been seeing some interesting people during your little sabbatical.'

'You mean my mother, of course. She's always interesting. Mostly she berated me for never going to Mass.'

'Oh come, come, don't be so modest. You know that's not what I meant. The White House . . . can't keep a thing like that secret in a gossipy town like Washington DC, you know.'

Wilde should have felt affronted but he wasn't surprised; that was the point of a secret intelligence service, wasn't it? He laughed. 'Well, Eaton, if you know so much you won't need me to tell you any more.'

'I'd have liked to have been a fly on the wall, that's all.'

'You mean you don't have the Oval Office bugged? Your friends must be slipping.' He was suddenly impatient to see the back of Eaton. 'Are we done then?'

Eaton's fingers tightened around his glass. 'There's something else, a little complication.'

'Go on.'

'Frau Haas's son, Albert. He's eight years old. He was coming out of Germany separately, to be met at Liverpool Street railway station by Miss Morris. We know he was put on the train. But it seems he was lifted from his carriage at the border when the train was about to cross from Germany into the Netherlands.'

'Lifted by whom?'

'Border guards . . . Gestapo, perhaps. Not certain.'

Wilde's mood changed. 'Good God, that is not a *little* complication,' he said angrily. 'It's a hostile act. An outrage! Where is the child now?'

'We don't know. We assume he has been taken back to Berlin. But so far we've had no word. It's as if he's vanished from the face of the earth. The embassy over there and the Quakers are looking into the matter with great urgency. Miss Morris and Frau Haas are extremely distraught.'

'This changes things, Eaton.'

'You mean you won't look after Lindberg?'

'Quite the contrary. It means I will do all in my power to help. If it helps, they can both come here until Lydia gets home. Now,' – Wilde got to his feet and ushered Eaton to the door – 'I have things to do.'

And thinking. Lots of thinking to do. There was still a nagging doubt. No one could have concerns regarding Eaton's enmity for Nazi Germany. But that didn't mean he was to be trusted.

Lydia sat opposite Bertha Bracey on the third floor of Bloomsbury House.

'Nothing,' Bertha said.

'What can we do?'

'The embassy is doing all it can. Miss Forster is in touch with senior members of the regime.'

'They won't talk to her, will they?'

'You'll be surprised, my dear. Strange as it may seem, many Nazis have fond feelings towards the Society of Friends. Anyway, we won't give up. Albert Haas must be somewhere – and so we shall find him and shame them into reuniting him with his mother.'

'We have to do something, Bertha. We can't just sit here and wait.'

'Patience, my dear. Make use of the patience God teaches us.'

Lydia shook her head. 'No. It's not good enough. I have to do something. Frau Haas can't go back to Berlin, so I will have to go.'

Bertha Bracey's shock registered in her eyes. 'Is that wise, my dear?'

'Wisdom has nothing to do with it. I accepted responsibility for the boy. Anyway, I know my way around Berlin. If Albert is there, I'll find him.'

'I need you here, Lydia. And—' She hesitated, her kind face concerned. 'Forgive me, my dear, but I ask this as a friend – what of Professor Wilde? He must have returned from America by now. Have you not been in contact with him?'

Lydia bristled. What had this to do with Bertha Bracey? 'I was going to call him this evening,' she said stiffly.

Bertha picked up the handset from her desk telephone and turned it towards Lydia. 'I'm just going out to the newsagent. You have the room to yourself for half an hour.'

Wilde was sitting at his desk when the phone rang. He picked it up.

'Tom Wilde.'

'So you came back.'

'Did you doubt it?'

'Well, it would probably have been safer to stay over there.'

She still knew how to rile him. But they weren't going to argue, were they? He softened his tone. 'Lydia. It's good to hear your voice.' Two and a half months was a long time in the history of a relationship, particularly one as difficult as theirs had been in the weeks before he left. 'When will I see you?'

She was businesslike. 'Soon. I gather Eaton will be bringing Herr Dr Lindberg up to stay with you. I'll be a few more days. Bertha Bracey needs me here.'

'I'm sorry about that—'

'It won't be long. Tell me about America. Did you have a good journey?' A pause and then the words he'd hoped to hear: 'I've missed you, Tom.'

He hoped she meant it. He wasn't sure. 'I've missed you, too, Lydia. I have a lot to tell you. Mostly, I just want to see you.'

'How was your mother?'

'Strong as an ox in her mind. But I wasn't convinced. She seemed frail. Look, Lydia, there's so much to tell – to talk about. I could catch the train down tonight. Lindberg isn't here yet, and Frau Haas is bedded down at the Bull. There's nothing to keep me here.'

No hesitation in her reply. Straight in. 'No, Tom. To be blunt, I'm working my socks off. I'm really not great company at the moment. Anyway,

Eva Haas needs you. You've heard about this frightful business with her boy? I've been glued to the phone and the wires – that's why I couldn't meet you off the boat. You understand, don't you?'

'Of course I do.' He wasn't at all sure that he did. 'But wouldn't it have been better if Frau Haas had stayed in London while inquiries are being made?'

'That was the original plan, but she insisted she had to go up there. I suppose she's right. There's nothing she can do in London – and she needs to work or she'll go mad. Cambridge is the place for her. I won't be more than a few days. Then we'll have the long vac to look forward to.'

She sounded distant, as if London was further away than America. There was something she wasn't telling him. He didn't doubt her fidelity, not for a moment, but he was missing something. 'Well,' he said at last, 'a thousand kisses.'

'And a million back.'

Just time for those three words, but she didn't say them, and neither did he.

'The days will fly by, Tom. You'll have to enjoy May Week for both of us.'

'Lydia, where are you staying?'

But the line had already gone dead.

Lydia looked at the phone. Tom had wanted her to go with him to America to meet his mother; she understood that. She understood, too, that with war looming it could be her last opportunity: Mary Wilde was not in the best of health.

But this was bigger, this work in London. This was about the fate of thousands of children. They had to come first, and if Tom and his mother couldn't see that, well there was nothing to be done.

Henty O'Gara wrenched open the rotting window on the ground floor of the boarding house, slipped out into the garden and made his way westwards through the maze of dirty, neglected streets from the railway track in Barnwell. In his pocket was a scrap of paper, part of an ordnance survey map of the town. It was, perhaps, the one thing that could cause him trouble if he was searched, but he could always claim that any tourist would have a bit of map like this to find their way around. It would be a poor piece of evidence to hold him on. The bag of explosives in his room was another matter, of course.

This was the route he had taken to the Free Library, but now he stopped short, at the edge of the park known as Christ's Pieces. He waited at the corner of Earl Street, just before the pleasant terraces of Emmanuel Road. They were nice houses, early nineteenth century, he guessed. A little like some parts of Dublin. He suppressed a laugh. The stamp of the British. The stamp of their fucking dominion over a quarter of the globe.

A group of men were finishing a game of bowls on the green and a policeman in his tall helmet was walking slowly across the centre of the park, hands behind back, looking all around him.

O'Gara stood and watched for five minutes, smoking a cigarette like any working man loitering between pub and home, until the constable turned away down Drummer Street towards the town centre. The bowls players were packing away their equipment. Dusk lingered this close to midsummer. O'Gara walked to the centre of the little park, where paths crossed. Through the trees, he caught sight of a church spire, a little way to the north and west. Lowering his gaze, he saw what he was looking for: the wall that separated Christ's Pieces from Christ's College. And in the wall, almost in line with the church spire, was a closed wooden door.

Checking that the policeman hadn't turned back, O'Gara strode towards the door in the wall. *Hold your shoulders back*, he told himself, *don't look furtive.*

The door was painted green, but he had no interest in it or what lay behind its peeling paint. It was the brickwork. Five courses up from the pavement, then fifteen bricks to the left. The one with barely any mortar. His hand went to it. It should be loose, but it wasn't.

He counted again and was certain he had made no mistake. Behind him he heard a sound. He turned, and flattened his back to the wall. Two undergraduates in billowing gowns were racing each other across the park, laughing as they went. He breathed again.

Taking a penknife from his pocket, he opened the longer of the two blades and slid it into the mortar to the right of the brick. With the fingernails of his left hand he got a grip on the other side of the brick and that was enough. It came out and fell to the ground, breaking in two with a dull crack.

O'Gara probed the hole in the wall and pulled out a small edge of cardboard, the cover for a book of matches. He turned it over, and there it was: a telephone number and a time. Picking up the two halves of the brick, he replaced them in the hole.

CHAPTER 8

The Deutsche Lufthansa flight took off from Croydon Aerodrome in bright sunshine at 8 a.m. On any other day, Lydia would have baulked at boarding an aircraft bearing a swastika on its tail, but this was the earliest available flight to Berlin, with just one stop, in Amsterdam. She had no option.

As the plane rose steadily into the cloudless sky, it occurred to her that the pilots could be transferred to the Luftwaffe at a moment's notice and be sent back to attack Britain along familiar and well-rehearsed routes.

Her seat was close to the front of the plane, beside the porthole window. She looked out and down through the light scattering of clouds as England turned into a green patchwork of fields and forests, rivers and roads. She had a book, but her eyes were heavy from lack of sleep and she kept it closed in her lap.

'Are you travelling for business or pleasure, young lady?' the man at her side said in precise English as the plane levelled off at its cruising altitude.

His voice startled her. He had arrived on board after she had settled herself in the window seat, and plonked himself down beside her. She had nodded to him and said *Guten Tag*, but then turned away, not wishing to engage in conversation. Now she found herself obliged to reply. She smiled apologetically. 'A little bit of both.'

'Amsterdam or Berlin?'

'Berlin.'

'Me too,' he said.

He was a pink-faced man, clean-shaven with a double chin nestling comfortably on the edge of his collar. She had already decided that he looked German, with his fair hair close-cropped. She guessed he was a businessman of some sort, but you couldn't tell in these feverish days. There was so much talk of Nazi spies, agents and fifth columnists. He offered her a cigarette and when she declined, took one for himself and lit it, blowing a cloud of smoke in her direction and making her feel queasy.

'I am going home before the war starts,' he continued. 'Much as I like England I have no wish to be stranded there, away from my family.'

'Perhaps there won't be a war.'

'Oh, there will be a war. Fortunately I am too old and fat to fight this time round.' His belly rumbled and he turned to face her and put out his right hand. 'Manfred Bloch, young lady. England representative for Seebald Royal Tours.'

His fingers were limp and podgy and damp. A wave of soapy eau de cologne wafted her way. 'Should I have heard of your company?'

He laughed. 'No, no. It is not the biggest of enterprises. We take holidaymakers on tours of the great houses and palaces of Europe – mostly England, France, Hungary and Germany.'

'And you gain access to these palaces?'

He laughed again. 'You have caught me out. No, young lady, we do not have access to Buckingham Palace or Balmoral – but where possible we show the exteriors from a distance. We make these restrictions quite clear to our clients, most of whom are German.' He lowered his voice confidentially. 'I must confess they tend to prefer Windsor Castle to Versailles. I think we have more kinship with England.'

'Then let us hope war can be avoided. Another great war would be a terrible tragedy.'

'Indeed, but we must be realists. I am certain I shall not be returning to your country this year.'

She felt herself drifting again. Yeats came to mind; slouching towards Bethlehem. She was writing again, more feverishly than she had done for years, but her publishing company was in the doldrums. Nothing had come her way that she loved and so she had published nothing. Her eyes were heavy. 'Forgive me,' she said. 'I must rest. I did not sleep well last night.'

Lydia had not told Eva that she planned to go to Germany herself, for Eva would doubtlessly have tried to dissuade her. She understood the German woman's need to work, to still her mind. *She has been through so much*, thought Lydia. Perhaps she no longer had the energy to keep on fighting. But she, Lydia, could not let it go. She had promised to keep Albert safe. If his mother could not go to Berlin then she would go herself. But she would not tell Tom, for he would move the very heavens to prevent her going. And if – *when* – she found Albert she would accompany him back to London personally. Eaton had been another matter. He had understood instantly why she felt she needed to go, and had offered her advice and the name of a contact.

The plane droned on. She closed her eyes and turned her head away from Herr Bloch. He left her in peace. Some time later, she felt a hand on her shoulder. 'Miss,' her fellow passenger said. 'We are making our descent.' She looked out of the window and saw the distinctive crescent of the aerodrome buildings at Tempelhof, close to the heart of Berlin. Everything was grey and cloudy. Smoke rose from a million chimneys, many of them industrial.

She was puzzled. 'What happened to Amsterdam?'

'You slept through it. I could see no purpose in waking you as we were not required to disembark.' He took a card from his pocket. It was embossed with his name and company details. 'Feel free to call if I can ever be of service, miss.'

She did not take the card. 'I do not think I will be going on any royal tours, Herr Bloch.'

'That is not what I meant.' He pushed the card closer then dropped it in her lap, just as the plane made its landing. 'Germany is a hard place for a stranger these days.'

She still felt groggy. The bouncing of the aircraft across the tarmac did not help, but she took the card from her lap. What exactly was he implying?

'I know people,' he said, his voice little more than a whisper, almost drowned out by the propellers as the plane taxied towards the grand terminal building. 'You never know when you might need assistance.' He lit another cigarette.

For some reason, she warmed to him. 'My name is Lydia Morris,' she said. She picked up his card and put it in her novel. 'Thank you. I needed a bookmark.'

In three years, the great city had undergone profound changes, even out here in the suburbs. From the back of the taxi, Lydia gazed at the swastika banners of red, black and white, that hung from every public building. She spotted a squad of brown-shirted men marching and she saw the smashed and boarded shop windows and knew what they were. Back in August 1936, when she had last been in Berlin for the Olympics, the persecution of the Jews had been hidden away, the *Stürmer* showcases put into storage so that the so-called newspaper's foul anti-Semitic message might be concealed for a while. Now there was evidence of persecution and militarism wherever she looked.

Lydia had wondered if there might be difficulties at the aerodrome, given the strained relations between Germany and Britain. Perhaps she would be detained by border control and customs officials and questioned for hours on end. In the event, the passport inspector had asked her business and she said she was visiting a friend, Miss Ulrike Forster, for a short holiday. He had asked, too, about her religion and race and seemed satisfied by 'Quaker, British', although, of course, the religious implication was not strictly true. The customs officer opened her case and sifted her belongings cursorily before closing it again and nodding her through. The official at the pass control, bored or indifferent, stamped her passport, intoned a perfunctory 'Heil Hitler', and waved her through, wishing her a pleasant stay in the new Germany. 'Heil Hitler,' she said back, knowing that others who failed to respond had been barred entry. At all events, it had been easier to get into the country, she suspected, than it would be to get out for most people.

Miss Ulrike Forster, one of the Quakers' organisers in Berlin, lived to the west of the city, in a villa near Schlactensee. She was a serious woman trying to maintain sanity in a world cheapened by brutality and tyranny. She threw the large, heavy door wide. 'Come in, Miss Morris, please come in.'

The house was enormous. From the outside it was overblown and intensely ugly, built to impress with baroque pretensions. Indoors, the rooms were high-ceilinged and cold, designed for another age. But they were furnished simply in the Quaker style. No extravagance.

Lydia hauled in her small suitcase. 'I'm sorry to land myself on you at such short notice.'

'All are welcome here, Miss Morris.'

'Thank you.' A question hovered on her lips, then emerged more in hope than expectation. 'Any news?'

'Nothing. Not a word. What must poor Frau Dr Haas be feeling? You know Albert really is the sweetest boy you could meet. I cannot imagine anyone would harm him.'

Miss Forster spoke in clear, textbook English with every consonant enunciated clearly, but her accent was pure German, having spent most of her fifty years in the country of her mother's birth. Tall and thin with not an ounce of fat on her, she wore her straight fair hair almost like a medieval helmet. She reminded Lydia of some of her father's more austere Quaker friends.

'We will talk over lunch. First, though, you must unpack and freshen yourself up. Is that well with you?'

'Thank you, Miss Forster.' Lydia hesitated. 'I really am very grateful. I know that you have done everything humanly possible to find Albert but I couldn't just sit there in London waiting. I had to come . . .'

'Well, I admire your spirit.' Miss Forster smiled and Lydia saw that her first impressions had been wrong; there was a great deal of warmth there. 'Lunch in half an hour, yes?'

'Yes, that would be lovely.' And then she would go to Tiergartenstrasse and talk to the man whose name had been given to her by Philip Eaton.

'Just a small word of warning, Miss Morris. You must realise that we are all watched. My house is observed, your entry into the country will have been noted and they will undoubtedly take an interest in you.'

CHAPTER 9

Sweat dripped from Wilde's brow and streamed in rivulets down his cheeks. His hair was soaked, and his bare, tanned chest glistened. He hit the punchbag with a machine-gun flurry of sharp jabs, then stood back, breathing heavily.

'You're out of condition, Prof.' The trainer raised a reproachful eyebrow. 'Slow.'

'Thanks for telling me, Joe. I think I'd worked that out for myself.'

'Don't they have gyms in Yankeeland?'

They had plenty, of course, and some pretty damn fine boxers, too, but Wilde had found his time in America eaten up by his lecture tour, and, of course, staying with his mother in Boston. He could have found an hour or two for himself, he supposed; perhaps he had been too lazy.

'Come on, let's spar a little, Prof. Three minutes. I'll go easy on you.'

'No, not today, Joe.' He had already untied the laces on his gloves and was removing them. He put them on the boards at the edge of the ring, then reached for his towel to wipe his face and body. 'I've got an eleven o'clock appointment.'

'I'll let you off then. Just this once.'

Wilde was a lean, powerful man, a middleweight, but he knew that he could never beat Joe Spinks in a fight, even though Joe was six inches shorter and two and a half stone lighter than him, as well as a couple of years older. Joe had been an Army champion before going professional, featherweight division. He'd been about to have a crack at the British title when he got sick. After three months out he had come back, but he never got another shot at the title. He still fought with the courage and ferocity of a terrier, though. Could still whip any man within two weight divisions in the eastern counties, amateur or pro. Most of all, he possessed skills and speed of which Wilde, though a fair amateur, could only dream.

He liked this little gym on the south side of Cambridge. It stank of stale sweat and leather and there were flecks of dried blood and plenty of dust because no one ever cleaned the place, which was all part of its questionable charm. Lydia, who considered boxing barbaric, would not have approved.

Wilde picked up the gloves and handed them to Spinks. 'Put those away for me, would you, Joe?' He nodded towards the wall clock. 'You keep that ten minutes slow, if I recall. I've got to make tracks.'

'Next week then?'

'Sooner than that, I hope. As you so bluntly said, I'm slow.' He was stripped to the waist, his trousers held up by a belt and secured at the ankles with bicycle clips, above bare feet. His shirt and tie hung like limp rags from a hook on the far wall. He pulled on his shirt, aware that he probably smelt like a raccoon. But there were no washing facilities here and he didn't have time to go home or to the college baths. Geoff would just have to take him as he was. He dragged on his socks and shoes. He didn't bother to knot his tie properly, just let it hang about his neck and tucked the ends down his shirt front.

He stepped outside into the balmy summer air. His motorbike was right in front of him, perched on its stand and he stood back for a brief moment to admire her. The Rudge Special. One hundred miles per hour guaranteed, as he had proved more than once when the summer roads were dry and traffic-free. He'd had the Rudge three years now and had grown to love her sensuous black body, her slender gold trimmings and her long chrome exhausts; she had served him well.

Pulling on his goggles, he kicked the bike into life and sped off up the road, his shirt billowing around him. Five minutes later, he wound his way down the narrow thoroughfare known as Free School Lane and drew to a halt outside the Cavendish Laboratory, a rather prosaic late-Victorian building that might have pleased a self-satisfied municipal worthy.

Inset high in the ornate gatehouse wall was a statue of the Duke of Devonshire, whose family name was Cavendish, and who had provided the cash to found this place of discovery and science. Its motto invited you in: *Magna opera Domini exquisita in omnes voluntates eius* – the works of the Lord are great, searched for by all who delight in them.

But fine words and a few noble carvings aside, the Cavendish was a dull building that had been blackened by soot in the half century since its construction. Nothing from the outside suggested that this characterless place had produced some of the most dramatic and astonishing scientific advances in human history; that it was, in fact, a place of magic.

Wilde pushed the Rudge through the wide oak gateway into a cobbled courtyard where a mass of bicycles crowded the walls. To his right he saw the rather incongruous new Mond laboratory with its crocodile motif (said to be have been ordered by the Russian physicist Kapitsa in tribute to the late Lord Rutherford); further along, there was scaffolding and the noise of builders at work.

He hoisted his motorbike onto its stand and strode into the main building. At the entrance, he spoke quickly to the porter, who pointed him in the right direction. He climbed up a flight of stone steps, two at a time, to a high, half-panelled corridor reeking of tobacco smoke and strange electrical smells, and he picked his way over a stone floor carpeted with discarded cigarette butts and ash.

Geoff Lancing was at his workbench in a small, chaotic office. There were books and papers everywhere. Sunlight flooded in through the curtainless window on to a collection of unidentifiable pieces of machinery and glassware, some seemingly broken, some held together with rubber bands or bits of string.

Lancing did not look up. 'You're late, Tom.'

'All of five minutes. How can I ever make it up to you?'

'I'll find a way, don't you worry.' At last he raised his eyes, and grinned.

'Is this really the place where they split the atom, Geoff? I rather think the Mad Hatter might have been at home here.'

'Out of chaos comes order.' Lancing backed his chair away from the bench and stood up. 'Actually, that's not entirely true.'

'Entropy.'

'You understand more science than you let on, Tom.'

'I sometimes think entropy applies as much to history as it does the real world. Things fall apart . . .'

'Well, you've obviously got a clear head this morning, which is a good start.'

'What's going on with that scaffolding outside?'

'An extension – the Austin Wing – paid for with a generous grant. Should be up and running as a high-tension lab in next to no time. A cyclotron has already been installed.' Lancing shook his head, but was still smiling. 'Some of us already think it will be too small for our needs.'

'A cyclotron?'

'A particle accelerator. Much better than the one Walton and Cockcroft used when they split the atom back in 1932, but a little off the pace in 1939. I know, I know . . . double Dutch. I'll try to keep it simple. If you're going to study atoms – or split them – you have to fire them in a well-defined beam from a radioactive element, so that you can engineer a collision with other atoms. The accelerator does that for you.' He clapped Wilde around the shoulder. 'Come on, I'll show you around, introduce you to some of the chaps, then we can retreat to the library for tea and buns and a layman's guide to the building blocks of the universe.'

To Wilde, the lab he saw was as mysterious as an alchemist's lair. And yet the work being done by the men hunched over tables, desks and workbenches was a world away from their forebears' idea of science.

Geoff introduced him briefly to Professor Bragg, who had succeeded Ernest Rutherford as director of the Cavendish. Bragg was clearly pre-occupied, but other senior men were more welcoming, as were the lab technicians whose immense skill in preparing radioactive materials enabled the physicists to do their work.

'These men are marvels,' Geoff whispered in Wilde's ear as they moved on. 'But they need to be careful. Old Crowe, Rutherford's assistant, burnt himself so badly handling radioactive materials without gloves that he needed skin grafts. Lost a finger, which did it for his piano playing.'

'What happened to him?'

'Oh, Crowe's still here. Still principal assistant.'

They ranged through the building, up three floors and then into the stuffy, over heated loft where new students learned the tricks of the trade in their first weeks. Wherever they went, rooms seemed crowded with dons and research students. 'There has never been enough space,' Lancing said. 'The Austin wing will help, but it'll still be a jam. Come on.'

Downstairs once more, Lancing pushed open a door to a room with bare brick walls and floors of wooden planks. At least two dozen men – and a couple of women – were packed into a space that should have housed no more than half that number. There was a low and constant murmur of voices and the buzz of high-voltage electrical discharges.

It seemed there was scarcely room to move. Glass-blowing equipment, lathes and vacuum pumps were crammed to the corners, while a jumble of instruments and appliances covered the solidly built workbenches. It seemed chaotic: retort stands for holding test tubes; electrical wires hanging and snaking from the walls in impenetrable tangles; pipes of all lengths and diameters, lights in the ceiling, lights on desks; ladders against walls and shelves; boxes of yet more equipment; dials; tubing; pulleys; levers; cogs; geiger counters and other measuring machines; soldering irons; condensers; transformers; yet more wires – nests of them protruding from the back of desks and dispersing like a delta; switches; generators; bottles; batteries.

And always that intense hum and scent of electrical burning, cutting through the layer of pipe and cigarette smoke.

An illuminated sign hung at an angle from the ceiling: TALK SOFTLY PLEASE.

'Like bees in a hive,' Lancing said. 'This is why we need the extension. Too many people, too little space – and since Lawrence Bragg took over, he's brought crystallography to the fore. There's a hell of a lot going on – I lose count of our research graduates.'

Wilde spotted Torsten Hellquist and Paul Birbach, working together at a bench. Hellquist waved him over.

'Ah,' Geoff said. 'You know our two stars. Brilliant, and as mad as kites.'

'Birbach's on the same staircase as me in college.'

'Of course he is.'

They wove their way through the chaos.

Hellquist shook Wilde's hand vigorously. 'Hello, Mr American, so you are back from your travels. To what do we owe the pleasure of your company at the Cavendish?' Hellquist was Swedish, perhaps six foot two in his brogues. An amiable elk of a man, large in girth and character, he spoke excellent English with an attractive lilt. Despite his extended belly, he was handsome; with fair Nordic features and clear blue eyes. He was often at Wilde's college, visiting his friend Birbach. Wilde had always liked Hellquist very much; he'd shared some pleasant and rather drunken sessions with him in the Eagle or the Bull – sometimes both in the same evening. Wilde thought back to his conversation in the White House: what had Dexter Flood said about Hellquist and Birbach? That they had 'dubious sympathies'? What had he meant by that?

Hellquist was certainly a much more imposing figure – and a better communicator – than his colleague, Birbach, who said little at the best of times and then with a German accent so heavy it was almost incomprehensible. A Jewish refugee from Göttingen, Birbach was perhaps a foot shorter than the Swede, and scrawny with it. His hair was dark and his short black moustache made him look like a cross between Hitler and a mouse. He looked up, but did not make eye contact. Without a word, he returned to his papers.

'I'm trying to make sense of what you all do here,' Wilde said. 'It isn't easy.'

Hellquist laughed. 'Particle physics in one easy lesson, eh? Good luck, Mr American.'

Wilde nodded to a glass and metal contraption on the desk. 'What's that thing?'

'Cloud chamber,' Hellquist said.

'It creates an artificial cloud in a glass case,' Lancing said. 'And then the condensation enables us to see the path of charged particles – particles so small that the most powerful of microscopes wouldn't get you close to seeing them. Charlie Wilson earned himself a Nobel for inventing that. He made the invisible visible as the saying goes.'

'What are you using the chamber for today, Dr Birbach?'

The German still did not look up. Hellquist cupped his hand and leant into Wilde's ear. 'Take no notice of Birbach. He is like this when he concentrates. You ask what we are doing with the cloud chamber? Nothing today. All we are doing is thinking and tinkering and scratching numbers down on paper.'

'They are trying to replicate and refine Otto Hahn's fission experiment,' Lancing put in. *Fission*. That word again. 'Is it dangerous, Dr Hellquist?'

Hellquist shrugged. 'Depends what you use it for. Like everything. For me, I see it as the solution to all the world's energy needs.'

There were a few moments of silence. '*We don't believe they're on our side*,' Dexter Flood had said, but all Wilde could see was that he was intruding on these men's work. 'Come on, Geoff,' he said. 'Where's that tea and cake you promised?'

At the doorway, Lancing stopped and nodded back towards the bench where Hellquist and Birbach were working. 'Those two,' he said quietly. 'You'd pass them in the street and never notice them, but they have two of the sharpest minds in the world. If anyone can find a simple way of turning fission into usable energy, it's Paul Birbach. And if anyone can find a way to make it and sell it for a great deal of money, it's Torsten Hellquist.'

CHAPTER 10

Wilde and Geoffrey Lancing sat facing each other at a small table in the Cavendish library, with a pot of tea, jug of milk, a bowl of sugar cubes and two cups. To Wilde, the word *library* conjured up a comfortable place smelling of dusty tomes and leisurely afternoons, but this place was rancid and dank, and smelt of rot. Lancing didn't appear to notice. He had a pad of paper in front of him. His thin fingers clutched a pencil. 'Perhaps you should bring your chair around and sit beside me, Tom? Then you can see what I'm writing and drawing.'

Wilde shifted around the table. He realised that he was about to be on the receiving end of the sort of supervision that he gave to his undergraduates.

'You will stop me if I'm boring you, won't you?' Lancing asked.

'You won't bore me, Geoff. Science is a wonderful thing. Where would we all be if Newton hadn't discovered gravity, for instance?'

'Floating in space?'

'Precisely.'

Lancing laughed. 'Sadly, not everyone shares your humour, however. Birbach wouldn't spot a joke if it punched him in the face. Do you know about his baths?'

'I've seen him trudging across the court in his dressing gown, clutching a towel.'

'He has four-hour baths. He says it's the best place to think. Think how cold and dirty the water must get, Tom. He's a true eccentric. But that aside, I'll be sorry to see him go.'

'Go? Go where?'

'He's been recruited by the even madder J. Robert Oppenheimer in California.'

'Hellquist not going with him?'

'Not to date. Perhaps he's not mad enough.'

Wilde grinned. 'What's *your* secret insanity, Geoff?'

'Oh, me? Flying, as you know. My sister Clarissa inherited all the family madness. I will always be the dull swot. Bloody awful at sport. Physics and aeroplanes, that's me summed up.'

Wilde looked at Lancing with a sceptical eye. He might have had a swot's brain, and be a little under average height, but with his swept-back fair hair, his open good looks and his easy manner, he looked almost as much a movie star as his famous sister.

'Come on, that's enough fun,' Lancing said, dropping a couple of sugar cubes into his tea. 'You want to know about particle physics. Believe it or not, it's actually quite interesting.'

He began drawing. A circle which he labelled as nucleus, containing twelve smaller circles, six of which he shaded and tagged protons and six more which he left unshaded and marked as neutrons. Then encircling it all he drew orbital lines with six dots which he called electrons. 'Imagine this as a carbon atom, Tom. This is gross simplification and still just theory, but this is how we believe it works. The electrons with a negative charge orbit the nucleus, rather in the way that the planets orbit the sun. The nucleus contains both protons – which have a positive charge – and neutrons, which have no charge at all. In the case of carbon, it's all quite stable – but when you get to the heaviest elements such as uranium, which have a lot more protons and neutrons, the nucleus becomes less steady. In effect it begins to decay spontaneously. Are you taking this in?'

'I think so.'

'It now seems that the instability inherent in uranium – particularly an extremely rare form of the element known as uranium-235 – makes an atom bomb possible. It is that instability which can lead to fission – the bursting apart of the nucleus, releasing huge amounts of energy. A concept that has been suggested for many years.'

Wilde nodded. 'H.G.Wells . . .'

'Quite. It now seems he was right when he imagined that one day atomic bombs might be dropped from planes. Harold Nicolson suggested much the same thing in his book *Public Faces*, describing an "atom bomb" the size of an inkstand having the capacity to destroy New York. That might not be so far-fetched. Yet even as recently as the early thirties when that was written, our own dearly beloved Professor Ernest Rutherford was writing off the atom as a source of energy. But Nicolson's grim prediction looks pretty accurate now.' Lancing poured them both another cup of tea. 'Have you heard of Leo Szilard?' he went on.

'Only through his work with the Society for the Protection of Science and Learning.'

'Well, he's Hungarian, a good friend of Einstein and as mad as Paul Birbach. In fact he's another bath-time thinker. He also happens to be one of the many Jewish scientists who fled Hitler. In Leo's case, he left Germany pretty much on the first train after Hitler was elected in 1933. Anyway, when he heard what Rutherford was saying about the atom, he had a eureka moment – while walking the streets of central London as it happens. He already knew from Cockcroft and Walton's experiment how much energy was released when a lithium atom was split. He was looking up at a traffic light on Southampton Row, apparently, when he suddenly thought this: what if there was an element which when its atom was hit by one neutron released two or more neutrons? His answer: there would be a chain reaction, liberating energy over and over again. This would all happen in a fraction of a second, of course – and the result would be a massive energy burst. An explosion of breathtaking magnitude. The equivalent of thousands of tons of high explosives.'

Wilde stirred his tea. 'A superbomb,' he said quietly.

'Indeed. And we now know there is an element to make it happen – uranium.' Lancing ran his long smooth fingers through his fair hair. 'But I don't want to alarm you. Fission wouldn't *have* to be used for nefarious purposes. If the explosion were controlled, it could become a fabulous source of power, perhaps even enough to provide electricity for a town.'

Wilde nodded and sipped his tea.

'Which takes us to Otto Hahn, Fritz Strassmann and a wonderful lady named Lise Meitner. Lise, being Austrian-Jewish, had to get out of Germany in a hurry after the *Anschluss* last year, but her name is forever linked to what Hahn and Strassmann achieved at their laboratory in Berlin. She was the physicist, they were the chemists. And you may have heard what Rutherford said on the subject – *all science is either physics or stamp collecting.*'

Wilde waited. Lancing was drawing again. This time his picture was very simple: a little figure *eight* laid on its side.

'Last December, Hahn and Strassmann artificially induced fission – though it wasn't a word they knew. They were firing neutrons at uranium. When the nucleus received the neutrons, it burst apart into new, lighter elements. That bursting is what we now call nuclear fission. A tremendous amount of energy is released – a million times more powerful than any other source. Two hundred million electron volts per atom, if that means anything to you. More importantly it releases two or more neutrons which can, in turn, be captured by other nuclei. Szilard's chain reaction.' He jabbed his pencil at the paper, scratching lines out from his double-bubble like a comic book explosion. He grinned sheepishly. 'The only problem now is how to harness that power. That's where we're at.'

'Thank you, Geoff,' said Wilde. 'I am indebted.' He meant it.

'You can teach me about the Armada one day.'

'So how difficult would it be to build a superbomb?'

'To be honest, I don't know. Birbach and Hellquist think it can be done quite simply. Personally, I think they're being rather optimistic. You would need a lot of high-grade uranium – and that's not easy to come by.' He stopped and looked around the room. 'I can't help wondering . . . maybe we shouldn't be talking about these things.'

Wilde followed his eyes. 'I thought spies were my line, Geoff.'

'I haven't told you any secrets but, well, one can't ignore the international situation. There's a lot going on at the Cavendish, as you might imagine. The secret boys have been up to say we have to be careful who we talk to and what we talk about.'

'They fear the Nazis will spy on you?'

'Possibly. The Cavendish has for years been at the heart of particle physics – the very nucleus if you like. And it's not just the Germans who are interested in the place. I expect Stalin would also like to know what we're up to. But look – there are specialisations within specialisations . . . The fine detail of fission isn't quite my line. I'm more of a wave theory man, though, of course there are close links.' Lancing gave a wan smile. 'You know, Tom, I hate to admit it, but I think the Cavendish's glory days are over. The big money and the big breakthroughs are more likely to come from America. Bragg has been steering us away from particle experimentation because he believes we can't compete. Our enemies might not know that, though, so we're still vulnerable.'

'And Hellquist and Birbach?'

'They're not the only brilliant minds left in the Cavendish. Dirac's still here having turned down Princeton. There's still good work being done, just not as showy as it was under Rutherford.'

Wilde knew all about Ernest Rutherford. Who didn't? He was the big, bold New Zealander who discovered the nucleus and its properties and who led the Cavendish so brilliantly for almost twenty years until his death in 1937. But Wilde wanted to know more about another man. 'Have you heard of a German physicist named Arnold Lindberg?'

'Of course. The world of physics is very small. Lindberg is – *was* – a brilliant man. He was picked up by the Gestapo two or three years ago. Haven't heard a dicky bird since.'

'He was in a concentration camp. But he's out now – and in England. He's coming to Cambridge – and he'd very much like to continue his studies here at the Cavendish. What are the chances?'

Wilde had expected enthusiasm, but Lancing was silent for a few moments. 'No,' he said at last. 'No, I'm pretty sure he won't be accepted here.'

'Really? Why not?'

There was an awkward pause. Lancing looked at the wall clock. 'Look, Tom, I have to dash. Hell of a lot to do today.'

He drained his tea and stood up. Wilde did the same, his question unanswered. They walked to the main door together, a sudden slight stiffness between them.

'Do you know, Tom,' said Lancing, 'there's only one bloody telephone here for scores of us? Our discoveries are the stuff of science fiction, but our damned facilities are medieval.' He forced a laugh.

'Sounds like Cambridge University through and through.' Wilde smiled. 'Thanks for showing me around. I think I almost got the hang of it.' He shook Lancing's hand and set off across the yard to the Rudge.

'Hang on,' Lancing called after him. 'I almost forgot! Clarissa demands your presence for cocktails and whatever this evening. Bit of a bash, I think. Not doing anything, are you? I'll pick you up. Best bib and tucker.'

So, he was going to come face to face with the famous Clarissa Lancing. Not only that, he would also be meeting Mr Milton Hardiman, the man with whom he was supposed to make contact. How very convenient.

Wilde climbed aboard the Rudge and kicked her into life. In his head, he was still trying to make sense of fission. Of course it didn't really matter exactly how fission worked, or even what it meant. What did matter was that the possibility of a superbomb was no longer the stuff of fiction. And Lancing's reassuring words that it could just as well be used as a peaceful source of energy, like coal, to power the nation was of little comfort. No wonder Dexter Flood in the White House had been interested in what was happening in the Cavendish.

And yet ... and yet it wasn't the prospect of a superbomb that came to mind when he thought of the looming war. It was a vision of the muddy fields of Flanders and the gas-poisoned trenches. History taught that one war was pretty much like the last; a depressing thought. He had been a schoolboy last time and his mother had taken him to America before he could get involved; this time he would stay and do what he could.

He was outside the lab now, back in Free School Lane, and was about to twist the throttle when he stopped. A man in his forties of middling height – perhaps five foot seven – with a thick wedge of charcoal hair perched on top of a severe short back and sides was heading towards Bene't Street. But it wasn't just the hair that Wilde noticed, it was also his legs, bowed and bandy like those of a cowboy who had spent a great deal too long in the saddle. He had not seen those legs since the summer of 1912.

Wilde shook himself. Of course it couldn't be him. Why would he be here in Cambridge after all these years? He lifted his goggles and narrowed his eyes. It *was* him, surely.

He accelerated and drew in a little ahead of the man, stopping to look back. The face was the same as it had been as a seventeen-year-old, although a little thicker, lined by the sun, and with a hint of jowls. 'Henty?' Wilde said. It was a question, not a statement. 'Henty O'Gara?'

The man stopped, too, his body immediately tense. 'Are you talking to me?' he said.

'You are Henty O'Gara, aren't you?'

'I think you've got the wrong man.' He was about to walk on, but then checked himself and jutted his chin out. 'And who might you be, mister?'

'Tom Wilde. Your cousin Tom.' Wilde had no doubt now. The accent was Irish, the tone soft, west coast Ireland; the voice was Henty's. No doubt at all. 'Summer of 1912, Galway Bay. Remember? I was thirteen, you were seventeen. You must remember it.'

O'Gara was thinking fast. Of course he recalled Tom Wilde and the County Galway beach house and the summer the two sides of the family had spent together, swimming and riding and fighting. It had been a good time, when even the rainy days seemed full of sun. But that was then and this was now, and he was on a mission under a different name.

His instinct, drummed into him, was that he must stick with the story and the *nom de guerre* Declan Burns at all times. But Tom Wilde wasn't about to wear that one, was he? This had to be sorted out more subtly. So Henty O'Gara he would be again for a few brief moments, and then he need never see cousin Tom again.

'Well, well! Is it really you, Tom? Jesus, look at you. You were a snotty little public school toff who wanted to learn to box last time I saw you.' He laughed and held up his fists. 'Put 'em up, Yank!'

Wilde removed his motorcycle gauntlet and shook O'Gara by the hand. 'Henty O'Gara, by all that's holy.'

O'Gara's astonished expression had creased into a grin. 'So it is now. So it is. What are you doing here, you Yankee bastard? I thought you'd be fighting your way across America, not consorting with the fucking English.'

'I'm a don. I teach history. What of you, Henty? What are you doing these days?'

'Horses, Tom. Always horses. I'm over here because I've got some nice runners at Newmarket and then Ascot.'

'You're a trainer then? Or jockey?'

'Neither. I own the fuckers.'

'And where are you staying?'

'Newmarket, of course – and I intend taking their English lordships for all they've got.'

'Then you have to give me a tip. I've got someone who'll love me forever if I can provide him with a sure-fire winner.'

'OK. It's a bit early, perhaps, but we have a lot of faith in Carthaginian Eye for the July Cup.'

For a few moments they just looked at each other. Their conversation hadn't even come close to bridging the years. Since O'Gara's father – Tom's mother's brother – had died during the Irish civil war, the two branches of the family had had little to do with each other. So what else had happened? Who was alive, who dead? Henty must certainly have made some money if he had racehorses. But how? And a hundred other questions. Was he married? Where did he live?

Wilde glanced at his watch. He could spare an hour. 'Can I buy you a drink for old time's sake, Henty? The Eagle's just around the corner.'

O'Gara was about to say no. This was already getting complicated. But then he let out a deep roar of laughter. 'Jesus, of course I'll take a drink off you.' Then again, no. 'What's the time, Tom?'

'Nearly one o'clock.'

'Ah, what a damnable shame, I'll have to stand you up. Got a meeting to get to. But give me your address and telephone number, won't you – and I promise I'll be in touch. We'll get together before I leave Newmarket, and then we can have a proper drink together.'

Wilde pulled out his notebook, wrote his details down, tore out the page and handed it to O'Gara. 'There you go. Come over any time.'

'I heard about your wife and child. Jesus, I was sorry to hear that. Are you married again, Tom?'

'Not exactly.'

O'Gara chuckled. 'I won't intrude. What about Auntie Mary, is she still . . .'

'My mother's well enough. Living in Boston, Mass. Just been over to see her as a matter of fact. Thought it wise before, you know – well, we all know, don't we, the coming war.'

'Indeed, indeed.' He held out his hand. 'You know, Tom, it's a real pleasure to see you again after all this time – twenty-seven years, Jesus . . . Where did the days and years go? Anyway yer snotty fucker, I'll be in touch with you soon.'

O'Gara watched Wilde ride away down Bene't Street towards the junction of King's Parade and Trumpington Street. Then he slipped into the telephone kiosk to the right of the pub and waited for the bells to chime one o'clock.

CHAPTER 11

The queues stretched all down Tiergartenstrasse, on the south side of the great gardens that breathed fresh air into the teeming centre of the city. The huge old mansions and palaces here were some of the grandest properties in Berlin, once the homes of the nobility and wealthy industrialists, but now they as likely as not housed embassies and their offices. In better days, their view over the park had been spectacular, even enjoyed by Boswell with a glass of cherry schnapps in his hand, yet now the outlook was distressing: a long line of downcast human beings, perhaps a mile long, quiet, orderly and patient, yet desperate. Most were women or elderly men, all Jewish, all seeking the precious visa that would enable them to leave this hellish country behind.

SS officers lounged back in an open-topped Mercedes, idly watching the waiting line, and occasionally taking notes or photographs. An open-topped carrier with yet more troopers pulled up, this time with the Brownshirts of the *Sturmabteilung* or SA.

A strange and horrible wailing rose from the long line. There were gasps and tears and quaking. Some people seemed close to collapse.

Lydia watched open-mouthed. She had heard of these things from Bertha, who had been here soon after Kristallnacht the previous autumn, but hearing things second-hand and seeing for yourself were very different.

The SA stormtroopers, all of whom had pistols and clubs, leapt from the rear of their vehicle and began to strut up and down the line, demanding papers. Lydia had stopped on the other side of the road. She felt both terror and fury at the sight of the tormentors with their shiny high boots, their brown shirts and the swastika armbands on their right sleeves.

One of the Brownshirts gently removed the glasses of a middle-aged woman and examined them closely. He said something to her, then held the glasses to his mouth and breathed vapour on the lenses before rubbing them against his tunic to clean them. He smiled and handed them back to her. She nodded her thanks and reached out to take them, but the SA man's fingers opened and the spectacles fell to the pavement, shattering the glass. He grinned and quite deliberately crunched the heel of his high boot into the broken and twisted remnants. Shrugging, he took hold of her nose between thumb and forefinger. 'They were too small for this thing anyway.' Laughing, he moved on to another victim.

Lydia wanted to slap this bully's face, but she knew it would not end well. She had to swallow her revulsion and concentrate on finding Albert Haas. As she was turning away she saw two black-clad officers climb out of the Mercedes car and approach the queue with a bucket. She was close enough to see them hand the bucket to an elderly man and to hear one of the SS men say, '*Säubern Sie das Auto. Bitte.*'

The old man, bewildered and shaking, took the bucket. He stood there, unable to move, clearly petrified.

'What are you waiting for, Jew? Get on with it.'

He upturned the bucket to show them. 'I cannot clean your car. There is no water in it. No cloth.'

'Do you not salute an officer?'

The old man's eyes flicked from left to right and back. The women and men around him averted their eyes, afraid to attract the attention of the SS. The old man held out his arm straight, as ordered. But it still wasn't enough.

'Say the words, kike.'

'Heil Hitler.' It was as if the words would choke him.

'You are Jewish, are you not?'

'Yes, sir.' The old man bowed his head.

'Then you should be circumcised.'

'Yes, I am, sir.'

'Show me.'

The old man was trembling. 'Sir, I cannot. There are ladies present.'

'Pah. I am sure they have seen such things. Down with your trousers – or would you like me to remove them for you?'

Gingerly, the old man undid his belt and fly buttons. Slowly, he lowered his trousers a fraction.

'Well? Where is it? Where is your Jew's cock?'

Shamed and humiliated, the man exposed himself. The SS officer leant forward and examined him. 'Yes,' he said at last. 'That is a Jew's cock. You smell disgusting. Now pull up your filthy trousers, find some soap and water and a cloth and clean the car. And make it shine. If I see any dust or grease, you will be on a charge. Next stop Sachsenhausen.'

'But, sir, if I go I will lose my place in the line.'

The other SS man took his Luger from its holster and pointed it at the old man's chest. 'I will count to five.'

The old man, still struggling with his trousers, waited until the count of three, transfixed by fear and confusion, then someone at his side suddenly pushed him in the back and he stumbled forward and began to move. 'I will go, I will go.' He could not go fast, no more than a shuffle. He walked on his old legs across the street, trying to button himself all the while, and Lydia saw now that he had a limp. He was going towards one of the great houses, to beg water and materials for his chore.

Behind him, the SS and SA officers were laughing.

Lydia was stiff with impotent rage. She knew in this moment that the pacifism of the Quakers was beyond her. She turned away, helpless. Looking straight ahead, she walked to the front of the seemingly endless line to the overblown stuccoed building that housed the British passport office. Those in the line eyed her with a mixture of envy and resignation as she went ahead of them, through the large gates, across the wide front courtyard and up the steps to the grand entrance.

She was directed to a small room on the first floor, with the words PASSPORT OFFICE stencilled on the wall beside the open door. People were waiting both inside and out. Lydia elbowed her way through to a desk where she presented herself to the secretary, a young woman who looked as if she should still be at school.

'Have you been called? Do you have your passport and exit papers?' She spoke German but was clearly English.

'I'm not after a visa. I'm British. I must speak with Captain Foley.'

'The director is very busy, I'm afraid.' She held up her palms and indicated the twenty or more people crowding around.

'I think he might have had a message about me from a mutual acquaintance, Mr Eaton.'

'Ah, are you Miss Morris?'

Lydia nodded. 'Yes.'

'One moment, please. He's just with someone at the moment, but I'll slip you in as soon as he's free. Do take a seat if you can find one.'

Lydia found a space to stand by the window, which was open to let in air. She thought of her conversation with Ulrike Forster over a lunch of salad, black bread and cheese.

'Frau Haas brought the boy to me personally,' Miss Forster said. 'He is a quiet, studious boy, very well-mannered. Well, they all are, of course. None of them deserves this.'

'And you saw him on to the train?'

She smiled grimly. 'It was one of the more orderly transports. The parents managed to hold back their tears and the children were generally obedient. Only God knows whether they will ever see each other again. You know, Miss Morris, this is all a dreadful mystery.'

'His visa and exit papers were in order?'

'Of course. There can have been no reason to remove him from the train.' She took a sip of water and gave her visitor a long look, half helpless, half pitying. 'Can I ask, Miss Morris, what do you think you can really do to find a boy in a city of four million souls? What evidence do you have that he is even here?'

Lydia had no evidence, but nor did she have any option. She knew she was being foolhardy in coming here, but there were times in life when one had to throw caution to the winds. The moment Eva had asked her to meet her son off the train, she had felt responsible for him. She could not simply wait in London twiddling her thumbs. 'At least I have a start,' she said. 'Philip Eaton gave me that much. And I was hoping you would give me some pointers, Miss Forster. If Albert is alive and in Germany, then someone must be looking after him. Where would the Gestapo take such a boy? An orphanage, perhaps? Would one of the Jewish leaders be able to help?'

Ulrike Forster reached across and laid her hand over Lydia's. 'Most of the Jewish leaders are in the concentration camps or in hiding. As for orphanages accepting Jews? Well, I am sure they would have told us by now if Albert had turned up. Let me make some more inquiries.'

'And what about the man who brought her here to you?' asked Lydia. 'Could I talk to him? He might know something.'

'Herr Baumgarten? I fear I have no contact details for him. It's safer that way. He was very brave in doing what he did, as it is.'

Lydia allowed Miss Forster to squeeze her hand. 'Thank you,' she said. 'I know how much you have on your plate.'

'We all do what we can, but it is never enough. And we have been accused of "going over to the Nazis" in our efforts to help. But please remember this, Miss Morris: when you deal with the Nazis, you must think how Jesus of Nazareth would have talked to them. We must believe there is some good there. *Der Mensch ist doch gut . . .*'

Now, looking from the window of this old lodge at the desperate people below, it was hard to see any good in the Nazi regime. Freedom seemed such a fragile thing. After five minutes the English secretary waved her over. 'He'll see you now.'

Frank Foley was a short, bespectacled man in his fifties. He looked unremarkable in his tweeds with slightly flyaway and thinning grey hair, yet even before he spoke he exuded an aura of warmth and understanding. 'Pleased to meet you, Miss Morris. I had a rather mysterious wire from our mutual friend, Philip Eaton, asking me to do what I can for you. He didn't say what you wanted. Perhaps safer not to . . .' He grinned. 'They read all our wires, you know. But if Eaton asks me to help, then help I shall. If I can. Please, sit down, won't you?'

Lydia was still overcome by the long line of human misery outside his door. 'All those poor people, Captain Foley. And those SS men, Gestapo, whatever they are . . . they are such bullies.'

Foley himself did not sit down. 'I only wish I could do more,' he said. 'All I can do is try to keep the line in order and take them water. They'll stay overnight, you know.'

'Do they all want to come to England?'

'They want visas to Britain or British territories. As Director of the Passport Control Office my job, of course, is to ensure that no one is allowed to come to Britain who might take a job from one of our own. But these people are desperate, so what am I to do?' He held up a pile of unfilled visas. 'And so I sign them at the slightest excuse, hand them out, mostly to Palestine – and damn the consequences. Failing that, their only hope is Shanghai, but our people are really under the cosh there.' He laughed. 'I'll probably get sacked, but the National Socialists have made it quite clear they want the Jews to die like dogs. So I try my best to get them out of the country. Better to die in freedom than as slaves in Dachau or Sachsenhausen, isn't it?' He afforded her a wan smile. 'But you're not here to listen to my problems, are you, Miss Morris? What can I do for you?'

'I'm trying to find a missing boy. A little Jewish boy named Albert Haas.'

Foley obviously knew of the *Kindertransport* and was aware of the Quakers' work even though it was not something in which he was personally involved. Lydia told him all she knew about Eva and the removal of Albert from the train at the Dutch border, but he had never heard of her or the boy.

'Can you think of anyone I might approach for information – anyone inside the regime? I'm told they are sometimes quite amenable to approaches from Quakers.'

Foley thought for a few moments. 'Actually, I have had an idea,' he said at last. He tore a piece of paper from a pad and scribbled a few words, then turned it to show her. 'Go to this place, the Taverne, nine-thirty or later. It's not far from here. The British and American journalists gather there every evening to exchange notes and gossip. They keep a table reserved. They're good people.' He pointed to the name on the paper. 'JT McGinn particularly, but if not him, then any one of them will probably offer you advice. Tell them I sent you. If they've heard anything about your boy, they'll help. But take care. There are some pretty unpleasant people in this city.'

CHAPTER 12

A spin out to cocktails with a famous movie star seemed a fair idea given the balmy weather. Apart from anything else, it would give Wilde the chance to make the acquaintance of Milt Hardiman. Wilde had spent the afternoon catching up on his college mail, seeking out his undergraduates and paying his respects to the master of the college, the senior tutor and the bursar.

What he found was an eerie mixture of reality and unreality. Yes, all agreed a war was on the cards and that it would be bloody awful, but no, they weren't going to mope. Summer was here, the May Ball was almost upon them and they were going to enjoy a damned good party. He smiled at the theme of the ball – black tie and gas masks. To hell with the future. The one question they all asked was: why hadn't he taken the opportunity to stay in America? He shrugged it off.

Coming down the stairs from his rooms he bumped into Birbach and Hellquist. They were arguing.

'Hello again,' he said.

Birbach looked away, surly and sullen, his mouse-like moustache quivering.

Hellquist threw up his arms. 'Ah, Mr American, help me here, please.'

'Help you with what, Dr Hellquist?'

'This fool!' He jabbed a chubby finger towards Birbach, not quite touching him. 'Tomorrow he goes to California. But why? Why does he split up our working partnership? Together we have all the answers. He is the theorist – and I am the practical one. Together we could give the whole world cheap free energy and make ourselves millionaires. Separately, we are but half of a whole. You are American – tell him he is a fool.'

'What has any of this got to do with me being American?'

'Nothing – but tell him anyway.'

Wilde laughed. It was not the first time he said seen these two fighting. He liked Hellquist, who made no secrets of his ambitions to be as rich as a Rockefeller or Krupp. Birbach was a different matter, a decidedly strange character. Wilde did his best to avoid listening to the tittle-tattle about his private life, but it was impossible to filter everything out.

'So you're off tomorrow, are you, Dr Birbach? Well, let me wish you all the best.'

'Pah!' Hellquist said. 'That will not help. Now he will think you approve of his move.'

'Then follow him, Hellquist, follow him . . . or perhaps he's trying to avoid you?' Without another word, Wilde strode off, leaving them to their squabbling.

Wilde hadn't worn his dinner jacket since Christmas. He pulled it out of the wardrobe and held it up to the light, dusting the shoulders. It seemed all right. He laid the trousers out on the bed and smoothed the creases. His dress shirt had been ironed by Doris, and she had put it away carefully. With black tie and cummerbund, he should just about pass muster. Probably wouldn't do in Beverly Hills, but this was Cambridgeshire.

Downstairs, there was a knock at the door. He frowned. Far too early for Geoff. He trundled down and opened the door to a man in uniform, proffering an envelope. 'Mr Wilde? Cable for you, sir.'

Wilde tore open the envelope. REPORT TO ME SOONEST RE C LAB STOP FEARS THIS END STOP FLOOD.

'Is there any reply, sir?'

Wilde scratched out a short cable. WHAT FEARS STOP NOTHING OBVI-OUS THIS END STOP. His pen hand froze in mid-air. He tore the paper in half and dropped it in the bin beneath the telephone table.

'Sir?' The telegraph boy looked anxious.

Wilde held up his palms. 'No, thank you. No message.'

He closed the door, then picked up the phone and tried to get through to Jim Vanderberg at the US Embassy. The receptionist said he would be unavailable until the morning. Wilde folded the telegram and put it on the hall table by the phone. Before replying, he would talk to Jim. He wanted his old friend's advice on Colonel Dexter Flood.

At eight thirty on the dot a car's horn sounded in the road outside. Looking out from his bedroom, he saw Geoff Lancing waving up to him from the rear window of a large and very fancy motor car. Powder blue.

The chauffeur wore grey livery with a peaked cap. He held the rear door for Wilde, who ducked in and took a seat beside Lancing. The upholstery was creamy white hide and the trimming of the interior was walnut; a well-stocked drinks cabinet held pride of place.

'Champagne?'

'It would be rude not to.'

Geoff already had a glass in one hand and a bottle of Veuve Clicquot in the other. He poured a slender crystal glass to the brim for Wilde. They clinked and both downed half the wine in one. Geoff immediately topped them both up.

'So what is this enormous beauty of a car?' Wilde demanded of Lancing, as the chauffeur, disconnected from them by a glass screen, did a U-turn and picked up speed towards the centre of town.

'Hispano-Suiza. A car beloved of movie stars and the Riviera set. Didn't you note the swanky stork emblem on the bonnet? Only the best for my sister's guests, Tom.'

'So I see. You're making me nervous.' He fiddled with his tie, wondering at what point expensive elegance slipped into over priced vulgarity. 'In fact I'm beginning to feel rather shabby.'

'Oh, good Lord, don't worry about that. We'll be the smartest chaps there. She's invited all sorts, including half the lads from the Cavendish. Wants to make her presence felt in the vicinity. This is just her way of announcing her arrival. Always has to be the centre of attention, my sis. Remember, though, just don't . . .'

'. . . mention the film? Don't worry, I won't.'

'That wasn't what I was going to say, actually, but never mind.'

They drove south and west, no more than ten miles into wide-open countryside. The evening was light and warm and Wilde gazed out with pleasure at the young fields of green, the trimmed hedgerows, the trees heavy with new leaf, the grazing of cattle and the slow winding of the river. They passed through ancient villages, mellowed by time, their thatched cottages unchanging over the decades and centuries. In the near distance, he spied gentle hills. This land was so very different from the endless flatness of the Fens to the north of Cambridge, and yet he loved them both with a passion.

When all those people in college and elsewhere asked him why he lived here rather than in America, he never gave these landscapes as a reason; if he said anything at all, he protested that it was because he needed to be close to his subject matter, the lands of the Tudors, in particular Sir Francis Walsingham and Sir Robert Cecil. That was true, but it wasn't the only reason; the beauty of this country also meant a great deal to him.

They pulled into a long driveway between rows of poplars.

Wilde was on his third glass of fizz and he felt at peace with the world. He was going to relax and enjoy himself and breathe the night air deeply. He thought of Lydia: his irritation with her for not meeting him off the boat had evaporated. If she wanted to miss an evening like this, that was her business.

'So this is Milt Hardiman's joint?'

'It's called Old Hall. Hawksmere Old Hall to give the place its full name. Milt and Peggy spend their summers here and their winters in Long Island or New York. This year they have my dear sister as their guest.' Lancing lowered his voice so that the driver wouldn't hear. 'They're not really my cup of tea.'

The lawns on either side of the drive, beyond the poplars, were perfectly manicured. A peacock strutted along beside them for a few paces, then wandered off. They drew up in a circular forecourt littered with Rolls-Royces, Bugattis, Lagondas, Bentleys and a host of lesser vehicles. The house looked late Elizabethan, almost a copy of Hardwick Hall, with tall windows, divided by transoms and mullions. Square and high, with tall chimneys, it must have been the home of someone important in Elizabeth's court. Wilde decided a lot of money had been spent on it in recent years, because it looked in very fine condition. Two footmen stood at the front door, beneath a wide portico with columns, both with a pair of identical fine-featured dogs on leashes, like sentries to the underworld.

'Borzois,' Lancing said.

'*Très chic.*'

'I think they've hired them for the evening. They're very showy people. As a pet, they have a rather fiercer looking animal. Alsatian, I believe.'

As they approached the door, one of the footmen opened it wide and bowed low with a sweep of his arm to bid them enter. Inside, they came straight into a large, square hall, probably eighteen feet high, lit by crystal chandeliers. Wilde estimated it was at least forty feet square.

At least they had refrained from adding any cod-Tudor styling, so no pikes or halberds, pennants or shields on the walls. The old panelling was still in place and had been restored and polished.

The hall was already filling up. A jazz band was playing in the far corner and servants were everywhere with trays of champagne glasses or canapés. Wilde took a glass and looked around, trying to catch a glimpse of the star of the show. Instead he saw a few faces he knew from the university and many faces he had only seen in newspapers and on newsreels – stars of stage and silver screen, politicians, some aristos, diplomats (Wilde was sure he spotted US ambassador Kennedy), and a couple of members of the exclusive Cliveden set (was that Nancy Astor and Lord Lothian?).

'So this is your idea of an intimate little cocktail do, is it?'

'Did I say that?'

'You implied it.'

Lancing took him by the arm and nodded towards the throng. 'Come on, Professor Wilde. Time for you to meet the star of the show.'

'Should I be intimidated?'

'Well, I've known Clarissa all my life – and she's always scared me.'

They wove their way through the guests. Wilde spotted several people he had met at the Cavendish earlier in the day, including Torsten Hellquist and, more surprisingly, the pinched little pencil that was Paul Birbach. Birbach had a woman on his arm. There were always surprises to be had under the heavens.

Lancing caught his eye and laughed. He cupped his hand to Wilde's ear. 'I'll tell you about Paul Birbach and his sexual proclivities later.'

'I think I've heard rather too much about his private life actually, so spare me the details. And he's off in the morning?'

'He'll be missed, especially by poor Torsten Hellquist.'

Clarissa Lancing was surrounded by men. Blonde, slender and taller than her brother, she had the predatory beauty of a Tallulah Bankhead or a Marlene Dietrich. But the men now hemming her in weren't about to heed any warning signs; they couldn't get enough of her.

Her eyes lit up when she saw her brother and Wilde. She cut the man talking to her dead and dismissed him with the lightest flick of the fingers. The disappointment as he slunk away was all too evident.

She proffered her cheek to her brother and he dutifully kissed it. 'Darling,' she said in the musky voice that had thrilled millions of cinema-goers, 'I thought you'd never arrive.'

'Well, here I am, sis.'

She wore an exquisite silk silver gown that moulded itself to her slim figure. Around her neck, a string of pearls. In the long, artist's fingers of her left hand she clutched an ebony and gold cigarette holder. Smoke slowly spiralled into the air and vanished.

'Allow me to introduce Professor Tom Wilde,' said Lancing. 'Tom, my sister, Clarissa.'

Languidly, her right hand snaked forward. He took it and rather got the idea that a handshake wouldn't do, so he kissed it. When he raised his eyes, he saw that hers were drilling into him and he froze. Her eyes were the eyes of Charlotte, the wife he had loved and lost in childbirth so many years ago. He had seen Clarissa's eyes on screen, but only in the flesh was the haunting likeness apparent.

Those eyes, their colour, depth and sparkle. Charlotte made whole again.

'So you're Tom Wilde. Well, well. Darling Geoffrey's reports haven't done you justice.'

'I don't know what he's been saying, Miss Lancing, but you must know that he's a fearful liar.'

Her soft, dry fingers were still in his hand and he gently released them. As he did so, they tightened on his and he found that they were holding hands.

She drew on her cigarette, removed the holder from her scarlet lips, pursed them into an O, and blew a smoke ring in his direction. 'It's such a lovely evening. Let's go into the garden. You don't need him, do you, Geoffrey? Go and talk Spitfires and atoms to one of your friends.'

With the gentlest of tugs, she began to steer Wilde away.

Wilde looked at Lancing and shrugged.

'You'd better do what you're told, Tom. She doesn't brook disobedience, you know. Not for nothing are the world's greatest directors and producers terrified of her.'

'Oh, Geoffrey, you tell such fibs.' She smiled at Wilde. 'Don't listen to him. I'm just a little giddy sometimes, that's all.'

From the hall, she led him through a large sitting room. The French windows had been thrown wide and guests and servants were drifting in and out.

Lawns swept down to the river where swans glided by, as though part of the landscaping. A vast and brilliant white marquee covered a swathe of the lawn to the west of the house. Another band with a female singer was outside the tent on a platform. They were performing 'Summertime'. Men and women were slow-dancing on the grass.

'Shall we?' Clarissa said.

'My pleasure.' He took her in his arms and their feet were instantly in time. Unbidden, her silky body pressed itself to his. He caught the scent of her perfume, just distinguishable from the smokiness of her hair.

Together, they moved as one to the heady music. He was vaguely aware that other dancers had stopped and were watching them. He was aware, too, of thoughts and sensations that were beyond all human control. This woman was intoxicating him and they had barely spoken a dozen words.

At one point, her fingers went to his temple and traced the grooved scar. The hair had never regrown there properly, but the hair above covered it amply. The delicate touch of her fingers was soothing, but the memories were anything but. He sensed again the hot rush of pain and blood, the stench of cordite in the alleyway at the side of his house as the bullet scoured a furrow in his skull. Clarissa didn't ask him about it; perhaps Geoffrey had told her what had happened.

Too soon, the song faded to its conclusion, but their bodies remained bound a little longer. Slowly, she withdrew from him, her eyes alive with sensuous mischief. 'You are very beautiful, Professor Wilde,' she said.

'What utter tosh.' He tried to laugh off the electricity he felt, but she mocked him with the flutter of an eyelash and the kiss-pout of her lips. 'Thank you,' he said. 'It's nonsense, but thank you.'

'You're wasted in your lecture halls and archives.' She clicked her fingers and a waiter appeared with a bottle of champagne and poured them each a glass.

He didn't want to think of Lydia tonight. All he wanted was to get tight and dance and listen to this fine music in the warmth of the summer twilight. 'There's a lot more to history than dusty tomes, you know?'

'Really?' Her delicate fingers touched his face again; her long nails tracing faint lines down his cheek. 'Then why do I sense that you are avoiding something? Some other path?'

He wondered what she had heard – but perhaps she was just mocking him. He looked away, trying to disengage himself from uninvited images of transgression. 'Tell me about this place. It looks very much like my period, late sixteenth century.'

'You'll have to ask Milt and Peggy about that.'

'I haven't had the pleasure yet.'

'Oh, you'll meet them soon enough. Now, Professor Wilde,' She held his face between her hands and kissed him full on the lips. 'Be good and look after yourself. I must circulate. Until later, yes? I promise that later you will have my undivided attention. Like a good student, I shall study at your knee.'

'You have to go?'

'Counts and countesses to entertain, prime ministers and movie stars. Needs must.'

She left him with his champagne. For a few moments he simply stood there like a fool watching her retreating back, her finely carved shoulder blades bare and lightly tanned. A servant passed and he put the champagne glass on the man's tray.

'Can you get me a whisky? A Scotch whisky? I'll be down at the river.'

He stood at the river's edge on a wooden jetty with a pair of rowing boats tied up, watching the sun set over the distant meadows. Fifty yards to his right a boathouse caught his eye. It was old and faded and romantic, redolent of long-forgotten love affairs and trysts. The servant arrived with his whisky and a decanter. Wilde knocked back a glass and held it out for a refill. 'Thanks,' he said.

So this was Milt Hardiman's place. Hardiman, the man he was supposed to work with, probing the secrets of the Cavendish. Well, it seemed Hardiman was well ahead of him: half the staff of the lab – including Birbach and Hellquist – were here. Not only that, but he was clearly close to Geoff Lancing through his sister. Wilde wondered whether any paltry efforts he might make would be redundant. Did Colonel Dexter Flood really expect him to provide information on the Cavendish, or was he just covering his bases?

Nonetheless, he did want to find Paul Birbach and talk to him away from the college and away from the Cavendish. He'd very much like to know why he had decided to leave. Were his loyalties really suspect? Something dubious about him that America should know of before he arrived there to work with Oppenheimer? Perhaps here at this party, with a couple of drinks under his belt, he might be less taciturn.

As the thought came to him, he saw Birbach's gaunt little figure emerge from the house on the arm of the woman with whom he had been earlier. They both looked out of place here. Birbach's dinner jacket was two sizes too big and he blinked with bemusement at the dancers and drinkers. His woman looked worn down and hard. Even from this distance, he could see the hem of her maroon dress was unevenly stitched, and he suspected her necklace was sixpenny paste from Woolworths. Wilde berated himself for being condescending, but he wasn't judging her, just observing.

Birbach was a pace or two ahead of the woman. He stopped until she was at his shoulder, then moved on again, his little legs taking odd, short steps that propelled him in front once more.

Nursing his glass of Scotch, Wilde began to amble towards them hoping to catch a few minutes of Birbach's time, but something told him they didn't wish to be disturbed just at the moment. He turned, instead, to listen to the band and watch the dancers.

He was feeling decidedly mellow. After a couple more tunes, the band took a break. Wilde looked around him. He didn't really want to engage in conversation with anyone just at that moment. In the dying embers of the sun, the boathouse caught his eye, a hundred yards or so upstream.

Glass in hand, he strolled towards the rather gorgeous old structure. He had always liked boathouses. There was something about the light in these places . . . He pushed open the slatted wooden door and heard the soft lapping of water against the hull of a rowing boat. And another noise. A brushing noise. He stood there, eyes acclimatising to the gloom, and was confronted with a sight that made his jaw drop.

The woman in the maroon dress was on her knees on the decking, the stub of a cigarette in the corner of her mouth as she scraped her hand in circles, making scrubbing motions on the slatted wood. But she had no brush in her hand. As Wilde watched, transfixed, Paul Birbach came into view. His trousers were around his ankles. He knelt behind the woman and lifted her skirt.

CHAPTER 13

The glow from the Italian restaurant spilled out on to the pavement in a side street close to Wilhelmstrasse. The good-natured maître d'hôtel spotted Lydia as soon as she entered and asked her, in German, whether she had a reservation. As soon as she said *nein*, he began to speak English.

'We are quite full, madam. Is it just you? I'm sure we could make space for you.'

'I was hoping to find a Mr McGinn. He's with a group of reporters.'

'Ah yes, they have a *Stammtisch* – a table reserved for them every night. A dozen or so members of the foreign press corps. Mr McGinn is here tonight. Let me show you to their table.'

Lydia had spent the past few hours on the telephone in a tiny room Frank Foley had arranged for her to use in the Tiergartenstrasse building. Foley's cheery young English secretary, Margaret, provided her with coffee and explained how the telephone system worked. She also provided her with the numbers of English and German contacts, all of whom seemed sympathetic but could do no more than say they would keep an ear to the ground. The secretary had warned Lydia that it was believed the Gestapo listened in to all their calls, so she was circumspect in what she said.

In the early evening, the secretary appeared again. 'No joy?'

She shook her head. She had run out of ideas and names to call.

'Well then, I'm taking you out for a quick bite to eat and a glass of wine. You'll work better properly fuelled.'

'I'd love a beer, but I need to go to the Taverne, to meet those journalists.'

'Oh, they won't be there for ages. They'll be writing up stories and filing copy for the morning editions at this time of day. Come on, you won't miss them – they'll all be there until the early hours.'

After a gentle twenty-minute walk through the grey streets, past the endless building work commissioned by Hitler in his extravagant plans for a Rome of the north, and across the grey waters of the canal, they made their way to the Romanisches Café in a lovely square near the

Zoo Station. Its echoing halls, once favoured by the country's artists and writers, were pitifully sparse. But the steins of beer they immediately ordered from the despondent waiter were as refreshing as ever.

As they talked of England and their backgrounds, they discovered they had both been to Girton. Margaret was twenty-six, three years younger than Lydia; their time at college had not crossed, but they were able to share stories of tutors' quirks, famous escapades and scrapes.

'So how did you end up here, Margaret?'

'You've heard of Kristallnacht?'

'Of course.'

'Well, I was working for the ministry in London. A few days after that horrible night, I was despatched out here. Poor Frank Foley was simply overwhelmed by the numbers trying to flee – and he needed help. So here I am.'

Lydia was relaxing after the stresses of the past hours. She enjoyed this brave young woman's company. They ordered some food and switched from beer to a half litre of house red. 'Shouldn't you be getting home?' Lydia asked. 'I'm sure I must be keeping you from something or someone.'

Margaret laughed. 'Don't worry about me. We're in the office until at least ten every night. And even then the queue won't have diminished.' Her face fell. 'It's simply bloody awful. The stories we hear!'

The waiter returned and they both ordered potato omelettes with salad.

'Tell me,' Lydia said.

'Are you sure? It can be pretty harrowing.'

'I need to know what's happening here.' She wanted to get an idea of how realistic the chances were of ever finding a little Jewish boy consigned to the hands of pitiless men.

The young secretary grimaced. 'Yesterday, we received a letter from a Bavarian farmer who lives in a village near Nuremberg. He was seeking visas for himself, his Jewish wife and their four children. His wife was driven out of the village by the local SA brigade last November.'

'They split up a family?'

'Yes, they really do such things – and there are no courts to stop them. All their belongings were smashed up and the poor Frau was beaten with sticks. Her husband could do nothing. The wife had to go to stay with Jewish relatives in Nuremberg and the husband was left alone to look after the farm and what was left of their little grocery business. They had, he said in the letter, been happily married for twenty-five years. Just an ordinary contented couple who had raised a family together and been good neighbours. He told us he had written to the district council leader begging for assistance, asking for permission to have his wife return in safety. The letter he got back from the council leader, a ghastly sounding party man named Seiler, was jaw-droppingly cruel.

'He told the farmer it was his own fault for marrying a Jewess in the first place and that no, she would not be given permission to return. The reply ended with these heartless words – and I made a point of remembering them word for word – "Your question regarding what should now happen to your wife is of as little interest to me as twenty-five years ago it was to you what would become of the German people if everybody entered a marriage that defiled the race."' She took another sip of beer. 'What sort of people are they, these Nazis? What is to be done about them?'

Lydia knew how the Quakers would deal with them: prayer and fasting. Perhaps Ecclesiastes was right after all; perhaps there was indeed a time for peace and a time for war. If so, then surely the second of those times was upon them.

'They enact new laws against the Jews every week,' Margaret continued. 'Some laws are designed to drive them out of Germany. Others make emigration almost impossible.'

'What will happen to this poor farmer and his wife?'

'All I could do was write back and say they would have to apply for visas in person. Their best hope is obviously to get out of the country, but it's a matter of finding places for them. Captain Foley bends the rules as far as he can, but there's only so much he can do. Visas are like gold dust.'

Now, three hours later, as the maître d' escorted her through the tables to meet the reporters, she found herself trying and failing to understand how an apparently civilised society could descend to such cruelty. At least this restaurant was free of men in uniform.

The maître d' came to a halt in front of a long table, weighed down by plates of food, overflowing ashtrays, bottles empty, full and half-empty, and endless steins and glasses of all denominations. Nine or ten men, all in three-piece suits and ties, sat around talking in loud voices, laughing, smoking and drinking. As she approached, they fell silent and one by one turned their attention towards the new arrival.

'Gentlemen, forgive me for interrupting, but this young English lady wished to talk with Mr McGinn.'

One of the men leant over and offered her his hand. 'I'm John Terence McGinn. Call me JT. Any good at poker dice, are you?' He was a young Englishman with a cut-glass accent. 'One Reichsmark ante.'

Another of the journalists, a tall, balding man of forty or so, stood up and pulled out the vacant chair beside him. 'Ignore him, sister,' he said to Lydia. He was an American. 'Take a seat. What can I get you to drink? Have you eaten?'

Lydia thanked him and sat down. She had probably had quite enough to drink already, but she'd heard that reporters determined a person's worth by their ability to hold liquor, so she asked for a schnapps.

'No, no, you're in a little piece of Italy here. Forget schnapps. Willy Lehman, who owns this joint, gets in the finest grappa. You gotta try it.'

'How can I help you?' McGinn said. 'Is it just me you want or can these reprobates listen in?'

Lydia looked around the table. They were an interesting looking bunch, with neat haircuts, most of them wearing spectacles, all smoking. There was a world-weary, jaundiced air to them, but a certain warmth, too.

'Well, my name is Morris,' she said. 'Lydia Morris. I was given your name by a mutual acquaintance, Captain Foley. I'm looking for a little Jewish boy called Albert Haas. He was on one of the train convoys to London, but was taken away on the German side of the Dutch border. There was no explanation and nothing has been seen or heard of him since. All our inquiries to the German regime are met with silence.'

'Our? Miss Morris. You said *our*. Who do you represent?' McGinn asked.

'I represent the mother, Frau Dr Haas, and I represent the Quakers who organised the transport. Frau Haas has made her way separately to London and was expecting to be reunited with him there. Captain Foley at the passport office suggested you might have contacts within the regime who might have heard things?'

JT McGinn turned to his colleagues. 'Any of you heard of this boy?'

They all shook their heads.

Lydia had expected as much. 'Perhaps I should tell you a bit more about the circumstances,' she went on. 'Frau Haas is a scientist, a physicist. She worked at the Kaiser Wilhelm Institute in Munich. She was driven out and moved to Berlin. A few days ago, she made her escape.' She lowered her voice, in case diners on nearby tables might be listening in. 'I have a horrible feeling that the boy was snatched to persuade her to return to Germany.'

'What makes you think that?' McGinn asked.

'Maybe they feared she had sensitive scientific information that they didn't want passed on? I'm sure it's some sort of blackmail. I saw her talking to someone in the street in London. I think he was putting pressure on her.'

'So she has some kind of expertise that the Nazis are reluctant to lose?'

'Something like that. There's another thing. When she escaped Germany, her uncle, Dr Arnold Lindberg, who is also a scientist, went with her. He had been in Dachau for three years. I'm not quite sure how she managed to get him out. Is it possible the Nazis abducted the boy in revenge for his escape?'

JT McGinn rose from his seat. He put his thumbs in his red braces and nodded to his comrades. 'I'm going to ask Miss Morris to come with me somewhere quieter, chaps. Not at all sure this is the place for a conversation like this. Do you mind?' He turned to Lydia and smiled. 'Miss Morris?'

Outside the Taverne, the air was cooler and mercifully less smoky. JT McGinn took her arm and guided her back towards Wilhelmstrasse. The night darkness added yet more menace to the swastika pennants that hung from the high buildings, gently fluttering in the light breeze.

'I'm staying at the Adlon,' McGinn said. 'I thought we could go to the bar for a drink, Miss Morris. I'm afraid there are plenty of brown spies there, too, but nowhere's clear of them in this town. We can find a quiet corner.'

The Adlon, next door to the British embassy, was considered Berlin's finest hotel. McGinn guided Lydia through to the piano bar where a slender young man in a white dinner jacket and white tie was mechanically pumping out some Nazi-approved piece by Liszt.

They found a table away from the music and other guests. 'You never got your grappa, Miss Morris,' McGinn said. 'How about your original choice, schnapps?'

'That would be lovely. Thank you.'

'Now then,' he said when the waiter had gone. 'I'm interested in this other character, Lindberg. I haven't heard of Frau Haas, but I've certainly heard of Arnold Lindberg. I think he survived the Deutsche Physik's purge of Jews pretty well for a couple of years, but then he was rather indiscreet and found himself hauled off to Dachau. Is that the way you understand it?'

'Yes, just about.' For the first time, in the soft light of the bar, she took a good look at JT McGinn. He wore round glasses. His fair, wavy hair, was casually parted down the left, and his blue silk tie set off a well-tailored linen suit. 'I suppose you'll be looking for a newspaper story from this?' she said

'That's always a bonus. It's the reason my masters in London pay me to live here in luxury, but despite what you've heard about reporters, I am not entirely without scruples. The fate of a little boy, whether he be Jewish or otherwise, should concern us all.'

The waiter arrived with two shot glasses of schnapps. McGinn put his hand up. 'We'll need a couple more after these.'

'Of course, sir.'

McGinn watched him go. 'He's a brown, paid to listen in to the guests' conversations, but he knows I'm wise to him, knows he'll get nothing from me.' McGinn threw back the drink, but Lydia sipped hers. She couldn't afford to get drunk.

McGinn moved closer so he was whispering directly into her ear. 'Don't tell a soul, Miss Morris, but I am myself part Jewish, on my mother's side. If Himmler and company found out, they'd have me on the next plane or train out. So this is personal for me. And I fear things are not looking good.'

'I've heard some pretty awful stories.'

He afforded a resigned smile, but he clearly wasn't amused. 'It's going to get worse. Much worse than the world realises. At the end of last year *Das Schwarze Korps*, the newspaper of the SS, spoke of "the vital necessity to exterminate this Jewish sub-humanity". Not *expel*, you'll note, but *exterminate*. America's consul general here in Berlin, Raymond Geist, has seen what's threatened, too. He has said he believes the Nazis mean to annihilate the Jews. That's his word, *annihilate*. We can't say we haven't been warned.'

'Why does one not read about this in the British press?'

'I'm afraid our editors don't have the stomach for it. Nor, perhaps, do our readers. That's why men like Foley are doing such an important job. He just says, to hell with it – have a visa and get out of this dungeon as fast as you can. So that's me. That's where I stand, Miss Morris. I'm not out to fill column inches with the story of Albert Haas. Unless it helps, of course. Sometimes a light shone on a subject is just what's needed. But to get back to detail, tell me this, just how did Arnold Lindberg get out of Dachau? To be honest, I'm surprised to learn he's still alive.'

McGinn took out a packet of cigarettes and offered them to Lydia. She was about to shake her head. She never smoked. Instead she took one and he lit it. She coughed and blew out a mouthful of smoke. 'Ugh.'

The reporter laughed. 'You're not a smoker, Miss Morris.'

'Pretty obvious, eh?' She sighed, but kept the cigarette. 'You asked about Lindberg. I have to say the story I've heard has more holes than a colander. Frau Haas says she was helped by some sort of agent from the Jewish underground. He dressed in SS uniform and fooled the guards at Dachau into releasing Herr Dr Lindberg. It all sounded thoroughly implausible.'

'Yes, I see your point. Did this fellow have a name, by any chance?'

'Baumgarten.'

McGinn's eyes widened. 'Baumgarten?'

'Do you know him? Does it mean something to you?'

'Oh yes, it means a great deal to me.'

The waiter arrived with their second glasses of schnapps. McGinn drank his in one hit and waved the waiter away. When he was gone, McGinn held a hand over his mouth and spoke so quietly Lydia had to strain to hear him.

'Baumgarten isn't one man, Miss Morris. It's a codeword. They think it's amusing. Baumgarten is the SD or *Sicherheitdienst*. It's Reinhard Heydrich's secret service.'

CHAPTER 14

Tom Wilde stood just long enough to see the diminutive Paul Birbach attach himself to the woman's naked haunches. With a grunt, the little German scientist pushed himself forward into her. She did not glance back or in any way acknowledge what he was doing to her, merely continued her scrubbing motion as he made quick little thrusts.

Outside, Wilde caught his breath and tried to make sense of the strange tableau that had just been acted out in front of him. He needed to hunt down a drink. Anything to get the Bosch-like vision out of his head.

His vow to cut down on alcohol could go hang itself tonight. This was May Week and Lydia was in London. Scotch would console him for a while. As he wandered towards the marquee, he signalled a champagne-toting waiter, the same one who had brought him whisky before. 'Why don't you leave the decanter with me this time.'

'I'll find you a fresh bottle, sir. Single malt, perhaps.'

'Oh yes, indeed. Good man.' He reached in to his pocket and took out a half crown, then placed it on the tray.

'Thank you, sir.'

As he watched the waiter make his way back indoors, Wilde was aware of someone at his shoulder and turned sharply to find himself confronting a man of his own height.

'You be careful, buddy.'

'What?'

'I saw you with her.'

'Who are you?

'Milt Hardiman. I own Clarissa Lancing – and I own this joint. You're Tom Wilde, right?'

'Pleased to make your acquaintance, Mr Hardiman. It seems we have friends in common back home.'

'That we do, Wilde. I've been looking forward to meeting you. Dexter Flood has told me great things.'

The men shook hands and sized each other up. Hardiman might have had a strong face and a powerful physique, but his thin black moustache gave him the look of a two-bit fairground hustler.

'How exactly do you *own* Miss Lancing?'

'My money made her a star. I can unmake her any time I want. But she's dangerous, Wilde. She'll eat you up and spit you out.'

'I have no idea what you're talking about.'

'You will. Soon enough. Anyway, it's good to have you here. You're a history man, yes?'

'I am. And you, Mr Hardiman?'

'I help America and I make money.' His moustache rose a scintilla as his lips curled into a grin. 'Clarissa Lancing is one of my investments.'

'Well, it seems you have spent it well.'

Hardiman shrugged. 'Maybe. By the way, what do you make of her brother?'

'He's a good friend.'

'I know that, for Christ's sake! That's not what I meant. I want to know about his science. Is he up there with the best of the atom boys?'

Everyone was clever at the Cavendish, but some were – Wilde thought of Birbach and Hellquist – well, different. Geoff Lancing knew his stuff, but he wasn't quite different enough, as he himself would probably admit. Nonetheless, his reply was circumspect. 'I don't know, Mr Hardiman, I really don't know.'

'Milt. The name's Milt. And that's this week's work for you – get the gen on Geoff Lancing's brain.'

For a few moments Wilde said nothing, hoping the waiter would hurry up and replenish his whisky. At last he spoke. 'This house of yours, late Elizabethan, I'd guess.'

'Yeah, Tudors. All those wives. Not quite Cliveden, but it suits us. Apparently, Queen Elizabeth slept here one time. Not sure who with.'

'I'd like to know more about it, explore the place – with your permission, of course. Do you spend much time here?'

'You know, we used to spend our summers at our Old Westbury spread, but we've been over here these past three years. Europe's the place to be right now. The sound of marching boots and low-flying fighter planes. I love it. Do you think the Limeys are going to fight?'

The suddenness of the question caught Wilde off-guard. 'You mean go to war?'

'What else would I mean? They won't, will they? They can't be so dumb as to stand in Germany's way. The Luftwaffe could do for this tin-pot nation in a week. The Brits would do well to listen to men like Joe Kennedy and negotiate for an alliance of the Aryan races, some sort of understanding against the Jews and the Bolshies and the Slavs. And the sooner they do it, the better it will be for all concerned. The biggest danger, as I see it, is Franklin D. Rosenfeld. Am I right, Wilde?'

'*What* did you say?'

'You heard. The Jew lover in chief.' Hardiman roared with laughter. 'Hey, feller – just kidding, right?'

Had he really said that? *No, I didn't mishear*, thought Wilde. The waiter arrived with a bottle of whisky and a glass. Wilde poured himself a large measure while trying to work out how to respond. Geoff Lancing had said Hardiman came from Long Island, but his drawl placed him deeper into the southern states of the US. Wilde raised his glass. 'Good health.'

'And you, Wilde. Do I shock you?'

'You know what, Hardiman, I think I'm probably a little tight for politics right now. Another day, perhaps?'

'OK, but just say yes or no. Will the Limeys fight?'

Wilde sighed. Everyone seemed to be asking him this question lately. 'I hope so,' he said. 'I really hope so.'

'Then you don't get it. You don't get it at all.' Hardiman slapped him on the back, then shook his head. 'Enjoy the party, feller. We'll certainly talk more another day. And bring me what you've got – names. That's what we need, the important names. And the lowdown on Lancing.'

'Why don't you just ask him to spy for you?'

'Because who would report on *him*? Look, feller, he's English and you're American. You're one of us, aren't you?'

Lydia tried to take in what JT McGinn had told her. If the man named Baumgarten was a Nazi agent, then what was going on? 'Baumgarten' was the man who had effected Lindberg's release from Dachau and had planned his escape through the mountains with Eva. It would certainly explain why the camp guards had been so easily persuaded to let Lindberg go, but why would the SD want him released? What was Eva's role? Did she know that Baumgarten was SD, or was she merely a pawn in a bigger game? What, for that matter, did Philip Eaton really know? And still the original question – why had Eva's son been abducted?

'I beg you, Miss Morris. I have this information in the strictest confidence from a very important source – a senior member of the *Abwehr*, who despises the SD,' McGinn said. 'He told me inadvertently and then realised his slip. It is not so much a codeword as a name that merits instant attention from anyone on the inside. If it got out, then not only would he be in grave danger – but I would lose a most valuable contact.'

By now, Lydia was exhausted and losing track, so the reporter asked the concierge to hail a taxi to take her back to Schlactensee. As McGinn ushered her into the back of a Mercedes cab, they exchanged telephone numbers and the reporter said he would be in touch whatever the outcome of his inquiries. 'Just be careful what you say on the phone.'

Henty O'Gara examined the Thompson's Lane electric power station from every angle. It was not an impressive building, just the one chimney belching out black smoke where Battersea had four. It was an easy target, but he was worried; there was too much to be done. He couldn't afford a hiccough.

It was late, after midnight. The drinkers from the St George and Dragon near the park tennis courts had long since gone home. Scudamore's punts beside Magdalene Street Bridge were all tied up for the night, covered in tarpaulins. The warmth of the evening had given way to a slight chill, but he didn't notice.

None of this was going the way he had hoped. The decrypted message in the book had taken him to Christ's Pieces, then the dead letter in the brick wall had led him to this afternoon's telephone call. The voice at the other end had been muffled and indistinct.

He heard three words, as though through a soup. 'The power station.'

'Is there only the one?'

'Thompson's Lane.'

'Can we meet? I need to talk to you. I need your local knowledge. I've got ideas. How to fuck the fuckers.'

There was breathing on the line but no reply.

'I can't do this on my own, mister. Jesus, we're fighting for the same cause! Let's have a pint somewhere.' He had looked from the telephone box towards the tavern. 'Tell you what. I'll be in the Eagle in the town centre at seven. I'll be by the bar with my left hand on a pint. And I'll be alone. Come and ask me if I've got a horse. How's about it, mister?'

The breathing continued for a couple of seconds.

'At least give me another way to contact you, won't you?'

The line went dead.

In the afternoon, he found the power station. It wasn't difficult to find, with its tall chimney, down by the river near Magdalene Bridge. But it was a hell of a public place, with working men's houses all along the lane, barely three or four yards from the outer wall. How could he breach that without being seen? At the eastern end, there was an open space with courts for lawn tennis. You could lay a bomb there, against the wall, he supposed, but would it even make a dent? The best way in was the main gateway where the coal lorries arrived to deposit their loads, but that would be manned twenty-four hours in the day.

At seven, O'Gara had gone to the Eagle. He had bought a beer in the public bar and stood there with his left hand on the glass, waiting like a jilted lover. Plenty of men came in and drank and went out again. One or two even tried to engage him in conversation, but none of them asked about horses.

And so he was still alone, still out on a limb. All he knew was one target: the power station. Jesus, you didn't have to be a strategic genius to come up with that one, did you?

The power station building was right on the river, on the far bank from Magdalene College, a little way north and east of the Church of St Clement and the synagogue and the Friends' Meeting House. Well, thought O'Gara, you'd have thought it would be safe enough with all those godly fellows around, keeping it in their prayers. Seemed almost a sacrilege to bomb it.

But then again, if O'Gara was honest, he would have to say that it would be a crime *not* to blow up the power station; it did nothing to add to the beauty of this ancient town, and it pumped out endless quantities of smoke and steam from its turbine. No one would miss it, would they? He laughed at the thought that the scholars in the college across the river might actually thank the IRA for their work when they had got over the inconvenience of having no electric light for their studies.

He made a decision. A boat was the way to do it. Not a punt, though. That was a craft with which he was unfamiliar. He had rowed plenty of dinghies in his time, even done a little sailing. But punting was not big in Galway.

One craft, however, had caught his eye – a canoe, tied up alongside the punts. And he had noted that a paddle had been left in it.

Whisky bottle in hand, Tom Wilde wandered around the grounds of Old Hall, trying to make sense of his conversation with Milt Hardiman. What exactly did the man stand for? Turning a corner, he spotted Torsten Hellquist sitting on a teak bench on the flagstone terracing that looked out on the lawn. His head was in his hands, his vast bulk hunched forward. Wilde sat down beside him. The Swede did not look up.

'I won't offer you a drink, Hellquist.'

'Give me a vodka.' He raised his head and Wilde saw that his clear blue eyes were bloodshot. 'Ah, it's you, Mr American.'

'It's me, without the vodka.' He held up the whisky bottle. 'Only this.'

Hellquist bent down and found an abandoned champagne glass at the side of the bench. 'Pour,' he said.

Wilde poured. 'I think we should make a toast,' he said. 'To the end of the war.'

Hellquist shook his head. 'No, the end of money.' He laughed, then they clinked glasses.

'I thought you liked money.'

'Then you don't know me very well. I want money, because I need it for the life I desire. But I despise it all the same.'

'I can lend you a couple of quid if you're short.'

'A couple of quid? That's funny. I need a lot more than that. Try a couple of thousand and you might be getting close. Can you lend me two thousand, Wilde?'

Two thousand pounds? 'That's quite a sum. What is it, gambling debt?' Wilde knocked back his drink. The whisky was talking tonight. Best keep his own mouth shut.

'No, no. Think of it as an investment. Perhaps I could persuade Paul Birbach to stay. I could pay you back very soon. Birbach and I, you know, we can be very rich if we continue to work together. He has found a way . . .' he tailed off. 'It means nothing to you.'

'Try me. Is this about fission?'

'Well, he's a clever guy. He's seen a short cut, a simple way to turn it into usable energy.'

'Or a bomb?'

Through the bloodshot gauze of his eyes, Hellquist looked at Wilde and frowned. He put his left index finger to his lips. 'Shh.'

They sat together in silence. It was the early hours now, and the band was still playing, deep, maudlin blues with dancers shuffling in circles on the lawn, holding each other up.

'No bomb, Mr American. Just power. Plenty of power for the whole wide world. If you were to lend me two thousand pounds I would be able to pay you back a millionfold. Energy is money. Look at the coal barons, the oil tycoons. I will be the first atomic billionaire.'

Wilde patted him on the back and laughed. 'And Birbach can do this for you?'

Hellquist's glass was empty, He dropped it and it shattered on the stone paving. 'Paul can do anything. Anything. Did you see him with that woman?'

'Who is she?'

'I don't know. A cleaner or a maid, I suppose. They always are. I'm pretty sure he pays them. Maybe his mother was a cleaner and abandoned him – isn't that what the psychiatric guys would conclude?' He looked beneath the bench and found another glass, intact. 'But, you know, when a man has a brain like Paul Birbach, you can forgive him things, yes?'

I wouldn't judge him anyway, Wilde thought. We all have our vices. And what might Torsten Hellquist's vice be that he was short two thousand pounds? Or maybe he really did just want to use it to pursue his dream of dazzling riches. He would not be the first man with such an ambition. Wilde poured a slug of single malt into Hellquist's new glass, then drained the bottle down his own throat.

'But there is one thing I can never forgive Birbach. He doesn't play chess! What sort of mathematician or physicist does not play a good game of chess, Mr American?'

Wilde rose unsteadily from the bench. Clarissa was walking his way. Not walking, sashaying; her dress shimmering in the light of the hurricane lamps dotted around the lawns.

CHAPTER 15

O'Gara cut the paddle into the water with care to avoid noise. Across the river, lights burned in the windows of the college that he knew, from his map, to be Magdalene. There was no other traffic on the water, but nor could he afford to be heard from the banks. He had untied the canoe at the quayside, to the east of the bridge and slipped away downriver into the darkness.

The great chimney of the power station loomed, black against the charcoal sky, no more than a hundred yards away. A couple of rowing boats and a large motor launch were tied up beneath its walls, at the foot of a flight of stone river stairs.

He lashed the canoe to one of the rowing boats, then picked up his bag from the belly of the canoe and climbed across to the steps. He grasped the metal handrail and, with only the slightest hesitation, climbed up into the main yard of the power station.

It was dark and quiet. A couple of coal lorries were parked. To his right, he could see the gatehouse, dimly lit, with a pair of heads just visible, unmoving. Perhaps they had nodded off. Well, he'd wake them soon enough. Loudest alarm call they'd ever have.

Now then, where to plant the bastard of a bomb for biggest impact? He liked the idea of bringing down the chimney, but he didn't have sufficient explosives for that. How about putting it by the coal pile? Perhaps it would catch fire. Couldn't guarantee it.

A dimly lit doorway beckoned to his left. He could slip in there, find the turbine room and plant the bomb to damage its blades. It was a tempting thought, but that wasn't the point of this operation. The chances were he would be spotted. If he was caught now, he would be incarcerated in the Scrubs or Dartmoor and be of no use to anyone. He had to stay free.

He was aware, of course, that he had been followed here. He had been shadowed ever since the Eagle. So they had been there after all, but had not thought fit to make contact. Perhaps that was wise, but it irritated him all the same. How could they be sure he would not mistake them for English agents, and either lose them or shoot them?

'Hey, you!'

A guard. Too late. No time to set the fuse. Then the sound of a whistle. O'Gara looked around. He couldn't go back the way he had come; a canoe on the river would be too slow. His only hope was to run. The lights of an approaching coal lorry lit the front gateway, which was gaping wide. Sidestepping the guard who was hurrying in his direction, he gripped his bag of explosives tight in his arms, and ran.

The music had long since stopped. Half of the guests had gone home or slipped off to find a bedroom. Wilde was lost in a whisky-fuelled embrace with the woman the whole world wanted.

To the east, the night sky had turned to pre-dawn pink. She took his hand and tried to lead him towards the French windows into the house. Through a fog of whisky, Wilde realised it was time for him to make his excuses and leave. Whisky kills conscience stone dead. Not remorse, though. That would be there come morning if he didn't go now.

'Good night, Miss Lancing,' he said. 'It has been a pleasure to make your acquaintance.'

'Don't you want some breakfast?'

'I'm spoken for.' What a strange, old-fashioned choice of words. What did it mean – married, engaged, courting? Anyway, there were times recently when he wasn't at all sure that he was *spoken for*.

'So that means you can't eat breakfast?'

'Breakfast?'

'Of course. What else were you thinking of?'

He laughed and followed her.

In the hall, the great staircase beckoned momentarily, but instead she manoeuvred him towards the front entrance.

'I thought you said breakfast.'

'Yes, but not here.'

Clarissa stopped on the front steps, whispered something to a footman, then turned and slid her silken arm under Wilde's, folding her slender silken body into his side. Her perfect nose tipped up towards his face and her eyes met his, and then closed as she kissed him on the lips.

In the back of the Hispano-Suiza, she sank into his shoulder as the driver pulled away. He seemed to know where he was going without any orders being given.

Wilde's first instinct had been right, of course. He should have just left her there and then on the lawn. But breakfast it would be. Where was the harm in that?

Within a few minutes, they had pulled off the main highway and were bumping along a poor road towards a couple of single-storey buildings with flat roofs. Beyond them, Wilde could see a small aeroplane. And, a little further on, a small corrugated hangar, with a wide entrance leading into a gloomy interior where he thought he recognised her brother's yellow Sopwith fighter, a relic of the Great War.

The driver braked slowly outside the first of the smaller buildings, then climbed out and opened the rear door on his mistress's side. Clarissa squeezed Wilde's hand. 'Your aeroplane awaits you, Mr Wilde.'

'Oh no,' he said, his head still a fog.

'You're not one of the *little* people, are you, Tom?'

'Maybe I am.'

'I don't think so. I really don't think so. Come on.' She was tugging gently as she backed out of the car. 'You don't strike me as yellow.'

A rusting sign over a doorway announced that this was Boldbourne Airfield. Inside the squat building, the chauffeur took a leather flying coat down from a hook. 'This should fit over your dinner jacket amply, sir.' He held it open and assisted Wilde to slip in his arms.

'Are you the pilot?'

'Madame will be flying you, sir. To breakfast, I believe.' He brushed down the sleeves on the nicely weathered leather coat. 'Perhaps the Ritz?'

When Clarissa reappeared on the concrete apron, she was attired in trousers, boots, short leather jacket and with goggles up on her forehead, her hair flowing down around her shoulders.

'Ready, mister? Let's fly.'

The whisky was playing havoc with his stomach and brain. Flying didn't seem like a good idea in the circumstances, but what the heck? 'Let's fly,' he echoed.

They strode across the apron to a green biplane with a two-seat cabin and a single airscrew. A mechanic in an oily blue boiler suit was standing to attention beside a small set of steps, and the prop was already turning, the engine idling. Someone at Old Hall must have called ahead to have the little aircraft prepared for take-off.

'All ready for you, ma'am. Full tank.'

'Thank you, Harry.' She turned to Wilde. 'Shall I be pilot or you?'

'Have you flown a plane before?'

'Of course. Geoff and I were brought up with them.'

'Well, then you have the edge over me. Are you sober enough?'

'We'll just have to find out, won't we? Anyway, there's not a lot of traffic up there. Nothing to crash into.'

Wilde wasn't convinced; there was plenty of *terra firma* to collide with.

She held his face in her hands and kissed his lips. Her lips were perfect. She pulled back slowly and met his gaze with her own knowing eyes. 'I knew you weren't yellow,' she said. 'You're a warrior, Professor Wilde. Just my type.'

Within minutes, they were settled into their seats; the chocks had been removed, the coolant temperature, magnetos and oil checked. A short taxi to the far end of the airfield, a turn, and then they were bumping across the turf and gathering speed into the wind. She looked sideways at him, grinned, then opened the throttle and, within thirty bone-rattling seconds, they were in the air.

The sun was to their left, just peeping over the horizon and the sky was cloud-free. The whole of England seemed to open up beneath them, a patchwork of lush greens, of empty roads and thin rivers.

There was no turbulence and Wilde was relieved to discover he was not nauseous. Perhaps he might just get through this flight in one piece. Clarissa seemed to know what she was doing at the controls. 'Are you going to tell me now, or must our destination remain a mystery?'

'Oh, I like mysteries, don't you? Fear not, it'll be worth it, Professor.'

'What is this thing?'

'De Havilland Hornet Moth DH87B. Lovely little two-seater flyabout.'

'Geoff's been up in Spitfires.'

'I know. Flashy little bugger. Actually, he's my darling boy. I love him to bits.'

'I think he's rather besotted with you, in a fraternal sort of way.'

She laughed. 'Oh, I drive him mad. Rather think I made his boyhood a misery. He was well rid of me when I went to Hollywood and now I'm back, upsetting poor Geoffrey's quiet little life.'

They were both silent for a while. The engine droned, the countryside opened up below them. Wilde was beginning to feel the effects of the whisky wear off, and it wasn't a pleasant sensation. He thought back to the night before and his encounter with the owner of the house, Milt Hardiman.

'Tell me about the Hardimans. I met him briefly, but not his wife.'

'They're friends. What more can I say? Milt is rich. Peggy is his chatelaine. She organises his life, and looks after the little boy, Theodore.'

'Is Hardiman a politician?'

'He has politics. Who doesn't? Politics is part of being alive. Even for dumb blonde screen goddesses. Or perhaps you think we should stick to lipstick and diamonds . . .'

'He called Roosevelt *Rosenfeld*.'

She was smiling. 'Really?'

'I don't think it's funny.'

'Don't be so dry, Mr Wilde. It's rather a good joke. You should lighten up. Are you strapped in? Yes? Good.' Smoothly, she eased back the joystick and the little Hornet Moth began rising in a sharp arc, struggling to gather speed as it hit vertical. And then, momentarily, they were hanging upside down, with the world where the sky should be, and Wilde's breath taken away. And then, just as quickly, the plane was going down, down, down – and levelling out. The loop completed.

'Thanks for warning me.'

She was laughing wildly. 'Well, at least I made sure you were strapped in. Sorry if I woke you.'

'I almost lost the contents of my stomach.'

'Oh, that's nothing. Wait till I try a roll or two.'

'Lucky I haven't had breakfast yet.' He looked from the window. From the position of the sun, he deduced they were heading southwards. She was flying low, skimming the ground at little more than a couple of hundred feet so that he almost felt he could lean out of the cockpit and touch the tops of the trees with his fingers. 'I guess we're on our way to London. Claridge's perhaps?'

'Keep on guessing. The Hornet Moth has a range of more than six hundred miles, so I suggest you just sit back and relax.' She reached into her flying jacket and pulled out a silver cigarette case. She opened it and was about to take one, but then looked at Wilde's reproachful eyebrow and snapped the case shut. 'OK,' she said. 'I'll let you off.'

'Thank you.'

The cabin was cramped but had a hint of luxury, with sprung leather seats, inlaid facings, lush carpet underfoot. Wilde closed his eyes, but the nausea was kicking in, so he forced them open again.

Half an hour later, the vast urban sprawl of London appeared beneath them. 'A nice gentle landing, please, Miss Lancing. My stomach won't take any more aerobatics.'

'Are you working up a good appetite, Professor Wilde?'

'Not yet.'

'You will.'

She flew on, and ten minutes later, they were almost past London and heading on southwards with no sign of making a descent. Wilde said nothing. When you have absolutely no control of a situation, panic or complaint are worthless responses. He'd find out their destination when it suited her. In another half hour or so, they were at the coast. From the panorama of the distant shoreline to the south, Wilde guessed they were somewhere near Dover.

'Do you see the white cliffs? Down there is the pretty little resort of St Margaret's Bay. Have you been there, Professor Wilde?'

'No.'

'I have many fond memories of St Margaret's. We used to go on holidays there every summer until . . .' she tailed off.

'Until what?'

'Oh, it's a long time ago . . . it must have been the last year of the war. We had a nanny called Tobin. Mrs Victoria Tobin. Geoff and I loved her dearly. But she'd lost her husband at the first battle of Ypres and she was – troubled. One day we went for a walk along the cliffs. We stopped for a picnic. Geoff and I were playing; Tobin was at the cliff's edge, looking out to sea. I looked up just as she stepped out into thin air. I watched her plunge to her death.'

'My God!'

'I can still see it in my mind's eye, Professor Wilde. It affected Geoff and me for quite some time.'

'That's simply ghastly. That poor woman! And for you two to have witnessed it . . .'

Clarissa gave Wilde a wan smile. 'I'm sorry. I should never have brought it up. Please don't ask me anything more about it. As I said, it was a long time ago.' She brightened. 'After all, this is supposed to be a day of fun and laughter!'

Wilde looked sideways at her, held his counsel.

Soon they were over the open sea, the Channel, and then over France.

'Let me take another stab,' said Wilde. 'Paris?'

'Well done! Just another hundred and fifty miles or so, travelling at, let me see, just over a hundred knots.' She looked at her watch. 'Estimated arrival time eight forty-five GMT, then a dash to the Rue Royale. How does Eggs Benedict sound?'

'I don't suppose they do kippers?'

'I doubt the French even know what a kipper is.'

'Then Eggs Benedict will have to do. But there's a problem, Miss Lancing. I don't have my passport.'

She opened a small handbag and pulled out a card. He was speechless. 'May I ask how you got your hands on it?'

'A little light burglary by my driver, Professor Wilde. No harm done.'

'You're simply appalling, Miss Lancing.'

'You don't know the half of it.'

The plane's landing at Le Bourget aerodrome was bumpier than the take-off had been, but perhaps Wilde was simply sobering up. A liveried driver was waiting for them beside an open-topped Bentley, engine running.

They stopped off at the customs and passport shed, where she was recognised and fawned over. When the passport officer asked her the reason for her visit, she said, 'Breakfast with my friend, the professor.' The official smirked and waved them through.

As Wilde settled beside her in the back seat of the car, he wondered what in God's name he was doing here. He had to see his undergraduates, he had to prepare for the imminent arrival of a refugee German scientist, and he had to make contact with Colonel Flood at the US War Department. No, on second thoughts, cancel the third of those chores. Before that, he needed to check in with Jim Vanderberg at the US Embassy in London.

Twenty-five minutes later, they were pulling up outside Maxim's right in the heart of the city, close to the Place de la Concorde and the Madeleine.

'You know, darling, I really think I've changed my mind. They'll be all over me here like a casting director's hands. They'll tell the press boys and they'll want my photograph to hang in the lobby.'

Wilde climbed out of the car. 'Well, no one's going to notice me – and I'm hungry now, so this suits me just fine.'

'You have no idea what a trial fame can be, Professor Wilde,' she said, sipping her second coffee. 'We've had reporters clambering all over Old Hall and the estates trying to get a picture of me. Thank God for Izzy!'

'The dog.'

'The boys with the cameras don't like Izzy. She has very sharp teeth – and she'll use them, too.'

Wilde had always wondered about the attraction of fame. Not to be able to walk down the street quietly and unobserved. Had she had enough of celebrity?

'Will you go back to Hollywood?'

'Who knows? But they'll have to get down on their knees. You know I get cables every day begging me. Scripts arrive and go straight in the garbage. The best – the *very* best – was turning down Selznick. Now he's stuck with some ghastly little nobody for his big colour film.'

'Why would you turn down something like that?'

'Darling, you don't know Hollywood. You don't know movies. The more you spit at them, the more they want you. My price goes up with every rejection.'

This certainly wasn't the way Geoff had told the story.

'Do you want to make love to me, Professor Wilde?'

For a moment, he was thrown. He met her eyes. 'Not while I'm eating my breakfast.'

'Perhaps you'd like me for lunch. You know Tallulah ate me for lunch. Or so I read in one of the scandal sheets.'

'Tallulah? As in?'

'Is there another? One name is enough in Hollywood. Greta, Marlene, Mae, Bette, Clarissa.'

'I suppose you must know them all?'

'In the carnal sense? No, not all. Most, perhaps – but it's not gentlemanly to ask.'

'I think you're teasing me, Miss Lancing. Your brother warned me you were dangerous.'

'Geoff said that? Disloyal boy. Anyway, he's always been the dangerous one.'

Wilde finished his coffee. 'Geoff dangerous?'

'Always. Even as a small child, you could never know what he was going to do or say next. Don't trust a word he utters, Professor Wilde.'

'Do you mean he was a danger to himself or to others?'

'He shouldn't be allowed near a lab. All those glass vessels, all those chemicals and gases and electricity. It's asking for trouble.'

Wilde laughed out loud. 'I think we're talking about different people.'

'You think you know him better than me, darling? I've known the bloody swot for thirty years. How long have you known him – three?'

Wilde realised he needed sleep. The coffee, strong as it was, would not keep him awake much longer.

She read his mind. 'We've got a suite booked at the Bristol, you know. Let's get over there and get you to bed. You're hung-over. And when you wake up, we can play a game. It's called Gone With the Wind. You can play Rhett and I'll be Scarlett.'

Share a room with Clarissa Lancing? He had sobered up enough for alarm bells to start jangling. A few hours ago at the Old Hall, he had thought . . . well, what *had* he thought he was going to do when they went indoors and he gazed up at the staircase? He shrugged off the difficult question. That was then and he had been as tight as a sailor in port. Now was different.

'Well? Shall we go?'

'I—' He stopped. What could he say? *Contrary to the impression I might have given back in Cambridgeshire, I have no intention of being unfaithful to my beloved Lydia Morris.* As it turned out, he didn't need to say anything.

'Don't be a bore, darling,' she said, heavy ennui in her voice. 'I'm not going to pounce on you and molest you.'

'I need to get back to Cambridge,' he said. 'I have a lot planned for today.'

What in God's name was he doing here with this woman?

'Well, you have three choices. Take the boat train, fly regular service from Le Bourget – or wait until I'm ready to go. For now, though, I suggest we shun the motor car and take a brisk walk over to the Rue du Faubourg Saint-Honoré. Then you're on your own. I'm off shopping.'

Back in Cambridge, Henty O'Gara stretched out on the rank bed. What a disaster of a night. The guards at the power station hadn't laid a finger on him, nor had they chased him through the streets of Cambridge, but they were now aware of an intruder. There was no longer any chance of catching them napping.

It was a matter of waiting for his contacts to come to him. But would they do that now that he had failed in his first task? Chances were, they'd simply cut him loose, write him off. He couldn't afford that. Only one thing for it: he had to find another way into the power station. Prove himself.

CHAPTER 16

Lydia arrived at the Adlon to find JT McGinn pacing up and down the lobby. He stopped as soon as she entered. He had called her at nine thirty that morning, just as Miss Forster's bible reading was finishing, and asked her to meet him at eleven. He had refused to say anything further on the telephone.

Taking her arm, McGinn ushered her out and around the corner on to Wilhelmstrasse. 'Just walk,' he said.

'Is something the matter?'

'Everything's the matter. I think I've stuck my finger into a wasps' nest.'

'Who have you been speaking to?'

'The thing is, you see, Miss Morris, whatever you might think, not all Nazis are cut from the same cloth. Even among the high-ups they come in all shades. There are the rabid ones, but there are also the career ones who find a lot of the worst excesses rather distasteful. There are the wives, too. Not all of them are as cruel as their husbands. Even Emmy Goering is said to have secretly helped a Jewish friend in need.'

He was looking around constantly, making sure they could not be overheard, trying to spot the spotters.

'I understand that, of course.'

'I have a friend among the higher ranks at No. 8 Prinz-Albrecht-Strasse. I can't give you his name. I called him at home last night from a public kiosk and asked him if he knew anything. He was very edgy, told me to shut up and said he would meet me at a cafe we both know on Matthäikirchstrasse this morning at eight thirty. It never occurred to me that they put taps on their own kind, but I was wrong.'

'What happened?'

JT's round tortoiseshell glasses had slipped down his nose; he pushed them back up. 'Oh, he was there all right, but he was very jumpy. He told me I should not be asking questions about such matters. He was furious with me for calling him at home. Previously we had always made contact at public events – embassy banquets, that sort of thing, where everyone talks to everyone. But I wasn't having it. I pushed him – hard. Played on his conscience. This was an innocent eight-year-old boy. We were entitled to answers. He just shook his head. And then the bloody Gestapo pulled up outside the cafe. I saw him go white. I told him to run, but he just shrugged. "It is nothing, old chum," he said. "I have told you nothing. They have nothing on me. I'll get a lecture for meeting you, but I'll brush them off with the usual excuse – I was intelligence gathering." And then, just before the Gestapo boys arrived at our table to escort him away for questioning, he whispered a name and telephone number to me.'

'Will he be all right, your friend?'

'Probably. But they'll give him a hard time. They'll want to know why he was talking to a foreign journalist without authority, but we already have a cover story for that. He will say that I had promised him information on a dissident who has now left the country. Easily checked – and part-way true.'

'What about you?'

'Oh, they just made the usual threats. Said I would lose my permit and be kicked out of the country if I stepped out of line again. I don't care about that.'

'Then we can phone the number, can we?'

He stopped, looked around again. Nodded in the direction of a man in a trilby and dark brown suit. 'That's the problem over there, Miss Morris. And others like him. I'm a tethered goat now. So are you. I have made contact from a public phone, but I don't want to risk another call.'

'Then what now?'

'He will meet you.'

'Will you be with me?'

'No. I've done all I can. This is the parting of the ways.'

'But you said you would help me.'

He shrugged. 'And I have done. If it's not good enough, then I'm at a loss.' His hands were in his pockets.

'So where do I meet this man – and when?'

'Keep your voice down, Miss Morris. Stay in the centre of Berlin today. Do tourist things. Go to galleries and shops. He will approach you if and when he considers it safe. If he thinks he's at risk, he won't come near you.'

She was aghast. McGinn was leaving her high and dry. Had she misjudged him so utterly?

He pulled his right hand from his pocket. 'Shake on it, yes?'

She took his hand. As he withdrew, she realised he had left a sliver of paper in her palm. Lightly, she curled her fingers around it.

'Good luck,' he said. 'And remember, you will be in danger, too.'

She watched him walk away, back into the hotel. Then she crossed the road on to Behrenstrasse, and sauntered eastwards past the Deutsche Bank. Was she being followed? She didn't dare look. She turned right down Friedrichstrasse. The broad frontage of the Schauspiel Cafe beckoned. She went in, took a seat and ordered herself a coffee. A copy of *Der Stürmer* had been left on the corner of the vacant table at her side. She picked it up. On the front was a cartoon of Neville Chamberlain with a prominent nose. She flicked through it and was appalled. It was nothing but an anti-Jewish rant.

In her hand, she still had the piece of paper McGinn had placed there. She hadn't dared look at it yet. The waitress arrived with her coffee. She asked if there were any lavatories and was directed to a door at the rear of the cafe. Once in the cubicle, she unfolded her hand. The paper said simply, 'Inside St Hedwig's. 6 p.m. Wear a hat with a feather. Destroy this paper.'

She tore it into little pieces and flushed it away.

The Scavenger. O'Gara had to find the Scavenger. Or to put it more precisely, the Scavenger had to make himself known, because otherwise there was no way of finding the fucker.

There was a knock at the door. He slid from the bed and lifted the latch. It was the landlady. 'Good morning to you, missus,' he said. He hadn't bothered to ask her name and nor would he.

'It's ten o'clock, Mr Burns. You can't stay in your room in the daytime. These lodgings are for working men.'

'Ah, is that really the time? I'll be out in a jiffy, missus.'

She had her arms folded across her bony chest. 'I thought I heard a noise coming from this room late last night. As though someone was messing with the window, climbing in or out maybe.'

'No, no, I woke up in the early hours and needed air. It was awful stuffy last night, missus. That's all. Sorry if my opening the window woke you.'

The landlady kept her arms folded. The corners of her lips were turned down. 'I need your room,' she said. 'I want you out this morning.'

'I paid for a week.'

'You'll get what's due if there's no damage.'

'And what if I stay put?'

'Then you'll be dealing with the constable, who just happens to be my own son. Out by midday, Mr Burns. I don't like your sort one bit.'

Alfie Carpenter unscrewed the Thermos flask and poured sweet, milky tea in two tin mugs. Beside him, Willie Smith stretched out on the river-bank with his hands behind his head, gazing up at the blue sky and the southward-scudding clouds. The tip of his rod rested on a home-made tripod, the line out to a float in mid-river with an earthworm on the hook below the surface. The fish weren't interested, but Alfie didn't care. This was the good life. Him and Willie and a sunny day by the river.

They were on the bank of the Cam halfway between Cambridge and Grantchester. Not too many people out yet, not too much river traffic to disturb them or the fish. They'd been here since seven o'clock in the morning but the only bite they'd had was a nibble of their own cheese and ham sandwiches.

'Cheers,' Smith said as he took the mug.

'What's that?'

'I said "cheers" – are you deaf, lad?'

'No, not you – *that*.' Carpenter pointed towards a riverside tree, twenty yards upriver. 'What's that thing?'

Smith was up on his elbows, peering at the curious object washing this way and that, caught up in the roots of the tree but not held firm. 'Dead body.'

'That's a dog.'

'I'm not so sure . . .'

Carpenter put down his tin cup and sauntered across the grass towards the tree, a weeping willow. He turned back, mouth open. 'Dear God, it *is* a body,' he said. 'A child's body.'

In the Louvre, Wilde stood a long time in a sort of trance, gazing at the Venus de Milo: a two thousand year old hunk of stone that was said to evoke intensely erotic feelings in men. Not in him, it didn't. He was intrigued by the statue, but it was the pale, living flesh of Clarissa that stirred him.

He went back to the Hôtel Le Bristol and lounged on an elaborately upholstered sofa in the lobby, reading the world's newspapers and trying to get his thoughts together for a lecture he had to give the following day. It would be easy enough – *The illusion of stability in late sixteenth-century England* – nothing too taxing, nothing he didn't know by heart. Finally he nodded off. He woke at midday, his head throbbing but his mind clear. From one of the bars he heard the strains of *J'attendrai*. His eyes drifted to the main doors. Clarissa was coming in, carrying a large leather shoulder bag and a smile that seemed to say Mission Accomplished.

'Well,' she said, 'are you ready to go? The car's waiting outside.'

He pulled himself to his feet. 'Yes, I'm ready. May I carry your bag?'

'Thank you, kind sir. Do you like it? I got it for a song in the flea market.'

He took the bag from her. It was so worn and scratched he thought it must be a hundred years old. Mostly, he was surprised by its weight. He frowned at her. 'You carry a lot of lipstick and mascara, Miss Lancing.'

'And you are exceedingly impertinent for even expressing an interest in the contents of a lady's bag. If you must know, it contains a couple of very expensive bottles – so don't bash it about.'

An hour later they were in the air. They were flying into a headwind and the flight was longer and less comfortable, but he felt grateful for the small mercy that she did not attempt any aerobatics. Over the din of the engine, he tried to make conversation. 'Why England, why now?' he asked.

'For the season,' she said. 'Aren't you glad I'm here?'

'War might come tomorrow.'

'One can but hope.'

'Are you serious?'

'Oh, Hollywood's so safe. No one's going to attack America. Europe's the place to be. Don't you hear the guns of war? Aren't you excited by it all? Goose-stepping into Austria and Czechoslovakia? He's like a medieval warlord, don't you think? A German Attila or Genghis Khan, off to conquer the world.'

'What will you do when he goose-steps into Cambridge?'

'I'll invite him to dinner, of course.'

He laughed despite himself.

They landed at five o'clock. The Hispano-Suiza was waiting. In the back of the car, she leant against Wilde's shoulder.

'Good adventure, huh? So where now, Professor Wilde – back to your stuffy books, or Old Hall for drinkies?' She patted her leather bag. 'Remy Martin Louis XIII.'

'Lucky I didn't bash it around then.'

'Wrapped and double-wrapped like swaddled babies.'

Her smile was serene. In the light of day, he studied her eyes again. In colour and shape, they really were remarkably similar to Charlotte's, as was the smile that played at the edges. But they were missing something: his late wife's warmth and kindness.

'Drinkies?'

'No. There are things I must do.'

'And to think Geoff told me you were Wilde by name, wild by nature. Well, you don't escape from me that easily. Come over tomorrow when the crowds aren't there. And wear your whites. Tennis and the finest brandy money can buy.'

'I'm expecting guests.'

'Bring them, Professor Wilde. Any friend of yours is a friend of mine.'

A note had been put through the letter box. It was lying there on top of the rest of his mail, a sheet of paper folded over.

'Dear Wilde,' it said. 'I'm at the Bull. Brought Lindberg up today. Apologies for the change of arrangements. Come over at your leisure. Eaton.'

Wilde screwed up the paper and threw it in the bin. He sighed. Yes, he'd agreed to this, but he enjoyed having his house to himself. Perhaps that was why he and Lydia had never set up home together, either with or without a gold band.

Damn it, he had no option. A promise was a promise. He wandered over to the shelf where the Scotch bottle was looking at him with a gimlet eye. It was still empty.

On the table, he couldn't avoid yesterday's cable from Colonel Dexter Flood. He read it again. 'Fears this end,' it said. What sort of fears?

He picked up the telephone and dialled a London number. The call was answered at the second ring. 'United States Embassy.'

'Jim Vanderberg, please. It's Thomas Wilde. He knows me.'

There was a pause, then the click of the call being transferred.

'Tom? You're back! Well, good. When are you coming down to see us?'

'Soon I hope. I want a good long chat about everything, but not right now. For the moment, can I put a couple of questions to you? What do you know of Colonel Dexter Flood from the War Department in Washington DC?'

'Hmm. No more than you, I guess. Soldier academic with an interest in European politics going back a few years. Why?'

'I met him at the White House. I didn't take to him.'

'The White House, eh? You're flying high, my friend.'

'You mean you didn't know? I rather thought you had been behind the invitation.'

'If I was, I wouldn't say. As for Dexter Flood – why do you need to know?'

'FDR wants me to maintain contact with him over certain matters here in England. Things I'd rather not talk about over the telephone.'

'Well, I've heard nothing bad. But I'll ask around, make a few inquiries for you.'

'Thank you, but be careful. I don't want to compromise you or your career prospects, Jim. This is *my* problem.'

'Have no fear. I'll be as discreet as a clap doctor.' Vanderberg laughed. He was Wilde's oldest friend. They had studied history and shared rooms in Chicago. They also shared an interest in espionage ancient and modern, and they had a similar world view. They had been fortunate in ending up in England at the same time. Now, though, Vanderberg's posting as an attaché at the US Embassy in London was unlikely to last more than a few more months; Ambassador Kennedy wanted shot of him because their views on Germany and England diverged too sharply. The pay-off was that Jim would be promoted to a senior role in the State Department back home while awaiting his first appointment as an ambassador in his own right.

'The other thing I wanted to pick your brain about was an American guy called Milt Hardiman and his wife Peggy. Have you heard of them?'

'Milt Hardiman? Sweet Jesus, yes, Tom. He's one of Kuhn's backers. You've heard of Kuhn?'

'The leader of the Nazis back home, the German American Bund?'

'That's him, Fritz Julius Kuhn. Well, Milton Hardiman is one of the big money men behind the Bund.'

Wilde found he wasn't surprised. 'He's here in Cambridgeshire for the summer. I went to a party at his swanky estate last night. I didn't like him, and I wasn't sure about some of his friends. He sneered at FDR, called him Rosenfeld.'

Vanderberg laughed. 'They all do that, all the German American Bund types. Their little joke. Do yourself a favour and stay away from him. He's poison.'

So why had FDR's man Flood asked him to use Hardiman as a go-between if he had unsound political leanings? 'I think I need to know more about Dexter Flood as a matter of urgency, Jim.'

'I'll call you soonest.'

'As to the Hardimans, there's a slight complication. Clarissa Lancing is staying with them for the summer. Her brother is my good friend Geoff Lancing. We sort of hit it off, I think.'

'Clarissa Lancing the movie star?'

'The same.'

'Well, goddamn it, Tom.'

He could almost hear Jim's disapproval at the end of the line. Vanderberg was a happily married man with children. He knew and liked Lydia. Wilde rushed to reassure him. 'Nothing like that, Jim. It's just, you know, she asked me over for tennis and cocktails. Lydia's in London. It's harmless, isn't it?'

'Who are you kidding, Tom? Not me, not you. Lydia's a good one; hang on to her. You want my friendly advice? Stay away from temptation, buddy. Keep away from the noxious Hardimans at all costs – and keep your pecker in your pants where it belongs. Do you read me loud and clear?'

Wilde heard him, but he wasn't at all sure he was going to heed him. What was that stuff about moths and flames? Well, Clarissa Lancing burned awfully bright.

CHAPTER 17

Lydia was at a loss all day. She wandered the centre of Berlin like a tourist, looking with vacant eyes at the shops and stores in the busy thoroughfare of Leipzigerstrasse. The city was a blaze of red and white and black – the ubiquitous swastika pennants hanging everywhere. And the streets below them were preternaturally litter-free; no one dared drop even a cigarette end.

In a department store, she bought a felt hat with a pheasant feather protruding at a jaunty angle, then walked along Unter den Linden. At the Brandenburg Gate she watched a troop of Hitler Youth march by in lederhosen with white stockings and tassels at the knee. She bought a brown paper bag full of birdseed from a frail old Jew. He held out his shaking hand for a few pfennigs, but she gave him ten marks. He thanked her profusely and scurried away, while she went off to feed the pigeons. She resisted the temptation to buy hot bratwurst for herself from a street sausage seller although it smelt delicious. Instead she took in the old and new museums by the Spree and found herself profoundly unimpressed by the Nazis' narrow vision of art. She also gazed with distaste up at the overweening Victory Column. In the afternoon, she refreshed herself at an outdoor cafe and listened to the soulful melody of a zither minstrel.

Wherever she went, she felt certain she was being followed. But was she being followed by Nazi agents or by the man who had agreed to meet her? Strangely, she felt least nervous outside the new Reich Chancellery building on Wilhelmstrasse; it was so outrageous in size and scale that it did not seem real; too cold and soulless and modern to be threatening. Gazing upon the home of the SS and SD on Prinz-Albrecht-Strasse was less comfortable. Who knew what horrors took place behind those baleful walls, in painted rooms along institutional corridors, and in grimly lit dungeons?

At teatime, needing the warmth of decent human company, she went around the corner to Tiergartenstrasse and dragged Frank Foley's secretary, Margaret Reid, out for coffee and cake. Margaret didn't need much persuading. The queue of people waiting their turn to beg for a visa had not diminished overnight.

'Another eighteen-hour day for Frank and me,'

'I wish I could help.'

'When you get home, kick up a stink. Tell them they need to allocate more visas to these people. Britain has an empire that reaches to all corners of the earth. Surely someone somewhere could provide a home.'

Margaret tried to turn the subject to the efforts to locate the missing boy, but Lydia hushed her. 'Do you think we're being watched here?'

'Perhaps,' Margaret said. 'To tell the truth I've given up caring. What are they going to tell their bosses? Today Margaret Reid went to work, then she went back to her flat, exhausted.' She laughed. 'Not very exciting, is it?'

'I need to know that I'm not being watched.'

'Oh well, that's easy.' She lowered her voice to a whisper. 'Come back to 17 Tiergartenstrasse with me. We'll slip you out the back.'

At five to six, Lydia found herself standing on the wide open space of Opernplatz, on the south-east side of the Unter den Linden. Opera-goers milled around waiting for the doors to open, either in evening dress or the uniform of senior military and *Schutzstaffel* officers. Lydia felt horribly conspicuous and was aware that she was shaking.

She kept her head down and walked towards St Hedwig's Cathedral, with its six-columned frontage and its distinctive dome. A line of teenage boys were tripping down the broad stone steps, like choristers who had escaped practice. Keeping well away from them, she headed up in the other direction. At the top of the steps she checked her watch. One minute to six. Bells were about to chime around the city; she had to be inside.

Don't look around. Walk straight in. She was supposed to wear her hat with the feather. But she couldn't wear a hat, could she, not inside a Roman Catholic cathedral? Or was it the other way round – was she required to keep her hair covered? She removed the hat and held it under her arm, with the feather visible and prominent.

Light streamed in through the high windows. Banks of long, smoothly carved pews ranged across the stone floor of the great rotunda, facing the high altar. She walked down the aisle between the pews, aware of the echoing click of her shoes at every step. She stopped, bowed and made the sign of the cross.

She heard the sound of other heels on the stone floor and turned to see a young priest in a cassock and lace-fringed surplice walking towards her. He bowed his head in her direction, but carried on towards the altar where he used a snuffer to extinguish two candles. Lydia sat down on one of the pews towards the left-hand side, wishing to be both easily visible and utterly inconspicuous. The air was heavy with incense. How very different this all was from the religion of her youth. No candles or incense or gold artefacts in the Cambridge meeting house of the Society of Friends. Such ornamentation was an affront to God, she had been told. And yet as she sat here in this holy place, she had to confess it had a certain attraction. Perhaps the spirit could soar here after all.

The priest turned away from the altar and walked back towards the rear of the dome, then disappeared into the sacristy.

She heard another sound behind her and half-turned. An old, white-haired woman, bent and in widow's weeds, had entered. She, too, made the sign of the cross, then went to a shrine at the side of the great rotunda, put a coin into a box and lit a candle that she placed among a blazing array of others. Each one represented a prayer, a request to God.

The young priest emerged once more and came her way again. This time he stopped beside her and asked her kindly whether she wished to be confessed. She said, '*Nein, danke*,' and he immediately smiled. 'Ah, you are English, yes? Can I help you at all? Vespers is hours away.'

'I just wish to sit for a while . . .'

'Are you Jewish? All are welcome, you know.' His eyes went to her trembling hands. 'Whatever your faith, you have no need to be nervous here.'

'No, it's not that. I just need some quiet reflection.'

He nodded, holding his hands together in front of him. 'Forgive me. I have intruded. I will leave you alone, of course.' He bowed again and left her to go about his business. She closed her eyes. Perhaps a prayer was indeed called for in this place, at this time. Tom should be here with her. What would he think when he discovered she had come to Germany without telling him? How would she feel in his place? Betrayed, of course.

She sensed she was not alone. She opened her eyes and turned briefly. A man had slid into the pew behind her. He was leaning forward, as though deep in prayer.

'Miss Morris, keep your eyes to the front if you would.'

She had seen enough of him. It was a face she would recognise again.

He was a man in his late forties, with short fair hair and a clear complexion. She imagined he would be big, for he seemed to be squashed into the pew rather uncomfortably. He was wearing a black suit, a white shirt and a tie, and she could smell his sweat.

'Can you help me?' she asked.

'That depends what you want. I can get you out of Germany. I can get anyone out, to the country of their choice, with a great deal of their jewels and gold. I am the Scarlet Pimpernel of Berlin. And my rates are very reasonable, considering the great risks I take. Fifty Reichsmarks for the exit papers, then fifty per cent of all gemstones, gold and currency smuggled out. It is a good deal, because the border guards would take one hundred per cent.' His voice was businesslike; then it softened. 'You can call me Fritz. It is what all you English call us Germans, is it not?'

'I don't want to get anyone out of Germany. I am trying to find a missing boy. A boy of eight named Albert Haas who disappeared from one of the *Kindertransports* en route to England.'

'Indeed, that was what I was led to understand. A boy named Albert Haas . . .' he said, as though mulling over the name.

'I was told you might be able to help.'

'All things are possible. How much money do you have?'

Lydia had not expected this. She was not short of cash because she had been left with a comfortable estate on the death of her parents when she was a child. She had brought fifty pounds with her to Berlin, half in Reichsmarks. Had she been so naive not to consider that bribes might be necessary?

'I have some money. Not much, but I could try to get more from the bank in the morning.'

'I have heard of this boy. It is a difficult, complicated matter.'

'What have you heard?'

'That depends who I am talking to. Who do you represent, Miss Morris?'

'I am representing myself. If you have information – or if you can get it – just tell me how much you want. I'll pay you, whatever it costs.'

'Are you MI6? Has the British Government sent you?'

'No, of course not. How could you possibly think I was MI6?'

He laughed.

She stiffened. 'How can you laugh? A boy is missing. His mother is terrified.'

'Of course, I am sorry. It is just the company you keep.'

'I don't know what you mean.'

He didn't explain, but pursued his question. 'I must ask again – who do you represent?'

She sighed deeply. This conversation, with her back to the man, was draining her and felt as if it was going nowhere. And yet, he knew her name, had taken the trouble to come to meet her. He had either been trailing her as an agent of the regime, or he could truly help her. Most importantly, he had said he had heard of Albert Haas.

'The Quakers,' she said finally. 'The Society of Friends. Perhaps you haven't heard of them.'

There was silence behind her. The young priest was walking past them again, this time accompanied by an older priest. The man behind Lydia waited until they were out of earshot, then he prodded her in the back with his finger. 'Take this,' he said. She put her hand to her shoulder and he slipped a piece of card into her fingers. Not just a card, a photograph.

The picture showed a young man and woman, both aged about twenty. Both healthy and smiling, lying on their backs on the grass, as though enjoying a picnic.

'My son and daughter,' the man said. 'They are twins, fine young people. There was a time after the war when they were wasting away to nothing. It was the Quakers who saved them from starvation in 1920. Your people provided milk each day. You saved many lives when the world turned its back on us.'

It was said that for five long years after the end of the war the Quakers fed a million German children every day with milk and rice, soup and bread. She looked at the photograph again, then handed it back.

'Then perhaps you could repay the Quakers by finding Albert Haas.'

'He was not taken from the train, I can tell you that much. And for you, Miss Morris, no charge.'

What use was this? 'He *was* taken from the train, sir,' she said, her voice insistent. 'It happened at the Dutch border. Other children in his compartment have testified that he was taken away by uniformed men.'

'Perhaps he was moved to another part of the train. I have certain knowledge that he made the journey to England as planned. He has been there all along.'

'No. That's not possible.'

'I swear it, on my own children's lives. You are wasting your time in Berlin, Miss Morris.'

She turned around to face him. 'Who are you? Why should I believe you? And how do you have the power to get people out of Germany?'

'Please, turn around. You are endangering us both.' She turned back away from him and he whispered hoarsely into her ear. 'My father was a writer. They burned his books along with twenty thousand other books on the Opernplatz outside this very church. And now, I pretend to be one of them, the Nazis. That is how I can do what I do. That is how I hear things.'

'Then if what you say is true, if Albert is in England, where exactly is he?'

'I don't know. But I must tell you one other thing.'

Once again, silence.

'Yes?'

A long pause, then a sigh. 'Perhaps I should not be telling you this, but I must caution you: Frau Dr Haas is not all she seems.'

The words might have chilled her, but she was already thinking much the same. If the SD was involved in Lindberg's escape, how could Eva not have known – or at least have suspected something? But these thoughts did not help with the immediate problem of finding Albert. 'Are you certain that the boy is in England?'

'I am certain he was taken there. After that, I cannot say.'

'Please tell me more, where did you come by this information? Who are you?'

'I will say only this: you should get out of Germany now, Miss Morris. It is probable that the only thing keeping you alive is that you are a Quaker. Even Heydrich respects your organisation. But it may not last.'

'Are you trying to scare me?'

'You should be scared. The whole world should be scared. Tell Foley to look into the activities of IG Farben and the work of Gerhard Schrader and Otto Ambros. They scare *me*, Miss Morris.'

And then she heard him rising from his pew, the scrape of his shoes on stone, and when she turned, he was gone.

After a minute, she rose and began to make her own way out of the Cathedral. The young priest was near the door. 'I hope you found the peace you were seeking,' he said.

She had found something. But it wasn't peace. 'Thank you,' was all she said.

'Go with God.'

From outside there was the muffled but distinctive sound of a gunshot. Their eyes met. Together, they hurried out into the evening air. From the top of the steps, they looked down at the body of the man who had called himself Fritz. Blood was pouring from his head onto the stone of Opernplatz, where, he said, his father's books had been burnt.

The sunlit square was teeming with opera-goers, early evening diners and sensation-seekers. They turned their eyes away, though all must have heard the shot and seen the man fall. No one approached. No one wanted to be involved. Among them was a large man in an unnecessary coat, silhouetted against the mass of people, the black shadow of a pistol dangling from his right hand as he lumbered away, unchallenged, towards Unter den Linden. Even at this distance there was something horribly familiar about him. She had seen him before somewhere, but where?

'What do we do?'

'You do nothing,' the priest said, putting his hand to her shoulder to guide her away. 'You go and make yourself safe. I will deal with this.'

'We must report it, Father.'

'To whom? I know that man,' he jutted his smooth chin towards the corpse. 'I have seen him before. I always thought he was one of them.'

'Gestapo?'

'Who knows? Gestapo, SD, SS, SA ... they are a many-headed serpent.' He nodded towards the retreating man, the fat killer. 'Same with him, I am sure.' He crossed himself. 'They burnt the synagogues. They will burn the churches next.'

As she looked down at the body and the pooling blood, Lydia thought her heart and lungs would burst from their casing. What had she got herself into?

CHAPTER 18

Wilde telephoned Philip Eaton at the Bull and told him to keep the Germans at the hotel overnight. 'I've got nothing here. No food, no beds made up. All I can offer them is whisky, and not much of that. I need to get our char, Doris, on board for the domestic stuff. Filling the larder, all that. I'm hoping she'll do a bit of cooking and baking for me, too.'

'Well, at least come over and say hello. They're understandably very nervous.'

'I will. I'll just nip into college for one or two things. Then I'll be with you.'

Wilde hastily tied his tie, then grabbed his jacket and walked into the centre of Cambridge. The weather was still fine. Every so often he saw someone carrying a gas mask. Not something he'd bother with for the moment. In the event of a sudden attack by a hostile power, Cambridge would be some way down the list of targets. His sense of peace was shattered by a thunderous roar, and he arched his neck to see a formation of Spitfires directly overhead. They kept low, barely two hundred feet above ground. Before he could count them, they were gone.

The head porter looked grim-faced as he welcomed Wilde. 'Evening, Professor.'

'You look as if you've seen a ghost, Scobie.'

'Not much to cheer the spirits in college today. Haven't you heard the news, Professor? They found poor Dr Birbach dead in the river this morning.'

'Birbach dead?'

'Couple of anglers found him. Thought he was a child at first, I believe. Well, he was small enough, wasn't he? He was supposed to be off to California today. The whole college is in a state of shock. Doesn't feel like May Week.'

'This is awful, Scobie. Was it an accident? Are the police involved? What happened?'

'I gather he drowned, sir. But I don't know anything more than that. Shocking news. Not that it ever felt as though Dr Birbach was truly one of us, if you know what I mean, what with him being a German gentleman. But still, it shakes you up a bit.'

Wilde trudged up the stairs to his rooms. On the way he passed Birbach's door, which was closed. He had been a strange man, perhaps every bit as brilliant as Geoff Lancing and Torsten Hellquist clearly believed, but Wilde's abiding memory of him now would be on his knees in a boathouse preparing to mount a woman playing the part of a cleaning lady.

Within hours, he had somehow come to his death in the Cam. Accident? Suicide? Murder? It was puzzling and disturbing in equal measure. Wilde wanted to know more.

He sat down at his desk and picked up his fountain pen, looking down at a pile of papers. He let out a sigh: the night and day had caught up with him. Bobby had left a bottle of whisky on the desk as promised, but it remained unopened. He couldn't work, couldn't look at any essays or deal with correspondence. God, did he really have to go and make small talk with the Germans and Eaton? He put down the pen, stretched his shoulders and yawned. Get it over with, he told himself.

Rising from the desk, he wandered to the window and looked out over Old Court in all its early summer finery. Ivy on the walls, the lawn a magnificent shade of green. Young men in gowns striding forth with purpose as Easter Term drew to a close. Among them he spotted the large figure of Hellquist waddling across the lawn. He ought to go and offer condolences. Perhaps, too, he might know something about the circumstances of his friend's death.

Hellquist had reached Birbach's door as Wilde was about to descend the stairs.

'Dr Hellquist,' Wilde called out.

The Swede, who was carrying a large leather briefcase, stared up into the gloom of the stairwell and squinted. 'Is that you, Mr American?'

'I saw you crossing the court. Please accept my condolences. I know that you and Paul Birbach were close.'

Hellquist nodded. There was sadness there, obviously, but something else, too. Anger? Or something akin to it.

'Thank you. You are a good friend. You know, Paul, for all his flaws, was the best of men. I rather think I loved him.' He sighed heavily.

Wilde rather thought Hellquist was about to cry, but instead the big Swede shook his head.

'Ah, this is so bad, so bad.'

Wilde nodded. No words of condolence seemed adequate.

'You know, Mr American, I was just going into Paul's rooms. There are papers he was going to give me before he left for California. I need them. Your head porter, Scobie, said it would be all right.'

'Of course. Can I help you with anything?' Wilde followed Hellquist as he opened the door and squeezed his great bulk inside.

He had never been in Birbach's set before and he almost laughed at what he saw. The main room looked like one big, incomprehensible mathematical puzzle. There were half a dozen blackboards of varying sizes, a couple hammered to walls, one on an artist's easel and the others propped against furniture. Every inch of them was covered in chalked numbers and letters and mathematical symbols and curious drawings. The floor was littered with sheets of paper, all covered in calculations.

'Don't worry. It all makes sense to me,' said the Swede.

'I'm sure it does.' Wilde looked around for some sign of a life outside mathematics. All he could see was a hard wooden chair and, ranged across the back wall, a single rather austere bed. 'I had no idea he lived like this.'

'He had a flat nearby, where he mostly slept and had immensely long baths and entertained his . . . his ladies. He was a man who split his life into pigeonholes, that is the best way to describe him.'

Every man had his secret passions. But that didn't explain how he had died. 'How did this happen, Hellquist?' Wilde asked.

'I have no idea.'

'I just don't understand how he could have ended up in the river. What time did he leave Old Hall?'

'I don't know. I suppose I saw him at midnight with that awful new woman of his. What do you suppose they talked about when they were not, you know, jig-a-jig?' He waved his large hands. 'I'm sorry. I liked Paul very much. I just didn't always like the company he kept.'

'Did he introduce her to you?'

'Not as such. Paul did not understand society's little courtesies.'

'Have the police said anything? Was it alcohol? It seems such a . . . such an extraordinary accident.'

Hellquist was scooping up papers from Birbach's desk and thrusting them into his case. He stopped and gave Wilde a strange look. 'Accident, Mr American? Paul Birbach's death wasn't accidental. He was murdered.'

'*Murdered*? I thought he drowned.'

'Well, if he did, then it was because someone held his face under water. A man like that does not die by accident. Birbach held the secrets of the universe in his head. Someone wanted to stop him in his tracks. They will try to get me next.'

'Are you serious?'

'Of course I'm serious. They will kill me because I was the only one here who understood exactly what he was doing. And so I think I might be safer elsewhere.'

It struck Wilde that Hellquist really believed his life was in danger. He intended to flee.

'Where will you go?'

'Who knows? Home to Stockholm perhaps. Or America, as Paul planned to. Best that I tell no one, I think. That way no one can betray me. I can trust you, Mr American?'

Wilde nodded.

'But still, it is safer not to tell you where I am going. First, I need to deal with all this.' He picked up a board rubber and began scrubbing out Birbach's blackboard equations.

'Dr Hellquist, I don't think you should be doing that.'

'No, Mr American? What would you do? Let it fall into someone else's hands?'

'But don't you need it?'

'It's already safe in my head. Much safer than being left here.'

The words in Dexter Flood's telegram came rushing back. *Fears this end.* Two Cavendish men: one dead, the other scared for his life. Perhaps Colonel Flood knew what he was talking about after all.

On his way out, Wilde called on Horace Dill. He pushed open the door to his rooms tentatively. Horace did not like to be disturbed at the best of times. As before, the place stank like a prep school sick bay. That and the sweat and the overpowering stench of stale cigar smoke, a smell that would never go away if the windows were to be left open ten years.

He entered on tiptoe. The mound of Dill's body beneath the bedclothes was not the size it would have been a few months ago; poor Horace was much diminished. His eyes were closed, so Wilde turned around to leave him to his sleep.

'I'm awake, damn you.'

'Ah, Horace. Glad to find you alive.'

'Have you brought my grapes?'

'No. They're not quite in season, I'm afraid.'

'Good. I hate the fucking things.'

'And I'm not lighting a cigar for you. But I do have news to cheer you up. Arnold Lindberg has arrived. He's at the Bull.'

'Arnold's in town? Well, why isn't he here?' Dill's voice collapsed into a rasping cough. His body shook violently beneath the covers.

Wilde found a glass of water on the bedside table and held it to Dill's lips. He tried to drink, but only coughed more. Wilde waited until the spasm subsided.

'Are you trying to poison me, Wilde?'

'It was water, Horace.' Wilde suppressed a chuckle. It occurred to him that Horace was rather enjoying his deathbed scene. He had always been one for high drama. 'Shall I ask Lindberg if he'd like to pop around and see you? How many years is it since you were working together for world revolution?'

Dill held up both hands with fingers splayed. 'Ten,' he said.

'You may not be able to have much of a conversation.'

'I'll be all right. For pity's sake bring along some ale. That fucking water will be the death of me.' Dill gasped and clutched his chest and fell into another bout of blood-flecked coughing.

Wilde would have liked to ask how Dill had come to be friends with Lindberg. All Wilde knew about him was that the German was a Communist, a Jew, and that he had tried to escape Germany in 1936 after falling foul of Himmler and being denounced by the *Deutsche Physik*, the Nazi-sympathising group of scientists who had 'cleansed' Germany's laboratories of non-Aryans. But it was clear that he wasn't going to be able to get much information out of Horace Dill at the moment.

'I'm about to go and see Lindberg now. I'll bring him back if you think you're up to it.'

'Just fucking go!'

Wilde went.

Henty O'Gara had found a hotel. Not a rooming house this time. He had hoped for anonymity in his lodgings, but instead his Irishness had been all too conspicuous. Well, he'd have to pay good cash for a room in a fine toffs' hotel. At least no one there would make a song and dance about his accent, no one would look at him sideways as though he had bombs in his bag. No one would treat him like a dog, and he wouldn't have to sneak in and out of windows.

The room was pleasant enough and he was able to take a quick bath and a shave in the bathroom down the corridor. Then he headed north-wards down St John's Street, past the great colleges, Trinity and St John's, to take another look at the Thompson's Lane Power Station. Once again, he sensed he was being followed every step of the way. He was just about to double back and see if he could spot his pursuer, when he felt a tap on his shoulder.

A sharp, urgent, whisper in his ear. 'Oi, mister! Come with me.'

O'Gara whirled round. A boy, barely in his teens. 'Who the hell are you?' he demanded.

'Sod that. Just follow me,' the boy hissed and set off back towards the river.

Swearing under his breath, O'Gara followed the youngster across Magdalene Bridge, and along Castle Street, away from the bustle of the town centre. Up past Castle Hill, he ducked into a side street and slid into a low-fronted public house. O'Gara did the same. If this lad was a copper's nark, he was done for – but, Jesus, there was a time in every man's life when the whistle blew and he had to go over the top.

'Over here, in the corner.'

The pub was heaving with drinkers: working men, bargees, drivers, he guessed. Rough types. Not a scholar in sight out here.

'What you drinking, mister?'

'Milk stout. Tell me, are you old enough to be in here, son?'

'Sod you, mister.' The boy sauntered off to the bar and returned with two pints. 'There you are. Don't say I do nothing for you.'

O'Gara relaxed a little; not too much. 'Thank you, sonny.'

'I'm not your sonny.'

'What's your name then?'

'None of your business.'

'Then sonny it is,' O'Gara said. 'Why have you been following me – and why have you brought me here?'

'You messed up Thompson's Lane, mister, that's why. You've got to get back in there.'

'Jesus, it's pointless. And keep your voice down, will you?'

The boy was shabby, his pores ingrained with dirt. He slouched like a burglar casing a joint, his fingers cupping his hand-rolled cigarette. O'Gara looked at him and was appalled. Was this kid really the best the IRA command could find in England?

'It ain't pointless, mister. We wanted you to blow the place to smithereens.'

'Well then, you'd better get me a barrel load of gelignite, because what I've got wouldn't do much more than knock a hole in a wall.'

'Well, do that then. You're supposed to be the sodding bombs expert.'

Oh, he was a bombs expert all right. The English had taught him that well enough in their war with Germany before he went home to a more important conflict – the war for Irish independence.

'I want to meet the Scavenger.'

'Scavenger?' The boy paused, suddenly alert. 'What're you talking about? What Scavenger?'

'You know very well who the Scavenger is. You wouldn't be here otherwise. Don't take me for a fool.'

The boy shrugged. 'It ain't gonna happen.'

'Then how can we plan a proper campaign? I was told contact would be made with the Scavenger, that there would be access to explosives from building sites or Army depots, that we'd work out a list of targets together. I can't work blind, sonny.'

'Well, maybe you'll get it when you show who you are and what you can do.' He lowered his voice. 'Yes, we've got something bigger for you, but first you've got to show us you can blow a hole in a sodding power station. Right, mister? Hardly like trying to blow up Buckingham sodding Palace, is it?'

'OK then,' O'Gara said slowly. 'OK, I'll do what you say. I'll blow a hole in an outer wall tonight. But there's no way I can get to the turbine or the chimney. It'll be symbolic, nothing more. Tell the Scavenger that, if you will. And then I want a meeting.'

The youth smirked, and then downed his pint of bitter in one. He took a last drag of his thin cigarette stub, dropped it to the sawdust floor and stamped it out. 'Be seeing you, mister,' he said.

O'Gara watched his receding back, took another sip of his stout and put down the almost full glass. As he slipped from the pub out into the street, he saw the youth loping away down the hill. A hundred yards on, he stopped, and began to roll another cigarette. O'Gara wanted to laugh. This would be easy.

CHAPTER 19

Wilde met the German scientist Arnold Lindberg and his niece Eva Haas at the Bull. They were in the reception area with Eaton when he arrived and all three of them stood up, as though on parade. Eaton made the introductions and Lindberg shook hands and made a sharp bow. Wilde half expected a click of the heels.

'Mr Professor Wilde, I am honoured to make your meeting,' Lindberg said. 'No, that is incorrect. I must say *acquaintance*. I am honoured to make your acquaintance. I have heard great things about your scholarship.'

'I am sure your English is a great deal better than my German, Herr Dr Lindberg,' said Wilde. 'And I too, have heard marvellous things about your scientific work.'

He noted the gauntness in the man's face, the close shaven stubble on his veiny head; he had suffered terribly.

Wilde turned to Eva Haas and smiled at her. She was not at all what he had expected. Small and earnest, she was deathly pale, and yet there was an exquisite luminescent quality to her complexion.

There was, above all, a hint of warmth in her mouse-like seriousness. She said nothing other than 'How do you do', so he tried to bring her out of her shell as they sat in the lobby with coffee.

'Tell me about your time in Cambridge, Frau Dr Haas. You were at Girton, I am told.'

Her eyes suddenly lit up as though recalling a better time. 'I remember English crumpets, Professor, with lots of melting butter. In the afternoons, we would gather in one of the young women's rooms and we would use forks to toast crumpets on the open fire. And we would drink pots of sweet and milky English tea. I enjoyed those days very much.'

'And I believe you knew Lydia Morris.'

'Of course. She was a wonderful friend to me. I was a little lost and hesitant with my English when I first arrived, but she gave me much assistance. I owe her a great deal.'

'Well, she should be up soon. And' – he hesitated – 'I hope you have had some good news about your little boy?'

Eva looked down and shook her head. There was an awkward silence.

Eaton put up his elegant hand. 'A quick word in private, old man.'

'Excuse us,' Wilde said, and followed Eaton through to the bar. 'What's going to happen now?'

'I'm going to leave them here overnight. Can you pick them up tomorrow when you've fixed all the domestic arrangements?'

'Will they be safe?'

Eaton sighed. 'To keep them completely safe, we'd have to put them in Pentonville. We're taking a gamble that Himmler's boys simply won't have the wherewithal to find them, particularly as no one will broadcast their presence.'

'What about Frau Haas? Do you think Lydia will be back tomorrow? I rather got the impression that she was staying in London for the duration. Doesn't seem quite right to leave Frau Haas all alone in Lydia's house.'

'Perhaps she could stay with you in the meantime. How many spare bedrooms have you got?'

'Two.'

'Perfect. One for each of them, then. She's a widow, so I doubt your charlady or neighbours will think it too scandalous. Anyway, I'm sure it won't be for long. Miss Morris will be back from Berlin any day.'

Wilde's brow creased. 'What do you mean?'

Eaton took a sharp intake of breath. 'Oh God, I wasn't meant to tell you.'

'What are you talking about?' Wilde demanded.

'I'm sorry. I think I've put my size tens in it.'

'Are you serious? Lydia in Berlin?'

No point in trying to dissemble now. 'I think she didn't want to worry you. She's gone to try to find out what happened to the boy. Personally, I doubt she'll get anywhere, but who knows, the German high command has a soft spot for Quakers. I'm sure she's in no danger.'

'This is madness, Eaton! Why did you let her go?'

'How could I prevent her buying an aeroplane ticket?'

'You could have called me – look, I've got to go to her.'

Eaton gripped Wilde by the arm. 'You'd have known nothing of it if I hadn't blabbed – and you would have had no cause for concern. She'll be back safe and sound in next to no time, you'll see.'

Wilde looked at his watch. Seven o'clock. When did flights start in the morning? 'Where can I fly from?' he demanded.

Eaton clicked his fingers to summon the barman. 'Forget it, you're not going. If necessary I'll have your passport confiscated.'

'You can't do that! I'm an American citizen.'

'Try me. You're an alien in Britain and I can make things very difficult for you. Think it through, Wilde. Your presence in Berlin would endanger *both* of you and do bugger all for relations with the German regime if you start throwing your weight around. Do you think you're not known over there?'

'But she could already be in danger.'

Eaton's voice dropped. 'My man Foley is looking out for her. Directs the passport and visa office. But that's just a cover: he's MI6 station chief in Berlin.' Eaton mouthed the words. 'His secretary, Margaret Reid, is also one of ours. They will have been pointing Miss Morris in the right direction – the safe direction. And they'll do a better job than you at keeping her safe, Wilde. Believe me. They know Berlin – you don't.'

Wilde could see the truth of Eaton's line. Of course it didn't make sense to blunder into Berlin after Lydia, but he felt sick with worry. And there was another thing: why *had* Eaton blabbed? He never said anything by mistake. Never. There was always an ulterior motive.

'When is she coming back?'

'She didn't say, but look, chances are she'll draw a blank. Either way, I'd expect her home soon. She can only delve so far in Berlin and she knows she's needed up here to look after Frau Haas.'

'Lydia's in a foreign country, a country we could be at war with at any moment, and you're saying there's nothing I can do?' Wilde was angry – and not just with Eaton. Why was he the last to know what Lydia was up to? The answer was obvious, of course – because he would have moved mountains to stop her going, and they both knew it.

'No, that's not at all what I'm saying. There's a great deal you can do to help.'

'Keep our German scientists safe. What about your offer of a gun?'

'As I said, that's up to you.' Eaton paused. 'There was something else, too, Wilde.'

'You surprise me.' Wilde raised an eyebrow. He should have known. There was never anything simple with Eaton.

'You've been consorting with the Hardimans out at Old Hall.'

Why did Philip Eaton always have the power to unnerve him? For a moment, Wilde considered punching him for being so bloody intrusive. Instead he laughed. 'Of course I shouldn't be at all surprised that you know that. And I suppose you want me to stay away from them, is that it?'

'Quite the opposite, old boy. I want you to get in there among them. Become thick as thieves with them. I want to know what they're up to, because I'm certain of one thing – they're not on our side.'

Not for the first time, Wilde wondered just whose side Eaton might be on himself – but he was pretty sure it wasn't Hitler's, so they shared that much in common. 'I've told you before, Eaton. I am an American. I'm not interested in working for the British secret service.'

'I know, I know. But I must tell you, I think we've all got reason to be worried about people like Milt Hardiman.'

'Because he's a Nazi sympathiser? Plenty of people are, you know.'

Eaton clicked his fingers again and finally the barman arrived. 'Come on, let's have a quick Scotch. I've been drinking coffee with our distinguished guests for hours, and I've had enough of it.' He ordered a couple of doubles. 'Look,' he said to Wilde. 'All I'm asking is that you accept their invitations. I'll be frank with you: we think Hardiman's here for a specific reason. He was linked to some unpleasant types in America – Fritz Kuhn's Bund, but others, too. Men who kept their heads down and didn't go shouting their heads off like Kuhn's bully boys, but were able to wield real influence. Much more dangerous.'

'But what exactly do you suspect?'

'If I knew, I'd tell you. But you have a way in. And you have certain skills.'

'Ah, you're trying to flatter me.'

'No, Wilde, it's the truth. I've seen it in you before. For God's sake, we need to find out what the bastard is up to.'

The whiskies arrived. They clinked glasses. 'To daylight,' Eaton said.

'Is that it? Your toast?'

'A terrible darkness is falling. Don't you feel it?'

Yes, he felt it all right. 'OK,' he said, trying to sound casual. 'I'll keep an eye on Milt Hardiman.' No need to mention that he had actually been instructed to work *with* the man. He also needed to discover the true nature of Colonel Dexter Flood. If Flood wanted him to work with Hardiman, and if Hardiman had Nazi sympathies, then what did that make Flood? And what game, if any, was FDR playing?

'I don't trust Hardiman,' Eaton continued. 'I don't trust his damned wife or anyone around them.' He gave Wilde a long and level look.

'Anyone? Are you including Clarissa Lancing in this?'

'Apart from fancying the pants off the girl, what do you think of her?'

'A little on the wild side.'

Eaton laughed out loud. 'That's the understatement of the year coming from a man who has just been flown to Paris for breakfast and back again. Come on, let's down these and get back to Lindberg and Haas.'

'There's something else. Did you hear about Birbach? Paul Birbach, the Cavendish scientist?'

'Should I have?'

'His body was fished out of the river.'

Eaton was suddenly alert. 'Why haven't I heard of this? Are the circumstances suspicious?'

'Not as such, but his friend Torsten Hellquist certainly has doubts. They were both at Hardiman's place for the big party. Along with a lot of other Cavendish and university people, I might add.'

Eaton took out a notebook and scratched a few notes in his elegant hand. 'It doesn't sound good. I'll look into it, Wilde. See what the police say and get back to you.'

'As for that gun . . .'

'I'll slip you my Walther.' Eaton got up, and tossed back his drink.

'One moment.' Wilde put a hand on his arm. 'I'll keep an eye on Milt Hardiman for you, provided you guarantee to get Lydia back safely. Can you promise me that?"

After Eva Haas had retired to her hotel bedroom, Eaton left, saying he had to get back to London. Wilde and Lindberg walked slowly to college. They spoke very little on the way. Lindberg had new clothes, a good suit bought in London, but it could not disguise his skeletal frame or sunken cheeks. He brightened at the sight of Horace Dill, however. The two comrades clutched each other's hands, tears in their eyes.

Lindberg had worked under Rutherford at the Cavendish in the late twenties and had come to know Dill through the Cambridge University Socialist Club; both had also been members of the Communist Party. Despite such a long association, however, conversation was difficult at first. If Lindberg had ever had the art of small talk, he had lost it in the brutal confines of Dachau; Dill was unable to say much without suffering a choking fit. Nonetheless, there was real warmth between them and for half an hour the two men reacquainted themselves, the tears falling liberally. Wilde had never seen Dill like this before.

He had brought two bottles of ale and handed the old friends one each.

At last they began to talk properly, and Wilde stood back and watched them, and listened.

'You know what they did, Comrade Dill? For a special treat, every Sabbath, they put pork in the broth, or so they said. In truth, I couldn't taste it, but every week they said it was there, just to torment the stricter Jews among us.'

'Bastards,' Dill rasped.

'For myself, I could happily have had more pig in my broth. Particularly bacon. I cannot resist bacon. I had it for breakfast with eggs this morning. It was like manna from heaven.' Lindberg laughed out loud and Dill managed a grin. 'But you know there were those who would not eat the Dachau broth for fear of offending God, and they were close to starvation.'

When it became clear Dill was fading into sleep, Wilde gently guided Lindberg back to the Bull. He would collect him in the morning. In the meantime, he had other things on his mind, in particular the troubling death of Paul Birbach. Did he die in some hideous accident, or had he been murdered as Torsten Hellquist suspected?

Lydia spent the evening with Frank Foley, first at the passport office and then at his home in Wilmersdorf, with his wife Kay, trying to make sense of the events at St Hedwig's Cathedral.

Foley listened carefully, smoking a succession of cigarettes. Finally he spoke. 'Of course it's possible that what he told you about the boy is true.'

'So Albert could be in England.'

'Yes, why else would he have been so certain? It would help, of course, if we knew who the man in the cathedral was. I'll make inquiries but don't hold your breath, Miss Morris. We won't see anything about it in the papers.'

'Won't McGinn know who he was?'

'His Nazi contact will know – but he'll have to keep a very low profile for a while.'

'What should I do?'

Foley lit another cigarette. 'The fact that they killed your man must be taken as a serious warning. Any goodwill felt for you because of your Quaker background can no longer be relied on. As you've seen for your-self, these men have no qualms in pursuit of their aims.' He drew a finger across his throat. 'You need to go home to England. We'll try to get you on the first flight in the morning.'

At 11 p.m., Foley stretched his arms and yawned. 'Enough,' he said. 'I have to sleep. Won't you stay the night with us here, Miss Morris? You know, I'm not sure it would be wise to travel across Berlin tonight, not after what you have witnessed.' He gave a half smile. 'To be honest, Miss

Morris, one is never quite sure who is driving the taxis. Kay will make you up a bed.'

'What about Miss Forster? She will be expecting me.'

'I'll call her. And I'll have the embassy driver pick up your bags.'

Earlier that evening, Henty O'Gara had been taking a solitary drink in the bar of the Bull when his long-lost cousin entered with another man. Wilde had been engrossed with his smooth-suited companion and didn't see him, so O'Gara threw his drink down his throat and slid unnoticed from the room and out onto Trumpington Street. He waited on the far side of the road, and watched. Tom Wilde would have to emerge eventually.

Half an hour later, Wilde stepped out with yet another companion, a frail man with a shaven head and a stoop. They moved along the road at a snail's pace, eventually entering the gateway of one of the great university colleges.

O'Gara was in two minds. He already knew where Wilde lived. But he wanted more than that. It was just possible he might be of some help. *Because, let's be honest, I need some fucking help.*

Jesus, Wilde was kin, wasn't he? And half-Irish to boot? And fate had thrown him into his path, so it had to make sense to use the fucker.

The problem facing him was his isolation. Whenever he dialled Dorian Hyde's number, the phone just rang and rang and rang. No contact for the best part of a week, and here he was all alone with the Scavenger in his reach. But what should he do if the phone was never answered?

Damn it. He had no option.

He waited until dark and returned to Thompson's Lane, this time carrying his bag. He didn't try anything fancy. Just set the fuse and dropped the bastard thing against the perimeter wall and walked on.

Two minutes later, the bomb exploded and blew a hole the size of a car in the wall of the Power Station. Across the road, windows were blown in. The occupants of the houses stumbled out. Some were in pyjamas. Children were crying. They clustered around the smoking mass of bricks in stunned horror.

Police officers from the St Andrew's Street station were on the scene within five minutes, followed by the fire brigade. There was no sign of any human injuries, but a stray mongrel was found dead on the other side of the road.

Henty O'Gara stood with his hands in his pockets watching the aftermath with grim satisfaction. It should be enough to keep the Scavenger happy, he reckoned. If anything would get him on the inside of the operation, then surely this would be it.

He lit a cigarette and slowly walked away to find a phone box. He had to try the number again.

CHAPTER 20

Wilde was too late for high table, so he ordered food in his rooms, then scribbled notes for his scheduled lecture until his eyes clouded over. It was only just dark when he gave up. Unable to face the trek home, he stripped off his clothes and took to his narrow cot bed.

He lay with his eyes open. Despite the exhaustion, sleep wouldn't come. The room was stuffy, even with the window open. He threw off the bedclothes and lay naked in the still, fragrant warmth of the night. His mind was hundreds of miles away in the capital of Germany with Lydia Morris. What had happened between them? Where had the trust and companionship gone?

In Boston, he had shown his mother pictures of Lydia and had talked of their hopes and plans. He knew his mother was disappointed not to meet her, but she came from a time when such emotions were held in, and so he had told her half the truth – that Lydia was working with the refugee council at a time when all hands were needed. His mother had seemed to accept it; or at least she hadn't asked the obvious questions: why hadn't they married? Why did they live next door to each other rather than together in one house? Did they not want children? They were not questions he could have answered adequately.

A restive sleep came at last but, not having drawn the curtains, he woke soon after dawn with sunlight streaming across his chest.

He clambered out of bed, splashed water from the basin over his face and body, towelled himself down and dressed in the clothes he had been wearing the night before. He needed to get home to prepare for his guests. He could bathe and shave and put on a fresh shirt there.

As he looked out of his door, he spotted Bobby, bustling about the gyp's room, across the stairway from his own rooms.

'Coffee, sir?'

'Thank you, yes, but it'll have to be very quick, Bobby. And very, very strong.'

'Of course, Professor. Black without sugar, as always.'

Wilde followed the gyp into his little kitchen and watched him as he prepared the coffee. The aroma of the new-ground beans was enough to spark life. It struck him that there was little going on in college that Bobby didn't know. 'Sad news about Dr Birbach, Bobby.'

Bobby drew back his lips from gap-toothed gums. 'Terrible, sir. My brother-in-law Willie Smith found the body while fishing. Proper shook him up.'

'Where was that?'

'Halfway between Cambridge and Grantchester, tangled up in the roots of a willow.'

'Any idea what happened?' He didn't mention to Bobby that he had seen Paul Birbach, very much alive, at a country house party some miles south-west of Cambridge just hours before his body was discovered.

Bobby shrugged. 'Accidents happen and people drown – especially after a few drinks have been taken, if you get my meaning, sir. Young gentlemen jump from the bridges or go swimming when they oughtn't to. Others fall from punts and boats. It's the booze, Professor, always the booze. Willie works for Scudamore's Punts, so he's found more than one body in his time. Mind you, he did say there was something a bit different about this one.'

'In what way?'

'Well, Willie was in the war, and he was surprised by the state of the dead gentleman's mouth. Don't know how long the body had been there, of course . . .'

Wilde broke in. 'What about the mouth?'

'He said it was blistered and raw, like it had been burnt . . .' Bobby tailed off.

'Go on.'

'Well, sir, as mad as it might sound, he said it was like the terrible blisters our lads got in the trenches – from the mustard gas the Hun blew their way.'

Wilde very much wanted to hear what the police had to say about Birbach's death. What about Rupert Weir, the police surgeon – had he seen the body? Perhaps Bobby's cousin had an over-active imagination, but it certainly merited investigation.

Doris was dusting the front room when he arrived home.

'Good morning, Professor Wilde.'

'And you, Doris. Actually, I need a quick word with you. Two refugees from Germany, scientists, are coming today. They are Herr Dr Lindberg and a lady named Frau Dr Haas. I'm sure Miss Morris must have spoken to you about her.'

'Yes, sir. She said her little boy would be staying with her for a while.'

'Well, the boy won't be coming as yet. And until Miss Morris arrives home, the Germans will both stay here – so I need beds made up in the spare rooms. And I wonder if you would provide enough food for break-fasts and perhaps prepare a beef stew or pot chicken for a couple of sup-pers. I'm sure they will both be out at lunchtime, so no need to bother about that.'

'Of course, sir. That will be no problem at all.'

Wilde showered, dragged a razor across his face, then dressed quickly; that was one thing he had learned at Harrow – how to get dressed in double quick time. The penalties for tardiness were not to be taken lightly.

Downstairs, he dialled Jim Vanderberg's home number in Chelsea.

'Ah,' Vanderberg picked up on the third ring. 'I'm glad you called me at home. I was trying to get through to you all last night. Been on the tiles again, buddy?'

'No, I stayed in college, Jim. But I do have a couple of things to talk about.'

'Before you do, I have something to say to you apropos of Milt Hardi-man. You recall I told you he was poison, a flag-waving American nasty, to be avoided at all costs? Well, forget that piece of bullshit advice. The exact opposite is the case.'

'You mean he's not a nasty?'

'No, I mean he's not to be avoided. I would very much like you to smarm up to him as though he's the most admirable man you've ever met. Can you hold your nose and do that?'

Wilde trusted his old friend implicitly, but this was just a bit too odd. A hell of a lot too odd. Why, separately, were Philip Eaton, a British MI6 agent, and Jim Vanderberg, a senior attaché at the US Embassy, both trying to get him to spy on this man Hardiman, a man he barely knew?

'You better explain where this is coming from, Jim – and what exactly you are hoping I might discover.'

Vanderberg lowered his voice. 'I got a message via my old pal Bill Donovan. It came here, to my home, bypassing official channels.'

'What is it?'

'This man Hardiman is a close associate of you know who.'

Wilde was exasperated. 'No, I don't know who.'

'Think about it. I don't want to say the name. OK, to hell with it – Joe Kennedy, my boss here at the embassy. Now, I'm not for a moment suggesting that he is anything but one hundred per cent loyal to the United States of America, its interests and people, but I'm damned certain that he doesn't give a monkey's armpit for Britain or the British.'

'I get it.' Ambassador Kennedy – Joseph Patrick Kennedy – had made no secret of his disdain for Britain, constantly talking the country down and letting it be known that Germany would crush the puny British Army and air force within weeks of war breaking out. And he seemed quite certain that the world would be a better place for it. The message to his homeland: don't get involved, America. Leave this next war to the Europeans. Make friends with Herr Hitler and let him have his way.

It was common knowledge that the White House was not too happy about his stance; and nor were some members of Kennedy's London staff, Jim Vanderberg among them. Relationships were severely strained at No. 1, Grosvenor Square.

'Hardiman's presence in England cannot be a force for good at this time, Tom. If you can be discreet, stick to him and find out what he's up to.'

'And why me?'

'Because you're already on the inside. You're in a unique position, buddy.'

'OK, Jim. I'll see what I can do. But look, I should tell you Philip Eaton has already asked me much the same. You remember him?'

'Sure. I thought you didn't like him too much.'

'Let's say my feelings are conflicted. My question is this: are you and the British working together on this?'

'No. But it might make sense to cooperate.' Vanderberg paused. 'So what was it *you* wanted to talk about?'

'Dexter Flood. You said you'd ask around.'

'What can I say? Sounds like a regular guy. War hero, trenchant views. Irish-American like you, Tom.'

'I had a cable from him. Wanted me to contact him soonest about the Cavendish Laboratory. His words were: *Fears this end.*'

'So did you contact him?'

'I wanted to talk to you first. What concerns me is his link to Hardiman. If Milton Hardiman is my enemy, how can Flood be my friend?'

'A good question. I'll do some more digging.'

'And I have to tell you that something's happened. A Cavendish physicist by the name of Paul Birbach has been found dead. Brilliant man apparently. Brilliant, but strange. The secrets of the universe at his fingertips. The thing is, his close friend and working partner, a Swede named Torsten Hellquist, says he was murdered – and he fears he will be next.' Wilde waited a beat. 'And the last time I saw Birbach was at Milt Hardiman's party, a few hours before he died.'

There was an intake of breath at the other end of the line. 'Wow. Is that a coincidence, or is something going on here?'

'I don't know, but I do know that Birbach was meant to have left for America by now – to work with one of the top men over there, guy by the name of Oppenheimer. Instead he was found dead in the river, and I aim to find out exactly how he died.'

'Do you think there's some link to Hardiman?'

Did he? His suspicions weren't really coherent as yet. First he needed to talk to the police and the pathologist. 'All I can say is that it's hard to imagine these events are isolated. There's something else. Two physicists have arrived from Germany. Jewish refugees. I've been put in charge of their safekeeping by, you've guessed it, Philip Eaton. The point is, these two are working on the same sort of stuff as Birbach and some of the other Cavendish guys. Atoms and all that – exactly the sort of thing Colonel Dexter Flood asked me to look out for.'

'And what are you suggesting?'

'I don't know – probably nothing at all. Except . . . One of the German scientists is a woman name of Eva Haas. Her son has gone missing on the way to join her in London. The only reason I could think for anyone to abduct a child would be either ransom or to exert control on the mother. It worries me.'

'What do you want from me then?'

'Well, that's it, Jim, I don't know. I really don't know. A steer, perhaps? Are these things I should be telling Colonel Dexter Flood? A missing boy, a murder . . . oh sweet Jesus, Jim, this isn't good.'

Tempelhof was busy and they were in plenty of time, so Kay Foley took her leave of Lydia outside the main doorway to the rather grand terminal building. 'Do stay in touch,' she said. 'I would so love to hear that you have found the little boy safe and well. If only we could protect all of them.' She smiled wanly and grasped Lydia's hands. 'This German situation isn't going to end at all well, you know.'

The two women embraced. Lydia went into the main foyer and found a seat where she could hear the speaker system. The plane wasn't due to leave for an hour and they hadn't started boarding, so she tried to read her book. She couldn't concentrate. While she was asleep during the night, her mind had been clear, but now it was full of blood and the ghastly image of a man dying before her eyes.

When the call came, she walked to passport control. The official, a thin man with half-moon spectacles, studied the document closely, raising his eyes from her photograph to peer at her face.

'Frau Morris?' he said.

'Yes.'

'Come with me if you would.' He spoke English fluently.

'My flight has been called.'

'There is still a little time. Leave your bag here. We will look after it.'

Ordering an underling to take over his duties, the official led her down a brightly lit corridor to a bland room with a table and two chairs but no window. 'Wait here, please, Frau Morris.' He clicked his heels, bowed politely and left, shutting the door after him. He had kept her passport.

Lydia waited. She looked at her wristwatch and saw the minutes ticking past. She badly wanted a cigarette. Or a drink. Her throat was parched. God, a neat Scotch would slip down well. She could not take her eyes from her watch. With ten minutes to go before the flight was scheduled to depart, she went to the door, half expecting it to be locked. It opened. She looked down the corridor, both ways. No one was coming.

What was she to do? She was almost certain that the seat reserved for her was the only one available that day. Kay Foley had told her she had only managed to book because there had been a cancellation. She couldn't afford to miss her flight.

To hell with it. She walked back to the passport desk. The official looked at her with cold displeasure. 'You must return to the room, Frau Morris.'

'I'm about to miss my flight. Please give me my passport and bag and let me through.'

'This is a serious matter and I have my orders. Officers are coming from Prinz-Albrecht-Strasse. It will be for the best if you stay where I have left you.'

'Can I make a telephone call?'

'That is for the officers of the *Geheime Staatspolizei* to decide.' He nodded to his underling and said, in brisk German, 'Escort this woman to the holding room. Stay with her. She is not to leave again.'

Lydia understood the command. 'This is ridiculous! You have no right to detain me. I am a British citizen. I insist you call the embassy. Talk to Captain Francis Foley at the passport office at Tiergartenstrasse 17.'

The officer dismissed her with a flick of his fingers. 'Enough.' His subordinate took her upper arm and pulled. She tried to shake him off, but he was too strong. What was the point in fighting? She didn't even have her passport; she wasn't going anywhere until these officials released her and returned her papers. Humiliated, she was aware that the other passengers were watching her surreptitiously. Once more it was plain; in a police state, no one wanted to get involved. She recalled a dark joke: *What is the difference between England and Germany? In England, if we hear an early morning knock at the door, we know it's the milkman.*

Fifteen minutes later, the door to the room opened. Two men in civilian suits entered. The bulges beneath their dark jackets gave away the presence of handguns. Both snapped a sharp 'Heil Hitler' to the guard, who saluted in return and left the room.

'Good afternoon, Miss Morris,' the shorter and older of the two new-comers said, smiling. He spoke almost perfect English. 'I am Rudolf Kirsch, *Kriminaldirektor*. I must apologise for this interruption to your travel plans, but we very much wanted to talk with you before your depar-ture. We have been looking for you since last night.'

'Not very hard. I haven't been hiding,' she said, and then wished she hadn't. It couldn't be wise to rile these men. She tried to smile, attempt-ing to conceal her irritation and charm them instead. 'I don't know what this is about, Herr Kirsch, but I think you've made me miss my aeroplane. I need to get back to England. Can you not help a damsel in distress?'

'We will get you on the earliest available flight – once this matter is sorted out to everyone's satisfaction. We are only doing our jobs, Miss Morris.'

'But what is this matter? No one has told me what is going on. The passport man said you were Gestapo. Is that true?'

Kriminaldirektor Kirsch took the second chair and sat opposite her across the table. He wore a good suit, dark grey, with a red tie. On his lapel, his party membership badge. The other detective, much younger than his superior and in a cheap brown suit, stood to attention by the door, his mouth firmly shut, his eyes bovine and dull. 'You were at St Hedwig's Cathedral on Orpenplatz last night,' Kirsch said. 'You were witness to a murder.' He waited, still smiling, watching her face closely. His dark hair flopped across his brow. Like his Führer, but without the moustache, she thought. 'Why did you not report this to police? Is murder not considered a serious crime in your country?'

'But I was still in the cathedral when the incident occurred. The square was full of people. Any one of them would have seen more than I did.'

'That is not the way I understand it. I am led to believe you came out of the cathedral with the priest, that you were at the top of the steps looking down at the dying man within seconds of the shot. You must have seen the gunman.'

'No.'

'Did you examine the injured man? Did you think to call for medical assistance? I do not understand why you would not do this.'

'My spoken German is not what it might be. There were others better placed than me. The priest, for instance.'

Kirsch rose and began pacing the small room. His colleague did not move.

'Can I make a telephone call, please?'

He ignored the request. 'Why are you in Berlin, Miss Morris? Why exactly did you come here?'

'I was visiting friends, and I wanted to see more of Berlin. I was here for the Olympics in '36 and I wished to see more of the city.'

'Which friends?'

'Quaker friends. I don't see what business it is of yours.'

'Ah yes, you are a Quaker. A pacifist, no doubt.'

She did not reply. The word pacifist was intended as an insult.

'And what, then, were you doing at the cathedral? St Hedwig's is not a Quaker meeting house but a Roman Catholic temple.'

'It is a beautiful building with a remarkable dome. I was told I must visit it. Quakers, too, appreciate beauty.'

'But you met someone there, you spoke to him – and then he was shot dead within seconds of leaving the building.'

'No,' she said. Lying did not come easily to her. 'No, I met no one. I sat alone in a pew and prayed for peace.'

'A man joined you. He sat behind you, talking to you. The man who was shot.'

'Who told you this?'

'Do you confirm it then?'

'No, of course not. No one spoke to me. I was aware of someone sitting behind me and heard some words. I turned to see who was there and presumed he was praying aloud. That is all. It was certainly no one I recognised, so why would I have talked to him?'

'Perhaps he had some information to pass to you. Secrets, for instance.'

'No, that's nonsense. Who was he anyway? Why was he shot?' And who had been watching us, she wondered? Who had reported her to the police? The priest? The old woman who lit the candle? Or the killer himself? Perhaps he had looked around the door and seen the self-styled

'Scarlet Pimpernel of Berlin' talking to her, then slipped out and waited on the steps for his victim.

'Indeed, those are interesting questions: who was he and why was he shot? We very much hoped that you would be able to help us with that, Miss Morris.'

'So you don't have a name for him?'

He shrugged, the smile still fixed firmly to his face as though it had been painted on. He did not answer her, simply peered into her eyes. Finally he stood up. 'I am sorry. I do not find your answers adequate. You will accompany us to Prinz-Albrecht-Strasse for further questioning.'

'This is outrageous! I have committed no crime. I am a British citizen. I *demand* that the embassy be informed – and that I be allowed to talk with them.'

'Don't make this difficult, Miss Morris.'

She walked between the two Gestapo officers along the corridor, then out into the main lobby of the aerodrome. There was no physical force used because there was no need. But nor could they disguise the fact that she was a woman being marched away by two law officers.

They were at the main doorway out on to the road where the taxis waited and big black cars dropped off wealthy patrons. There were few clouds now; the morning was brightening up. Above them, a three-engined plane droned monotonously as it made its approach to land.

'Miss Morris?'

She stopped and turned at the unexpected voice. So did her escorts. A large figure towered over all three of them, seemed to cast them into shade.

'It is Miss Morris, is it not?'

'Yes.'

'Perhaps you do not recall me? Manfred Bloch. I was with you on the flight from London.'

She put a hand to her chest as realisation dawned. He had been a travel agent, hadn't he? Now she remembered. 'Of course, Herr Bloch. What are you doing here?'

'I was about to catch the Munich flight. More business. Always business. But what is this?' His eyes flicked from Lydia to the two police officers. 'What is happening here?'

'Excuse me, sir.' Kirsch took her arm and inserted himself between her and the newcomer. 'This lady is coming with us.'

Bloch looked bewildered. 'Who are you?'

'*Kriminaldirektor* Kirsch, *Geheime Staatspolizei.*' He stressed the words, presumably accustomed to the very mention of the Gestapo wreaking terror. 'Now, if you please, sir, go about your business.'

'I know this woman. Is she being detained?'

'Good day, sir.'

She was being pulled away now, towards a black Mercedes, a driver in the front seat, its engine running.

This was her chance. 'Call Captain Foley at the British passport office. Tell him—' But before she could say any more, she felt a hand push down on the top of her head and she was being forced into the smoke-filled back seat of the car.

She looked out from the closed window. Manfred Bloch was staring at her from the aerodrome entrance. She mouthed two words. *Please help.* But he wouldn't, would he? No one dared help in a police state.

But he nodded. Then he started to walk towards the car as though he still had something to say to her captors. It was a mere twenty metres, but in those few strides she became aware of something familiar in the way he moved.

Kirsch climbed in beside Lydia and slammed the door shut. His junior colleague took the front passenger seat. 'Go,' Kirsch said. The driver crunched the Mercedes into first gear and released the clutch. The car juddered forward and within moments they were out on the road, heading into the heart of the city.

Her mind spun. Nothing made sense. *Something in the way he moved.* Manfred Bloch had a distinctive rolling gait. Sometimes you could recognise a man by the way he moved as clearly as by his face or fingerprints. She had seen that gait twice before. First in London, outside Bloomsbury House with Eva Haas – and then last night in Orpenplatz, walking away from the cathedral, a pistol dangling from his hand.

CHAPTER 21

The lecture was supposed to last an hour, but Wilde wound it up after fifty minutes, exhorting the young men and women to use the long vacation to good effect, to visit as many historic sites as they could, to avail themselves of whatever contacts they had to gain entry to the great houses, to use their eyes and ears and critical faculties.

As he spoke, he realised for the first time that there was a very real chance that some of these young people might not be here at Michaelmas; the government had already introduced a limited form of conscription. The thought of them in uniform, going off to war, brought him up short. For a moment he stopped in mid-flow and gazed out at the banks of bright faces in front of him. He feared for their futures. 'Look,' he said. 'You all know that I don't go along with Henry Ford. History is not bunk. But in days like this, well, I suggest you enjoy the present too.'

His subject had been *The illusion of stability in late sixteenth-century England*. In three hundred and fifty years, the world had learnt nothing. Stability? There was no longer even an illusion of such a thing; the world was crumbling before their eyes.

At the end of the lecture his parting words were: 'God bless you all.' He tried to look away as two of his undergraduates cornered him, but if they saw the dampness in his eyes they said nothing. They had been disappointed that he had been away these past months, they said reproachfully. Would he be kind enough to give them an hour or two before the long vac? He would be delighted, he said. He would be in touch with a convenient time. 'And I will set you plenty of reading for the days when you are basking at the seaside. No novels for you two.' They were good students; a light supervision was quite adequate in their case, and his two months' absence would not have affected their degrees.

When he got back to his rooms, he found Bobby waiting for him, with a small, grizzled man who seemed nervous.

'This is Willie Smith, my brother-in-law, Professor,' said Bobby. 'Married to my sister, Marjorie.'

Wilde shook the man by the hand, felt the trembling. A rarely used word came to mind as he assessed his visitor: meek. Willie Smith was a meek man. 'Pleased to meet you, Mr Smith.'

'Thank you, sir. It's an honour to be here, sir.'

'Nonsense. Come in. Would you brew up a pot of tea for us, Bobby?'

'It's already on the go, Professor.'

Wilde indicated to Willie that he should sit on the hide sofa, and tried to put him at ease. 'Feel free to smoke a cigarette. I'm afraid I don't so I can't offer you one.'

'That's all right, sir. I think I've probably smoked enough this morning. The missus is always telling me to cut down.'

'Well, we both know why you're here. Bobby tells me you and your friend discovered the body of poor Dr Birbach in the river. You noted something about the mouth, I believe.'

Bobby returned with the pot of tea and two cups.

'And one for yourself, Bobby,' Wilde said. 'Come and sit with us if you would.'

Bobby fetched himself a cup and gingerly took his place next to his brother-in-law. He poured the tea.

Wilde turned back to Smith. 'We were talking about the man's mouth.'

'Yes, sir. It was blistered and raw. Swollen with ulcers, like he'd been drinking in mustard gas. I saw the effects of that in the war, sir. Not the sort of thing you forget.'

'You pointed this out to the police, I take it?'

'Yes, sir.'

Bobby held up a hand, like a pupil in class. 'If I may just say, Professor, the police was here this morning. Carted a lot of stuff away from Dr Birbach's rooms.'

Wilde nodded. He wondered what sort of police had been involved. Philip Eaton's sort, perhaps? It did not sound the sort of operation a local copper would have authorised. He wondered, however, whether anything of value had remained to be removed after Torsten Hellquist's little pillaging exercise. No one would have known better than Hellquist what was actually of any value. He returned to the matter of the corpse. 'What was the state of the remainder of the body? Was it fully dressed – and if so what clothes?'

'The deceased was wearing a white shirt, sir. I think you would call it a dress shirt. That's all.'

'So he was naked from the waist down?'

'Yes, sir.'

'Did you spot any other injuries?'

'No, sir. Not as such.'

'What do you mean *not as such?*'

'Well, I mean obviously he was drowned, so that's sort of an injury in itself, isn't it, sir?'

'Do you think he might have died in some other way, though. You mentioned mustard gas. Could that have killed him?'

'Mustard gas *can* kill a man, but you'd have to get a bad dose. It couldn't happen in Cambridge, though, could it? I've never heard tell of mustard gas since the war. How would it be here in England? Left it all in Flanders, thank God.'

Wilde wondered about those missing hours in the life and death of Dr Paul Birbach. Wilde had seen him in the boathouse at sunset, so that must have been about 9.30 p.m. He hadn't seen him again after that. According to Bobby, Willie Smith and his friend had discovered the body the next morning at about 10 a.m. So that meant there were twelve and a half hours missing. A lot could happen in half a day. A man could fly to Paris and back in that time. He wondered if Geoff Lancing knew what time Birbach and his lady friend had left the party.

'Is that all, Professor?' Bobby said.

Wilde shook his head. 'I'm sorry, I was elsewhere for a few moments. So, Mr Smith, what time did you arrive at the river?'

'Seven, sir. We'd been there three hours when Alfie spotted the corpse. It was tangled up good and proper, so it must have been there all along.'

Wilde suddenly recalled that Hellquist had said he had seen Birbach at midnight. So that narrowed it further; there were *seven* missing hours, from midnight to 7 a.m. 'What did the police say to you, Mr Smith?'

'Not much, sir. It was only a couple of constables. A man drowned in the Cam isn't usually big news.'

'What did they say when you mentioned mustard gas?'

'One told me to stay off the sauce, sir, but the other one agreed that the man's face looked a bit of a bleeding mess – excuse my language, Professor Wilde, but those were his words. We didn't discuss it any more than that.'

Wilde, who was sitting on his desk chair, picked up his cup and took a sip. The other two followed suit. 'Well, Mr Smith, I must thank you for taking the trouble to come here to see me. If anything else comes to mind, I would be grateful if you would tell Bobby here and he will pass it on.'

Bobby nudged his brother-in-law. 'Go on, Willie, tell the professor.'

'Yes?'

'Well, there was one other thing. When we dragged the body out and laid him down on the bank, I did notice his wrists were black and blue.'

'As if he had been bound?'

'I'd say so, sir, yes.'

This was no simple accident.

Wilde found Rupert Weir at Addenbrooke's Hospital on Trumpington Street. He was taking coffee alone in the doctors' common room and immediately rose to shake hands. Weir and his wife Edie lived in a large and splendidly appointed Edwardian house on the outskirts of Girton. They were two of the most delightful people Wilde knew.

'Coffee, Tom?'

'Love one.'

Weir was large of girth with a large appetite and a larger than life character to match. Even in midsummer, he wore tweeds with a bulging waistcoat. He summoned the tea lady and ordered another pot.

'How was America?'

'Wonderful, thank you.'

'Well, you must tell me all about it. In fact, come out to Girton and have some supper with us. Edie will want to hear everything and pester you with questions.'

'I would love to – perhaps next week? But, in the meantime, I need to pick your brains.'

Dr Rupert Weir had two roles in the community. One was as GP, serving the needs of families for everything from coughs and colds to the care of the old and dying. The other role was police surgeon, in which role he was called upon for many tasks, from assessing the inebriation of car drivers, to producing reports on times and causes of death for the coroner.

'You're welcome to them.'

'I gather a body was dragged from the river yesterday – a man from my own college. Dr Paul Birbach.'

'Ah yes, the little German gentleman. Got him here in the mortuary. Strange case.'

'What's strange about it?'

Weir raised an eyebrow. 'What's your interest, Tom?'

'He was on the same stairs as me at college. There's a lot of disquiet about the place. I wanted to get to the bottom of it.'

'Fair enough.' Dr Weir paused. 'What do you know about the case?'

'I know he was half naked, and that his mouth was blistered as though he had inhaled poison gas . . .'

'And?'

'And it seems quite likely that he was bound before death.'

'Good. Then you know almost as much as I do. Come on, let's pop down and you can take a look. Got a strong stomach, have you?'

Birbach's chest had been opened up and his organs exposed. His face in death looked nothing like the Birbach that Wilde knew. The intelligence was gone; the expression was bland. Nothing of his great mind was left behind.

'See the blistering around the lips, Tom? Classic signs of vesicant inhalation.'

Wilde studied the body as though it were a waxwork. The sweet smell of decay did not trouble his stomach; it was the coldness of the room that made him shiver. 'You were at the front, weren't you, Rupert?'

'Yes, I worked in a field hospital. First saw mustard gas at Passchendaele. Yellow stuff. Not hugely effective for killing, but caused a great deal of panic and discomfort. Ghastly days. Never thought to see it again.'

'Strange way to kill someone, isn't it?'

'Certainly not very efficient in the short term. There are much quicker, cleaner ways to commit murder. But if you wanted to terrorise someone, to panic them . . . well, it would do that.'

'Torture.'

'Exactly. Terror is what gets us – the fear of asphyxiation. Gasping for breath. Enough to break the most resolute man, I'd say.'

Wilde nodded. He thought of Horace Dill and the panic in his eyes as he struggled to suck a little air into his corrupt lungs.

'But it wasn't the gas that killed your friend Birbach. Have a look here.' Weir prodded the dead man's lungs with his index finger. 'They're as pink and sweet as a baby's. Dr Birbach was not a smoker and nor did he actually inhale this stuff. His throat and stomach were clean too.'

'What did kill him then?'

'Heart attack. He already had heart disease. It's possible that stress might have brought on the attack.'

'The stress of someone trying to force him to inhale gas, for instance?'

'It's certainly a possibility.'

'So how might the gas have been delivered?'

'Directly to the mouth through something like a frogman's oxygen mouthpiece? But clamped over the lips rather than inserted in the mouth. His eyes were not affected, which means he was not in the middle of a gas cloud. There were other injuries, too,' Weir continued. 'Burn marks to the chest as if he had been touched with cigarettes. Definitely torture. I suspect the heart attack cut his torturer's efforts short.'

'So what are the police doing about this?'

Weir pulled the sheet back over the corpse, and ushered Wilde from the mortuary. 'They're investigating, of course. Actually, I think they're a bit overstretched what with the IRA setting off a bloody bomb, but don't worry – Detective Inspector Tomlinson's not a bad sort. Just a little lacking in imagination. I made it quite clear to him that this was a priority.'

'Do you think you could get an interview for me? I'd really like to talk to him.'

'I'll ask him and let you know. By the way, who exactly was this fellow Birbach? One of those smart-arse scientists from the Cavendish, wasn't he?'

'Among the very smartest.' Wilde said quietly. 'The sort of man with secrets to torture and kill for.'

Weir's easy-going demeanour vanished. 'In that case, Tom, I wonder if this might not be a bit too big for Tomlinson and our local boys. I'm going to put through a call to a Special Branch chum in Scotland Yard.'

O'Gara had never felt so alone in his life. He had tried every hour on the hour, then every half hour, yet still the phone just rang and rang without reply. Where was Dorian Hyde? Without him, there was no point to his being here. O'Gara had what was wanted now, the information. The question was what to do with it when the big man wouldn't answer his phone and there was no other way of making contact.

His mind kept returning to Wilde. He had a brain on him, for Christ's sake. If he were on side, he'd be a help. Well, he knew where Wilde was at least, and he was accessible. It might be a risk worth taking. Jesus, he was beginning to think he would have no option. Not for the first time, it occurred to him that he wasn't cut out for this sort of work. But there were times, as the cowboy said, when a man had to do what he had to do. Or something like that.

Wilde took a detour via the St Andrew's Street police headquarters. No, he was told, Detective Inspector Tomlinson, was not available. And no, there was no one else with the time to speak with the professor unless he had information he wished to provide. The whole of the Cambridge Constabulary was up to its neck in the bomb outrage on Thompson's Lane and the curious death of a scientist in the Cam. Not a man to spare.

Five minutes later, Wilde found the two Germans sitting in the lobby of the Bull. For a moment, he had a strange feeling that they had been there all night – for they were in exactly the chairs they had occupied when he met them. They both rose at his approach. Arnold Lindberg had a valise; Eva Haas had a knapsack. He guessed they hadn't managed to carry much in the way of belongings on their trek across the mountains.

He did his best to give them a friendly welcome. 'I'll get the concierge to call a taxi and we'll be on our way.'

On the journey to his house, Wilde sat in the front beside the driver. Dr Lindberg leant forward. 'Please excuse me, Professor Wilde, do you think it would be possible to go to the Cavendish Laboratory today?'

'I'll call my friend Dr Lancing, see what he says.'

'I cannot tell you how much I am looking forward to seeing the old place once again.'

As the cab dropped them off, he pointed out Lydia's house, *Cornflowers*, next door. 'Of course it's empty now with Miss Morris away.' Should he mention that she was in Berlin? How much did Frau Dr Haas know? Best thing was to let her bring it up. 'And so, for the moment, you will both be staying in my rather more modest home.'

He spotted Doris through the window and within moments she was opening the door to them and taking control. She bustled around, showing the visitors all the rooms, pointing out the bathroom amenities, the tap that always stuck, how to operate the window latches, the location of the laundry baskets and the kitchen equipment available to them. 'And you must tell me your likes and dislikes regarding food,' she added, stressing every syllable like an elementary school teacher talking to a pair of six-year-olds.

Wilde meanwhile telephoned the Cavendish. Lancing sounded less than enthusiastic. 'It's not a great day for visitors, Tom. Not a lot of smiles around here, what with the terrible news about Paul Birbach. I gather Torsten Hellquist is beside himself with grief.'

'Of course – I understand. How about tomorrow?'

Lancing heaved a resigned sigh. 'Oh – damn it; bring them today, after lunch. I'll have a little talk with them, give them the lowdown. The truth is, of course, that they are far from the first German physicists seeking a place here. We've already had to turn away rather a lot of them. Best that I'm open with them straight away rather than raise false hopes.'

'Any chance of them seeing the boss?'

'I'm sorry, Bragg's in London for a few days. I know he'd love to help everyone who comes through his door, but of course he just can't. You saw how crowded this place is, Tom. But, look, I'll try to let your friends down gently.'

'Thank you, Geoff. I owe you a drink.'

'Tell you what – pay me back this evening by thrashing Milt Hardiman on court. He's a smug bastard when he's got a racket in his hand. You've got an open invitation to Old Hall, you know.'

Wilde seized the chance. He very much wanted to hear what the inhabitants of Old Hall recalled about Dr Paul Birbach's last night on earth. 'Yes, of course, I'll come – but I'm not sure about the tennis. I haven't played since last summer.'

'Then drink him under the table instead.'

Wilde put down the telephone and sought out Lindberg and Eva. 'We'll set off for the Cavendish at 2 p.m.,' he said. 'I'll have to leave you to your own devices until them, I'm afraid. Anything you need, just ask Doris.'

Eva nodded. 'Uncle Arnold will stay here. I wish to go to the new synagogue, not far from the Magdalene Bridge. Is that fitting for you?'

'If you don't mind motorbikes, I'll give you a ride down there.'

Wilde brought the Rudge to a halt outside Antonio's Café. 'Before you go your own way, can I take you for a coffee, Dr Haas?'

She looked slightly wary at the suggestion. 'I wanted to make myself known at the synagogue. I have Jewish friends in Cambridge.'

'Ten minutes, maybe a quarter of an hour? Best coffee in town here.'

She bowed politely. 'Of course, Professor Wilde. I should be delighted.'

They entered Antonio's and found a good table, with a white cloth and a choice of Italian coffees, including espresso, which Wilde ordered. Eva asked for a hot chocolate.

'I just wanted to say hello, really. Tell you a little about myself. Welcome you to Cambridge. I know you've lived here before, at Girton, but the circumstances must be very strange for you, not to say distressing.' He smiled at her and his voice softened. 'Tell me about your boy. I cannot imagine how dreadful this must be for you.'

She looked strained. 'I do not know what to say about him. It is all so . . . so terrible.'

'Even if the Nazis have taken him, I'm sure they won't hurt a child.'

'I pray you are right.'

'Have you notified the police?'

She shrugged helplessly. 'Which police, Professor Wilde? The Gestapo, perhaps?'

He saw her point and changed the subject, asking her about her friendship with Lydia.

'You know, she was always a good friend. Not everyone was so welcoming to a German Jewish girl in those days. And then I was so pleased when she agreed to meet Albert and look after him until my arrival. I knew I could trust her.' She shifted uncomfortably in her chair. 'Now I feel she blames herself somehow for what has happened. But, of course, that is not the case.'

Their drinks came. They talked more about her time in Cambridge, the rigours of Girton and the lectures she attended by the men who had split the atom: Rutherford, Cockcroft and Walton.

'Were you there when it happened?'

She laughed. 'No, but when I heard their lectures I was beguiled by their magic. No one has ever seen an atom, and yet they, in their own separate ways, brought these minuscule particles to life for me. I knew then what I wanted to do with my life.' She managed a small smile. 'But you know it has been difficult these past few years with the sanctions in Germany. I should have stayed in England after Girton, but my husband wanted me back home. Klaus had a good job with a chemical concern. The deal was that I should complete my studies and then return and we would be a family.'

'Of course, I understand. And where is Klaus now?' Even as he asked the question, he knew the answer. He had endured the same loss himself, and it left an indelible mark.

Her hand came across the table and touched his. 'I see it in your eyes, Professor. You have suffered the same thing. My Klaus was taken by TB two years ago.'

'I am sorry.'

'Of course, thank you. And you?'

'Childbirth. My wife and our child. It's a long time ago.'

'But the wounds do not heal so easily. Anyway, as you know, life became intolerable for us these past few months. Albert had already been banished from his school for the crime of not being wholly Aryan. And then Kristallnacht. I knew we would have to leave.'

After they finished their coffee and chocolate, Wilde walked her to the synagogue. As he left her, he couldn't help noticing that a dozen or more police officers were milling about Thompson's Lane. He approached a tall, uniformed constable who was standing guard, hands clasped behind his back.

'What's going on, constable?'

The policeman looked suspicious. 'Are you Irish, sir?'

'The accent's American.'

The constable visibly relaxed. 'There's been an IRA outrage you see, sir. Irish beggars let off a bomb outside the power station.'

Ah, so this was what they were talking about at St Andrew's Street. 'Anyone hurt?'

'A dog, sir. As to the damage, it'll be the work of a week to put it right, including the broken windows.'

'How do you know it was the IRA?'

'I believe they sent a message to the newspapers. Could have saved the ink, though. It's *always* them, isn't it, sir?'

CHAPTER 22

Wilde rode his motorbike to the Cavendish and found Geoff Lancing. He was sitting at his table in his room, smoking a cigarette. He seemed a long way away.

'I'm sorry, Geoff. Have I interrupted you?'

Lancing shook his head. 'Forget it,' he said. He sounded resigned. 'Just events. Have you brought the Germans with you?'

The death of Birbach had obviously hit Lancing hard. The most easy-going, cheerful of men, today he looked utterly despondent. 'You were very unsure when I called,' said Wilde,

Lancing put his cigarette hand to his brow. Smoke curled up slowly through his fringe. 'It's complicated, Tom. More complicated than you can imagine.'

'Try me.'

He drew deeply on his cigarette, then exhaled a cloud. 'It's Lindberg. Some people are unhappy about him. His past.'

'You mean because he's a Communist?'

'No, no one gives a damn about that. This is the least political place in Cambridge. Outside these walls there is sound and fury – the whole world in a rage about ideologies and God knows what else – but in here, we delve quietly into the heart of the cosmos. Tory or Labour, Communist or Fascist? Do you think those distinctions amount to anything in the vastness of the universe?'

'I take your point. But of course, Lindberg has already worked here. I wonder what has changed?'

Lancing looked pained. 'We all know he's had a hard time, but frankly, Tom, he wasn't totally honest with Rutherford when he was here before. It's his work at the end of the war, I'm afraid. You probably wouldn't know about it.'

'Then tell me.'

'He started life as a chemist. In early 1918 he volunteered to work with Fritz Haber in the Chemistry Section of the German War Office where they were developing gas weapons. He was at the Kaiser Wilhelm Institute in Dahlem and later he joined the Bayer Chemical Works in Leverkusen. Apparently, he came up with some lovely ideas involving phosgene, chlorine and the mustard gases. And you know what – they all bloody knew it was against the Hague Convention.' Lancing sighed. 'I'm sorry, Tom, it makes me bloody mad. My old man's brother was gassed. Survived, but God he was a ghost of a man.'

'It was war, Geoff. The British used gas too.'

Lancing snorted. 'But while the poor bloody infantry were drowning, blistering and choking, the men who designed these gases survived and prospered. Haber won the Nobel prize in 1918 for pity's sake. Otto Hahn was one of them, too – and now he's acclaimed for his fission work! The world is upside down, Tom.'

'Look, I'll keep Lindberg away.'

Lancing stubbed out his cigarette and reached for another. 'No, you're right. It's just me and this damnable day. Lindberg can come and work in the library, do some reading. I'm sure he's a fine chap and he doesn't need me to judge him after what's been through in the concentration camp. I'm sure he's atoned. Who knows? He might even come up with some sound work for us. But I'm not letting him near any of our equipment. Apart from anything else, the secret boys wouldn't allow it; they were rather wary of Birbach, if you must know.'

'Understood.' Wilde waited until he could be sure the worst of Lancing's anger had dissipated. 'Look, Geoff, I want you to tell me about Birbach – who he was, where he came from. I lived and worked only a dozen steps away from him, but I knew nothing about him.'

Lancing gave a brief resumé of Birbach's career: hounded out of his job at the University of Munich, he'd worked in Italy with Fermi and in America with Oppenheimer, before arriving in Cambridge three years earlier.

'And he was supposed to rejoin this Oppenheimer fellow?'

'Exactly. And I could quite understand why. America's the coming place for particle physics. I know I've told you this before, Tom, but I can't stress enough what a remarkable mind Birbach possessed. He saw things with breathtaking clarity. He was convinced he had come up with a feasible way to create an energy source – for good or ill – with a minimal amount of radioactive material, perhaps no more than five pounds of uranium. At any rate, a great deal less than the tonnage most physicists have been imagining. He also believed that it might be terrifyingly simple to make a bomb with the power to destroy an entire town or city. Even Werner bloody Heisenberg could do it, he said.'

'Hellquist was working with Birbach. Does he understand it?'

'That's not entirely clear. Torsten Hellquist is a difficult man. He seems open, but in fact he keeps a great deal to himself. He never had Birbach's insight, but he is quick on the uptake and sees ways of applying theory to practical use. He has dreams of supplying the world's energy needs, making himself a millionaire. I know he had been working on some technical drawings with Birbach but I don't know whether they had actually solved all the problems.'

'Is it possible Birbach died for his knowledge?'

'It's hard not to be worried, isn't it?'

'What are the police saying?'

'I don't think the local cops have a clue. Not their fault, really. Probably not more than a couple of dozen people in the world understand what we're doing. Anyway, I've put calls through to Scotland Yard and the War Office. They'll be sending somebody up.'

'Soon, I hope.'

'Today or tomorrow, hopefully. But who knows? Special Branch and the secret service have other priorities at the moment.'

Wilde grunted. Perhaps Rupert Weir's call or Eaton's influence might shake them out of their torpor. He began to move towards the door, unable to endure any more of Lancing's smoke. 'I'm going to take you at your word, Geoff, and bring Lindberg and Haas along. Maybe Lindberg will surprise you. But before I go, there was one other matter. The woman Paul Birbach took to the party, do you know who she was?'

Lancing laughed. 'She was a cleaning woman. All his tarts were cleaners or barmaids or laundry women.' He clapped a hand to his own mouth. 'God, I sound a snob. I'm sorry, that was uncalled for. But the truth was he did have a pattern.'

'Did this one have a name?'

'Do you know, he *did* introduce her to me in an offhand sort of way. Now what was it? Ah yes, Mrs Winch, that was it. Annie Winch if I'm not mistaken.'

'Do you know anything more about her? Where she worked, for instance?'

Lancing rubbed his cheek. 'No,' he said at last. 'No, that wasn't her name – not Annie Winch, *Fanny* Winch.'

'Well, someone must know. Perhaps Torsten Hellquist. Is he here?'

'No, haven't seen him today. I imagine he stayed in his rooms back at St John's. It would be understandable if he was too distraught to work. But whatever you do, don't forget tennis and cocktails this evening. Hell hath no fury like a Clarissa scorned, you know.'

Lydia was left alone in a plain room, cold, with a smell of sweat, cigarette smoke and cabbage flatulence. The whole building at Prinz-Albrecht-Strasse seemed to echo with footsteps and muted voices. She knew this to be the home of the SS, the SD and the Gestapo. She wasn't sure whether it was fevered imagining, but every so often she thought she heard screaming from a long way away, reverberating like the wailing of long-dead ghosts along corridors and through walls. Perhaps it was the height of the ceilings and the shine of the institutional paint that made this place so sinister.

If this solitary treatment was supposed to break her down, it was working. She even wished Herr Kirsch would visit her so that she had someone to plead with. All she wanted was a telephone call.

It was late afternoon when Kirsch returned. He was smiling and apologetic. 'Have you been fed, Miss Morris?'

'No. No one has been here. I have not even been allowed to go to the lavatory.'

'I shall arrange that for you in a moment, and then I will have food sent to you. Perhaps a cup of tea and some cigarettes, too.'

'What I want most of all, Herr Kirsch, is to be allowed out. You must know that I have committed no crime and that I have no further information to give you about the murderer or the man who was killed.'

Kirsch took out a packet of cigarettes and offered her one. 'The priest, Father Schwartzmann, says you were deep in conversation with the man who was killed.'

She suspected that was a lie. Kirsch was fishing. She had no reason to think the priest would betray her in such a manner. She shook her head, slowly and very firmly. 'No, we both know that isn't right. The priest would not have said such a thing, because it is untrue.'

Against her better judgement, she took one of his cigarettes. He reached over with a lighter and she drew in the smoke. It was ten years since she gave up smoking and here she was smoking her second in two days. It tasted foul but she didn't stub it out.

Kirsch slid a paper across the table so that it lay in front of her eyes. 'That is his statement and his signature. You clearly have a reasonable knowledge of German. Read it.'

She raised her gaze, refusing to look at the words. 'No, I won't read it. You could have written that yourself. You are trying to scare me into making a false statement. Now, I would like to go, please, before you show the Gestapo and your country in an even worse light.'

He sighed. 'You are making this very difficult for yourself, Miss Morris. I shall go and order your food and find a female member of staff to accompany you to the toilet.'

'Where is the priest? Have you arrested him, too?'

'On what charge?'

'I have no idea. I thought you didn't need little things like criminal charges to arrest people.'

'No, he has not been arrested. He voluntarily made his statement and returned to the task of tending his flock.'

There was a knock at the door. Kirsch pulled it open. A young uniformed officer executed an exaggerated Hitler salute and handed him a note. Kirsch read it slowly, then nodded to the younger man in dismissal. He turned back to Lydia. 'Well, well, Miss Morris, you are free to go.' He seemed disappointed.

'What was that message?'

He ignored the question. 'One of our drivers will take you where you wish.' He consulted his wristwatch. 'I fear you will have no flight from

Tempelhof today, but I will make sure you have a seat on the first flight in the morning. We will collect your passport and luggage on the way out.'

'I want to go to Captain Foley's house in Wilmersdorf.'

As they were about to leave the holding cell, she saw Kirsch pick up the so-called statement by the priest and scrunch it into a ball. He tossed it into an empty wastebin.

The car was waiting outside the main entrance on Prinz-Albrecht-Strasse, a uniformed driver at the wheel. Kirsch opened the rear door and she climbed in. She leaned over and said, 'Lessingstrasse, Wilmersdorf, if you please, driver.'

Kirsch was still holding her door. 'I wish you well on your onward journey, Miss Morris,' he said as the door clicked shut. Lydia leant back on the rear seat and breathed a sigh of relief. Frank and Kay Foley would look after her.

Suddenly she sat up. There were no handles on the inside of the doors. What sort of car had no handles for the passengers? Kirsch had gone round the front of the car and was leaning into the driver's window.

'Ravensbrück, driver,' Kirsch said. 'For attention of Baumgarten.'

Lydia's muscles contracted. She caught the driver's eyes in the rearview mirror. Manfred Bloch was looking back at her. The car pulled out into traffic.

CHAPTER 23

'Colonel Flood, this is Professor Wilde.'

At last: Flood's voice, metallic and distant.

'Where have you goddamn been, Wilde?'

'I got your cable.' He wasn't going to make excuses to Colonel Dexter Flood: he owed him nothing. 'You mentioned fears.'

More crackling. This was a world away from the ease and convenience of a telephone system along wires. You could talk to a friend in London as easily as you could over the garden fence with a neighbour. Radiotelephonic communication across continents was not so easy.

'Yes, goddamn it, what have you discovered in the Cavendish?'

'The physicist Paul Birbach has been murdered. He was about to go to America to join Robert Oppenheimer.' Give a little information that is already public knowledge. Put Flood at ease. Tease him out.

The line went silent. Wilde wondered whether they had been cut off, but then Flood's weirdly mutilated voice returned. 'For God's sake, Wilde! When did this happen?'

'A couple of days ago.'

The gap seemed to lengthen. 'And you only tell me now? He's one of the guys I told you to keep your eyes on. What happened?'

'I don't know.' Wilde wasn't about to reveal the little he knew to this man until he understood a little more. 'Now – about those fears you mentioned. Hadn't you better tell me what's going on over *there*?'

'Heisenberg's here. You heard of Heisenberg? The Germans' top uranium man. He's touring American universities, asking questions. Some of the academic guys don't like it – they think he's trying to find out what we know, maybe how close we are to a superbomb. Most of our men are keeping shtum. But what I want from you, Wilde, is the lowdown on Cambridge. What are they saying about this guy Birbach? How was he killed? Goddamit, Wilde! You need to get off your ass, buddy.'

Wilde did not reply.

Another crackling silence, then. 'Are you listening to me, Wilde?'

'I'm listening.'

'Well – find out what's going on at that lab! What about the other guy I mentioned: Hellquist? Where's he in all this?'

It was a good question. Had he already left Cambridge? Perhaps he was already en route home to Sweden. His college might know.

Flood was still snapping out questions like a machine-gunner loosing bullets. 'Who else is working there? How close are they to a bomb? I want a list from you of everyone who works there. Get it to me, soonest.'

'I'm not doing that.'

'Goddamn it, that's an executive order from your government.' More crackling, then the ghostly voice came back yet again. 'And keep me in the loop on the dead guy. This is for America, Wilde. You remember, America, don't you?'

Wilde put down the telephone and let out a long breath. Eva Haas and Arnold Lindberg were in the sitting room with the door closed. He left them there and went to the kitchen.

'Coffee, Doris. For the love of God, a cup of very strong black coffee.'

'Five minutes, Professor Wilde. Is everything all right, sir?'

'Nothing's all right, Doris. It might help if Lydia was here but I haven't heard a word. I don't suppose she's contacted you.'

'No, sir.'

'You know she's in Germany?'

'No, sir, she didn't tell me.'

Wilde snorted. 'No, she didn't tell me either.'

A quarter of an hour later, with coffee burning him from the inside, he was sitting in the front of a taxi, with Lindberg and Haas in the back. The best of the good weather had passed over, leaving a solid bank of white cloud. There would be no rain, though, so tennis would be on.

At the Cavendish, he took his guests straight through to the library and sat them down at a table to wait for Geoff Lancing, who was being hunted down by one of the porters. Given their earlier conversation, he was worried about the warmth of Lancing's reception, but in the event he approached with a bright smile and an extended hand.

Wilde made the formal introductions, first Eva, then her uncle. Wilde noted how Lancing's gaze lingered on Eva. He glanced up at the wall clock.

'Geoff, I've got things to do . . .'

'Leave Dr Lindberg and Dr Haas with me,' said Lancing.

The porter at St John's shook his head. 'Sorry, sir, Dr Hellquist is not in his rooms.'

'Are you sure?' Wilde said. 'I'm told he hasn't been at the Cavendish today.'

'I'll double-check for you if you wish, sir.'

'Please do that, porter.' Wilde slipped a shilling coin from his pocket.

The porter touched his bowler and his military moustache bristled. 'Very grateful, sir.'

Five minutes later he returned, shaking his head once more. 'No sign of him, Professor, but I did happen upon his bedder in Second Court and she said his bed wasn't slept in last night.'

'Do you know where else he might be? Does he have outside lodgings?'

The beetroot-faced porter appeared to weigh up his next words carefully. He moved closer to Wilde and whispered into his ear. 'Not really my place, sir, but I believe he does have a lady, a *married* woman, if I'm correct. Perhaps her old man's away.'

'Where would I find her?'

'That I couldn't say, Professor Wilde. Tends to keep his private life private, does Dr Hellquist. The married woman is only rumour, I'm afraid.' He gave his nose a knowing tap. 'But in my experience there's rarely smoke without fire.'

'Would you let me know if he returns?'

'Of course, sir. I know where to find you. Oh, and the bedder did say something else. Said there was a smell of burning in the room – and some soggy ashes in the basin.'

Wilde stood on St John's Street looking up at the ornate towers. He was angry with Hellquist for not being there, and he was angry with Lydia for not being here in Cambridge. What on earth was he doing with his inept investigations into a murder that did not concern him and his amateurish plan to infiltrate the world of an American Nazi?

He was a history professor, for God's sake. Stick to the supervisions and lectures and writing, Wilde. If you want a bit of adventure, delve into an archive and get your hands dusty. Live vicariously through the lives of Drake and Raleigh and the heroes of antiquity. And then it struck him. There might be a way to find Fanny Winch, the lady friend of Paul Birbach. If she was, indeed, a cleaning woman, then there was every possibility that she and Birbach had met either at college or at the Cavendish. It was worth a go. Someone might know her.

Wilde strode southwards down King's Street, past Trinity, Caius, the Senate House, then onto King's Parade with the towering beauty of King's College chapel to his right. On his left was Bene't Street, leading onto Free School Lane and the Cavendish, but he carried on.

The town was in midsummer mood. With the long vacation looming, most undergraduates had given up on their studies and were in whites wandering towards the tennis courts on Midsummer Common, or Fenner's, the university cricket ground, past Parker's Piece in the south-east of the town. Others carried towels and hampers as they headed down towards the river for games and picnics and punting. Innocent fun. Wilde wanted none of it, not this year. Let the young enjoy this time; they had most to lose in the coming months and years. Anyone who thought otherwise was deluding themselves. Since Hitler marched into Prague back in March surely even Neville Chamberlain must be resigned to war.

At college, he cornered Scobie in the porter's lodge and got straight to the point. 'Dr Birbach had a lady friend, a Mrs Fanny Winch. Have you heard of her, Scobie?'

'No, sir. Should I have?'

'It's possible she worked here, as a cleaner perhaps, or in the sculleries.'

Scobie took off his hat and scratched his head. 'No, sir, I think I'd remember a name like that. And I'm certain I know everyone who works here, by name and by sight.'

Of course he did. It was his job to have control of who came in and who left the college grounds. Wilde thanked him and retraced his steps along Trumpington Street, then turned right past the Eagle to the Cavendish.

In the past few days the lab's porter had come to know Wilde by name. 'Fanny Winch? Yes, I know her. Been cleaning here two or three weeks now.'

'Is she here?'

'No, no. Early morning shift before most of the gentlemen arrive.' The porter paused. 'Is this about Dr Birbach?'

'They were seeing each other.'

'That's one way of putting it, Professor. Would you like me to leave a message for her when she comes in? I imagine she's pretty upset. Must have thought she'd caught a handsome earner in our Dr Birbach.'

'I don't suppose you have any details? I'd like to talk to her.'

The porter pulled a black book down from a shelf. 'I like to keep track of everyone, telephone numbers and such like in my book. If not, the head of housekeeping will likely have it.' He flicked through the pages. 'No, sorry, no telephone number. Ah, but there is an address.' He stabbed his finger at the page. 'Swaffham Lane. I believe it's off the Newmarket Road, towards the edge of town before you get to the new builds. No. 16, Swaffham Lane. Any help?'

'Thank you.' Wilde fished for a coin, realised he didn't have one. The porter put up his hand. 'No, no, sir, don't think of it. I hope you find her.'

Wilde collected the Rudge, then rode out eastwards. Swaffham Lane was a narrow, mean street of slum houses. Children were playing in the road; a couple of small girls were barefoot. There were few cars here, a beaten-up Ford Ten, an Austin that had seen better days. There were no trees or front gardens. The front doors, paint peeling, stood directly on to the narrow pavement.

He parked on the kerb in front of number 16. A group of boys, aged about ten, came to examine the Rudge Special. 'How fast does she go, mister?'

'Hundred,' he said.

'Hundred miles an hour?'

'Hundred miles an hour.'

'Cor! Can I have a go, mister?'

'No. But you can sit on the saddle if you want. Take it in turns, but be careful to keep it on its stand. Look after her for me, will you?'

As the boys scrambled over the bike, Wilde knocked on the door. It was a tiny terraced house, no more than fourteen feet wide, perhaps two rooms on the ground floor and another two upstairs. All built to the most basic standards; there would certainly be no indoor lavatory.

The door opened. A boy of twelve or thirteen stood there, glaring at him. 'Yeah?'

'I want to speak to your mother.'

'Mum!'

The interior was dark, but Wilde could see three other children clustered around a table in the corner. He guessed their ages ranged from about two to ten. The far door opened and Fanny Winch emerged, wiping her hands on her apron. He recognised her from Old Hall.

She squinted, then nodded. 'I saw you at that fancy do,' she said.

'My name is Wilde. Thomas Wilde.'

'Well, hello, Mr Wilde. I won't shake your hand because I've been doing the washing. Do you want to come in?'

'Thank you.' He stepped inside. The room smelt of tobacco smoke and burnt cooking fat. The elder boy had rejoined the other children at the table. They were all watching him, in silence.

'Horrible, isn't it,' she said. 'Best I could get for ten shillings a week.'

She was right. It was horrible. The walls were damp, the windows ran with condensation, the paint was flaking. And, above all, that stale stench of grease. No amount of detergent and scrubbing would rid this house of that.

'It's about Dr Birbach,' he said.

She shook her head. 'Terrible shame. Topped himself, so I heard. Chucked himself in the river.'

'You must have been one of the last people to see him alive.'

Her initial warmth was suddenly gone. 'What is this? You sound like the coppers.'

'Have the police spoken to you?'

'No. Why should they? It's nothing to do with me.'

Her arms tightened across her chest.

'Is this difficult for you?' he indicated the children. 'I'm just trying to find out what happened, that's all. Dr Birbach and I were college neighbours.'

'Well, I know nothing, Mr Wilde. We had a good time, the German fellow and me, then he brought me home. That's it. Nothing serious between us.'

'I'd really like to ask you a few more questions.'

'Well, I've nothing to say.'

He took a ten shilling note from his wallet. A week's rent.

She didn't take the money, but she did remove her apron. 'You're right. I don't want to talk here. Not in front of them. There's the Queen's Head along the way. The landlord'll let me in.'

'Take it.'

'No. You keep your money. I don't need charity.' She turned to the twelve-year-old. 'I'll do your tea in a short while, Michael. Keep them out of mischief.'

'Yes, mum.'

In the daylight, outside, Wilde found himself walking beside a presentable woman in her mid-thirties. She was fair-looking in a worn-out sort of way. Worn out by manual work and by four children, he supposed. Probably no man in her life, either; no steady man anyway. Her nails were rough-edged from her work, but she was otherwise neat and tidy.

When they arrived at the Queen's Head, the landlord let them slide in. They settled into a corner seat by the window, and he fetched a couple of small whiskies.

'Tell me about Paul Birbach,' he said, handing her a Scotch. 'How much did he pay you?'

'Are you suggesting I'm a tart?'

'I'm suggesting that a good-looking woman like you wouldn't have had anything to do with a man like Birbach unless it was a business arrangement.'

'He was nice to me. And you're bloody rude, Mr Wilde.'

'I saw you in the boathouse. That was more than you just being nice.'

She shrugged. 'Well, you're the dirty bastard for watching. Anyway, we all have our little peculiarities. That was his.' She laughed. 'Happy to oblige a fine gentleman like Dr Birbach.'

'That's bullshit, Mrs Winch. But don't get me wrong, I'm not your judge. We've all got to earn a living somehow – and it must be tough with four kids in the house.' Who the hell wouldn't go on the game if they were landed with four hungry mouths and the meagre wages of a cleaner?

'Think what you like.'

'Talk to me straight. If you know something then tell me and I'll make it worth your while. How does a fiver sound?'

'I already turned down your ten shillings, didn't I?'

'I'm sure you'd like to buy the kids something nice. New shoes perhaps. Cap guns, bows and arrows?'

She drank her whisky. 'You can get me another one of these for starters.'

Wilde went to the bar and bought her a double but nothing for himself. He took the whisky back to the table and set it down in front of her, then slid a fine white five-pound note beneath the glass. She did not push it away.

'What happened?' he asked.

'It was a strange night all right,' she said. 'We got a taxi home from that party and then he came in for a cup of tea. Nothing more, mind. You never know when the small ones will wake up and try to crawl into bed with you. He was just saying goodbye because he was supposed to be off to America in the morning. We kissed goodbye and I went to the front door with him, to see him off. I thought he'd be walking home but there was a big black car outside. We don't get fancy motor cars in Swaffham Lane, as you might have noticed.'

'Did you notice the make?'

'Do I look like the sort of person who'd know one make of car from another? It was big and black like I said, and it had two men in it, that's all I can tell you. I thought he must have arranged for his mates to pick him up, but he hadn't told me.'

'So what happened?'

'The driver wound down his window and said something to Dr Birbach.'

'Did you hear what he said?'

'No. I think it was foreign.'

'German?'

'Probably. I know he was German and didn't speak English well. But who knows? A foreigner's a bloody foreigner. I couldn't tell a Fritz from a Frog. But he seemed to understand, so you might be right.'

'What's your own accent, Mrs Winch? I'd say you're from Liverpool.'

She seemed taken aback. 'What's it to you?'

'Nothing – just interested. You're new to Cambridge, then?'

'You're right. Born and bred a Scouser, but there's no work for a cleaner up there. Thought I'd try here where all the fancy folks send their young gentlemen. Men with a shilling or two in their pocket, men with fine motor cars.'

'Back to the black car and the two men. You must have heard more. Did they use his name?'

'Yes, I think they did. They called him over. One of them got out then. That's when I went back in the house and shut the front door. I didn't like the look of them. There was something about them.'

'What time was this?'

'Don't know.' She shrugged. 'Twelve thirty at a guess.'

'You must have looked out the window?'

'Yeah, I looked out the window. By then he was in the car with them and they drove off. I thought they must be his friends. That was the last I saw of the car and the men; last I saw of Dr Birbach. Anyway, what's any of it to do with you?'

'Because he was my neighbour and he was murdered. And by the sound of it, you saw the murderers. And so I need a description of them – and I need the car's number plate. And then you'll have to tell all this to the police.'

Fanny Winch threw back the double Scotch and gasped from the shock of the neat spirit. 'You're scaring me, Mr Wilde.'

'I'm sorry,' he said. 'I didn't mean to do that.'

But if she could identify the men who had tortured Paul Birbach and then dumped his body in the river, she had every right to be afraid.

'I am going to get you out of Germany,' Bloch said without turning around.

Had she heard right?

'Herr Bloch?'

'Keep calm. Keep looking ahead as though you are my prisoner. If we are stopped, say nothing.'

'Are we not going to Ravensbrück?'

'No,' he said.

'I don't understand. I thought . . .'

'I think I know what you thought, Miss Morris. But there is much you don't know. You thought I killed that man in the Orpenplatz, but you were wrong.'

'But I saw you with a gun!'

'Of course I had a gun. There was a killer.' He glanced at her over his shoulder. 'But for now there is little time. You must leave Germany with great haste. If Kirsch discovers that you are not on your way to Ravensbrück he will circulate a description of this car and its number. All ports, stations and aerodromes will be put on alert.'

'Don't you think you owe me an explanation, Herr Bloch? I saw you in Bloomsbury, then on the plane, then Orpenplatz and again Tempelhof. Now you have been ordered to drive me to Ravensbrück but you say you are going to get me out of the country. What is happening? Who *are* you?'

'Bloomsbury? No.' He shook his head. 'Look, all you need to know is that I am on your side.' His hands gripped the wheel in frustration. 'God in heaven, this traffic!'

'Please take me to Frank Foley's apartment in Wilmersdorf. I beg you, Herr Bloch!'

They were now stationary at the back of a line of cars and trucks. Bloch turned around again. 'That is impossible,' he said. 'It would delay you. Anyway, his house is watched. I am going to take you to Tempelhof. You have a reservation for this evening's Zurich flight. It is your only hope.'

'The passport man will remember me.'

'No, his shift will have ended.'

'Mr Bloch, I trust Captain Foley. Give me one reason why I should trust you.'

'That is simple; because I am *not* taking you to the concentration camp.'

It was something, but it wasn't much. There were many ways to squeeze information from someone, one of which was to fool them that you were on their side. But what information could they want from her? They must know that she had not seen the murder. And this, surely, could have nothing to do with Albert Haas? Unless it was an elaborate ruse to get her to reveal the location of Eva and Arnold Lindberg?

'You must take messages for me,' Bloch said. 'To Philip Eaton.'

'*Philip Eaton?*'

'We work together.'

'He would have told me.'

Bloch gave a dry laugh. 'When did Philip Eaton give out more information than was absolutely necessary?'

'If you want to take messages to Philip Eaton, do it yourself. Why should I believe a word you say, Herr Bloch? I have had enough of your charade.'

'This is no charade. And I cannot return to England. I must stay in Germany now. I will be needed here when the war comes.'

'What are these messages?'

'I will tell you at Tempelhof. It is safer that way . . .'

He meant that if she was caught before reaching the airport, she might reveal information about Bloch and his contacts. If she knew nothing, she could reveal nothing. And in the meantime, she was beginning to realise, she had no alternative but to place her trust in him. She had to get out of Germany. The man in the cathedral had said the answer to Albert's disappearance did not lie here, and she had believed him.

The cars began to move again. Forty-five minutes later, they pulled up outside the terminal building at Tempelhof.

Manfred Bloch switched off the engine and turned around to face her, holding out her passport. 'When you get out, I will walk you to the door carrying your bag. There, I will hand it over to you. You will not have long to wait, so go straight to passport control. I will be watching. If I am wrong, if the passport control man from this morning is still there, I will intervene on your behalf. If I have to do this it will expose me. But if it has to be done, I will do it.'

'Are you "Baumgarten"? Are *you* the man who got Lindberg out of Dachau?'

'No more questions, Miss Morris. Now please, the message for Philip Eaton. Remember this carefully. Do not write it down. Tell him Seamus O'Donovan was here again, a guest of the *Abwehr*. And this time he has not been buying arms for the IRA. This time, he was finalising details for a major, joint attack on Britain. Some place of importance. This is all I know.'

'Who is this O'Donovan?'

'He's the man behind all those bombs that have been going off in England these past few months. He allies himself with the Nazis against the British, and the Nazis happily take his side. Do you have my message clear?'

She nodded meekly. 'Yes, Herr Bloch. I will tell Eaton. A major attack on Britain . . .'

'One more thing. Tell him he must break the habit of a lifetime for a Six man – and cooperate with Five on this. I have reason to believe they have an agent somewhere on the inside.'

CHAPTER 24

'Well, Tom, you look the part. But can you play the game, that's the question.'

Hardiman sized up his opponent with undisguised disdain, his gaze ranging from the top of Wilde's head, down his billowing white shirt and long white trousers to the tip of his tennis shoes.

Wilde ignored him and proceeded to remove his racket from its press. He held it flat in front of his eye, examining it for warping. It was old enough to be consigned to the lumber pile as firewood, but he had a soft spot for it: the racket had served him well. It seemed straight enough, considering it had not been out of the cupboard since last September. He tested the gut strings; they were a little on the loose side. Should have done something about that before coming here but it was too late now. In any case, he had more to worry about than the strings.

Milt Hardiman was flexing his elbows and wrists, rotating his right shoulder. He was almost as tall as Wilde and had the physique of a sports-man. He had half a dozen rackets on the bench, along with a tube of balls, fresh, white and virgin. He picked out one of the rackets, then tossed a couple of balls to Wilde. 'Your racket's pre-war, Tom. Want to borrow one of mine?'

'No, thank you, Hardiman. I like it.'

'Milt. The name's Milt. We're Americans aren't we? None of this damned English stand-offishness. Where have you played?'

'School. University. Lawns like this.'

'Is that it? Geoff Lancing told me you were a player. No Wimbledon?'

'Geoff might have exaggerated my skills.' Last time he had played with Geoff, he had beaten his old friend in straight sets. But beating Geoff Lancing did not, sadly, make him among the greatest of players. 'I'll try to give you a game, Milt. I can promise nothing more.'

'What's the stake?'

'Let's say half a crown, shall we?'

'No, goddamn it, Tom! Let's make it worthwhile. Five hundred.'

Wilde laughed. 'Five pounds is my limit. Guineas if you must.'

'Bullshit. What do you drive?'

'I have a motorcycle, a Rudge Special.'

'Can't you afford a motor car? What sort of man doesn't drive a car?'

Wilde was getting bored with this. 'I happen to like my motorbike.'

'What do you do when it rains?'

'I get wet.'

'More fool you, buddy. OK, your bike against my Lagonda. Sports tourer, four and a half litres.'

'No, the Rudge is more valuable to me than any car. Five guineas is my max.'

Hardiman's son, Theo, was buzzing around them like an irritating fly. Every so often he kicked the newly marked chalk dust on the baseline of the court. His father ignored him.

Wilde had said hello to Theo when he arrived at Old Hall with Lancing. The boy had been kicking up gravel in the drive. As the car with the newcomers arrived, he had grabbed several handfuls of stones and chucked them at the bonnet and windscreen. When Wilde tried to introduce himself, the boy had replied. 'Don't know you, mister. Tradesmen at the back.'

Now he was busy scuffing his shoes on the white lines. Perhaps he would be put to work as ballboy. Wilde hoped not.

Hardiman walked purposefully down to the far end of the court. There was a very slight incline, and Hardiman had chosen the high point. If he served from there, the balls were liable to skid down the lawn without enough height to reach Wilde's hitting zone. It was something to bear in mind.

'Five minutes knock-up, then straight in. Best of five sets.'

'Fine by me.'

They started knocking up gently, close to the net. Wilde immediately realised his lack of practice was affecting him badly. While Hardiman hit the sweet spot time after time, Wilde messed up. The ball was coming off the wood and the grip of his racket was slipping through his fingers. And when he did catch the strings, he was still failing to get the satisfying sound a ball makes when it brushes up from the very centre. He fought to concentrate, to focus on the ball, to move quickly and accurately, but his muscles were tensing, which is no good for tennis.

Hardiman's son, Theo, aimed a ball at Wilde's head. Wilde put up his left hand and caught it easily. The boy sneered. 'You know what, mister? Our dog, Izzy, could beat you.'

The dog, a powerful and vicious-looking German Shepherd, had greeted their arrival with a volley of bare-toothed barking, straining at its handler's leash.

'You may well be right, Theo,' Wilde said equably.

'Even Bee could beat you.'

'Who's Bee?'

'My new friend.'

'Is Bee a boy or a girl?'

Theo looked at Wilde as though he was dense. 'A boy, of course. He's very clever, but I don't think he's very good at sport.'

Wilde looked around. By now, the other guests had emerged from the house and were sauntering down the lawn towards the court. Both Clarissa Lancing and Peggy Hardiman were wearing calf-length tennis dresses and carrying rackets. If they thought there would be time for a game of women's singles after this match, they clearly didn't have much faith in his holding out against Hardiman for long.

But it became evident that they had other ideas. Clarissa joined Wilde and presented her cheeks for kisses, while Peggy walked over to her husband at the far end. Hardiman seemed put out. 'What the hell's this?' he demanded. 'We're playing men's singles here.'

'No,' said Clarissa, approaching the net. 'We're playing mixed doubles – Professor Wilde and myself against you and Peggy.'

'No, no, no,' Hardiman insisted. 'We've got a wager running. We're not playing goddamn girls' stuff.'

Clarissa smiled sweetly. 'If there's a bet, Professor Wilde and I will take it on against you and Peggy. OK? What is the bet, by the way?'

'My Lagonda against his miserable motorbike.'

'The hell it is,' Wilde said. 'I agreed five guineas. And that's it.'

'Boys, boys,' Clarissa said. 'I have a better idea. Your Lagonda, Milt, against my Hispano-Suiza, which, I am sure you will agree is the far superior motor car.'

Milt's face was red with rage. 'You two can get off my lawn right now. I'm playing this know-it-all professor and I'm going to give him a whipping.'

Clarissa laughed out loud. 'Oh, listen to yourself, Milt. This is tennis and cocktails, not Wimbledon!'

His wife took his arm. 'Milt, honey, let's just play a nice soft game, then we can all have drinks.'

Wilde had seen Peggy Hardiman only briefly at the party. Now he had a chance to look at her. She was very thin, tall, fair-haired, with a Long Island sheen that told of a lifetime of privilege. Her husband might be of indeterminate provenance, but *she* was undoubtedly old money and Old Westbury. Her voice was quiet and very much to the point; her conversation would centre on gossip about mutual friends and enemies. You would not want to be one of her servants. That quiet voice would not tolerate inefficiency or idleness.

Just then, Geoff Lancing emerged from the house, Eva Haas at his side. When they were about fifty yards away, Hardiman growled at Clarissa in a voice loud enough for everyone on court to hear. 'What in God's name made your excuse for a brother think it was OK to bring a goddamned kike here?'

Peggy tried to pull him away. 'Please, Milt, honey, don't make a scene. Not tonight. Let's just play some tennis, have some horse's necks and play some records. Please, honey.'

He wrenched his arm away from her grip and stalked to the back of the court. 'OK then, play. My Lagonda for your Hispano. And you, Lancing!' He hailed Geoffrey. 'Leave that damned woman alone and come over and umpire. Theo, you're ballboy.'

'How much do I get?'

'Ten dollars.'

'Twenty.'

As Wilde walked back to his baseline he spoke in Clarissa's ear. 'What was that? Did he really say that about Dr Haas?'

'Oh, don't make a fuss, Wilde. And to be honest, Geoff was a bit out of order just turning up with her.'

Under other circumstances Wilde might have made his excuses and left, but he had to swallow his revulsion and stay here. He changed the subject. 'I don't mind playing tennis, but I really don't want to be part of any bet.'

'You don't have to be,' Clarissa said. 'It's my bet. Anyway, we'll win very easily. Keep the ball on Peggy's backhand, which is kitten-weak. It'll drive Milt insane. He's a very fine player but we'll cut him out and then he'll lose all control. And tennis, my dear Professor Wilde, is all about control.'

She bestowed her movie-star smile upon him and he found himself wishing to kiss her. Like millions of other men.

As soon as the match proper started, Wilde realised that his tennis wasn't as bad as he had feared. By playing steadily and carefully, using a great deal of topspin and simply getting the ball back in court without going for outright winners, he and Clarissa were holding their own. She was a fine, strong player. By the time the first set was five-all, he saw that her tactics were paying off. Peggy was struggling with her backhand and Hardiman, seeing the danger, kept trying to poach balls that might have been better played by his wife. In doing so, he was over-reaching himself and leaving open court.

'You see,' Clarissa said smugly when she and Wilde sewed up the first set eight–six. 'Don't you want to join that bet now?'

'You were right. But no, the bet is yours.'

The next two sets were easier and by the end of the third, Hardiman had smashed his racket into splinters on the ground and had had to fetch a replacement from his chair. When Wilde and Clarissa took the final point, he refused to shake hands.

'Take the goddamn Lagonda! Useless Limey car anyway.' He clicked his fingers and a servant came running. 'Get cocktails, get music on.'

'Yes, sir.'

'And deposit some of Izzy's turds in the Lagonda.'

'Sir?'

'Forget it.'

The four players, along with Geoff and Eva, ambled up towards the terrace. Theo trailed alongside them, kicking a tennis ball as he went. 'I'm bored,' he said.

'Then go and play,' his mother said.

'Bee's asleep.'

'Oh, Theo, don't be a pain.'

The boy hunched his shoulders and sidled towards his father.

'Bee's his friend, right?' Wilde said. 'Is he staying here?'

Peggy Hardiman raised her pencilled eyebrows. 'His *imaginary* friend, Mr Wilde. Don't you know anything about kids?'

'Does he have any brothers or sisters?'

'Theo's enough for any mother.'

They sat around a marble-topped table laden with olives and canapés and game chips. A servant took their drinks orders. Hardiman, who hadn't said a word on the way from the court, said he was going to change and strode off into the house.

'Oh, don't mind Milt, Mr Wilde,' Peggy said. 'He's always been a sore loser. Clarissa knew what she was doing, you see – she knows all my weaknesses. And his for that matter.'

Theo was grabbing all the game chips from the table. He kept looking at Eva, who was sitting beside Geoff Lancing. Their conversation – all about science – went straight over everyone else's heads. Theo went up to her.

'What are you talking about, lady?'

'The atom.' Eva said. It occurred to Wilde that Theo could not be much older than her own son.

'Pa says you're a dirty Jew.'

There was a united gasp from the adults. Peggy Hardiman got to her feet and grabbed her son by the wrist. 'What did you just say?'

'Well, he did. He said she was a dirty Jew. Ask him.'

'How dare you!' She slapped the boy's face, and he yelped. 'You're going to your room, young man. Your father never said anything of the kind.' She turned to Eva. 'I'm sorry, Dr Haas. My son has a vivid imagination – and he hears terrible things at school.'

Eva nodded. 'Thank you, but please don't punish the boy. I have heard worse, much worse.'

Their drinks arrived and Hardiman returned, changed from his tennis whites to grey pants and a light blue shirt. 'What's the problem with the boy?' he demanded of his wife.

'He was rude and he told lies, Milt.'

Hardiman parked himself next to Wilde. 'We were going to continue our talk, as I recall, Tom. You were dog drunk on my whisky last time we met.'

'Then I apologise.'

'Nothing to apologise for. I was dog drunk, too. How did you find Paris?'

'We turned left at London and headed due south.'

'Oh, you're the funny one.'

'To be honest I was too tired to notice Paris. Apart from the Louvre and the Eiffel Tower I could have been anywhere in the world, but I suppose it was an adventure.'

Hardiman lowered his voice. His eyes indicated Eva Haas. 'This woman with Geoff, she's a German Jew, right? What in God's name is going on here?'

'She's a scientist. A very fine physicist.'

'I guess she's one of the Cavendish mob. They let in all sorts there, from what I hear.'

'Not all sorts,' said Wilde. 'Only men and women with very big brains.'

'But the Jews, you know ... From what I hear the big news from Germany is that an Aryan guy, Otto Hahn, is the one who made the big breakthrough. You know, made a bomb possible. The Jewish science is all bullshit.'

'Einstein's Jewish.'

'He's a fake. The Deutsche Physik guys have disproved all his crazy ideas.'

'Well, what of Hahn's collaborator – she was Jewish.'

'And as soon as she snuck out of the country, Hahn made his break-through. Think about it, Tom. Was the woman a help – or a hindrance?'

'I'm surprised you're aware of all this, Milt.'

'What? You think money men can't understand science? You'd do well to stay on the right side of a guy like me. We need men like you.'

'We?'

'You know what I'm talking about. America, buddy. Dexter Flood got you on side, right? Got to be on the right side of history, Tom. You're a historian – you know all about that. If you're a true patriotic American, you'll be with us. Don't get sentimental about the kikes, because they sure as hell wouldn't cross the road to help you, unless you opened your wallet. You're not British, so you get to choose your side. Choose the right one.'

It occurred to Wilde that Eva Haas must be able to hear a lot of this rant. And yet she seemed deep in a conversation of her own with Geoff Lancing. He glanced over at them and began to wonder. Well, why not?

He turned back to Hardiman. 'Did Geoff tell you that one of your party guests was found murdered?'

'Burbank – no Birbach. Another goddamned Jew scientist. What happened to the guy?'

'It seems he might have been gassed.'

'You mean he put his head in the oven?'

'No, I didn't mean that. I meant it looked as though he was fed gas. Not town gas, either – but some kind of blistering agent. I was wondering: can you recall the exact time he left your party? Did he have his own car – or did you lay one on for him?'

'You sound like a policeman, Wilde.'

'He was my neighbour in college.'

Hardiman shrugged. 'You saw me at the party, buddy. How can I remember what time some little science guy left? I could barely remember my own name come morning.'

'I spoke to Dexter Flood today. He's interested.'

'Then you better see what you can find, I guess.'

'Perhaps your wife knows.' He noticed that Peggy had been listening in to the conversation. 'Mrs Hardiman?'

'I'm afraid I don't think I noticed the man at all. Was he alone?'

'No, he had a woman friend with him, name of Mrs Winch. Fanny Winch.'

Peggy frowned, then shook her head. 'I'm awfully sorry. No, they mean nothing to me. But you know, Mr Wilde, there were over two hundred people at the party, and to be honest with you, I didn't know who three-quarters of them were.'

'I'll call Dexter myself,' Hardiman said. 'Make some inquiries of my own. Thanks for bringing this to my attention, Tom. You hear anything else, let me know, right?' Hardiman stuck an expensive cigar in his mouth, and then offered one to Wilde, which he declined. 'What I do recall, Tom, was that you were mighty interested in the history of this fine house.'

Clarissa had had enough of being excluded from the conversation. 'Are you going to hog Professor Wilde all night, Milt?' she broke in. 'Come on, Tom, dance with me.' She signalled to a servant. 'Put on some band music. Dance music. And turn it up loud.'

Wilde danced on the lawn with Clarissa. Hardiman did not dance. He nursed his brandy and ginger ale in silence, watching the dancers through a wreath of cigar smoke.

After the number ended, Clarissa led Wilde back to the table. Hardiman grunted at them. 'Tom still wants to know about the house, Clarissa.'

'Then tell him all you know, Milt.'

'Why don't you show him? Let him see for himself.'

Clarissa was still holding Wilde's hand. 'Well?'

'Lead on.'

'I'll keep your drinks warm for you,' Hardiman said.

Clarissa led him into the hall. 'Apparently this place was in ruins,' she said. 'They were talking of pulling it down after the war because no one wanted it. Or they couldn't afford it.'

Wilde ran his fingers along the smooth, sensuous grain of the ancient panelling. He paused before the magnificent stone fireplace, as high as it was wide, deserving of a single blazing ash log on an autumn day. He gazed up at the slightly threadbare tapestry of some mythical scene dominating one wall. 'Well, he's done a good job,' Wilde said in honest admiration. 'Good restorative work, I'd say. It's easy to get Tudor houses wrong.'

'There's plenty more upstairs. Come on.' In front of them the curved staircase, crafted from oak, beckoned. They climbed to the first floor. On the south side was a long room, perhaps fifty feet, with a ceiling of intricate plasterwork and bookcases full of leather-bound volumes from Italy and Spain and England. Wilde wondered how many of them had actually been read. How he would love to dig deep between their dusty covers for a few weeks or months in search of hidden gems of history and art. Perhaps that was not such an impossible idea.

The insanity of his situation struck him. He had been asked to spy on Milt Hardiman – and to spy *with* him on the Cavendish. But spy on him doing what? Playing tennis, drinking brandy and displaying vicious anti-Semitism? None of that, as far as Wilde knew, was a crime.

'The boy, Theo . . .'

'Is a spoilt brat.'

'He has an imaginary friend called Bee, it seems.'

'Really? I just ignore the tedious little swine.' Clarissa pushed open a door. 'And these,' she said, 'are my rooms. Enter, dear Professor Wilde.'

'A lady's private boudoir is exactly that, Miss Lancing – private.'

'I need to change out of my tennis things.'

'Then I shall leave you to it.'

'And I might need a little assistance with hooks and buttons.'

'I shall fetch you a maid.'

She gave him an old-fashioned look. 'Oh, just wait outside then. Don't run off now.'

As he waited, he leant his back against the wall. He felt apprehensive. He looked outside into the darkening sky. A few hundred yards in the distance was a group of outbuildings. One of them, an old barn, had lights on. There was a vehicle there – a van, and two men, carrying something heavy inside. Farm workers, he supposed. Working late.

Clarissa's door opened behind him. 'Oh, Professor Wilde,' she called. 'Where are you? I'm ready.' Her eyes peered around the jamb. 'I just need one last button seeing to.'

He sighed, and took two steps back to her door. She was standing in front of him naked and unashamed.

Her body was perfect in every detail: no man could have torn his eyes away. His gaze dropped from her eyes, down the slender contours of her neck, to the twin pink buds of her nipples. His eyes held there a moment, then dropped again down to the light, wispy curls of her sex and her endless, flawless legs. Desire surged and he knew he was lost.

'Well? Are you going to help me with that button or are you just going to stand there as though you've seen a ghost?'

'I see no button.'

'Then I suggest you come and find it.'

CHAPTER 25

The hours ticked by and the aeroplane droned ever on. Unable to relax, unable to read her book, all Lydia could do was gaze from the window at the lights of German towns below. She was still not safe. The five-hundred-mile flight was scheduled to take five hours; they would not be out of German airspace until the last half hour.

Kriminaldirektor Kirsch could raise the alarm at any moment, of course, once he realised that she had not arrived at Ravensbrück concentration camp. It would be a matter of minutes to work out that she had taken this flight from Tempelhof to Zurich; she had used her own passport and name. And all the while the plane was over Germany, the pilot could be radioed and told to land at the nearest airfield. It was a Lufthansa flight. German airline, German pilot. There would be no argument.

This time she had no companion, which was a small blessing. But nor did she have any other way of passing the eternity of the flight. She took a pen from her bag and her small black notebook. Unconnected words: *blood, sky, darkness, fear, stone, dome, Baumgarten*. A poem without verbs. She tore the page from the book and crumpled it in her hand and stuffed it in the ashtray.

She looked at her watch. They had been going four and a three-quarter hours now and the ride had become increasingly bumpy as they met the mountains south-west of Munich. And then, at last, she felt the nose tip down and the descent began.

A quarter of an hour later, they landed and the plane taxied to the terminal: the word ZÜRICH was painted in large letters on the main building. But it was not until the engine had stopped and the steps had been placed against the doorway that she felt safe. Now all she had to do was get to England.

In the terminal building, the clock told her it was 10 p.m. Swiss time. She spoke to the Swissair desk and the uniformed clerk told her there would be a flight to London the next day, at midday, and yes, there would most certainly be a seat available for her. In the meantime, would madam wish for a hotel room? A hotel room was exactly what she wanted, along with a bottle of decent wine, good food and a telephone.

'You've come all the way from Germany then, Dr Haas? Things got a little too hot, huh?'

'Given my circumstances, what would *you* have done, Mr Hardiman?'

'If it was truly my home, I'd have stayed put. But you Jews, you're just guests everywhere – and then you want to move the furniture around. You attach yourself to the host body like a parasite and then mutate it.'

Geoff Lancing slammed his hand down on the table. 'I say, steady on, Milt!'

Eva put her own hand over Geoff's. 'Don't, Dr Lancing. I can look after myself.'

Hardiman glared at her. 'Go on then. Let's hear your sob story.'

'I think you know exactly what is happening. I lost my work and my home. My child was deprived of his schooling and his friends. Things will only get worse.'

'These are small points. Inconsequential. Hitler's a good man. He's given Germany back its pride. Nobody messes with Germany these days.'

'There will be a war. A terrible war.' Eva was beginning to shake.

'Oh hell, yes, there'll be a war all right. But terrible? God no. No trenches this time. The whole thing will be over in weeks. In the meantime, you're here along with plenty of others like you. You're hoping for a job at the Cavendish, yes? Will that be forthcoming, Geoff?'

Geoff was fighting to regain his composure. 'I don't know,' he said coldly. 'But I suppose the runes aren't that good. Even Leo Szilard couldn't get a position. Rutherford wouldn't have him.'

'I've heard of Szilard. The chain-reaction guy.'

Geoff Lancing looked surprised. 'You are well informed, Milt.'

Hardiman waved his hand and changed the subject. 'Say, where's your friend and your sister? They must be looking around the house in fine detail. Go find them, Peggy.'

His wife stayed put. 'They'll be back in their own sweet time, darling. I think Clarissa knows her way around well enough.'

Hardiman smirked. 'Knows her way around every man in Hollywood. Didn't get her the *Gone with the Wind* number though, did it? Can't swing it when I'm not writing the cheques.'

Peggy gave his hand a sharp slap. 'That's a horrible slur, Milt.'

'Which one – the sleeping around or her failure without my backing?'

'Take it all back this instant.' Two spots of pink had appeared above Peggy's high cheekbones. 'Apologise to Geoff for saying such a thing about his sister, who is our beloved guest.'

'OK, let me correct myself. Clarissa Lancing is as pure as fresh-fallen snow and the world's most talented actress to boot. So please, Geoff, accept my apologies if I gave any impression to the contrary.'

Lancing forced a laugh. 'I think I know my dear sister well enough. Ah – talk of the devil.'

Wilde and Clarissa had just emerged from the house.

'Oh my *goodness*,' Hardiman said nastily. 'Don't they look flushed.'

Wilde needed to get away from this place. 'Milt,' he said, 'I'm afraid it's time to go. I have another guest and it would be too rude of me to leave him any longer.'

'OK.' Hardiman shrugged. 'I'll have to whip your ass another day.'

'Forgive me for dodging the men's singles. It wasn't my idea.'

'I'll meet you man to man soon enough. And I always win. But in doubles you're only as good as your partner's backhand – isn't that right?'

Wilde took his leave of Peggy Hardiman. She clutched his hands as though he were an old and treasured friend. 'You don't get away from us so easily, Professor Wilde,' she said. 'We're off to the Newmarket races tomorrow – you must come.'

Wilde was about to decline, to say he had other things to do; but Jim had asked him to stay close to these people. So had Eaton. Thus far he had discovered nothing apart from Milt Hardiman's anti-Semitism and poor sportsmanship, but both the British secret service and Jim Vanderberg believed there was more to Hardiman than met the eye. So Wilde had a responsibility. 'I'd love to come,' he said.

'Pick you up at noon then. We'll have lunch there. Don't forget your field glasses.'

His departure from Clarissa was more awkward. He thought of Jim Vanderberg's warning words. How the hell was he supposed to stay away from her? He was a human being, not a saint. Jim might have seen her on the silver screen, but he hadn't had to endure her naked body offered up to him.

She presented her cheek for a kiss. 'Sleep well, Professor Wilde,' she said as he gave her the lightest of pecks. 'Keep those pyjama buttons done up tonight.'

Wilde, Geoff Lancing and Eva Haas were driven back into Cambridge in the Hispano-Suiza. Wilde sat in the front alongside the driver. In the back, Eva was smoking a cigarette, frantically blowing smoke from the window. Whatever attraction there was between her and Geoff, it was no concern of his, yet he wondered how there could be anything between them when all her thoughts must be on her missing son.

He wondered, too, about the harsh reception she had endured from Milt Hardiman. Why had he been so overtly unpleasant to a woman he had never met before? Was Wilde missing something?

He turned round to Geoff. 'I went to St John's to talk to Torsten Hellquist, Geoff. No sign of him. I don't suppose you know where he's got to?'

Had he run for safety, as he intimated? Lancing also had rooms at St John's, close to the Swede.

'No, I haven't seen him either. I imagine he needed to get away. He must have been devastated by Paul Birbach's death. Well, we all were, of course. But with Hellquist, it was a great deal more intense. In science, they were like two halves of a whole. In their personalities, too. You know he had been hoping to follow Birbach to California?'

'No, I didn't know that.'

'Not sure Oppenheimer was interested though. He had worked with Birbach before, but doesn't know Hellquist.'

Wilde sensed Eva's interest. She was saying nothing, but she was listening. He rather thought that Frau Dr Haas might be *very good* at listening.

Albert Haas did not understand the people who were taking care of him. They came and they went. They brought him strange food and they spoke in a foreign tongue that he did not understand. He had learned a little English at school, but these people spoke so fast. Occasionally one of them, usually the woman, would break into her poor German to give him an order: *zu bett gehen* or *gehen sie schlafen* – go to bed, go to sleep.

He understood he must be in England. All he had been told was that if he was a good boy he would see his mother very soon. He had been told he should write her a letter, and so he had done so. It was very formal – addressed to *My Dear Mother*. Not *Mummy* or *Mum*. It said he was being well treated in his new country, that he was being fed well, that she must not worry.

But he *was* worried, because he had no idea when he would see her again. He had been so scared when the two men – one in uniform, one in a suit – and the pretty woman in a bright summer frock took him off the train. For an hour, he had been held in a room at the station, alone. The label around his neck was removed and he was told he would have new papers. His name would now be Friedrich Schulz. He must remember it and use it at all times if asked. It was the only way to get him to safety in England, he was told.

He obeyed, of course. He always obeyed adults. It was the way he had been brought up.

From the little station room, he had seen the train depart. Then another one had arrived and he was taken to it, accompanied by the pretty woman with the fair hair. She was German like him. 'You must call me *mummy*,' she had told him as they settled into their seats. 'Until your mother arrives in England. Do you understand, Friedrich?'

'Yes,' he had said, nodding uncertainly.

'Yes, Mummy,' she said, frowning. 'Try again.'

'Yes, Mummy. I understand.' It seemed wrong to call anyone else by that name, especially one as stern as this woman. And surely a boy had only one mummy?

At the end of the train journey, he had been taken to a hotel. Seagulls perched on the ledge outside the window, and in the distance he could see ships and the sea. There was no sign of the other children from the transport.

The following day, after breakfast, he and the woman had embarked on a ship. They were at sea for hours – he lost track of time. When, at last, they reached land, the woman had put him in a car with another woman, who was not German. He was told he must call her Mrs Jones. She spoke little on the journey. All she did was hand him a sandwich with some meat of a kind he had never tasted before. He was hungry so he ate it, but he did not like it.

And now here he was, still waiting. They were not unkind; they did not hit him. But nor were they warm towards him. Why was he not allowed out? All he could do was look out of the window.

Even though he was not big for his age, he was a brave and clever boy. Every night, he said a prayer that *Mutti* would come for him in the morning, and then he cried himself to sleep.

Lydia's call was put through very quickly. 'Mr Eaton?'

'Miss Morris! Where are you?'

'Zurich, Mr Eaton. I am coming back to England tomorrow. I need to give you some information. I'm not sure it can wait.'

'Are you in a hotel?'

'Yes.'

'Then I implore you, say nothing more. Whatever it is, it will have to wait until tomorrow. Are you coming by air?'

'I could go to the consulate in the morning, call you from there?'

'No, please don't do that. You must wait.'

'Swissair then, twelve noon departure. I'm not sure about the time of arrival.'

'I'll find out and meet you.'

'Would you do something for me?'

'Of course.'

'Call Tom, and tell him I'll be home tomorrow evening.'

CHAPTER 26

The morning was less bright. A cool wind had got up overnight, but in the porter's lodge, Scobie assured Wilde there would be no rain. 'My father's a ploughman, Professor, finest in the Fens in his day. No one reads the Cambridge weather like a Fenland farmboy. He says there won't be a drop of rain all week, which should at least see us through the May Balls.'

'Any word on Professor Dill, Scobie?'

'The doctor called on him this morning, but he didn't say anything. Oh, and sir, you might be interested to know that a coroner's inquest is to be opened this morning on Dr Birbach.'

'When and where, Scobie?'

'Eleven. Town hall. Open to the public.'

'Thanks.' Wilde carried on through the gateway into the New Court. On another day, he might have ambled slowly across the lawn and basked in its summer brilliance, but today he was in a hurry. Almost immediately, Scobie called him back.

'I'm sorry, sir, I nearly forgot. There was a call for you twenty minutes since. A Mr Philip Eaton. Wondered if you would oblige him by calling him back at your leisure. And he left a message – said Miss Morris was out of Germany and would be back in Cambridge as soon as possible. He said you'd know what he was talking about.'

'Thank you, Scobie. Thank you.' The day wasn't hot, but he was. His head was down as he hastened across the New Court into the Old Court, his black gown catching the breeze. Lydia's face came to mind, her tangled hair and bohemian clothes – an old darned shirt of her late father's perhaps or a painter's smock she had found in a shop in Cornwall last year. Her face. The face and mind he loved, the face of a poet and a lover, the very antithesis of glamour. And then the image vanished like smoke before his eyes and Clarissa appeared, beckoning.

When he reached his stairs, he noticed that the door to Birbach's room was wide open. Inside, Bobby was directing a couple of cleaning women who were wielding mops and brooms . . .

'This is a sad sight, Bobby.'

'The world moves on, Professor Wilde. These rooms have been used by many generations of great men and I am sure they will be used by many more.'

'Very philosophical.'

'Can I get you a cup of coffee, Professor? If you don't mind my saying so, you look in need of a pick-me-up.'

'Yes, coffee would be fine. And look, I'm being taken to Newmarket races this afternoon. I've never been before. Anything I should know?'

'Keep your wallet well concealed about your person, Professor. Keep your eyes peeled for pickpockets and don't play Find The Lady, sometimes known as the three-card trick. It's a fix – you can't win.'

'I'll bear that in mind. And what about a bet on the horses? I think you owe me a winner, Bobby.'

The gyp grinned, revealing his remaining front tooth. 'Well, Professor, if you're inclined to place a wager, I'd suggest Divine Tragedy in the three o'clock. Lightly raced two-year-old by Hyperion. If you can get a hundred to thirty, you'll be doing well.'

Torsten Hellquist wasn't at the inquest. Perhaps fear had, indeed, made him leave town. Nor was Fanny Winch there. Wilde surmised that she didn't want to have anything to do with the police, and who could blame her given the prostitution laws?

Birbach had no relatives in the country. His only acquaintances were from college or the Cavendish Laboratory and none of them except Wilde had turned up. The only other people there were the police surgeon, Rupert Weir, a reporter from the *Cambridge Daily News* and two police officers, one uniformed and one plain-clothes.

At the last moment, Geoff Lancing arrived and took a seat next to Wilde in the public gallery.

The coroner introduced the inquest by saying this was merely a preliminary hearing and that a full inquest would be held at a later date. He then called on the police to give a brief report on the discovery of the body and what was known. The plain-clothes officer gave his name as Detective Inspector John Tomlinson and described the position of the corpse in the river, and the condition in which it was found.

He said that it was immediately treated as a death in suspicious circumstances and the police surgeon, Dr Rupert Weir, had been called on to examine the body and, if necessary, to perform an autopsy. The result of that, as the coroner would hear, was that foul play was suspected and that it seemed likely that Dr Birbach had suffered poisoning by military-grade vesicant gas, though that was not the cause of death.

Police inquiries were proceeding. Friends and colleagues of the dead man were being questioned. The War Office in London, and Special Branch at Scotland Yard, had been contacted to discover the most likely source of the gas and to make their own inquiries. As yet there were few leads, but a Special Branch officer was expected in Cambridge imminently.

According to Dr Weir, who was called next, the gas used was almost certainly sulfur mustard, commonly known as mustard gas, for the blistering effect was typical. It was highly unlikely, though not impossible, that it had been self-administered or ingested accidentally, so it was right that the case be treated as murder.

Dr Weir said the victim had not ingested a large quantity of poison gas into the lungs. If it was forced on him, he would have resisted inhaling for as long as he could, perhaps a minute and a half. But then he had suffered massive heart failure – caused by shock and an existing heart condition – and death would have been sudden.

Tissue samples were being sent to the police laboratories at Scotland Yard for further investigation. The coroner listened carefully while taking notes, then adjourned the inquest *sine die*.

On the way out, Wilde and Lancing cornered the police inspector.

'Detective Inspector,' Wilde said. 'If we might trouble you for a minute? Dr Lancing here worked closely with Dr Birbach at the Cavendish Laboratory. I knew Birbach from college, where our rooms were on the same staircase. We would both very much like to talk with you.'

John Tomlinson was a stiff, bespectacled officer. He shook hands with the two academics. 'It is a most unfortunate occurrence, gentlemen,' he said. 'As I said to the coroner, we are desperately short of clues, not to mention manpower. It has been suggested that Dr Birbach's dreadful death was in some way connected to the work he was doing at the laboratory, but as yet that has been of no help to me. If either of you have any leads, I would very much like to hear them.'

'Who have you talked to?'

'The college master, and I have spoken on the phone to Professor Bragg.'

'Have you worked on Dr Birbach's last hours?' asked Wilde. 'You know, I suppose, that he attended a party at Hawksmere Old Hall just south-west of Cambridge, not far from Boldbourne? It is owned by an American couple, the Hardimans.'

'Yes, sir, I do know that. I'm sure the Special Branch officer will want to talk to Mr and Mrs Hardiman.'

'He attended the party with a woman named Fanny Winch. You will find her at No. 16 Swaffham Lane. Have you spoken with her?'

'All in good time, Professor Wilde. All in good time. Step by step.'

'I *have* spoken to her. She says that after he dropped her off he was picked up in a car by two men.'

'Then I will most certainly be asking my officers to interview the young lady.'

Wilde exchanged glances with Geoff Lancing. 'I suspect if you find that car and those men, you will have found the killers.'

'I'm not inclined to jump to conclusions, Professor Wilde. However, your point is taken.' The officer took out his notebook and scribbled the name and address of Mrs Winch. He also asked Wilde and Lancing for their own contact details, then thanked them again for their help.

Wilde watched him with despair. 'Far be it from me to tell you your job, Inspector Tomlinson, but has it occurred to you the political and security implications of this murder, given the work Dr Birbach was doing and the fact that the country is on a war footing?'

Tomlinson spoke as though addressing a slow child. 'Indeed, sir, which is why Special Branch and the War Office have been made aware of the death and its circumstances. In the meantime, I also have other important matters to attend to. Cambridge has suffered an IRA attack, one of many around the country. I should emphasise, perhaps, that we are all working under extreme pressure. Special Branch and the intelligence services lack resources, and so we must do what we can with the men available. I can promise you, however, that the killer or killers of Dr Birbach will be brought to court and will suffer the full and dread consequences of their abhorrent act. Good day to you both . . .'

They watched him turn and go. 'He's utterly lost, Geoff,' said Wilde as they, too, walked out. 'Doesn't know where to start. I rather suspect Inspector Tomlinson has never investigated a murder before. Paul Birbach was tortured and died – yet no one in authority seems to be asking the obvious questions.'

'It's a filthy can of worms, isn't it? Hopefully the Special Branch man will inspire more confidence.'

'If he ever arrives. God, though, I'd like to talk to Torsten Hellquist. He's the one who first suspected murder.'

'I'm beginning to get worried about him. He could at least have left a note to say he was going away, or made a phone call.'

Wilde grunted. He was becoming worried, too.

'Anyway, Tom, I've got to get back to the lab. I'm taking Eva – Frau Dr Haas – into the working areas. She wanted to see the high-tension laboratory.'

'Is that acceptable? I mean without clearance.'

'Why on earth not? I took *you* around, Tom.'

'Not quite the same thing, is it? Pretty clear I was in no position to glean secrets. What about Lindberg – are you taking him too?'

Lancing laughed. 'Oh, he's happy enough in the library. Trying to catch up with his reading after three years out of things. I'm afraid it's not going to happen. Whatever they did to him in that place, it's blunted his intellect. Dr Lindberg's days of cutting-edge physics are over.'

'Geoff—' Wilde paused. This was awkward. 'Why *did* you take Eva to Old Hall? Wasn't it obvious that Hardiman would be vile to her?'

Lancing looked puzzled. 'I took her because Clarissa *asked* me to bring her.'

A boy of twelve or thirteen approached them. He was in his Scouts uniform with a gas mask fixed to his face, giving him the look of an undersea creature. From behind his back he produced two cap guns. He pointed them at Wilde and Lancing and pulled the triggers. There was a crack and the whiff of sulphur. His laugh was distorted by the mask. Then he pulled it up from his face and ran away whooping.

Wilde had to laugh, too. But he couldn't help wondering how long it would be before the boy was required to tote real pistols. Nor could he help wondering about Eva Haas and her visit to Old Hall. There was something he didn't quite understand. It was almost as if Milt Hardiman already knew Frau Haas. But that, surely, was impossible.

CHAPTER 27

Everyone who was anyone was at the races. The women wore light summer frocks and sunhats. The men wore boaters and blazers, panamas and linen suits. They carried wallets bulging with cash and wore binoculars around their necks: no gas masks here. In the Members' Enclosure, they drank Champagne and fine Cognac and argued endlessly about the prospects of their horses.

It was a day for spotting the great and the good. Was that the Aga Khan cheering on his horse? Good Lord, isn't that Clarissa Lancing stepping from a powder-blue car and waving to the crowds? And who's the lucky man at her side?

At Newmarket races, a mere dozen miles east of Cambridge, men and women of noble birth mixed with brash new money and the lowest in the land – the tricksters, the unemployed, the drunks and the ex-cons. The only people missing were those who sniffed at the races and at gambling: the prim, disapproving middle classes.

Wilde immediately felt at home. He, Clarissa and the Hardimans (along with Theo, who smirked knowingly at Wilde) had enjoyed a fine lunch of lobster thermidor with a couple of bottles of vintage Krug in the members' dining room. Every so often a trainer or owner or course steward turned up to pay their respects. Milt Hardiman was well known in this fraternity. Was it the man they admired or his money?

The crowd was in high spirits, for this was quality racing, perhaps some of the last of its kind for years to come. Wagers were large and optimistic: eat, drink and be merry, for tomorrow we go to war. This might not have been Tom Wilde's usual habitat, but the spectacle of the shiny horses and the mad hubbub of the racegoers caught his imagination.

After lunch, they stayed at their table, sipping coffee and brandy and smoking Havana cigars. Hardiman and Clarissa were arguing. 'Goddamn it, Clary, it's always want, want, want with you. You want the whole world! Well, I've got news for you, sister, I've already given you the whole damn world.'

'Well, up yours, too, Milt.'

Peggy was studiously ignoring them. Wilde had no idea what they were talking about, but he suspected it was something to do with a movie deal. For a moment, he thought Hardiman might raise his hand to strike her. What was Clarissa to him? His pet movie star. Not just an investment, surely. Were they lovers, present or past? Whatever it was, Peggy Hardiman seemed entirely indifferent.

Wilde was sitting with Peggy to his right and Clarissa on the left. Peggy, tall and thin, leant over in his direction like some kind of languid stick insect. 'Aren't you going to have a wager, Professor Wilde?'

He responded to her silent plea for a change of subject. 'There's a horse in the next race I might go for.'

Clarissa turned her head sharply away from Hardiman and glared at Wilde. 'What's that?'

'I said I might have a bet in this race.'

Wilde had merely watched the first two races, but then he looked at the card for the third and spotted the horse Bobby had mentioned, Divine Tragedy. He placed his finger on the page.

'That's the one,' he said.

'Not a chance, darling,' Clarissa said. 'The favourite's odds-on and everyone says it's a cert. Anyway, you've gone for a Hyperion colt, so it will want further.' She turned to Hardiman. 'Isn't that so, Milt?'

Hardiman was only half-listening. He had turned away and was looking out the window, gazing deep into the crowd. 'What's that, Clarissa?'

'I said Divine Tragedy will want further than six furlongs.'

'You'd think so. But a Hyperion colt won the Gimcrack over six.'

Peggy patted his hand. 'Don't listen to these two know-it-alls, Professor Wilde. You put your money down on whichever horse you fancy.'

Clarissa nuzzled closer to Wilde. 'I still say you'll lose, Tom. Let's have a little side bet on it. Your horse wins, I do anything you want. *Anything.*' She lowered her voice. 'All the things you wouldn't let me do last night . . . The favourite wins and you're my slave for the day – and then you'll find out what *I* want.' Her hand was on his thigh beneath the white linen tablecloth, stroking. He needed to move away. He couldn't help his arousal;

that was beyond his control. And yet her scent no longer intoxicated him. Instead, it unnerved him. Every caress reminded him that Lydia was due home.

'And what would that entail, being your slave?'

'Do you really want me to spell it out?'

Wilde disengaged her hand from his thigh. 'My gyp says Divine Tragedy's the one, and I trust him.' He rose from the table. 'I'm going to put a fiver on the animal.'

'Go ahead and waste your money.' She drew on a black Sobranie in a long white holder, then blew a thin trail of smoke towards his eyes. 'What about our bet – is it on?'

She was angry, but he wasn't sure why. Was it something Hardiman had said?

He shrugged. 'How can I refuse?' he said, and immediately regretted it.

As he wandered down to the rails bookmakers Wilde wondered why in God's name he had agreed to be here with these people, with this woman. Jim Vanderberg had a lot to answer for. More bewildering was why these people wanted him along. He could not quite believe that he had the presence or charisma to entice a woman like Clarissa Lancing, a film star who had Hollywood at her feet, a woman who had been linked with Gary Cooper and Clark Gable, among others. Was she just playing games with the little people – or was there something going on?

The bookies were offering three-to-one against Divine Tragedy, so he took the odds, then watched the horses parading. Never having been to the races before, he was beguiled by the brilliance of the jockeys' silks, the glistening majesty of the thoroughbreds and the strange magic of the bookies' men with their secret tic-tac language of hand signals. A man could easily get drawn into this, he thought.

The race was a straight dash to the winning line. Wilde tried to listen to the tannoy, but the race commentary was as incomprehensible as a railway-station speaker, and he had no idea what was happening until they came into the last hundred yards and flashed past the winning post. Divine Tragedy, yellow silks shimmering in the sun, was well ahead of the rest. He had won.

Wilde laughed out loud. He wandered back to the bookie, who counted out four white five-pound notes. 'There you are, sir, five pounds at carpet, threes, plus your stake. My nippers won't eat tonight.'

Wilde very much doubted the children would starve. The bookie was puffing on a fat cigar, his enormous stomach protruding behind a loud scarlet waistcoat with a gold fob chain hanging between pockets. Wilde grinned, thanked the man, then strode off to the winner's enclosure to watch the hero of the hour being paraded. A stable handler who looked no bigger than a ten-year-old but had the wrinkles of a fifty-year-old was throwing buckets of water over the horse's steaming flanks as it performed a victory turn around the ring.

As Wilde lingered, pleased to be away from the tense atmosphere around the Hardimans' table, he was surprised to spot Henty O'Gara, standing on the far side of the winners' enclosure.

But of course he'd be there. Henty had said he had horses. That was why he was over from Ireland. He had said, too, that he would be staying in Newmarket. Wilde took a step round the picket fence and was just about to hail his cousin, when he stopped, and dropped his hand.

O'Gara wasn't alone now. He had approached Milt Hardiman and they were talking.

Wilde slid back and away, out of their line of sight. He shrank back into the shadow of the doorway to the jockeys' weighing room. He stood, unseen he hoped, and watched.

What on earth was the connection between Hardiman and O'Gara? But then, he told himself, the racing world was small, like a village. Everyone would know each other. Hardiman was a keen racegoer, had horses of his own in training, though none here today. But even though Wilde could see this was logical, it didn't seem quite enough.

Wilde was too far away to hear a word the two men said, but he could tell that Hardiman was irritated. O'Gara was spreading his hands as though explaining something unpalatable. And then Hardiman's mouth opened and clenched into the familiar syllables of a two-word expletive, his thin moustache seeming to slither over his mouth. He ran his fingers through his hair, then turned and stalked away.

As Wilde watched, O'Gara didn't move for a few moments, then he too began to walk away, heading in his direction. Stepping out from the doorway, Wilde set off with his head down. At the last moment, he looked up and his eyes widened as though he had only just seen O'Gara.

'Henty?'

O'Gara jerked to a halt. 'Jesus, what are you doing here?'

'Well, that's a fine welcome! Watching the horse racing. Same as you, I imagine. Have you got horses running?'

'We've got a couple.'

'We?'

'Me and my partners in Ireland. To tell the truth, I don't own them. I'm just their agent . . .'

'Let's go for that drink, Henty. We didn't get it before.'

'Aah . . . aah, I don't know, Tom. I'm a little busy at the moment.'

'Are you with someone?'

'No, but I need to be there for the trainers, you know. Our horses are lodged in Newmarket yards, so I'm the liaison man.'

Wilde clapped a hand on his cousin's shoulder. 'Come along. One drink. You could join my party if you like.' He cupped his hand to O'Gara's ear. 'Come and meet a famous Hollywood actress.'

O'Gara sighed in resignation. 'No, but I'll have a pint with you at the bar. Let's go through there.' He nodded towards the cheaper silver ring where ordinary racegoers crowded the stands. 'Too many fucking county snobs, dukes and earls around this neck of the woods.'

CHAPTER 28

The barroom was long and low and reeked of beer and smoke. The place was packed with racing men. All men. No women here. It took five minutes to order drinks and when they arrived, the tankards were slapped down carelessly, beer slopping all over the bar. It wasn't worth complaining. Wilde paid, then slid O'Gara's drink sideways across the soaking bar top. 'There you go, cousin.'

O'Gara grunted.

Wilde watched him expectantly. O'Gara seemed to have something on his mind; he seemed to be weighing up the pros and cons of talking. Something told Wilde this wasn't about horses.

'What is it, Henty?'

'Nothing.'

'You're preoccupied.'

'Ah, hell, can I ask you a question, Tom?'

'Of course. Fire away.'

'Whose side are you on?'

The question should have taken him by surprise, but the truth was, it didn't. Something was troubling Henty O'Gara. 'How do you mean exactly?' Wilde spoke calmly.

'I mean, do you have politics? All this European stuff – Nazis, commies, fascists, Trots and anarchists – where do you stand? Is it all bullshit or am I missing something? Tyranny or nothing, is that the way it's to be?'

This was a strange turn of conversation for the races. Wilde might have laughed, but he could tell that his cousin was struggling, looking for answers.

'Well, you know, I'm an American and I have a soft spot for democracy. Very old-fashioned and dull.'

'But you're Irish, too, Tom. Your mother's Irish. You can't escape that so easily.'

'No, I can't – and nor do I wish to. I'm very happy with my Irish blood. Very proud of it. But how do you get onto Ireland from talking about the far left and the far right? There's no great dictator in Ireland, Henty.'

A racegoer barged into O'Gara's back. He turned on him as though bitten by a snake, fist raised. 'Watch yourself, mister.'

The clumsy Englishman puffed out his chest. 'Fucking Mick.'

Even as a boy, O'Gara had not been one to shy away from a fist fight. Wilde put his arms between them. 'It was an accident, Henty. Let's not go down this road.' He tried smiling at the interloper. 'There's going to be no fighting, OK?'

The Englishman spat on the floor, then shouldered past Wilde and disappeared into the crowd.

'Thank you, Tom. I would have dusted the feller and ended up in clink on an assault charge.'

'Back to what you were saying, Henty . . .'

'Well, what I really want to talk about isn't just Europe, you see. I'm thinking of Ireland. Others have interests in the old country, not always benign.'

'Who exactly are we talking about?'

'You know what I'm on about, Tom. The bombs, the S-plan – the sabotage plan. Seamus O'Donovan and his bombing campaign.'

Wilde was assessing the situation fast. Henty O'Gara from the far west of Ireland turns up in Cambridge. An IRA bomb goes off in Cambridge. The dimmest constable on the beat would see a possible link, even if it turned out to be a false trail. 'Is this something you're involved in, Henty?'

O'Gara didn't answer directly. 'What about Germany, Tom? Do you think Hitler might help the Irish win the Six Counties back from Britain? You know, there are Irishmen who believe he would – and some who would happily make a pact with the Nazis if it meant kicking the British out of Ireland.'

'I imagine there are. But if you want my honest opinion, I'd say doing a deal with Hitler would be a bit like asking Satan into your house to chase out an old toothless dog. You might get rid of the dog, but you'll be left with something far worse, with sharper teeth and razor claws. There are no spoon handles long enough to sup safely with the Nazi devil.'

O'Gara took a long, deep draft of his beer, and then spat some of it back. 'Jesus, what is this stuff? How do the English drink it?'

'Do you want a whisky?'

'No, not now. Ah, dear God, Tom, I'm in so deep I don't know where to turn. I'm not made for this sort of thing. You know me – I like an honest fight the same as the next man. But deceit and all that, Jesus – it's another world. And now I don't have friends on any side. Can I trust you, Tom?'

'That depends.'

On what you're dealing with, Henty. On who you've become.

O'Gara stared into the unappetising beer, the glass still gripped in his right hand. The echoing din of the long barroom was almost drowned out by the brooding silence.

'I'd like to think so,' Wilde continued. 'I'd like to think you can trust me. But I don't really know what you're talking about. Is this something to do with Milt Hardiman? I saw you with him.'

O'Gara hesitated for a beat. Wilde remembered that look, more than a quarter of a century gone. They'd been out scrambling along the jagged edge of sea rocks on the cliffs near Doolin when O'Gara – who was ahead – got into trouble. He had panicked, but managed to haul himself up from the waves. Fortune had favoured him then, but for all his bluster, for all his readiness for a fist fight, Wilde knew he had never been the most confident of men. Nothing had changed, it seemed.

It was the name Hardiman that did it. The Irishman's hand tightened on the pint glass and crushed it. Glass fell in shards at his feet. He looked at his hand. Two or three slivers were embedded in his flesh. Blood and beer dripped to the floor. He plucked the pieces of glass out one by one. Then he took out a handkerchief and clutched it in his palm to staunch the bleeding.

'There must be some sort of first aid here for the jockeys. Shall we go there, Henty?'

'No, I'm all right. It's only a bit of blood. What do you know of Hardiman, Tom?'

'I'm here with his party. I know a bit about him. What do *you* know about him Henty? What are *your* dealings?'

O'Gara shook his head grimly.

'Should I be reporting you to the police? Does Thompson's Lane mean anything to you?'

O'Gara was clearly in some terrible torment.

'Henty? Talk to me. You said you wanted to trust me.'

'I do, I do.' O'Gara looked around the great teeming barroom. 'I need the help of a good man.'

Wilde gripped his arm. Hard. 'Do you want to get out of here, Henty? Find a quiet corner to talk?'

'No. This is better. No one'll hear us above this din.'

'Then if you've got something to say, say it now.'

'OK, feller, OK. There are no horses. Does that suit you? The horses were all bullshit, a cover story.'

'Thompson's Lane? The power station?'

O'Gara snorted. 'Maybe I need that whisky after all.'

'You can talk to me, Henty. I don't give a damn about the power station wall, and I'm not going to turn you in, because you'll get caught soon enough anyway. But Hardiman . . . I would like very much to know about your dealings with Milton Hardiman. What's your interest, Henty? Or rather, what's *his* interest?'

O'Gara tried to wrench his arm free, but Wilde's grip was tight and he wouldn't let go.

'That hurts, Tom. You're not the squirt any more, are you?'

Wilde released his cousin's arm. 'Henty?' Their voice were low. There was a crush of drinkers, but they wouldn't hear a word of this above their own din.

With his uninjured hand, O'Gara pulled out a cigarette and found his matches. Wilde took them from him and struck a light.

'It might as well come out,' said O'Gara, breathing deeply on the smoke. 'Either way, I'm a dead man. I've been working for this lot, that's what.'

'This lot?'

'The British. MI5. Working against my own people because I couldn't stomach Seamus O'Donovan's deals with the Nazis. And you know what? I've found stuff – but the British have hung me out to dry. I've lost my contact, so who do I talk to? Tell me that, Tom. I've discovered important stuff and I've no one to tell. Just a telephone number that rings and rings and rings . . .'

Four days earlier, when Captain Dorian Hyde arrived at the farmhouse along the coast from the town of Galway, Connell had not been alone. Now Hyde's body lay deep in the sea, ten miles west of the Aran Islands, wrapped in chains and weighted with rocks.

He shouldn't have been in Ireland, because he was needed in England, in London, acting as sole contact for MI5's most valuable property, an IRA man named Henty O'Gara who had turned on his comrades because, he said, they were dealing with the *Abwehr*, Germany's military intelligence. The story was that he hated the British, but he hated the Nazis more.

There was a problem, though: Captain Hyde of the British secret service – Military Intelligence, section Five – had not trusted O'Gara, and the feeling was mutual. O'Gara resented the Englishman's public school accent and his disregard for Ireland. Hyde simply saw all Irishmen and Irishwomen as the enemy because he was Anglo-Irish gentry, from a family whose once fine Kildare estate had been burned to the ground during the Irish War of Independence.

But O'Gara and Hyde were important to each other, and they had had to put aside their innate antipathy. They had a common enemy – the hardliners within the IRA who were willing to deal with Hitler.

With Britain preparing for a full-scale European war, it could not afford the disruption caused by the IRA's bombing campaign, with gelignite and potassium chlorate and Mills bombs exploding every day. Power stations, electricity pylons, water supplies, underground stations, shops, petrol stations, even Buckingham Palace were on the target list. At times, there were five attacks a day. And Germany's *Abwehr* was backing the IRA campaign with weapons.

O'Gara had offered to go to England and help break the bombing campaign. He said he had enough information to find the IRA's chief of staff on the mainland, the Scavenger.

Captain Hyde ran Henty O'Gara alone, his identity carefully guarded, for even MI5 had leaks. Yet still Hyde feared his own judgment; trust was a luxury he couldn't afford.

'Never turn your back on an Irishman,' his father had once told him, long before the bastards burnt their fine house down, 'or you'll have a knife in it.'

It had even occurred to Hyde that O'Gara might be the Scavenger himself. He had to check and double-check. Couldn't afford not to.

And so with O'Gara already in England, Captain Dorian Hyde ventured to County Galway in search of a defining clue to the true nature of the elusive Henty O'Gara. One man was sure to know the truth – a man named Connell, a senior IRA figure on the west coast.

Hyde had recruited Connell in London five years earlier when he was up on a charge of armed robbery. 'Work for me. Go home to Ireland and provide me with information on the IRA and we'll let the charge lie.' Connell had accepted the offer with apparent gratitude and relief. Hyde had sent him on his way with a warning: 'Do the dirty on me, Connell, and I'll feed you to the wolves.'

In the event, it was Connell who was the wolf. He took his freedom courtesy of MI5; he even took their money. Sometimes he even fed them half-truths and disinformation. But he was an IRA volunteer through and through.

Hyde's journey to Galway was supposed to be an in-out operation. No more than two days. Speak to no one but Connell. Hand him some money. Use him to uncover the true heart and nature of Henty O'Gara, then back to his phone in England.

Connell played with Captain Hyde like a cat with a mouse. He lured him to a remote farmhouse, not far from the sea, where his friends were waiting. They turned the MI5 officer into meat for the fishes. They did things to his body with knives and sticks that a medieval torturer would have been ashamed to admit to.

When he was all but gone and there was no more information to be had, they shot him in the head, wrapped him in chains and took him out in a boat to drop him in the sea. His body would never be found and no one save his killers would ever know his fate.

And in London, the telephone in the small service flat retained for his exclusive use – the number he had given to Henty O'Gara – continued to ring and ring and ring. And no one answered.

'What I need, Tom, is another contact. Something must have happened to my man Hyde.'

'I don't know anyone in MI5, Henty. But I know someone who will help. Foreign intelligence service.'

'Do you trust him?'

Did he trust Philip Eaton? In this case, yes. The truth was, he *needed* Eaton. O'Gara was linking the IRA to the Nazis and there was a connection to Milt Hardiman. Wilde nodded. 'Yes,' he said. 'I'll talk to him.'

'Then tell him I'm about to find the Scavenger,' O'Gara said. 'See if that means anything to him.'

'Scavenger? What or who is the "Scavenger"?'

'The Scavenger is the IRA's chief in England, director of the bombing campaign.'

'Do you mean Milt Hardiman?'

O'Gara looked doubtful, then shook his head and dismissed the idea with a wave of his hand. 'I suppose it's possible,' he said. 'But he's not Irish, is he?'

'Then what are you talking about? What connection does Hardiman have to all this?'

O'Gara hesitated again. He had a nervy glint in his eye.

'If you want my help, Henty, you have to put some faith in me.'

'OK, Tom. I was following a feller, you see. Someone I knew would lead me to the Scavenger. And I think he will. Maybe he already has – I'll know this evening. This morning the feller brought me a message at my hotel saying I'd be met tonight. I wanted to know what I would be meeting, so I tailed the feller. He had a bike; I have a car. So I followed him – and the fucker rode here.'

'And Hardiman?'

O'Gara laughed. 'I didn't know who he was. I'd never seen him before, but I saw my feller talking to him briefly. I wanted to know the big guy's name, so when the feller left, I stayed. And for what I did next you can call me a fool if you like, but I went up to the man and told him I had a message for him. Hand it over, he says. Could you confirm your name, sir? says I. Hardiman, he says, Milton Hardiman. Oh, Jesus, says I, I've got the wrong man. I was looking for Mr Henry Redmond. That's when he tells me to go fuck my mother's dog.'

'So you're suggesting Hardiman is somehow linked to the IRA.'

O'Gara shrugged. 'I'm not sure what to make of him, Tom. In fact I'm not sure of anything anymore. Jesus, I should never have told you all this. Probably put you in danger, too. But I was desperate . . .'

Wilde gripped his cousin's uninjured hand between both his. 'I'll do what I can, Henty. My contact will know what to do. You'll come around later?'

O'Gara nodded slowly. 'And I'll have more, I'm sure of it. You can tell your secret service friend he'll have it chapter and verse tonight.'

They parted in the bar. Wilde rejoined the Hardimans and Clarissa in the members' dining hall just before the fourth race.

'I thought you'd run away and deserted me, Professor Wilde,' Clarissa said.

'My first time at the races. I just wanted to wander. See the horses in the stables, mix with the people. Soak up the colour.'

'Well done you with your winner. I am now your slave girl. What do you have in mind? Something very improper, I trust.'

'Something outrageous.'

'Will you come to Old Hall this evening?'

'I don't think I can.'

'Hey, sure he's coming,' Hardiman said. 'We have a men's singles to play.'

'It will have to wait,' Wilde said. 'I have things to do.' *Call Philip Eaton. Wait for Henty O'Gara to make contact. Welcome Lydia home.*

But he did want to go to Old Hall. There was something there. He felt it. There was the house itself, inadequately explored. Things unspoken and unseen, haunting him. Secrets that his good friend Jim Vanderberg wanted. There were those outbuildings, too – best part of half a mile away from the main house. He was missing something, wasn't he?

Clarissa's hand beneath the table was at his trouser fly. Wilde put his hand over hers to stop it.

She feigned hurt. 'They're only buttons, Mr Wilde. It's what slave girls do for their masters.'

'And this is a very public place, Miss Lancing.'

Hardiman wasn't watching, nor was his wife. But their son Theo was.

CHAPTER 29

When Wilde arrived home, he called Philip Eaton's London number and left a message with his man Terence Carstairs. 'Tell him I need to speak to him soonest, if you would, Carstairs.'

'Of course, sir.'

'Do you know if Miss Lydia Morris has arrived?'

'All is as you might expect.'

Wilde took the reply as a Yes. He badly wanted to see Lydia, but he was also riddled with guilt. The fact that nothing untoward had happened in Clarissa's bedroom did not do much to lessen his sense of shame. The woman had been naked and he had been in her room. It was his bloody fault for allowing himself to be compromised.

Seconds after Wilde put the phone down, it rang.

'Hello?'

'Professor Wilde?' Not Eaton, but a growling voice of indeterminate provenance.

'Yes, who's that?'

'Detective Chief Inspector Northgate, Special Branch. I've been trying to contact you for a couple of hours.'

'Ah, I take it you've arrived to investigate the murder of Dr Birbach.' *You could have been here a great deal earlier*, Wilde thought.

'Indeed, sir. And I would very much like to talk with you.'

'Of course.'

'Could we agree to meet in the morning, perhaps? Say nine o'clock?'

'We could talk now if you want. Are you at St Andrew's Street? I could ride over. Or come here if you like.'

'Tomorrow at the station would be more convenient. I have several people to talk to this evening.'

'Well, I'm here if you change your mind. And make sure you interview Mrs Winch. She's among the last people to see Dr Birbach alive. She told me she saw him getting into a black car with two men.'

'Yes, sir, I've already interviewed her – and that's exactly what she told me. I now have descriptions of the men and our constables have been furnished with the details. We will find the car.'

At last something was happening. 'Nine it is then.'

'Thank you, sir.'

Dr Lindberg was sitting alone in the sitting room, listening to the wireless. He rose from his armchair and bowed formally. Wilde urged him to sit back down.

'Have you had a good day?' he asked.

'Indeed, thank you. But your phone has been ringing. I did not wish to answer it, so I let it ring.'

'That's all right.'

'Good, good. Well, as to the Cavendish, I have done much reading in the laboratory library. So many papers, in both German and English! It is not easy to catch up.'

'Is Frau Dr Haas not here?'

'She remained with Dr Lancing.' Lindberg smiled uncertainly. 'I think perhaps I am a little envious of her. He trusts her more than me, I think.'

Wilde nodded and excused himself. In the kitchen, he discovered that Doris had left a casserole dish with instructions in capital letters on how to heat it up: Lancashire Hotpot – mutton and potatoes. He lifted the lid. It looked and smelt good and reminded him of school lunches. Better than lobster bloody thermidor any day.

He thought back to the drive home from Newmarket with Clarissa. It had not been easy. She hunched away from him, deep into the corner of her seat, her gaze fixed firmly out of the window. In a child, he would have called it a sulk; in a movie actress, he supposed it was par for the course.

'What were you and Milt fighting about?' he asked.

'Oh that. It was nothing.'

'To an outsider, you don't seem to have much in common with the Hardimans,' he ventured.

'And what do you know about it, Professor Wilde?'

'Just what my eyes tell me.'

'Perhaps you need a pair of spectacles.'

And that had been the sum of their conversation until they reached the eastern outskirts of Cambridge. Then, 'What do you think of me, Wilde?' she had asked quietly, her face still fixed on the window and the landscape outside.

At first he thought he had misheard. 'What do I think of you?'

'Do you like me?'

A hard question. 'I think you are very demanding.'

'And do you think I've slept with every director in Hollywood?'

'I've no idea, but we've all heard of the casting couch, I suppose.'

'You mean where young women offer their bodies to men in exchange for roles in movies.'

'I suppose so, yes.'

Her head and shoulders shook. For a moment he thought she was crying. But surely Clarissa Lancing didn't weep unless the script called for it. He put out a hand to her and then pulled it back.

'That's not the way it is. They rape you, Mr Wilde. And then they pass you on. That's the way it is.' Her voice was deep and bitter.

She had said no more, not even responding to his 'Thanks for the outing – hope you have a good evening' as he climbed from the car.

Now he looked at his watch. It was seven thirty. He guessed Lindberg must be hungry. If Eva Haas arrived in time to eat, all well and good. If not, there would be leftovers. He still had no idea when Lydia would arrive.

Lindberg was amenable to the idea. 'You know, Professor Wilde, I do indeed have an appetite. In the KZ it was merely hunger. A constant gnawing at the stomach. But now, at last, I am regaining my healthy appetite. English food is not so bad.'

Twenty minutes later, they sat down together at the kitchen table. The food was good and Wilde opened a couple of bottles of beer, which also pleased Lindberg. They clinked glasses.

'Do you want to talk about it, Herr Dr Lindberg, your time in the KZ?'

'No, sir, I want to forget about it. But it is very hard, especially at night when I lie in a comfortable bed. In the Dachau camp, I fell instantly asleep through physical exhaustion, even though the beds were nothing but a thin horsehair mattress on hard planks of wood. Since I have been in England, I have lain awake every night on soft feather mattresses, thinking. Thinking too much about the futility of life and the dark heart of humanity. Last night I was still awake when the sun rose and the birdsong began outside my window.'

'I am still puzzled as to how you escaped Dachau.'

Lindberg shook his head. 'I feel the same, Professor. I never expected to get out of that place.'

'But how did they manage it? I have heard of men being freed when they secure a sponsoring country, but in your case I understood they had barred every request for you to leave Germany. Did they have a change of heart?'

'No, I am certain not. Baumgarten told them I was to be taken to another camp nearer Berlin. But it is a mystery to me how the Dachau commandant was so easily deceived.'

'This Baumgarten . . .'

'He pretended to be an SS officer. He also supplied us with false papers and explained in great detail how we were to pose as hikers and find our way through an alpine smugglers' pass. I must be thankful to him, but I did not trust his motives. That sounds extremely ungrateful of me . . .' Lindberg trailed off uncertainly.

'But it turned out OK.'

'Perhaps. Perhaps not. In truth, I do not know what will happen now.' He had already cleared his plate of every scrap of food. Now he downed the last drop of beer. 'This is very strange beer. Not like the beers I had when last I was in England.'

'It's called light ale.'

'Not that I am complaining about the beer, you understand. I don't want you or the people at the Cavendish to think me ungrateful. You are giving me shelter and Herr Dr Lancing is giving me some space to study. My dearest wish would be to find some post at the Cavendish. Is that asking too much?'

It was plain that Lancing hadn't broken the bad news. 'You know, Herr Doktor, I fear that's extremely unlikely. As I understand it, many refugee scientists have inquired after places at the lab, but only a tiny number have been accepted. Mr Eaton would certainly like you to remain in England, but from what Geoff Lancing has told me, you might have more luck at one of the American or French laboratories.'

'Lancing thinks I am not up to it. I see that.'

'I believe it's a matter of space more than anything.'

'And my war work with gases?'

Wilde said nothing.

Lindberg waved his hand in dismissal. 'Ach, the English used gases, too, and the French. I was in the Imperial German Army when I was deputed to the work. They told us the French were firing gas shells and we had to respond. They told us our work would shorten the war and save many German lives. Of course we knew it was against the Hague Convention, but what were we supposed to do? A man could not disobey orders.'

Lancing had suggested Lindberg had *volunteered* for the work, but Wilde did not want to get into an argument. 'These are not matters for me,' he said shortly.

'I may not be the man I was, Professor, but I fully understand such things can be held against a man.' He rose from the table, and gave a brief bow of the head. 'And now if you will excuse me, I think I will go to bed and read. I am not senile yet.'

'I hope that has not been implied. You are still a young man, Professor. You have plenty of years of important work ahead of you.'

'Thank you for your kind words. But you are wrong. Forty is not young in physics. In history, perhaps, but most physicists are past their prime at my age. Good night, Professor Wilde. I shall see you in the morning.' He clicked his heels and shuffled away.

Wilde tried to read, but to no avail. He played some music on the gramophone, quietly, but he wasn't in the mood. He rolled up his sleeves and removed his tie, then paced the house with a glass of whisky in his hand. The evening was warm and heavy. He looked at the telephone, which remained silent. If Carstairs had got through to Philip Eaton, his message was being ignored.

What was he supposed to tell O'Gara when he turned up? *If* he turned up. And where was Eva Haas? He was responsible for her safekeeping here in Cambridge, had promised he would look after her and her uncle. How could he do that when he didn't know where she was?

At half eleven, the phone still hadn't rung and Eva Haas had still not arrived home. Wilde looked at the whisky bottle. It was half empty, but he was stone sober and his mind was racing.

He stepped out into the back garden and looked up at the sky. It was clear now and the night was starry. He breathed in the scents of flowers from the surrounding gardens: wisteria, fragrant roses, trying to calm himself.

This was intolerable, this waiting. He gripped his hands into fists and jabbed at the night. Shadow boxing. Passivity wasn't in his nature: attack, not defence, was his style, and had too often left him open to an uppercut. He knew all too well that the adage about attack being the best form of defence wasn't always true. But tonight, he needed to do something.

Back inside, he picked up his keys and walked around to the side where he kept the Rudge. He knew he ought to stay and wait for the phone call, wait for the arrival of Henty O'Gara, wait until Frau Haas arrived home, stay in the house while Lindberg slept. But he was too restless.

He wheeled the motorbike down the front path on to the road, and fired her up. He was still in his shirt-sleeves, top two buttons undone, no goggles to shield his eyes from the breeze. He eased open the throttle and felt the familiar surge beneath him as he cruised down to the main road, then opened up along Jesus Lane towards town.

Even at this time of night, Cambridge was alive. This was May Week – the week in June when the colleges staged their famous May Balls. Revellers wound their way around the narrow streets: drunken young men in dinner jackets, bow ties awry and a champagne bottle in their hand; women unsteady on their feet in satin and taffeta and glittering inherited jewellery. Those in their last term sang for joy at the end of the restrictions imposed on them by their colleges, or sang with tears in their eyes at the end of an era and the coming of uncertain adulthood.

He pulled to a halt outside St John's. The Great Gate loomed from the darkness of the night. The late porter tipped his hat to him.

'Is Dr Lancing in his rooms, do you know?'

'I'm not sure, sir. I wouldn't wish to disturb his sleep, but I could look to his window to see if he has a light on.'

'I'd be grateful if you would. If he's there and awake, could you say Tom Wilde would like a word?'

Two minutes later the porter returned. 'Yes, sir, Dr Lancing is in his rooms and asked if you would care to join him.'

Geoffrey Lancing was in striped pyjamas, buttoned up to his neck. Wilde was always astonished at how neat and homely he kept his rooms. You would know his passion in an instant, for it was all around you – framed photographs and watercolours of aeroplanes on almost every inch of wall. None of the physicists' paraphernalia that Birbach had kept in his college rooms.

'You're out late, Tom. I was just off to bed.'

'So I see.'

Lancing grimaced. 'Don't worry, I wouldn't have slept. I keep thinking about atomic bombs.'

'Will it really happen?'

He shrugged. 'It's unthinkable.'

'But possible?'

'Yes, possible. Come here.' He went to his desk and opened a note-book. He picked up a pencil and drew a circle. 'That's Cambridge,' he said. Then he scratched a skull and cross bones over the whole page. 'And that's what just one atomic bomb would do to the town. Most people would be killed outright. The survivors would suffer severe burns. Over half of England would be contaminated by radioactive dust for months to come. All from one bomb.'

Lancing began stabbing the page with his pencil. Wilde removed it from him. 'Come on, Geoff.' He put an arm around his shoulder. 'You should have gone to Old Hall and got tight.'

'You know, Tom, there are times when I find the company of my sister and the sinister Milton Hardiman a bit on the rich side. I prefer my own nightmares.'

Wilde smiled. He knew what he meant. After a day at the races with Milt Hardiman and the added complication of Clarissa Lancing's insistent advances, he had been glad to get away. 'Geoff, what in God's name does your sister have in common with Hardiman? How did they ever get together?'

'That's easy. He's backed all her movies with millions of dollars. It all began with her first effort, an awful B-movie called *The Dark Lady*. You won't have heard of it, because it sunk without trace. But Milt Hardiman kept the faith.'

'Nothing to do with politics?' Wilde tried to keep his tone light.

'I suppose they do both seem to admire the likes of Benito and Adolf, but I wouldn't worry too much about that. Clarissa gets her teeth into a cause, shakes it to death, then moves on.' Lancing threw Wilde a sharp look. 'And that will include you, I'm afraid. You could fill an ossuary with the skeletons of her cast-off lovers.'

Wilde shrugged. 'I wouldn't put myself in that category,' he said. 'Anyway,' he went on, 'I did come for a reason. Frau Haas hasn't come home and I don't know where she is. I'm responsible for her. I thought she might be with you.'

Lancing looked surprised. 'Really? How odd. I thought she'd have got home hours ago.'

'When did you last see her?'

'Well, after the Cavendish, we went for a drink at the Eagle at about six, but we weren't there more than half an hour or so. Hour at the most. She was in rather a bad way actually – frightfully jittery. Didn't want to socialise with the other chaps, just me. She's fearfully worried about her boy, you know. One moment she's been throwing herself into work to dull the pain, the next she's in the depths of despair.'

'How did you leave things with her?'

'I offered to take her home, but she said she wanted to be alone and walk a bit. You don't think she's . . . you know . . . done something foolish?'

The thought had crossed Wilde's mind that she might be suicidal, but he didn't want to alarm Lancing. 'No, Geoff, I don't believe we've any worries on that score. I would venture to suggest that she is made of quite stern stuff.'

'Where is she then?'

'Perhaps she went to the synagogue to pray for her boy's return, or seek comfort from old friends? One of them might have offered her supper.' Wilde was aware he didn't sound entirely convincing, but Lancing nodded.

'Yes, that'll be it.' He went to one of his carefully organised shelves and pulled out a bottle. 'I need to get tight. One for you?'

'Uh-uh.'

Lancing poured himself a large measure, looked at it critically, then topped it up.

'You like the girl, don't you, Geoff?'

'I suppose it's pretty obvious.'

Wilde smiled. 'I'm pleased for you. But look, are you sure you're being wise to allow her into your inner sanctum at the Cavendish? How much do we really know about her?'

If Lancing was affronted, he didn't show it. 'Well, I know she's a refugee from a murderous regime and I know she's a superb physicist. A genius in the making.'

'That's not the point. I'm talking about her loyalties.'

'I know you are, Tom. But I trust her.'

'Fair enough. But what of your colleagues? What do they think when they see her working with you? What does Professor Bragg think?'

'I've had no complaints to date.'

'I'm sorry to have to speak like this, but from what you yourself have told me, the Cavendish has secrets which need to be protected. Paul Birbach has died – probably murdered. Was that for his secrets? And where's Torsten Hellquist? Why hasn't he got word through to say he's safe?' Wilde stood up.

'You're right – he should have called. But I think you're wide of the mark with Dr Haas.'

Wilde made for the door. There was no more to be said. 'Then I'm sorry to have barged in on you, Geoff. She'll probably be home by now.'

'No doubt about it. And I'll see her in the morning because we're meeting for breakfast.' Lancing knocked back his whisky. 'You know, Tom, studying bloody Walsingham has given you a suspicious mind.

Sometimes you just have to give someone the benefit of the doubt. She's a good one. I'm sure of it.'

On his way home, he noticed a small black car parked badly outside Lydia's house. The driver's door was open and the headlights were on, but there was no one about. Had Lydia arrived? He went to the front door and rang the bell. There were no lights on and no one answered. It was pretty clear the car wasn't hers. Perhaps it had been stolen and abandoned. He went to his own house next door.

There was no sign that Eva had returned. Wilde listened outside Lindberg's door again and was reassured by his thunderous snoring. He checked his watch. 12.15 a.m.

Removing his shoes, he padded upstairs to her room, which was next to the bathroom. He put his ear to Eva's door. Utter silence. As quietly as he could, he twisted the door handle. The door opened without creaking and he put his head around. 'Frau Haas?' he said softly, little more than a whisper. No response. Peering into the darkness, he said it again, a little louder. Nothing. He switched on the light. The bed hadn't been slept in.

Eva's knapsack was on the floor. The buckles were broken and the straps were loose. Without moving it from its position on the floorboards beneath the window, he flipped the top and looked in. He didn't want to disturb anything if he could help it, but he slid his hand past a couple of books, a crumpled cardigan, some underwear and some pieces of jewellery. Was that really all she had in the world?

There was another pocket on the front of the knapsack. There were papers in there – in another name and containing German stamps. An envelope, too, with a letter. He slid it out carefully. The envelope was plain white: no name, no address, no postmark.

It had already been ripped open. Inside was a sheet of paper. A one-page letter written in German in a child's careful hand. It was from Albert. Wilde knew enough to understand the gist. It began *My Dear Mother* and said he was being well looked-after, that he was being fed enough though he didn't like the food very much, that he was missing her. The sort of things Wilde himself had written to his own mother from boarding school. Boys of eight or nine are stoical creatures. They do not tell their mothers how homesick they are. Would not mention their tears. The letter ended as formally as it had begun, *Your devoted son, Albert.*

It was painful to read. Wilde was about to fold it and slip it back into the envelope, when he spotted something written on the reverse side. In a different hand – a plain adult hand, forward sloping – were two sentences that froze his blood.

Jew, your son will die if you do not do exactly as we say. Go to Cambridge and wait to be contacted.

CHAPTER 30

Wilde read the note again. So the boy was, indeed, being held hostage – and his mother knew it. Why had Eva not confided in someone? Why had she not called the police? Had she let Lydia go off to Berlin blind? Perhaps he was being unfair; perhaps she didn't even know Lydia had gone to Germany. One thing was certain: her precipitous journey to Cambridge must have been the result of the demand in the letter.

There was something else, though. With no address or name on the envelope, surely that meant it must have been delivered to her by hand. By whom? Where? When? Had contact already been made in Cambridge? Might that explain her disappearances, or even her present whereabouts? The most important question, of course, was what was wanted of her. But you didn't have to be a scientific genius to work out that it had to be something to do with the Cavendish Laboratory.

Wilde's mind was racing, gathering disparate information into a narrative. The death of Dr Paul Birbach; his presence at the home of Milt Hardiman. Hardiman's link to Henty O'Gara and the IRA. The disappearance of Torsten Hellquist.

The disappearance of Torsten Hellquist.

Hellquist had said he was getting out of Cambridge fast; he'd been worried for his own safety. But perhaps he hadn't been fast enough. Hellquist and Birbach – two men who believed they held the secrets of the superbomb: the theorist who knew how a device could be made relatively simply and the technician who could make it happen. How dearly would Hitler and his generals like to get their hands on such knowledge?

And now here was another strand: Frau Dr Eva Haas under duress. A mother trying to protect her child.

Wilde placed the letter back in the envelope, slipped it back into the front pocket of the knapsack and buckled it up as he had found it. He took a last look around the room, switched off the light and closed the door.

Downstairs, he dialled Eaton's number again. Once again, Terence Carstairs answered.

'I'm sorry, sir. It's most unlike him, but he has not called me. And until he does so, I have no way of making contact.'

'When he does, you must stress the urgency. Tell him I have a grave situation here in Cambridge.'

Wilde put the phone down. The whisky bottle had lost its allure. He needed a clear head. He was just about to return to the sitting room, when he heard a noise, a scratching and a soft cry. It seemed to be coming from the back garden. Eva Haas?

Wilde, still in stockinged feet, strode through the house. Opening the back door, he stepped out and almost stumbled over the body of a man, collapsed on the pathway.

Bending down, Wilde recognised Henty O'Gara. He could smell blood and felt its slippery stickiness on his hands. A lot of blood, on his body and hands and face.

'Henty – in God's name what's happened to you?'

The man was gasping for breath, trying to say something. Wilde couldn't make it out.

'I'll call an ambulance.'

Wilde was getting to his feet, but O'Gara's fingers curled around his wrist. His grip was desperate, but weak.

'I've been shot, Tom.'

The words were faint but Wilde heard them. He leaned closer.

'Who shot you?'

'Scavenger,' O'Gara whispered.

'Henty, give me a name . . .'

O'Gara's breathing was coming slower and shallower, now. His grip on Wilde's wrist loosened and his hand fell away.

'Henty, I've got to get help. Hold on. I'll be back in less than a minute, I promise you.'

He ran indoors and got through to the police straight away and told them to send an ambulance. Throwing the phone down, he grabbed a torch and clean tea towels and ran back outside. O'Gara was still breathing but he was now unconscious.

'Hold on, Henty,' Wilde urged. '*Hold on!*'

O'Gara had been shot at least twice, once in his chest and once in his upper left arm, but there was so much blood, Wilde couldn't tell where else he might have been injured. He tried to staunch the blood flow from the chest wound, reasoning that would be the most life-threatening.

The ambulance arrived within four minutes of the call. Wilde heard it pulling up, and ran down the side of the house.

'Over here!' he shouted.

Two ambulance men hurried round the corner, stretcher at the ready.

They were too late. Wilde had lost O'Gara's pulse two minutes ago.

Lydia was wide awake. Eaton had given her two pills, which he said were amphetamines. They were in a comfortable sitting room in Chelsea. Just Eaton, Lydia and a man named Davis.

It was 2 a.m. They had been here four and a half hours.

'I'm sorry about this,' Eaton said before the questioning started. 'But it's important that we get every last detail out of you while it's still fresh in your mind. From what you have told us, there could be real danger to our country. Mr Davis is an expert at discovering anything that might help us – even things you think unimportant or that you might have forgotten.'

Lydia sank into an ancient sofa of fine but very scratched morocco. Davis, a balding, grey-bearded man of about fifty, sat opposite her on a Victorian dining chair, leaning forward so that he was peering down at her with his warm but intense grey eyes. His gaze was comforting rather than disconcerting. She noticed that the phone was off the hook.

He wanted a full rundown on her time in Germany, hour by hour, minute by minute. All the events, all the people – Manfred Bloch on the plane, Miss Forster. Frank Foley, JT McGinn, the murdered man who would only give his name as Fritz, the priest at St Hedwig's, the Gestapo officer Rudolf Kirsch, and then Bloch again.

For much of the time Davis listened, scratching notes constantly, but every now and then he would put in a question. 'Describe the man in the church again, if you would, Miss Morris.'

Eaton stood near the unlit hearth saying little, watching and listening. Occasionally, he brought tea and biscuits from the kitchen.

The longer the questioning continued, the more detailed it became. Gradually Davis honed it down to five specifics: the suggestion that Albert Haas had come to England after all; the allegation that Eva Haas was not all she seemed to be: 'What do you think was meant by that, Miss Morris?' he asked, head tilted to one side; the IRA's involvement with the *Abwehr*; the possible threat of a big attack in Britain; and the veiled warning about IG Farben and the work of men named Schrader and Ambros.

Much of his line of questioning went over Lydia's head. She had no idea who Schrader or Ambros might be or even if she had remembered their names correctly. Davis did not seem inclined to tell her.

Eventually, Eaton brought the session to a halt. 'I think we've had enough for one night, Davis,' he said, looking at the clock on the mantelpiece. 'Miss Morris needs her sleep.'

'Actually, I don't need sleep at all. Something stronger than tea, perhaps?'

'Not sure how alcohol mixes with amphetamines, but if you're willing to risk it I'm pretty sure there's some whisky about the place.'

'Is this your house, Mr Eaton?'

'Indeed it is.'

'It's gorgeous. You live in some style.'

'Thank you. I inherited the place from my father. Chelsea might not be the smartest part of town, but I have always loved it. My father was an artist, you see. His daily routine involved home, the studio at the back and the Arts Club in the next street.'

'And your mother?'

'She bolted with an army officer when I was twelve. I didn't see a great deal of her after that, what with Eton, then Cambridge. My holidays were all spent here or in the south of France where my father painted every summer.' He smiled and turned to Davis who was waiting by the door, briefcase in hand. 'Got what you need, Davis?'

'I'll have a full report sent over to Carstairs first thing, Mr Eaton.'

After he had gone, Eaton put the telephone back on the hook, then poured drinks.

'I don't suppose you have a cigarette?'

He flipped open his silver cigarette case and she took one. He struck a match and she drew in the smoke. Just this one, she thought.

Eaton downed his whisky in one. 'Look, I know it's damnably late, but I'm worried about Cambridge. Baumgarten mentioned a big attack in Britain – and I know there are thousands of potential targets – but I can't help thinking of the Cavendish. I want to drive up there tonight. The choice is yours. You can stay here and have the run of the place or come with me.'

'I'll come with you.'

'Good girl. Just one more thing. Are you absolutely certain that the man who first identified himself as Manfred Bloch, and subsequently as Baumgarten, was the same man you saw in the street outside Bloomsbury House with Eva Haas?'

'I thought so – but I'm so tired and confused, I'm no longer sure of anything, Mr Eaton.'

Eaton smiled. 'I understand. But you can be sure of one thing. You are alive and free only because they believed you were a Quaker. Without that they would not have hesitated to detain you or worse, simply for prying.'

Detective Inspector Tomlinson removed his spectacles, blinked in the harsh light and rubbed his tired eyes. There was no lampshade in his office, merely a bare hundred-watt bulb dangling from a wire in the centre of the ceiling.

Wilde had him down as a precise, unimaginative man. A man of honour, no doubt, who worked hard, but not someone who could cope with anything that did not fit the rule book. Special Branch officer Ted Northgate, the third person in this room, was another matter.

'So how exactly did you know the dead man?' Tomlinson asked Wilde for the third time.

'I've told you, Inspector Tomlinson.' Wilde was trying hard not to lose his patience. 'Henty O'Gara's father was my uncle. We're first cousins. As boys, we spent a holiday together in Galway, western Ireland. This week, we ran into each other again by chance and he told me he was here for Newmarket. As I said before, we hadn't seen each other for over a quarter of a century.'

The conversation was pointless. Wilde badly wanted to speak to Eaton.

'Did you know that we were looking for an Irish bomber, Professor Wilde?'

Wilde could not prevent his eyes drifting heavenwards. 'Yes, of course. The Thompson's Lane explosion.'

Northgate who had listened in silence for ten minutes stepped forward. 'Inspector Tomlinson,' he said, 'I think I'll take this over, if you don't mind. Perhaps you could make contact with your beat officers, see if any of them might have information on Mr O'Gara's movements. It is entirely possible his car was seen in the hours before his death.'

Tomlinson stiffened, painfully aware that he was being dismissed from his own domain. 'Yes, sir,' he said.

'Thank you.'

When Tomlinson had gone, Northgate ran a hand across his smooth, completely bald pate and smiled at Wilde. 'I'm sorry, Professor, it's late. Everyone's tired and Inspector Tomlinson has a lot on his plate.' His voice was soft and deep. Some might call it a growl.

'Of course.'

'Not often Cambridge has one murder, let alone two.'

Wilde was sitting on a straight-backed wooden chair in front of Tomlinson's desk. Northgate now took the chair facing him. 'Indeed not. But I'm afraid there's not a lot more I can tell you about Henty O'Gara. Our two sides of the family had drifted apart in recent years.'

'I understand. But you must see our interest in the connection between you and the deceased gentleman. He died in your garden, Professor Wilde, and you share Irish heritage.' The Special Branch man sighed, sucking air through his brown front teeth. 'And this at a time when certain Irishmen have been causing mayhem in mainland Britain.'

Wilde almost laughed. 'Well, I'm not a member of the IRA, Detective Chief Inspector. I'm afraid I can't vouch for my cousin.'

'As he was dying, you told my colleague he said something. The word Scavenger. Yes?'

'Yes.'

'Did the word mean anything to you?'

Wilde hesitated, then shook his head. 'No.'

'You don't seem sure, sir.'

'I'm sure.'

'Then let me enlighten you. We know that the Scavenger is the *nom de guerre* of the IRA's chief man in England, the one directing their bombing campaign. We would very much like to find him and put him away. It would be fair to say he is the most wanted man in Britain.'

Wilde said nothing. Waited.

'We are greatly stretched, Professor. Bombs are going off in every corner of the country, almost every day. Cinemas, bridges, hotels, airports, railways. I have not seen my children in three weeks. I would very much like to put the Scavenger away. For good.'

'Of course.'

'So any help you can give me . . .'

What could Wilde say? Not the whole truth, certainly. 'Henty knew where I lived. Perhaps I was the first person he thought of when he needed help. An act of desperation by a mortally wounded man.'

Northgate eyed him as though he knew he was holding something back. 'Your cousin's mention of the word Scavenger suggests one of two things to me. Either he was referring to himself – confessing that he was the Scavenger. Or – and I rather think this is more likely – he was shot by the Scavenger or one of his lieutenants. A falling-out among villains perhaps. The doctors tell me he was hit by four bullets. Chest, upper left arm, left hand and thigh. As yet, I have no calibre for the bullet nor a likely make of weapon, but we'll know soon enough. I am also extremely keen to discover where the shooting took place.'

'Of course.'

'No thoughts?'

'None.'

'And then there's the other thing, isn't there? The death of your colleague Dr Paul Birbach. You seem to be having rather bad luck with your friends and relations, Professor . . .'

Wilde went silent again. This really was stuff he needed to discuss with Philip Eaton. The whole question of Birbach, the Cavendish, the missing Torsten Hellquist, Eva Haas and her son, the White House mission and the people at Old Hall. These were not things to be spoken of here and now. Not without the say-so of Eaton at the very least.

'Professor?'

'I hear you, Detective Chief Inspector – and I am as bewildered as you are. No, that's not the half of it. I am devastated by the violent deaths of the two men I knew. Harsh things have been said about my cousin, but I believe he was a fine man.'

Northgate had thick shoulders and a head that disappeared into his neck, like a blunt artillery shell. He looked like a rugby forward, a man accustomed to intimidating less physical men. 'In the case of Dr Birbach, you have taken it upon yourself to do a little amateur investigating, I believe.'

Wilde was not intimidated. 'If you mean that I wasn't paid, yes, it was amateur. But something needed to be done. Very little effort seemed to be emanating from this place.' He looked around the musty, smoky office.

The Special Branch officer allowed a smile to cross his lips. 'Well, *I'm* here now.'

'Which is all to the good,' said Wilde.

Northgate ignored the unspoken criticism. 'Talking of Dr Birbach, there is the matter of yet another rather important scientist to be considered. You have under your roof a certain Dr Arnold Lindberg, a German national – and this at a time when relations between our countries are, to say the very least, fraught. Coincidence upon coincidence.'

'And you have him here in this police station, grilling him no doubt. Herr Dr Lindberg is a frail man who has endured Dachau concentration camp for the past three years.'

The big Special Branch man shrugged his heavy shoulders. 'Needs must, I'm afraid.'

'Do you know Philip Eaton?'

'Military Intelligence Six? I know of him.'

'I think he should be included in this conversation.'

'Where is he then?'

'With luck he's on his way to Cambridge. Let's resume this conversation when he arrives, shall we, Detective Chief Inspector? Perhaps you would provide a car home for Dr Lindberg and me.'

Back at home, he helped Lindberg up to his room. The German looked shattered.

'Goodnight,' Wilde said. 'I'm sorry you have been subjected to this.'

The police had made a cursory search of the house. One of the coppers had drunk the tumbler of whisky he had left on the kitchen table, but fortunately no one had discovered the loaded Walther that Eaton had left for him. It was hidden beneath some old rags in the cupboard beneath the kitchen sink.

It was 2.30 a.m. Outside the streets were unlit; it would be getting light in a couple of hours. Wilde couldn't sleep and nor could he let this lie. He put on his leather jacket, slipped the gun and torch into the pockets, donned his goggles, and went out into the silence of the road.

Sitting astride the Rudge Special, Wilde tickled her into life and growled off into the last of the night.

CHAPTER 31

He came to a halt outside Old Hall's perimeter wall, a hundred yards to the south of the estate's main gate, then hid the bike off the road in a copse. Crossing the road, he clambered over the wall, a construction of brick and flint, no more than four feet high.

The driveway up to the Hall was about six hundred yards long. To the south was the river and the boathouse. To the north-east was the lawn and tennis court. But he was heading to the back of the house, to the out-buildings he had spotted on his last visit.

The sky was dark grey with the faint pre-dawn glimmer of a June day, not far off midsummer. Enough light for him to find his way along the edge of the driveway. He moved steadily, neither fast nor slow, keeping to the grass behind the trees that lined the drive. From the house up ahead, there was a dim glow at three windows where the curtains hadn't been fully drawn. And then, on the forecourt, three hundred yards away, he saw movement and heard the distant hum of voices, followed by the slamming of car doors and the firing up of an engine. The yellow beam of a car's headlights lit up the scene.

Wilde watched from the cover of an oak as the car circled the fore-court, and then headed up the drive towards the main gateway. As it passed, he thought he could make out two passengers in the rear seat. One of them small. Was that Eva Haas? He couldn't be sure, couldn't make out the face, but it certainly could be her. In which case, why in God's name would she be here? He wanted to dismiss the idea, but found that he couldn't. Not quite.

At the gate the car turned left onto the Cambridge road. He waited until the smooth purr of the engine receded, and then was gone.

Wilde moved on towards the northern side of the house, passing within a hundred yards of the forecourt, which was now deserted. The Lagonda, the open-topped Bentley and the Hispano-Suiza were parked in line. Passing them, he worked his way round to the rear of the property towards the outbuildings. A large barn, store-rooms, all the structures necessary to the running of a large estate. And inside them, lights blazed.

In his pocket he gripped the stock of the Walther PP semi-automatic pistol, forefinger feathering the trigger.

To the south, towards a bend in the river, there was woodland. Keeping low, he made his way to the shelter of the trees, before edging closer to the outbuildings. The pre-dawn sky was a shade less dark: the sun would be up within an hour and he had to be away while he still had a semblance of night for cover.

Two figures in silhouette were standing outside the broad doorway to the large and ancient brick-built barn. One of them, the taller, strode into the building. From the way he moved, Wilde was sure it was Hardiman. The one that remained outside was smoking a cigarette, blowing spirals of smoke into the grey.

He had been right to come here, thought Wilde. Something was happening, and his instinct told him it wasn't farm workers making an early start. He needed to get closer.

The professor began moving again, continuing on through the woods until he was fifty yards to the rear of the barn. After a moment's hesitation, scanning the open space left and right, he broke from the trees and ran, fast and low, to the back wall of the barn. He threw himself into the darkness of the high building, back to the wall, quickly regaining his breath. He looked up. High above him there was a shuttered opening, but without a ladder he had no hope of reaching it. He dropped to the ground and began to crawl through the grass and dust to the corner of the barn. At first everything seemed to be clear, but then he heard something that threatened to stop his heart: the growl of a dog. The Hardimans' German Shepherd, Izzy, chained to a ring in the wall.

There was another sound, too, echoing inside the barn. Nothing to do with the dog. A low, gasping moan. Panic? Pain? A human sound, yet terribly inhuman.

As he watched, the dog raised its snout, sniffing the air: a guard dog, trained to warn of uninvited presence. It let loose a frantic volley of barks.

Wilde had no option. Jumping to his feet, he sprinted back towards the woods, bent forward. Behind him, he heard the barking, frenzied now, then men's voices. 'Who's there? Unleash the fucking dog!' Hardiman, he was certain.

Flashlight beams swept the open ground. The dog was loose and after him. He couldn't outrun a dog. He pulled the gun from his pocket.

The floor of the wood was full of dead leaves, rotting windfall branches, roots and brambles. Wilde stumbled; almost fell. Turning, the dog was within twenty yards and closing fast. Wilde fired into the air, hoping to frighten the creature away but it wasn't deterred. It came on in the gloom, teeth bared.

Wilde fired again. This time to kill. The bullet hit the dog full in the head, killing it instantly.

He was fairly deep in the woods, but there was movement and light amid the undergrowth at the edge nearest the outbuildings. He had to go deeper. He heard the crack of a gunshot, then another. Goddamn it, they had guns too! Of course they did.

He ran on through the bracken, the ground slipping away in front of him, down to the river. It was no more than forty feet across. He pulled back his arm like an outfielder on a cricket pitch and flung his gun across to the other side of the river. Then he took a breath and dived into the water head first.

Wilde was a strong swimmer and he thrashed his way across to the far bank, scrambling up, through the mud and weeds. He found the gun almost instantly, then dived into the cover of a tree and lay still, panting.

From the woods on the far side, he saw the disconcerting sweep of torch beams and heard more shots. But they were speculative. Hardiman was still shouting and swearing. Wilde heard another voice and thought he recognised one of the chauffeurs.

'I think it's a poacher, Mr Hardiman.'

'Since when do poachers carry automatic weapons? That's no fucking poacher.'

Another voice, lower and muffled. 'Leave them to it, Milt. We got work to do.' There was something familiar about it. Who the hell was it?

'OK,' Hardiman barked. 'Fred, Gus – find him and bring him to me – hog-tied or dead. And then bury the damned dog.'

Wilde could hear the searchers' voices from the other side, the brushing of undergrowth. He had to move, and soon. If he was still around when the sun rose, he would be as good as dead. Stealthily, he crawled away from the tree. The woods quickly thinned out on this bank of the river and gave way to a field of young barley shoots. Not high enough to offer any cover to a running man, but if he stayed on hands and knees and moved slowly, it would be difficult for anyone to see him.

The searchers were now not far from his crossing point. 'We'll have to go over,' one man said.

'To hell with that!'

Wilde continued to crawl until he reached the field. He was moving faster now. Halfway across the field, he decided to risk it. He rose to his feet and began to run.

Two shots rang out. They'd seen him. But at least it was still too dark for them to make him out clearly. He had a head start. Then from behind him, the roar of ignition. Twisting his head, he saw that one of the cars on the forecourt was moving.

Wilde threw himself over the wall and landed on the grass verge with a shoulder-crunching thud. His eyes swept the road. Which way was the bloody copse? The silver birch – that was it.

The Rudge was there, safe and sound. He climbed on, said a split-second prayer that she wouldn't let him down, then kicked her alive. As always, she started first time, the beautiful beast.

The front wheel rose from the tarmac as he twisted the throttle and accelerated through the gears. The speedo was racing up. Fifty, sixty, seventy. He glanced back. Behind him, the car was turning out of the gateway. He put his head down low over the handlebars. Eighty. Ninety. Thank God the road was dry. He was taking the bends at suicidal speeds, pulling away from the car with ease.

On a straight stretch, he took her up to a hundred. The car was nowhere in sight now. A left, then a right, then a left again. A gap in a hedge. He took it, sliding up onto a farm track, then bumped along the hard tractor-worn furrows. Coming to a halt in the shade of the tall hedgerow, he killed the headlight but not the engine. He waited. A minute. Two minutes. Five. He'd lost them. He breathed a deep sigh of relief.

What the hell had been happening in that barn?

CHAPTER 32

His house was silent and dark, but there was movement and light in Lydia's house next door. The sun was about to rise; the streets of Cambridge were coming to life. Postmen, milkmen, bakers, all doing their early morning rounds. The clanking of milk bottles on the carts. The smell of new-baked bread in the air. No sign of any of the cars from Old Hall.

He parked the Rudge at the kerb and gave her fuel tank a pat. Then he knocked on Lydia's front door. Eaton answered it.

'Lydia? Is she here?' Wilde demanded. He had to see her.

'She's having a well-deserved bath. You look drenched too, Wilde. Come in, we need to talk. She'll be down in a while. What's going on?'

'I've been to Milt Hardiman's place.'

'Invited – or otherwise?'

Wilde took the Walther PP from his soaking jacket pocket. 'Definitely not invited.'

Eaton ushered him in. 'There's a lot's going on, Wilde. Lydia got out of Germany by the skin of her teeth. Coffee?'

'Make it very, very strong.'

'Have you killed someone?'

'A dog. He'd have had my throat. Something's going on at Old Hall.'

'Did they see you?'

'Oh yes, but it's possible they didn't recognise me. Although they would have seen me riding away. And Hardiman knows I have a motorbike.'

'Many people have motorbikes.'

Wilde told him everything: his conversation with O'Gara at the races, O'Gara's murder, the latest news on Birbach's death and the disappearance of Torsten Hellquist, the arrival of the Special Branch officer. 'And now Eva Haas has vanished,' he finished up. 'And I have discovered evidence that she's being blackmailed by the people holding her son.'

Eaton frowned. 'Eva Haas is fast asleep in your house. As is Professor Lindberg. We looked in on them when we arrived half an hour ago.'

'She wasn't there an hour ago.' Had she been at Old Hall? Was she in the car that departed soon after he arrived? Was she connected to events at the barn? What was happening there?

'Then we'd better find out where she has been.'

'And Lydia? Why wasn't she back sooner?'

Eaton had that look Wilde knew so well, weighing up what he needed to reveal and what to keep to himself.

'Come on, Eaton,' he said. 'None of your bloody tricks. Don't give me any bullshit.'

Eaton laughed. 'Am I that obvious? Let's just say we have been interviewing Miss Morris – and that her experience ties in with yours. She was told Eva Haas might not be all she seems. She also learned things that dovetail with what your cousin O'Gara told you. The IRA is in the *Abwehr*'s pocket. The Germans are smuggling arms to them – and the IRA have something big planned by way of repayment. One might very well speculate that the Cavendish Laboratory could be the target given the presence of O'Gara in Cambridge and his connection to Hardiman. The atom bomb thing . . .'

Wilde had no doubts. 'If Hitler thinks there are people in the Cavendish who could produce a nuclear device before his people come up with the goods, he would want them eliminated.'

'You're right, of course. But he might also want to find out what they know first. The attempt to torture Birbach, for instance? The disappearance of Hellquist?' Eaton was pouring two cups of black coffee. 'You wouldn't want to go to war unless you were pretty sure your enemy was well behind you in the race for the big bomb.'

'We need to go back there – to Old Hall. Something's happening.'

Could Hellquist be there? The agonised moan in the night . . .

'You're right, Wilde. But not you. I'll take your friend Detective Chief Inspector Northgate and a couple of local men.'

'I should come, too. I know the place.'

Eaton raised a decisive hand. 'No. You stay here. If they didn't recognise you, then you've still got an inside track on the Hardimans.

Let's keep it that way. We'll search the whole place. No stone unturned.
You stay here and find out what Frau Haas has been up to. Also, I want
you to draw me a map of the estate and the relative position of all the
buildings. Where you were – and exactly what you saw.'

Wilde glared. He didn't like this arrangement one bit.

Eaton smiled. 'You need to get dry. And you need to spend a little time
with Miss Morris. Now if you'll excuse me for five minutes, I'm going
next door to wake Frau Haas.'

They hadn't seen each other since March and things had not been easy
between them even then. There was no straightforward reason for the ten-
sion. He had been involved in some difficult late editing of the Robert
Cecil biography; she had been working hard trying to find young poets for
a planned anthology; he had wanted to go to America to see his mother
and to promote his book; she had been desperate to help the refugees.
Nothing unreasonable: just the fracture line of busy lives.

'I think you'd better kiss me, don't you?'

He saw the tears in her eyes and his doubts washed away. He took her
in his arms, smelt her fresh-cleaned hair, touched the bath-warmed skin
of her shoulders and back, kissed her lips, heard her sob.

'I was so scared, Tom. In Germany . . . I wanted you there so much.'

'Don't ever go and do anything like that again.'

'Do you still love me?'

'Yes . . . but I was afraid I had lost you.'

'I should have come with you to America. I'm sorry.' She was racked
with sobs. 'What must your mother have thought?'

'She understood.'

Lydia nodded, barely able to speak. 'Oh, Tom, what a mess I've made.
I hope I haven't missed my chance.'

'You'll meet her.'

'Can we go to bed? Please.'

He kissed her again. Her eyes and cheeks were wet, her lips salty. He
stood back from her, holding her gently at arm's length.

'I want to do that more than anything,' he said, eyes searching her face
as if learning her beloved features all over again. 'But Eaton will be back

any moment. There's something we have to do. I found something among Frau Haas's possessions. A letter from Albert – and a demand. The boy is being held hostage.'

Just then, the front door opened. Eaton stood there in the dawn light with Eva, fully dressed, at his side. She looked smaller, more mouse-like than ever. She kept her head down, refusing to meet their gaze.

Eaton waved the letter that Wilde had found in her knapsack. 'I've told Frau Dr Haas what you found. I've also told her we believe she was at Old Hall tonight. So far, she has said nothing.'

'What is happening, Eva?' Lydia asked, reaching out to take the letter.

'I have done nothing wrong. I am the victim. My son is missing.'

'Where were you tonight, Frau Haas?' Wilde said.

Lydia looked up from the letter. 'Oh my God, Eva, what have you been doing?'

'I have nothing more to say until my son is safe.' Eva's arms were wrapped around her slender frame. Tight and defensive.

Eaton tapped his watch. 'I've got to go, Wilde.' He nodded to Lydia. 'For heaven's sake talk some sense into her, Miss Morris, otherwise this is going to end very badly for her. Find out what the hell she's been up to.' He turned to Eva. 'We're on your side – but we won't be for long if you're working against us.'

Eaton parked outside the University Arms Hotel and raised his hand in greeting to the man waiting at the doorway. Leaning over the passenger seat, Eaton opened the door for Detective Chief Inspector Ted Northgate.

Northgate squeezed in and the men shook hands.

'A pleasure to meet you, Mr Eaton. I have heard about you, of course.'

'Not too much, I hope,' Eaton said.

'So, you'd better fill me in. Professor Wilde hasn't been terribly forthcoming.'

'Of course. You have the search warrant, I take it?'

Northgate let out a gruff laugh. 'The justice wasn't at all pleased to be removed from his bed. But yes, I've got it.'

Eaton pulled away and drove to St Andrew's Street where a police car with two uniformed constables was waiting. He signalled to them and they followed in his wake.

The morning was bright and fresh, the roads clear as they made their way south.

At Old Hall, there was no sign of life as the vehicles trundled up the long driveway and ground to a halt on the gravel forecourt. Eaton went to the front door with Northgate.

One of Milt Hardiman's men opened the door. After a brief exchange with Eaton, he disappeared indoors and returned in the company of his master. Hardiman snorted with derision. 'Well, good morning, and what the hell sort of boy scout deputation is this?'

'Mr Hardiman?'

'Who wants to know?'

'My name is Eaton, and this is Detective Chief Inspector Northgate. We're here to search your property.'

Hardiman was in his tennis whites. 'I'm eating my breakfast, goddamn it. Then I've got a coaching session. I say again, what is this?'

'A child is missing. We're having to search all properties in the area. Also outbuildings. It has been suggested he might have been seen in this area.'

'Is this really how you do things? You just turn up at my house?'

'We have a warrant. Just carry on with your breakfast, Mr Hardiman. If everything is in order this won't take long.' He turned to Northgate. 'Detective Chief Inspector, why don't you drive up to the farm buildings with one of the constables. Look through the woods, too. I'll take the house with the other officer.'

Hardiman pushed out his chest and glared at Eaton. 'Look, buddy, I understand you need to search the countryside. But inside my goddamned house – what's that about?'

'Just being thorough, Mr Hardiman.'

'The only child in this house is my son, who is presently eating breakfast with us.'

'We'll be fine – you carry on.'

'Am I suspected of something? Should I be calling my lawyer?' An edge of anger now.

'That's up to you. But if you've nothing to hide, then why waste your money?'

'Well, I've nothing to hide.' He glared at Eaton. 'Is this the way you usually treat guests to your stinking little country? Just march into their house like Stalin's secret police?'

Eaton shrugged off the remark and stepped into the hall with one of the constables, while Northgate clambered into the police car and set off across the parkland.

Nothing. They found nothing. The barn was empty save for a rusting nineteenth century plough, a modern tractor and some other farm equipment. The other outbuildings contained stores of various fertilisers and weedkillers and more farm gear.

'There was a scrubbed area of concrete floor, which smelt of disinfectant,' Northgate told Eaton when they met up half an hour later. 'That suggested to me that there had been some hurried clearing up – but no proof of anything untoward.'

The house had been just as unfruitful. He entered all the rooms, tried every cupboard and larder, looked in every hearth and coffer. He looked under beds, in all the drawers, all the while wondering: was it possible that the German boy was kept here? Or Birbach, or Hellquist? What exactly was he looking for? What was Hardiman concealing? In his mind, he was in no doubt that Wilde had stumbled onto something during the night – but what?

Wilde had told Eaton that he might run into the movie star Clarissa Lancing. He found her at the breakfast table with Hardiman and the other occupants of the house, Hardiman's wife and son. He questioned them all. There was a missing child in the area – had he been here? The physicist's sister laughed at him, the American boy asked the constable if he could try on his handcuffs, Hardiman's wife offered Eaton coffee, which he declined.

'My dog ran away last night,' the boy said. 'Mom says I can have another. We're going to the pet shop.'

'I said no such thing, Theo. I said Izzy was sure to turn up soon enough. Are you sure you won't have that coffee, Mr Eaton?'

Eaton had looked at these people and had not been put at ease. In his head, he could see the coming war in all its horror; never had he been so sure of anything. What use would boxes of masks be when the gas bombs rained down? He thought of his old mentor, Horace Dill, on his deathbed and thought he might be better off in the void. This was not the way it was supposed to have been. He, Eaton, had been part of that generation told that the war to end all wars had been fought; he was of the generation that believed the ideologies of brotherhood and common wealth could solve all mankind's problems. He had lived a life of privilege and had felt shame for the ease he had always enjoyed. Now he felt sick at heart and helpless.

As they drove away mid-morning, Eaton sat in silence for a few minutes.

'If you ask me, Mr Eaton,' Northgate said, 'it was all a bit stagey. Too perfect.'

Yes, it had been. But that was no help. He felt hollow. 'I think we need to increase security at the Cavendish.'

The letter was on the table between them. Lydia and Wilde on one side, Eva Haas facing them.

'You had no right to go through my things.'

'You were missing. I was worried.'

'I was late, not missing. Is this prison – or boarding school? Perhaps I am back at Girton.'

'This is avoiding the point,' Lydia said. 'Your son has been taken hostage – and demands have been made of you. But you told no one.'

'You have read the letter. Would you risk a child's life in such circumstances, Lydia?'

'What have you been asked to do?'

Silence.

'Eva, this is not good enough. We are desperate to help you and find Albert safe and well – but you must help us.'

'You don't know what you are dealing with.'

'I think we have a pretty good idea.'

'Do you think they won't kill him?'

This time it was Wilde and Lydia's turn to be silent.

Eva continued. 'I have lived under the rule of the Nazis for six years now, Lydia. A Jew is a Jew to them, whatever their age. We are vermin, subhumans, to be driven out or destroyed.'

Lydia dropped her gaze. She had seen the endless line of desperate people on Tiergartenstrasse. She had seen the way the SS and the SA tormented and bullied them. And all the while, the world stood by. But she could not let Eva dodge their questions. 'Tell me about Baumgarten,' she said. 'Describe him to me.'

Eva shrugged. There was a full cup of coffee in front of her, and half a packet of Woodbines. 'What is the point?' she said, reaching for the cigarettes.

'Did you know it was a joke among the SD – that they call themselves "Baumgarten"?' Lydia asked. 'A code name. Something foolish like that.'

Eva lit her cigarette and drew deeply. 'Are you saying that the man who helped Uncle Arnold escape was from the SD?'

'I'm saying exactly that. His escape was staged.'

'But the man was a Jew! He spoke Yiddish!'

'I'm not sure that proves anything. I speak French – that does not make me French.'

'But why would they help us escape like that? If they wanted us out of Germany, they could just have put us on a train.'

'Don't be disingenuous, Eva,' Lydia said. 'You know very well what I'm saying. I'm saying they offered a way out for you and Dr Lindberg and your son in exchange for something. Something you would do for them in this country. A little espionage, perhaps. But what you weren't banking on was that they would take Albert hostage, just to be sure you didn't renege on the deal.'

Eva turned her head away, then snorted. 'If you think you know so much, why ask me?'

'Because we need to know what they are planning,' Wilde said. 'We need to know exactly what they have demanded of you – and who is behind it. Is it Hardiman?'

Silence.

'We are aware that there may be some connection to the Irish Repub-
lican Army, who seem to have sold their souls to the German foreign
intelligence service. Have you had anything to do with them?'

Silence.

'There are only two reasons they would need to use a physicist like
you,' Wilde said. 'Firstly, to get inside the Cavendish. Secondly, to
understand what is happening there.'

Smoke spiralled from the edge of her lips.

'Lindberg was never important, was he?' Wilde said. 'Because of his
reputation, he seemed useful to the British – a reason for them to grant
refuge to you.'

'What do you want me to say, Professor Wilde?'

'Confirm it.'

She shrugged again. Another silence. She stubbed her cigarette in the
ashtray. The room stank of stale smoke and ash.

'Have you met an Irishman named O'Gara? They have killed him. Did
you know about that?'

Wilde watched her. She was a tough one all right: obdurate, secretive and
ferociously protective. He had seen her soak up the vicious anti-Semitism
of Milt Hardiman at Old Hall. But how much of that was the armour that
every mother in the world adopts when her child is in peril? The problem
here was that Eva Haas might be doing her son more harm than good.

'Have you seen Albert?' Wilde said. 'Have you been given further
proof that he is alive?'

Silence. A tear bubbled up in her left eye. She quickly brushed it away.

They had been here over an hour. The questions were repeated; the
answers either didn't come, or were evasive. Eva's untouched coffee
was cold but her cigarette supply was depleted. Wilde wondered if he
should wake Lindberg. Did he know anything? Might he persuade his
niece to talk?

The telephone rang. Wilde left the two women in the kitchen and went
into the hall to answer it.

'Wilde?' It was Eaton. 'We found nothing. The whole place is as clean
as a whistle.'

'What now?'

'I'm in a kiosk over the road from the police station, and I'm on my way to the Cavendish to work on some better security with them. At the moment, they have one uniformed constable stationed outside the gate, and that's it. How have you got on with Dr Haas?'

'She's saying nothing, but she's clearly desperately upset. I'm going to bring Lindberg into the conversation. I'm not sure he'll help, but it's worth a try.'

'And if no joy, then what? Keep her holed up, I suppose.'

Wilde had thought about that. He eyed the door to the kitchen. It was shut, but he lowered his voice anyway. 'No, we can't keep her prisoner. Better to let her go – and follow her.'

Eaton understood instantly. 'Take her to the Cavendish and leave her there. If she slips out, we'll be watching for her. Whatever else she is, I doubt she's an expert in avoidance strategy.'

'And will you be her tail?'

'She knows me. Not sure any of the local coppers would be up to it. Stick out like sore thumbs.'

An idea struck. 'My gyp, Bobby. He's a good man. Very sound.'

'Brilliant. Fix it, Wilde.'

When Wilde knocked at the bedroom door, he found Lindberg sitting on the side of his bed, holding his head in his hands. He looked up.

'And to think I was having a decent night's sleep before the Gestapo dragged me out of bed.'

'They are nothing like the Gestapo. The British police do not even carry guns.'

'Forgive me, but I am like a bear disturbed in its hibernation this morning. I think I need coffee.'

'Come downstairs,' said Wilde. 'I'm afraid I have to tell you a few things about your niece.'

Philip Eaton checked his watch as he stepped out of the telephone kiosk. He was more worried than he had been in a long time. This was all spinning out of control: he felt outnumbered and outgunned.

They were being attacked. He knew who was behind it – and he had not a shred of evidence.

He needed to protect the Cavendish. They couldn't surround it by armed guards, they needed something more subtle. Someone inside the building, perhaps. Northgate was supposed to be on the case, but did he have the resources?

Eaton stepped from the kerb to cross St Andrew's Street. The delivery van hit him at fifty miles per hour – far too fast for a street like this – hurling him up and onto the vehicle's roof, then dashing him to the ground. It happened in a fraction of a second. The van didn't stop or slow down. Dozens of shocked people saw the collision, but no one got the make or number plate of the vehicle. Nor did they note the driver with the fixed eyes, the turned down mouth and the gingery-red shock of hair.

Eaton's limp body lay discarded like a child's toy in the centre of the road.

CHAPTER 33

Lydia was exhausted. Questioning Eva had taken its toll of all concerned. Dr Lindberg had done nothing to persuade his niece to provide more information.

'Eva,' he had said. 'What is going on?'

She had shaken her head irritably. 'Oh, uncle – go back to bed!' she said, as if he were a senile old man. Lindberg had looked hurt and said nothing more.

Wilde had chased off to college to recruit Bobby, but before he went he took Lydia aside and explained the plan to follow Eva. He told her that Bobby was under instructions to telephone Cornflowers the moment he discovered anything. They discussed whether Geoff Lancing should be informed, but given his association with Hardiman and Old Hall – as well as the presence of his sister – Wilde decided it was politic to leave him in the dark. Just for the moment.

Lydia had waited until the late morning, before she appeared to relent. 'Oh well,' she said. 'You're obviously not going to say any more and you're not a prisoner. Come on, I'll take you to the Cavendish. I'm going into town anyway – and there can be no harm in you using the lab's library.'

'Thank you,' Eva Haas said. 'I am indebted to you, Lydia.'

Bobby was not the sort of man you'd notice on the street. Short and wiry as only jockeys and ex-jockeys can be, he held his cigarette cupped in his hand and avoided eye contact with passers-by, lounging with his back to the wall of the Cavendish Lab. He didn't even turn his head when Lydia Morris passed by with the German man and woman, but from the corner of his eye he glanced at the German woman. She would be easy to remember.

Miss Morris made sure Eva and her uncle were inside the Cavendish, then turned to leave. This time she nodded to him and he nodded back.

Now it was just a matter of waiting.

A pair of policemen now stood by the main gate. Eyeing Bobby suspiciously, one of them came over and told him to move on. 'You're not picking any pockets here, sunshine, not on my watch.'

'It's a free country,' Bobby said truculently. "I'll stand where I bloody well like!'

'Name?'

'What is this? Nazi bloody Germany or something? I'm waiting for a mate. We're going to catch a bus to Newmarket for the second day of the meeting.'

The officer grumbled and moved back to his post.

Lydia wanted to see Horace Dill, but not just yet. Eaton had told her how ill Horace was, and he was a good friend of hers; they shared a fondness for left-wing politics, although Horace had always sneered good-humouredly at her wet Fabianism. But after a night without sleep, she felt too exhausted to cope with a desperately sick man: she needed sleep. Badly.

Instead, she went straight home where she found Wilde in her bed. He, too, had been awake all night. Undressing, she slipped between the covers beside her lover's sleeping form. His body was warm; she had almost forgotten the warmth of the human body these past months. She curled against him and breathed deeply; she had not forgotten his particular earthy, manly scent.

Lydia nestled deeper against Wilde's back. She wrapped her arms around him and cupped his prick and balls in her hands. He moaned softly in his sleep. She closed her eyes and pressed even closer to him, badly wanting him inside her. But exhaustion took over from anticipation and she drifted off. Still holding him. She wanted him to wake like that.

The German woman reappeared at the Cavendish door an hour after entering the building. She stopped and looked around. She didn't appear to notice Bobby. She lit a cigarette, hands shaking, then walked at a brisk pace up Free School Lane and left into Bene't Street.

Bobby hobbled after her. His joints weren't what they were, but he could move quickly enough when necessary. He didn't want Professor

Wilde or anyone else at the college thinking he wasn't fit enough to do his work. This was no time to be signing on at the Labour Exchange, not with good jobs so hard to come by. And the college position *was* a good one – warm, plenty of food and gifts at Christmas courtesy of the dons and the undergraduates, some of whom had wealth enough to share around.

And so here he was, with a fiver from the professor burning a hole in his pocket just for tailing this woman. He rather liked the look of her. She was small like him, smooth-skinned and she had a good figure. Professor Wilde had told him not to follow her on to any private property but just to make a note of the address and report back from the nearest telephone kiosk. If she got in a car, he was to make a note of the number and try to get descriptions of any other occupants. Whatever happened, he was not to put himself in danger.

He wasn't worried. No one noticed Bobby or his ilk. Most of the clever men and boys who infested this town looked straight through the college servants. Professor Wilde was a bit unusual like that in the way he would pass the time of day with you. As for the German gentleman, Birbach, well, he had been a decidedly odd one. Never said more than the occasional word to Bobby. 'My bulb light is *kaput*,' perhaps. Or 'Fetch I a box of chalks.' No pleases, no thank yous, no 'Nice weather today.'

'This isn't linked to poor Dr Birbach, is it, sir?' he had asked Wilde.

'No questions, Bobby. Just keep it simple.'

Ahead of him, the German woman turned left on to Trumpington Street, then right on to Silver Street, past Queen's College and down towards the river by the weir. Halfway across the bridge, she stopped and looked north, gazing at the intricate puzzle of the Mathematical Bridge, a footbridge made of wooden struts. She threw the stub of her cigarette into the slow green waters of the Cam and lit another one.

Bobby spotted a lad he knew who worked on the punts. He stopped for a chat while keeping one eye on the woman.

She was there fifteen minutes, during which time she got through two cigarettes, gazing ahead of her along the river with its avenue of ancient buildings, its high elms and weeping willows. A stream of walkers and cyclists crossed the bridge. The whole area was crammed with students enjoying their last days before the long vac. Some were swimming. Many more were punting or rowing, perhaps practising for the May Bumps. On both banks of the river, picnic blankets were being unrolled, and corks popped.

Just then, another woman appeared. The German woman glanced at her quickly, then looked away. It was clear they knew each other. Bobby clapped his mate on the arm, told him to stay honest, then walked on to the bridge, stopping briefly close to the two women.

The newcomer was blonde. Not blonde like Jean Harlow, but upper-class blonde, in a blue and green, short-sleeved summer frock. She was on the tall side, probably half a foot higher than the German woman, and she was as thin as a punting pole.

'Come with me. We have to go back there. You know what we need.'

'I can't. They know.'

'No. They think they know, but they don't know. Come along, Haas, make it easy. And then soon, you'll see him.'

'How soon?'

'As soon as everything is verified. I promise. I'm a mother, too, you know.'

The German woman reached out and, for a moment, Bobby thought she was going to grasp at the taller woman's dress, like a beggar. But the other woman had already turned away, going back the way she came.

Bobby tried to keep the conversation straight in his head. He thought he had it, but he wasn't sure. One thing he was sure of, however, was that the tall thin woman wasn't German. And from her accent, she wasn't British either. American, he guessed.

He waited, watching the German woman. The American didn't even look back, but walked slowly onward, going west, over the river. At last the German woman, dropping her head like a recalcitrant schoolgirl, set off after her. By the time she had caught up with her companion, the crowds had thinned. Bobby kept a hundred yards back from them. At the side of the road, two hundred yards on, a black car was waiting. He couldn't quite make out the number plate or the make of the vehicle and started moving faster. He was only thirty yards from them now. Twenty, ten – and then the American woman turned around and met his eyes. She smiled.

The club hit him full force on the back of his head and he fell to his knees. He was still conscious, could hear a voice, but he could do nothing to prevent the second blow.

Wilde and Lydia woke at five in the afternoon and made love. It was sweet and gentle. She told him she loved him and said sorry and he said the same.

Afterwards, they lay on the rumpled bed, all the blankets kicked to the floor, their breathing subsiding with each passing minute. He didn't want to be anywhere but here in this room with Lydia's scent, and warmth and breath, but his mind was elsewhere, miles away, at Old Hall. In the outhouses, on the lawns, in the woods, inside Clarissa's bedroom.

'Do you want to tell me something, Tom?' Lydia said, her voice soft.

He hesitated, and knew that in doing so he had already probably revealed too much.

'Tom? Is something worrying you?'

He knew that she had to hear it from him, not from anyone else. 'I hope you'll think it's nothing.' He paused, looking for the right words. 'I guess Eaton has told you about the set-up at Old Hall?'

'Geoff's sister is there, isn't she?' Straight to the heart of the matter, either by chance or a lover's intuition.

'She . . . she came on to me.' No. He couldn't phrase it like that. He couldn't make himself the innocent player in all this. 'It was complicated. But nothing happened,' he said.

'You're talking in riddles, Tom. If you've got something to say, tell me in simple English.'

'Nothing happened – but the thing is, it *might* have done. I might not have resisted – and I feel terrible guilt.'

She clutched his hand.

'I'm sorry, Lydia. We were so distant. I began to wonder about us.'

As had she. 'But nothing did happen?' It was a question, not a statement.

'I didn't make love to her, but it was there on offer to me and if I'm honest, I wanted it. Or, at least, my body did.' He paused. 'I wasn't going to tell you.'

She wished he hadn't, but the genie was out of the bottle. You couldn't unknow something, could you? She felt numb, not angry. She wanted to be rational and modern, but old-fashioned jealousy and need for sole possession were not so easily pushed aside. 'What stopped you? She's a beautiful movie star, after all. Any man in the world would have fucked her given half a chance. Why didn't you, Tom?'

He knew he was supposed to say 'because I was thinking of you. You are the only one I have ever loved.' But he couldn't say that because they both knew it was a lie. He had loved before, had been married and fathered a child. He had come this far with the truth, so he should continue. 'Because it would have degraded me. She invited me in and she was naked, and like a dog following a bitch on heat, my first instinct was to accept. But if I had, then I would have been no more than a dog. As it happened, the Hardimans' brat, Theo appeared – and thank God that he did.'

'Are you suggesting you were saved through divine intervention? Not sure how that one will go down on judgement day.'

'That's not quite fair. I've told you everything now. I've been avoiding her. I swear, Lydia, that I am filled with regret and remorse.'

Silence descended. Her anger and heartbreak washed over the bed in waves.

'You must have given her some cause, I suppose,' she said in a small voice. 'A woman doesn't just take off her clothes on the off-chance that the nearest man might like to have her.'

'Actually, from what I've heard, that's exactly what she does. It seems she doesn't get all her Hollywood roles by accident.'

'The casting couch. What a bloody cliché. So she's manipulative and you're easily led. I never knew that about you, Tom. I thought you were the one who didn't follow the herd. The one who thought things through before he acted.'

'I made a mistake. Or I nearly did. We all make mistakes, Lydia.'

'*You* made a mistake, Tom. And don't you think you should have told me all this *before* we made love?'

He had no answer. In the silence that followed, the telephone began ringing from downstairs.

'I'll go,' he said, rising from the bed and pulling on trousers and shirt. 'It's probably Eaton.' Or Bobby. He should have called by now – unless Eva hadn't left the Cavendish.

'Maybe it's your fancy woman,' said Lydia sarcastically. 'I can't wait to meet her.'

CHAPTER 34

Both bells were ringing. The front doorbell and the telephone. Wilde picked up the phone to silence it.

'Tom, it's Jim Vanderberg.'

'I'll be with you. I'm just answering the door.'

'I've got to warn you . . .'

Wilde opened the door, the telephone grasped in his hand, the cord stretched to its limit.

A familiar face stood before him. At first, he couldn't place it, but he recognised it all right. Narrow cheeks and jawline, a mass of red freckles – and a shock of ginger-red hair. Initially, out of context, he couldn't work out who the hell it was. His confusion lasted all of two seconds. And then he recalled the mysterious voice in the night.

'Colonel Flood,' Wilde said. He had last heard him in the Old Hall woods while he was on the run from Hardiman and his men, but he had last *seen* him in the Oval Office at the White House. He had been in uniform; now he was in a light grey suit and striped tie and his brow had a film of sweat. 'What are you doing here?'

'Surprised to see me, huh? The new clipper service is going to be a wonderful thing. I have just been guest of honour on the test flight – USA to England. Soon every millionaire in Europe and America will be using it. Yesterday I boarded the plane at New York, stopped off at Canada and Ireland and today we came to a perfect touchdown on the still waters of Southampton Harbour. So here I am. Now, are you going to invite me in?'

Wilde stood back to let Dexter Flood pass, momentarily forgetting that this wasn't his house.

Flood strolled into the kitchen. 'Nice place,' he said, waiting for Wilde to follow him.

Wilde put up a hand to acknowledge the comment, but stayed where he was. He pressed the phone back to his ear. 'Hello?'

'Tom, is that who I think it is?'

'You tell me, Jim.'

'Is that Dexter Flood?'

'Carry on.' The visitor was still in earshot.

'He's gone rogue. Believed to have wangled himself aboard some kind of flight to Britain. Watch your back.'

'Yes, of course I'll do that lecture. Can you tell me a little more about the subject?'

'FDR has had him sacked. Wants him investigated over passing state secrets to a foreign power. Turns out he's a fully paid-up member of the German-American Bund and a committed Nazi. Didn't put that on his curriculum vitae. FDR won't knowingly have Bund men near him.'

'That's understandable.'

'There's something else. It has emerged that he's a pal of Seán Russell. Heard of him?'

'Yes, of course.' Russell was the Nazi-loving chief of staff of the IRA and was presently in the USA, drumming up support among Irish Americans.

'You're going to need help up there, Tom.'

'I know that to be the case, Jim. Well, thanks for letting me know. I'll be in touch about the lecture.'

'Wait, Tom. Whatever purpose he thought he had for you, it might have passed. I say again – be very wary.'

'Oh, I'm sure that's true. Don't worry, I'll bear all that in mind. I know how difficult these things can become when college bursars stick their oar in.'

He put down the phone. He thought back to the White House. It had been Dexter Flood who urged him to report everything he could discover about the possible development of atom bomb technologies at the Cavendish. *If anyone in Europe looks like they're gonna get their hands on a superbomb, I aim to make damned sure the USA gets there first,* he had said. Except that wasn't the truth, was it? He was going to make damned sure the *Germans* got there first. That was why he wanted Wilde to keep his eye on the Cavendish. He had evidently got wind of his friendship with Geoff Lancing; perhaps he knew, too, of Philip Eaton's plans to bring Eva Haas here. The circle was closing. This had always been about just one thing: ensuring that Germany stayed ahead in the superbomb race. Flood and Hardiman were in it together. And Eva Haas was their instrument.

And Wilde's role in it? They simply needed to keep him under close observation, because it had been arranged in advance that Eva and Lindberg would be staying with him and Lydia. They had been playing with him like a cat with a mouse, keeping him firmly within the compass of their claws. Or so they thought.

'Perhaps I can fix you a cup of coffee, Colonel Flood. It'll have to be quick, though – I'm going out.'

'Somewhere nice?'

Wilde ignored the question. 'How do you take it?'

'Strong, with cream. Plenty of sugar.'

'You might have to settle for milk instead of cream. By the way, how did you find me?'

'Oh, simple enough, Wilde. I called in next door and the cleaning lady said you were here.'

'And may I ask why you are here in England?'

Flood tapped the side of his nose, then winked. 'You know how it is, Wilde. Things are getting critical. A European war is on the horizon and we've got to be sure there's no blowback across the pond. Special assignment. Can't say more.'

'When we last met you assured me there would be no war.'

'Well, that was then and this is now.'

Wilde wondered whether Lydia would come down. She must have heard some of this from upstairs. As he prepared the coffee, he tried to make small talk. 'You know, colonel, I attended one of your lectures a few years back. *Friends and enemies, fascism and bolshevism in the old world*, it was called, if I remember correctly.

'I gave that talk quite a few times. What did you think of it?'

'I thought you went a little easy on Mussolini.' Thinking back on it, Wilde realised that Flood had been making the case for fascism as a bulwark against bolshevism. He was an apologist for Il Duce and the Führer, and all their acts and atrocities committed in the name of law and order and bread for the workers. How had FDR been blind to the man's politics? Wasn't the FBI supposed to take care of things like that?

Wilde handed Flood his coffee and passed the sugar bowl across the table. Flood put in three teaspoonfuls.

'So let's get this straight. There's one man down, Birbach, probably murdered. What else has been going on in this town? You have been very slow to report back.'

Wilde poured himself a coffee. 'As you know, Colonel Flood, I am not employed by you or the US government.'

'But you're a patriot? We've all got to work for America. You've been in contact with Milt Hardiman, right?'

'I have. And he has treated me royally – tennis, drinks, the races.'

'To hell with that. I'm not interested in your social life, Wilde. What have you discovered about the Cavendish lab – that's what America needs to know.'

'Excuse me a moment, I just have to take this coffee to the owner of the house.'

'That would be Miss Morris, right?'

'You do seem to know a lot, don't you, Colonel Flood?'

He took the coffee upstairs. Her door was closed. Under other circumstances, he might have walked in unannounced. Today he knocked at the door. When she said 'Enter' he walked in and put down the coffee on her bedside table.

Lydia was at her dressing table. She watched him in the mirror.

'I've made you coffee.'

'So I see. That will make everything right, won't it.'

He didn't respond to her sarcasm. 'We have a visitor.'

'Yes, I thought I heard voices.'

'Be careful what you say. I can't explain everything now, but he's not on our side.'

'Well – get him out of my house then!'

Watch your back. That's what Jim Vanderberg had said and Jim never overstated his case.

It must mean they were both in danger. Leaving Lydia's coffee on her bedside table, he went back downstairs.

'Where are you staying, colonel? The Hardimans?'

'No, no. Haven't called in there yet. I'm at that hotel in the centre of town. What's its name?'

'The Bull?'

'That sounds like it. Crummy joint.'

Wilde ostentatiously glanced at his watch. 'Look, I'm going to have to ask you to go. I have things to do. Perhaps we could meet up later.'

Flood drained his cup and grimaced. 'Call this coffee? It tastes like dredged Ohio mud.' He rose and swaggered to the door. 'I've got your number, Wilde. I'll call you with a time and place.'

At the front door, he turned around and shook his head. 'How about that, then, Wilde? New York to Europe in a matter of hours. If they can do that, how long before warplanes fly the Atlantic and drop superbombs on New York? That's why America can't stay aloof anymore. We need to know what's happening here.'

Wilde called Jim Vanderberg back.

'Flood was checking on you. You're his man.'

'Hmm. I don't get it.'

'Or maybe he wanted to kill you but something changed his mind.'

The thought had occurred to Wilde. 'Has a warrant been issued for him?'

'No, Tom. Neither here nor America. He might be a treacherous sono-fabitch, but I think the FBI want to be sure of their ground before hauling him in. In the meantime, should I come up to Cambridge?'

'No. I've got Eaton and Special Branch.'

Wilde put down the phone. He called out a 'goodbye' to Lydia, but received no word in reply. He went next door to pick up the pistol, and then stuffed the weapon in the pocket of his jacket. Outside, he wheeled the Rudge to the road, and started her up. He was about to set off when Lydia appeared at her front door.

'Where are you going, Tom?'

'To the Cavendish. I've got to relieve Bobby. Poor bastard must have been there all day. I also need to find Eaton.'

'Can you give me a lift to college? I want to see Horace.'

'Of course.'

She straddled the pillion seat. He turned to look at her and kept his words simple and direct. 'I know this is going to take a while to mend, but I have to try. You see, I love you.'

'Just ride. I'll find some way for you to make it up to me. Perhaps I'll get you to dig me a bomb shelter in the garden. I'll find something to suit your meagre talents, don't you worry.'

He managed a smile. One way or another, they'd get through this. For the moment, though, they had more immediate concerns.

Wilde left Lydia outside the college gates and told her to use his rooms if she wanted to wait for him there. Then he rode around to the Cavendish. There was no sign of Bobby. Puzzled, he spoke to one of the police officers stationed outside the main door.

'We've only been on duty less than an hour, sir,' he said. 'Haven't noticed any man matching your description in that time, I'm afraid.'

'Who was on duty before you? Would I be able to find them, do you think?'

'You could try the station, but it's been quite a day, sir. All the lads in the vicinity were called on to deal with a very nasty accident in St Andrew's Street. Shocking, it was. Pedestrian hit by a delivery van. Driver didn't even stop. He'll go down for dangerous driving when we catch the bugger.'

CHAPTER 35

Wilde parked the Rudge outside the Bull Hotel. The evening diners and drinkers were beginning to arrive and the lobby was busy, but he pushed his way through.

'Is Mr Eaton in his room? Mr Philip Eaton?' he asked the concierge.

'No, sir, haven't seen him since this morning.'

'Can I leave a message?'

'Of course, sir. I'll get it to him as soon as he arrives. I know he's booked in tonight.'

Wilde tore a sheet of paper from the counter pad: *Eaton – alarming development. Call me soonest, Wilde.* Wilde folded the note and sealed it into an envelope and watched as the concierge tucked it away in the pigeonhole under Eaton's room number.

'One more thing,' Wilde said. 'Do you have an American in residence, name of Flood? Colonel Dexter Flood.'

The concierge flicked through the guestbook. 'We have no one of that name here, I'm afraid, sir. No American gentlemen at all, to my knowledge.'

Somehow, Wilde wasn't at all surprised. As he turned around to go, Ted Northgate pushed his bulky way through the hotel's front door.

'Detective Chief Inspector?'

'Bad news, I'm afraid, Wilde.'

'What?'

'Eaton's been hit by a van. He's badly injured. Not looking at all good.'

'Good God.'

'I wouldn't like to bet against it being deliberate.'

'Is he . . . will he . . .'

'I think he'll survive. He's at Addenbrooke's – probably under the knife even now.'

This was shocking news. Wilde had to go to him, but in Eaton's absence, he needed to talk with Northgate first. 'Eaton had already told you everything we know, hadn't he?'

Northgate nodded.

'Well, there's something else.' Wilde quickly told him about the arrival of Colonel Flood from America.

'I'd like to speak to this man. Do you know where I might find him?'

'He said he was staying here, but they have no record of him. I would venture to suggest Old Hall – but what sort of excuse are you going to find to go back there again?'

'Let me worry about that, Professor Wilde. One other thing: from what you say, there is a grave possibility that you might be in danger yourself. Please leave this to the professionals from now on.'

Wilde shrugged. 'Of course. That's all I ever wanted.'

Before going to Addenbrooke's, Wilde rode back to the college, where he waylaid the head porter.

'Has Bobby been back, Scobie?'

'Bobby, sir? Haven't you heard? He's in hospital – up the road.'

The words hit Wilde like a physical blow. 'Bobby in hospital? How? Why?'

'He's got a sore head, that's about the sum of it. He was set upon by some young hooligan, I believe. I know he asked for you to be contacted. I'm very sorry if you didn't get the message.'

'I haven't been in my rooms, or at home.'

'Well, I'm sure a visit from you would be most kindly received.'

Two men down. If this was a battlefield, the day would be almost lost.

Wilde found Bobby sitting up in bed, his head swathed in bandages.

'I'm very sorry, Professor. I was beaten from behind with some sort of cudgel.'

'What do the doctors say?'

'I was a bit dazed. The docs were worried I might have a brain injury, but in the event they couldn't find one.'

Wilde grinned. If Bobby had retained his sense of humour, that had to be a positive sign.

'I think I was out cold for a minute or two. A baker passing by got me to hospital in his van in next to no time. I woke up to the smell of fresh-baked bread. And I'm still hungry, because I missed the hospital lunch round and all I've had is a cuppa and biscuits. What I wouldn't give for a slice of bread and dripping.'

Wilde sat on the edge of the brass bed. The ward was clean and bright with daylight slanting in. The sheets were starched and white and the blankets brisk and functional, tucked in with painstaking neatness. 'You'd better tell me exactly what happened. Was this outside the Cavendish?'

'No, sir. The German lady left on her own, as anticipated, then went down to the Queen's bridge on Silver Street. Once there, she stopped halfway across and just gazed at the water and the wooden bridge – the Puzzle Bridge, as I call it – smoking non-stop. After ten minutes or so, another lady came up and engaged her in conversation so I tried to get near enough to listen.'

'What did you hear?'

'The other woman told the German woman to go with her, but she didn't want to. She said *they know* – those were her exact words. The other woman said that they only *thought* they knew, but they didn't know.' Bobby scrunched up his eyes. 'Hang on a minute, sir, I'm trying to get this straight. She definitely said something else.'

'Take your time, Bobby.'

His eyes lit up. 'Now I remember, sir. The other woman said she'd see him soon. Him – she didn't say who *he* was, but she said she promised and that she was a mother, too. That's it.'

'Can you describe the other woman?'

'Tall, thin, with an accent. American, I think, sir. I'm not good on accents, but that was my reading of it.'

'And that was when you were attacked, was it?'

Bobby shook his head and immediately winced and clutched his temple. 'Oh, I shouldn't do that, sir. No, it wasn't on the bridge. The thin one set off, going westward. After a while the German woman followed her, and I tailed them across the bridge. They were just about to get in a car, when the thin one turned round and smiled at me. I was nearly close enough to read the number plate when I was hit over the head. That didn't knock me out, but the second blow did.'

'I'll make this up to you, Bobby.'

'No, sir, you've already given me more than enough. But you know, I think I heard her voice again, just between the first and second blows to my head. I think she was talking to the driver.'

'Did you hear what she said?'

'Two words, sir – it sounded like *bow bone*. But that doesn't make no sense now, does it?'

After some persuasion, Wilde managed to make contact with the consultant who had seen Philip Eaton on his arrival by ambulance. Dr Howell was a man of fifty with thinning hair and serious eyes.

'Before I answer any questions, Professor, may I ask your connection to Mr Eaton?'

'Think of me as his nearest of kin locally. We go back a long way.'

'That doesn't really answer my question, but in the circumstances – the circumstances being that we have no other name for a next of kin – I suppose it will have to do.'

'Well, Dr Howell?'

'Mr Eaton was hit with great force on his left side, and fell very badly, causing massive damage to the upper arm. I'm afraid we've had to remove his left arm, close to the shoulder. His left leg is fractured in several places. We are confident we can save it, but he'll have a limp.'

'Can I see him?'

'No. He's still out. Quite honestly, he's lucky to be alive.'

'When *can* I see him? It's urgent.'

'I'm really sorry, not today. He was a long time on the table, under a general anaesthetic.'

Northgate had said Wilde had no more part to play. But the professor knew that simply wasn't true. He couldn't sit at home, cowering, praying they wouldn't come for him and Lydia. He couldn't stand back when friends and colleagues were under attack. His hand went to his jacket pocket and he cradled the Walther.

The two women could not take their eyes off each other. Here in Tom Wilde's college rooms, Lydia sized the woman up and wondered what it was about her that made men go weak at the knees. Did men not look for kindness in a woman's face? There was none in this woman. Lydia forced herself to smile.

'Can I make you tea, Miss Lancing?'

'Oh God, what am I doing here, thrusting myself onto you like this? Is there something a little stronger than tea? And please, do call me Clarissa. I've rather fallen out of love with all this English reserve since being in America.'

Under the circumstances, Lydia would have preferred to stick with surnames. This woman had offered herself naked to Tom. Were they supposed to be best friends now? Lydia recognised the humbug in her jealousy. Wasn't she supposed to subscribe to a modern world view where vows of fidelity were old hat? She was discovering that it was one thing to be sophisticated, but quite another to have the other woman push herself into your space. She was far too well mannered to say these things, of course, so all she said was, 'Very well – then I'm Lydia. I'll see if I can find a little whisky. Tom usually has a bottle somewhere around the place.'

'I can't . . . I can't ask this of you.'

Lydia scanned the room and spotted the bottle standing on the desk, beside a pile of papers. Running some glasses to earth in the gyp room, she brought a couple back and poured two healthy measures. 'Water?'

'Oh, no water. Definitely no water.'

Before meeting Clarissa, Lydia had spent an hour with Horace Dill. It was exceedingly painful to see him brought so low. She thought he had very little time left. Weeks perhaps, but certainly not months.

'Don't you think you'd be more comfortable in hospital, Horace?' she had asked.

'No. Now light my fucking cigar, Lydia Morris – and find me something to drink.'

Horace managed to get it all out, then fell into a vicious coughing fit. After that, he couldn't manage to say more than the occasional word. He was so thin she thought his bones would snap with the spasms. She lit his cigar because there was no point in denying it to him. Hands shaking, he had tried to take one puff, but that was all he could manage. He held it between his thin, mottled fingers even after it went out.

At the end of the hour, in which she did her best to find out what she could about his friendship with Arnold Lindberg, she took her leave and said she would visit him again tomorrow. As she was crossing the Old Court towards Tom's stairs, the porter had caught up with her.

'Miss Morris, there's a young lady at the gate, wishes to see Professor Wilde, but he's not here. Called in and left again half an hour ago. She's in a bit of a state, I'm afraid. Knowing you were on the premises I wondered whether it was something you might help with.'

'Who is this young lady, Scobie?'

'She didn't say, but of course I do know.' Scobie lowered his voice as though imparting a grave secret. 'She's the Hollywood movie star Clarissa Lancing, miss. Everyone knows she's in town. I believe her brother's a fellow at St John's.'

Clarissa Lancing? Lydia had been both unnerved and intrigued. 'Did she say what she wanted?'

'No, miss, but she looks a bit the worse for wear. It's not quite the sort of thing I know how to deal with . . .'

'Very well, Scobie. Perhaps you'd escort her to Professor Wilde's rooms?' Lydia was both bemused and fascinated; she was about to come face to face with the siren who had attempted to lure her man on to the rocks. 'I'll wait for her there.'

Now here they were.

Clarissa's hair was all over the place, her mascara was streaked and she kept clutching and unclutching her beautiful fingers. She stood up and began to pace the room, frequently stopping at the window to peer out.

'Do you know when he'll be here, Lydia? I'm scared.'

'What are you scared of? Talk to me if you like. Tom and I are . . . neighbours. Why don't you sit down?'

Clarissa fell onto the sofa again and arranged herself like a tragic heroine. She fished in her handbag and produced a carton of cigarettes. She took one and lit it with trembling hands, then offered the packet to Lydia.

Black Sobranie. Temptation came in too many forms. Lydia took one of the cigarettes.

'Sweet Jesus,' Clarissa said. 'This is so awful. What must you think of me? You won't breathe a word to anyone, will you, Lydia? This could do terrible things to my career. You don't think the porter . . .'

'No, he's very discreet. But what are you scared of?'

Clarissa clutched the cigarette to her mouth, then exhaled smoke, gasping as she did so. 'Oh, something bad is happening and I don't know what! I'm caught up in the middle of it. There are bad people and I don't know how to get away.'

'Have you tried the police? And what about your brother? I know Geoff quite well myself. I'm sure he could help you.'

'There were shots in the night, you see. At Old Hall where I'm staying. And then this morning the police came around. It was terrifying. Searching everywhere and questioning everyone, demanding answers. Then after they went, he turned on me . . .'

Lydia waited.

'I suppose I'd better tell you. It's Milt Hardiman. I'm sure you've heard of him. Everyone has.' She turned her left cheek to Lydia. 'That's where he slapped me. Is it red? He called me a treacherous bitch and threatened to kill me. He said he'd shoot me in the head and bury me with the dog. It was all so out of the blue – I still don't know what he was talking about.'

'Do you want me to call the police? A threat to kill is a criminal offence.'

'He wouldn't do it, would he, Lydia? Please tell me he wouldn't kill me.'

Wilde called Eaton's office from the phone box on St Andrew's Street. It was answered immediately.

'Mr Carstairs, it's Professor Wilde again. Have you heard the news about Philip Eaton?'

'What would that be, sir?'

'I'm sorry to have to break this to you, but he's been badly injured – knocked down by a van. Clearly deliberate, whatever the police say.'

'This is very bad news, sir. Where is Mr Eaton presently?' Carstairs remained imperturbable.

'Addenbrooke's. They've had to amputate his left arm. Look, Detective Chief Inspector Northgate of Special Branch is already up here, attached to Cambridge police headquarters, but I wanted to be sure you'd heard the bad news.'

Barely a pause. 'Someone will be in touch, sir. Thank you for the call.'

Dexter Flood looked down at the mutilated corpse of Torsten Hellquist, spreadeagled on an old wooden door on the floor. His wrists were bound to nails at the top, right and left, but the hands were broken, bloody mincemeat, the result of repeated hammerings; his naked torso was spotted with black burn marks and streaks of blood. One of his eyes had been gouged. The ankles were bound to nails at the bottom of the door. 'He's fucking dead! You damned halfwit – now you've gone and killed both of them.'

Hardiman bristled. 'Don't talk to me like that, Flood. We got all we could from him. And if he's dead, so what? That's what we want, isn't it?'

'When we had every last piece of information from them, that was when they were supposed to be killed. How much did you get from Birbach? Whose fucking idea was it to use mustard gas?'

'He had a heart attack. We couldn't know that would happen. Anyway, Hellquist's told us everything. The *Uranverein* guys will make sense of it. He knew everything Birbach knew. I'd swear my life on it.'

'Believe me, it may come to that,' said Flood.

'From what we know, Hellquist was the building-blocks man. He had ideas about taking Birbach's theories and making them actually work.'

'Which is the whole fucking point, Milt. Making it work. That's what Berlin wants from us. And now you've killed him . . .'

'But I think we got it all.'

'You think . . . you think. Stop thinking, Milt. It's not good for you.'

They were in an aircraft hangar, the vast folding doorway closed and locked.

'The question is how far they've got. Could the Cavendish men really build one of these things?' Flood continued.

'The Jew woman says it might be possible.'

They glanced over at Eva Haas. She was sitting at a table near the door, under a bright table lamp. She had a pile of paper and a couple of pens and was writing, slowly and deliberately under the watchful eye of Peggy Hardiman and her chauffeur.

'How long? Are we talking months, or years? And if years, how many?'

'That's for Diebner and Schumann to evaluate.'

Flood jutted his chin in Eva's direction. 'When will she have finished?'

'She says it'll take her a few hours yet. This is complicated stuff and she has to make sense of what Hellquist said. It came out in fits and starts.'

'If she thinks she can fool us, put in some damned nonsense . . .'

'With her boy's life at stake, Dexter? Don't worry yourself on that score.'

'Do you think she's dragging it out?'

'Possibly, but I doubt it. She knows she doesn't get the boy back until this has been verified.'

They had little option but to trust her. But when she had outlived her usefulness, well, that was another matter.

Suddenly, Flood hammered his fist into his palm. 'Damn it, Milt, let's move on this! We can't wait for her.' He jerked his head in the direction of Eva. She looked up, fear in her eyes. 'Give the Scavenger the nod, Milt. Get this thing finished off.'

'There are loose ends.'

Flood snorted with derision. 'Forget them. I'll be safe in Germany while you and Peggy are drinking Manhattans in Manhattan. As for Wilde and his woman, they're going to have the hangover to end all hangovers. Come on, Milt, let's get out of this place. You need to think about making tracks. Your driver can guard the woman.'

CHAPTER 36

He was almost at the college gate when it hit him. *Bow Bone*. Bobby had misheard. He was dazed by the first blow and her accent had made it worse. It was just one word, not two: *Boldbourne* – the airfield. The Hardimans' private airfield, from where he had flown to Paris with Clarissa.

Where better to go if they needed space? The barn at Hawksmere Old Hall was no longer safe, so they had to go somewhere else. What did they have there? Were they keeping Hellquist prisoner? Was the boy, Albert, there, too?

Wilde accelerated down Trumpington Street. The Rudge purred beneath him.

There was still a grey light as Wilde dumped the Rudge against a wire fence, half a mile from the airfield, and began to edge his way across open land. Ahead of him he could see the hangar and the other buildings, lights showing through doorways.

His right hand gripped the stock of the Walther hard. He knew the weight of the trigger now and he knew the kick the gun would give when fired. He hoped he wouldn't have to use it.

In a few minutes he was at the hangar. The big main doors were closed, but a small postern door was wide open, yellow light flooding out. First he wanted to investigate one of the the admin blocks. He moved towards it, and flattened himself against the front wall. He moved closer to the open doorway and could hear voices: American voices. Dexter Flood and Milt Hardiman. He was in no doubt the others would be there, too: Hardiman's wife, the drivers from Old Hall, the ones who had hunted him in the woods less than twenty-four hours earlier. And Clarissa? He couldn't hear her, but whatever they were up to, she surely had to be a part of it.

He heard footsteps and shifted away fast, into the cover of the second administrative building. He watched and waited, but no one was coming out. Not yet.

To his right, he noticed a van. A very ordinary-looking delivery van, except for the badly dented front bumper and the smashed headlight.

It would be interesting to do a fingerprint test of the interior of *that* vehicle – and a forensic examination of the bumper and the headlight. But that was something for another day.

Wilde edged closer to the doorway of the admin building, tried to listen again. This time the voices were clearer but still difficult to follow. The voices came in and out of focus. He heard 'Berlin' and 'Cavendish' – and he thought he caught his own name.

Once more he heard footsteps. He loped back to the hangar and listened for a few moments, straining for sounds. No voices. With the gun up, alongside his cheek, primed to swivel, aim, fire, he advanced into the postern doorway and looked inside.

The taller of the two drivers was standing not six feet away from him, back turned, facing a small table where a woman sat, writing slowly on a pad, surrounded by papers. Eva Haas.

She looked small and lost in this large space, full of yellow light and shadows

The man guarding her had a gun in his belt, on his right side.

Eva stopped writing, arched her back and yawned. A natural break. She looked at the man, then past him and her eyes widened at the sight of Wilde. He put a finger to his lips.

Wilde touched the muzzle of the pistol to the stubbly hairs at the nape of the guard's neck. 'If you turn around or try to do anything,' Wilde said, 'I will fire.'

Wilde's gun was in his left hand. His heart was thundering. Blood surged through him. He reached his right hand forward, removed the pistol from the guard's belt and thrust it in his own pocket.

'Raise your hands where I can see them.'

The man did as he was told, said nothing.

'Down on your knees.'

'Fuck you.'

Wilde kicked his calf muscles. The man stumbled and staggered. Wilde grabbed his shoulders and forced him down. He stepped in front of him and put the Walther to his right eye. 'Do you think I haven't killed a man before?' He fished out a handkerchief from his pocket. 'Open your mouth.'

'Fuck y—' the guard began. He didn't finish the word. Wilde's fist crunched into his face. A boxer's punch. Blood flew from the shattered nose. The guard gasped as he fell backwards. Wilde followed him down. This time he hammered the face with the pistol. The guard was gasping for air, but Wilde pushed the handkerchief into his mouth.

There was none of the elegance of the boxing ring about this. This was brutal, visceral and very messy.

Wilde stood up and looked around for something to bind the man. That was when he saw the corpse of Torsten Hellquist. 'Oh, Jesus Christ, what have they done?' He felt faint with horror. 'What in God's name has been happening here?'

'They tortured him to make him answer questions.' Eva spoke in a flat voice.

'What bloody questions?'

'Questions about fission, Professor Wilde.'

'And you went along with this barbarity?'

'I had no choice. They have my son.'

The guard was trying to struggle to his feet. Wilde kicked out at his chin and the man's head smacked with brutal force into the concrete floor.

Wilde went over to Hellquist and looked down into his pitiful, mutilated face, his gouged eye. He couldn't look at the rest of the body: they had made an obscenity of a decent, kind man. As quickly as he could, he unpicked the cords that had tied Hellquist to the door and went back to the guard. Not caring how tightly he pulled, he bound the man's hands and feet, then wound a cord around his face to ensure he could not spit out the gag.

'Come on, Dr Haas, we're getting out of here.'

She hadn't moved from the desk.

'Come on, get up!' He grasped her upper arm and tried to pull her to her feet, but she resisted.

'No.'

'What do you mean, no?' He pointed to the corpse. 'You'll end up like Hellquist if you stay here.'

'I *can't* go with you,' she hissed. 'They have my son. They will kill him.'

'We have to go. They could come over any moment.'

'You don't understand, Professor Wilde. Not even Lydia understands. I am a mother. A mother will do anything for her child.' She picked up a scrap of card from the table, almost lost among the papers scribbled with complex equations. She held it up so that Wilde could see it. 'That is why I cannot leave this place.'

It was a photograph of a boy with metal-rimmed spectacles. There was something about the child's face. For a second, two seconds, he tried to place it. Then he knew: he had seen this boy. He had seen him not far from here, in the company of three other children – children he had assumed to be the boy's siblings. Four children in the front room of a poky two-up two-down in a Cambridge back street.

'This is Albert?'

'Yes, that is my son.'

'I've seen him. I know where he is.'

'This cannot be so.'

'I swear it. He is at Number 16, Swaffham Lane, Cambridge. We must go.'

Eva's hand went to her mouth. 'Is this true?' She rose, and then gestured at the papers.

Wilde scooped up the scattered pile, folded them into a rough bundle and thrust them into her arms. 'Bring them.' He raised the gun. 'I need my hand free for this.'

CHAPTER 37

Fanny Winch trudged through the streets of Cambridge. A sudden flash of fireworks at a May Ball lit the darkening sky, from the direction of the river and the Backs. With luck, the children would have seen it. She had left them in the backyard, told them they could watch out for fireworks, but that they had to be in bed by ten thirty, no later.

Near Emmanuel College, she spotted a policeman. He was in his thirties, well-built and not bad looking. He smiled at her, the way men usually did when they fancied you.

'Evening, love.'

'Evening, constable.'

'Where you off to, then? One of the May Balls, eh?' He eyed her up appreciatively.

'Chance would be a fine thing.'

'You'd be the prettiest lass there, you would.'

'Cheeky bugger.'

'No, straight up. You got the looks.'

'Then why haven't I been snapped up by a duke? My lot in life's charring. I char for the young college gentlemen at the Cavendish after their day's work's done and they're off supping champagne and what have you. Bloody messy lot they are. Mind my language.'

'Don't fancy a quick cuppa before you start, do you? There's an all-night caff not far from here.'

'What's the time?'

'Ten. Come on, love.'

'Ah, no, I'm on me own tonight. Perhaps another time.'

She left him and turned into Downing Street, shopping basket in her right hand.

At the Cavendish, the night porter told the duty officers that Mrs Winch was authorised to be in the building. 'You're late tonight, Mrs W.'

'Couldn't get the little one to drop off, Mr B. I think she's caught something.'

'And no sign of Mavis neither.'

'Still got the bug? Ah well, I'll just have to work twice as hard. A woman's work is never done. I'll be glad of a little overtime, truth be told. Three kids at home – that's a lot of mouths to feed.'

'You're a saint, Mrs W.'

'And you're a married man, Mr B – so keep your sweet talk for your missus.'

'I'm just brewing up. Would you like a cuppa?'

'I won't say no. Just go and leave my bag. I'll be with you in a mo.'

She had the whole laboratory complex to herself. She went into one of the offices, put down her bag and lit a cigarette. She didn't want to open the bag just yet. It contained five sealed quarter-litre bottles and a rough map of the layout of the Cavendish with five Xs marked.

Each of the specially constructed bottles had a timer, detonator and a very small amount of explosive attached. Just enough to fracture the glass and release the contents into the air. It was a brand new poison gas called sarin, she had been told, devised by chemists in Germany.

First things first. She was dying for her cuppa and she always enjoyed Mr B's company down in the porter's lodge. There was plenty of time, because she had already decided she couldn't be arsed to do any cleaning this evening.

Wilde did not knock at the door of Number 16. He turned the handle and it opened. He had his right hand in his pocket, clasping the butt of the Walther PP.

Eva was just behind him, her small, slender figure quivering with anticipation.

'Is he really here?'

'I hope so. He certainly was.'

Behind them, the Rudge was parked at the kerb, the scientific papers Wilde had gathered up stuffed in the saddlebag. He and Eva had managed to creep from the hangar and make their way across the airfield undisturbed. It wasn't until they reached the Rudge that they heard the distant sounds of discovery. Within seconds they had been speeding along the road back to Cambridge.

Now Wilde stepped inside the house, followed by Eva. The twelve-year-old who had answered the door when Wilde first came around, was in the front room.

'What the hell?' He looked up, startled.

'Is your mother here?'

'What's it to you? Oi – I've seen you before . . .'

'My name's Mr Wilde. What's your name, lad?'

'Michael.' He was a tousle-headed boy with intelligent eyes. 'Now sod off, mum's out working.'

'Where's the German boy?'

'Eh?'

'You heard me.'

'Don't know what you're talking about, mister. Just the three of us here. Now, piss off or I'll call a copper.'

Eva had had enough. She walked past the boy and peered along the narrow corridor towards the tiny kitchen. On her left was a steep flight of wooden steps.

'Albert,' she called out. Then louder: 'Albert!'

The boy Michael shot up from his perch at the front room table and tried to wedge himself between Eva and the staircase. 'You can't go up there, missus!'

For a moment, Wilde thought the woman and boy were about to fight, but then he heard a small voice from above.

'*Mutti?*'

A bespectacled face appeared at the top of the stairs.

Eva Haas pushed Michael out of the way and held out her arms as her son ran down the stairs, two at a time, and threw himself into her embrace.

Elbowing Michael aside, Wilde touched Eva on the shoulder. 'Frau Haas,' he said urgently. 'We have to get out of here. It's too dangerous to stay a moment longer.'

Clutching her son to her as if she would never let him go, Eva followed Wilde out of the mean little hall and into the night.

Fanny Winch laid the first of the bottles at the top of the building, in the attic room the young scientists referred to as 'The Nursery'. It was here the new recruits were taught the basics of dealing with radioactive substances. She, too, had had to learn a little about them when she arrived; they didn't want the charladies burning their hands touching things they didn't ought to touch. The young men – and a few young women – who had to spend their first few weeks there looked like a load of snotty swots to Fanny; playing with string and sealing wax and rubber bands.

But the word was that these kids had big brains. Word had it that they might have the wherewithal to build a weapon that would stop the Germans in their tracks. Fanny didn't give a fig for Hitler and his unpleasant bunch, but they were supplying arms to the IRA and they had promised that if war came, they would liberate the six counties and make Ireland whole again. And that, after all, was what she had been fighting for every waking hour of her adult life.

The timers had already been set for 9.15 a.m. All Fanny had to do was activate them and then place each device in its allocated place. In the Nursery, that would be at the top of the cupboard set against the wall opposite the window. 'This substance is colourless and odourless,' Hardiman had told her. 'The small explosive device on each bottle will release it and turn it to vapour. Being heavier than air, the droplets will drift down through the building. It is a great deal more toxic than cyanide – and a few drops will kill a man. Or woman.'

She had no idea if the death it brought was painful. Why should she care? Who in England had cared when the firing squad's bullets ripped into her father's body in Kilmainham Gaol, Dublin, in 1916? Him and the other brave martyr boys from the Brotherhood and the Volunteers . . .

She had been a girl of nine. In her head she could still hear the screams of her mother and aunties, and then the horror of discovering that Daddy would never come home. She hadn't cried or screamed, but she had sworn vengeance; she had sworn that she would complete her daddy's work.

Her mother took her to Liverpool. But Fanny never forgot. She might have lost her Irish accent, but she never lost her Irishness or the fire that burned within her heart. At seventeen, she had met Diarmuid Winch; they were of one mind.

Now Diarmuid was in Dartmoor Gaol, serving time for carrying explosives, and it was up to her to continue their work. She would fight until her last breath to avenge her daddy and the other bold boys, what-ever it took; even dealing with the Nazi devils. And if some members of the IRA thought they would be dirtying their hands by dealing with such men, then so be it. She was the Scavenger – and scavengers had to do the foulest of work in the filthiest of places. Clearing up stains of humanity like that traitor Henty O'Gara. Jesus, it had been easy seeing him coming. The boys in Galway had marked her card about that fellow.

She lit a cigarette and consulted her pencil-drawn sketch plan of the labs. She had worked it out to achieve a nice spread of the gas as it floated down through the stairwells and ducts. Mr Hardiman had said the Germans were almost certain the gas would be effective, but it was unproven under such conditions. Fitting that the experiment should be carried out in a place where other potentially deadly experiments were already being carried out. Well, they'd find out soon enough if it worked.

Cambridge. A civilised town in a civilised country. Yet how was Wilde to keep Eva and Albert safe? He would have to go to the police in time, of course: they would have to be told of the murder at Boldbourne airfield. But he had little faith in the police's ability to understand the magnitude of what was at stake. Nor was he certain about the Special Branch man. He called Wilde 'amateur', yet Northgate, the so-called 'professional', hadn't found Boldbourne and hadn't seen through Fanny Winch and her invented story about the black car and the two men abducting Dr Birbach. The truth was clear now: Birbach had never left Old Hall that night. He had been taken to the outbuildings, tortured and murdered for what he knew.

Wilde couldn't go home because Hardiman and Flood knew where he lived. There was one place, however – one place he doubted they would consider.

From Trumpington Street, he rode north along King's Parade, then up Trinity Street into the lee of St John's College, Albert and Eva huddled together behind him on the pillion seat. A few drunken revellers in evening dress staggered along the centre of the road, but he wove round them without difficulty. He stopped outside the gates, looked around for watchers, then killed the engine.

'Geoff Lancing has his rooms here,' Wilde said as he dismounted and helped Eva and Albert to climb down. 'Do you trust him, Frau Haas?' He set the Rudge on its stand, in the shadow of the ancient walls.

She bowed her head. 'Yes.' She stood there, arms around Albert, stroking his hair.

'Good. So do I.'

She hesitated. 'Professor Wilde, there is something I need to say. I have seen terrible things. I have deceived you. When we were at that house for the tennis, I had to pretend to be a stranger to those people – but the truth is they knew me already. I saw Dr Birbach die and then that poor man, Dr Hellquist, tortured like that . . . but what could I do? I was trapped. Would they not do the same things to my son?'

'Why you?'

'Because I speak German – and because I understand their work. I was also ordered to go into the Cavendish and find other secrets for them and other scientists who might hold the sort of information they desired. But I told them there was no one else, not even Geoff Lancing. I hope I saved them . . .'

Wilde said nothing. Who was he to judge her?

'Come on,' Wilde said. 'Let's hope Geoff's in. I think you'll be safe here.'

'What about the papers?' Eva said.

'Should we just burn them?'

'No, they are of great value. The result of many hours' work by Dr Birbach and Dr Hellquist. These papers are their legacy to the world.'

'I have an idea. Tell me which are the most important and I'll look after them.' He unhooked the saddle bags and slung them over his shoulder.

If Geoff Lancing was surprised by the arrival of Eva and Albert, he recovered well. He shook the boy's hand and introduced himself in imperfect German. Albert clung to his mother's skirt as though he would never let her go.

'I think we should leave them together for a few minutes, don't you, Geoff?' suggested Wilde.

Outside, Wilde and Lancing paced round the ancient court, while Wilde brought his friend up to date, the full story of Colonel Flood and events at Boldbourne airfield. Geoff Lancing listened with growing horror as Wilde told him about the terrible death of Torsten Hellquist.

'God, Tom, this is simply awful! Have you told the police?'

'I'll call them as soon as we've finished here. In the meantime, I don't want anyone to know where Eva and Albert are. Not even the police. We have two overriding concerns, Geoff: to protect the Cavendish and to protect Eva and Albert. It's vital you keep them here until you hear from me, personally, that the danger has passed. Have a word with your porters – they mustn't tell a soul, nor admit anyone they don't know. I don't even want the police to know that Frau Haas is here. Got that?'

They returned to his rooms to find Eva and the boy curled up together on Lancing's bed. Wilde called the police from the sitting room and told them to contact Detective Chief Inspector Northgate. He should go to Boldbourne airfield with an armed patrol. There had been a murder and the killers might still be there. He told them, too, to go to Number 16, Swaffham Lane and arrest Fanny Winch on suspicion of child abduction.

Wilde shoved his hand in his pocket and removed the gun – a Luger – he had taken from the guard in the hangar. 'Do you know how to use this, Geoff?'

'Oh, yes.'

'Then take it. Just in case. I've got another one.'

'There's one person you haven't talked about, Tom. My sister – what part does she play in all this? She's part of Hardiman's set . . .'

Wilde grimaced. He had hoped to avoid the subject. 'I'm afraid I fear the worst, Geoff. To tell the truth, I don't even know where she is right now.'

Lancing looked through the open door to the mother and son wrapped in each other's arms. 'The thing is, Tom, I know her better than anyone in the world. I knew her when she was a child. And I have no doubts about her. No doubts whatsoever.'

CHAPTER 38

As Wilde rode south, the town was quiet, the revellers dispersed. A half-moon cast silver light into dark corners. His mind was swirling with the story Geoff Lancing had just told him, a version of the account Clarissa had given as they flew over St Margaret's Bay and out across the Channel towards Paris. A very different version . . .

'We had a nanny,' Lancing began.

'Nanny Tobin,' Wilde said. 'Clarissa told me. A tragic tale.'

Lancing raised an eyebrow, and continued.

'Her husband had been an officer, but she was left destitute after he was killed in the War. What could she do? There were few men left to marry a well-bred widow in her thirties. So she had to become a governess or a nanny – a not uncommon tale. By the time of the events I'm describing, Clarissa and I were off at our respective prep schools, but my father kept Tobin on because she had become part of the family and, well, he was a widower. It never occurred to me at the time that there could be anything between them, but looking back I can't help wondering whether they didn't bring each other some comfort. I hope so.'

Wilde looked at his watch. 'Carry on, Geoff – St Margaret's Bay.'

'Before the war, most of our summer holidays were spent there, but it was shut up for the duration. By late August 1918 the war was moving eastwards and so it opened up again and we were brought down by Tobin to spend the last couple of weeks of the summer holidays there. Father had a few days leave and hopped over from France and, with the benefit of hindsight, I'd say he probably hopped straight into bed with Tobin. I suspect Clarissa rumbled them somehow – whether she actually caught them in bed I have no idea – but it makes sense . . .

'One morning, Clarissa said she wanted to walk along the cliffs to Dover and then play some tennis. Daddy could send a car over with our rackets and the driver would wait around to take us home later. Of course, he never refused her anything and it sounded a pretty jolly idea.'

'What happened?'

'Clarissa insisted that Tobin came with us – and Daddy agreed. So she made a picnic and we set off. Some way along the cliff path we stopped to have a slice of pork pie and look out to sea. It was a glorious day, but Clarissa was playing up, asking Tobin about her dead husband and when she was going to find another. Even at nine, I could tell she was out of order. When Tobin said she didn't want to talk about it, Clarissa began to sulk and wandered over to the cliff edge. Tobin became very agitated, told her to come back, that the cliff could crumble beneath her. Clarissa sat down with her legs dangling over the edge. The cliffs are high and sheer there. It was very, very scary to watch.

'Tobin begged her to come back; Clarissa studiously ignored her and just carried on swinging her legs in space. Tobin moved nearer and – it's a bit of a blur – the next moment she was no longer there. I'm not sure whether I saw murder committed or not. Have I blanked it out? Clarissa stood up, looked down to the bottom of the cliff, then turned, smiled at me and put a finger to her lips. "Oh, dear," she said. "I think Tobin's killed herself." '

Wilde gasped. 'Good God!'

'We ran home. Clarissa was in tears, collapsed at daddy's feet, told him Tobin was dead. "She said she couldn't take any more and just leapt. Geoffrey saw it, didn't you, Geoffrey?" I said I hadn't seen or heard anything. One moment Tobin was there, the next she wasn't, that's all I could say.'

'There must have been an inquest and a police investigation.'

'Of course. But without a suicide note, the verdict was open. I have had twenty-one years to think about it, however, and now I'm sure that Clarissa killed Tobin because she was jealous of my father's affection for her.'

'Do you think he suspected her?'

'Lord no, he's always worshipped the ground my sister walked on . . . as did I, Tom. She was perfect in my father's eyes. He began to give her flying lessons when she was fourteen and she was a natural. Bloody fine aviatrix from the word go. Superb navigational skills too. The other thing she's good at, of course, is acting. Wonderful actress, Clarissa, and not just on stage and screen.'

'You've no proof of any of this nanny stuff, of course. No evidence, nothing.'

Lancing gave a resigned smile. 'You're right, of course, Tom. But I know it's true. She came to me one night, a few years later, and said, "She thought she could fly, little brother. But we're the only ones who can fly." Just that.' He took Wilde's hand and held it between both his. 'I feel enormous guilt, Tom. Guilt for poor Tobin – and guilt for dragging you into this ghastly world. I'm sorry I ever got you involved with her and the Hardimans. She wanted you to come to Old Hall and, well, I'm so used to doing her bidding, I didn't really give it a second thought. It never occurred to me, of course, that she would set her sights on a grumpy, motorbike-riding, oddball history professor. You're not her usual type.'

'Thanks for the flattering vote of confidence, Geoff.'

The story was still there, stuck like a record in his head, as he arrived at the college. He spotted a car parked on the other side of the road, not more than thirty yards away. Two men sat, statue-like, in the front seats. It was Hardiman's Lagonda and Wilde recognised the two men from Old Hall. He smiled grimly: the guard at the airfield wouldn't be out and about for a while. Not after the hammering Wilde had meted out.

There was no way of avoiding being spotted, so Wilde didn't try. He parked the motorbike at the main gate, tucked the saddlebag under his arm, exchanged pleasantries with the night porter, and walked across the New Court through into the smaller Old Court. The college was deathly silent, the wisteria heavy with scent, the dark sooty walls silhouetted in the moonlight. On the west side of the Old Court, he climbed the smoke-stained staircase to Horace Dill's rooms. The door was open and a light was on, so he knocked and then walked in.

Dill was awake, propped up in bed with a book in one hand and a dead cigar in the other. His eyes met Wilde's and he smiled.

'Come to watch me die, Wilde?'

'What are you reading, Horace – Marx?'

'Too late for that. At this stage, it has to be Shelley. My life began with him, and so must it end.'

'What specifically?'

'You'll laugh . . . "The Triumph Of Life".'

Wilde raised an eyebrow. It was obvious that death was close to winning the battle in Horace's case. 'I'm sorry to call on you so late,' he said.

'Time's lost its meaning, Wilde. Anyway, I fear to sleep in the night.' He was about to descend into a coughing fit, but he put down the book and held his hand to his chest, took a few short, rasping breaths and managed to calm the storm.

Wilde held up the saddlebag. 'There are papers in here, Horace. Important papers. Can I hide them here? Some of them at least. I doubt anyone would think to look in your rooms.'

'What papers?'

'The work Hellquist and Birbach were doing at the Cavendish. Don't ask me to explain it, but both men are now dead because of this work. The Nazis did for them, Horace, and they would kill again to get their hands on these papers.'

Dill's rasping laugh descended into yet another fit of coughs. 'They're more than welcome to kill me,' he said when he could speak again. He eyed the room. It was as shabby and cluttered as it had always been. Books and papers everywhere, piled high, spilling from shelves, filling the space beneath his brass bed and beneath his table. Barely a spare space for a man to tread. 'Over there,' he said. 'Among my manuscripts.'

Wilde removed half the papers from the saddlebag, and crossed the room, sliding them in among other papers in a three-feet high pile. It would take a long time to find these.

'Thank you, Horace.'

'Well, with any luck, your Nazis will come and put me out of my misery with a bullet to the head. You know, Wilde, you do seem to attract trouble.'

'And you don't, of course, Horace.'

The older man grinned wolfishly, then grew more serious. 'Can you spend a little time with me?'

Wilde removed a pile of books from Dill's desk chair, moved it across to his bedside and sat down. 'Perhaps you'll beat it, Horace. Your cough doesn't sound as bad as it did.'

Dill ignored the bromide; he knew the truth. 'Do you want to tell me what this is all about?'

'Not really.' Wilde was thinking of Philip Eaton. Dill had been his mentor. Would the dying history professor wish to know what had happened to his favourite pupil? It seemed kinder not to mention it, and yet he found himself saying: 'Eaton was run down a few hours ago.'

'No, surely not?'

'He's alive, but he's lost an arm. It was the same people who want those papers. It was made to look like a road accident, but it was attempted murder.'

'Philip . . .' Dill was shaking his head, drifting into a reverie of many years ago.

'Do you want me to light your cigar, Horace?'

'No. It'll ravage my throat and stop me talking to you. Ah, Philip, Philip . . . he was the best of my undergraduates, you know. He's always been one of us – a great believer in social justice and a better world. He can do great things for this country.' He shook his head in despair. 'I'm not sure I'll be sad to leave this fucking life, Tom. So much unmitigated misery.'

Wilde took hold of Dill's thin hand, all skin, bone and sinew. He had always suspected, of course, that Eaton was a crypto-communist, recruited to the cause by Dill. That didn't mean, however, that Eaton didn't also have his own country's interests at heart.

They talked for an hour until the light in Dill's watery eyes began to fade. His breathing was slow, each breath more shallow than the last, rattling in his throat. When his eyes finally closed, Wilde stood up, put the book of Shelley verses on the bedside table, but left the dead cigar in his hand.

Before leaving the college, he visited his own rooms. On the table was a piece of paper, folded in half. He opened it: Lydia's handwriting. 'I was here,' it said. 'Your tart turned up in a bit of a state and I looked after her. She is very worried – seems you are her only hope. I have no idea where you are and we've given up waiting for you and gone home. At least I know you're not with her! Kiss kiss.'

When he left the college, the car was still there. Unhurriedly, he replaced the saddlebag on the bike, climbed aboard and set off southwards, keeping to thirty miles per hour, aware that the car was on his tail. Once outside town, he turned the throttle and accelerated. The road ahead was empty and soon it was empty behind him, too.

He looped eastwards and northwards and came back into Cambridge by way of the Ely road. His first stop was the Cavendish. Had the cleaning woman Fanny Winch been in? Indeed she had, the night porter said, but she had now gone home. Why, was there was a problem?

Wilde wasn't sure. 'Just take a look around, would you?'

'What am I looking for, sir?'

'I wish I knew. But if anything seems out of place, call me – or the police. Yes?'

'Very well, sir.' The night porter seemed less than impressed.

Arriving home, he half-expected to see the Lagonda outside his house. But there was no sign of it. He had to see Lydia, to talk with her, but first he parked the Rudge and went to his own front door, turning the key quietly.

Upstairs the quiet was broken by the soft murmur of Arnold Lindberg's snoring; at least he was safe and well. But none of this had ever been about him. His supposed escape from Dachau had just been a ruse by the Germans to get Eva Haas to England and inside the Cavendish Laboratory.

Wilde deposited the saddlebag with the remainder of the papers, carefully selected by Frau Haas, left his jacket and pistol on the bed and went to the bathroom. He washed his face in cold water and soap. His chin was rough and he considered shaving to keep himself awake, but the phone was ringing. He hurried downstairs.

'Professor Wilde?' A man's voice.

'Yes. Who's that?'

'Guy Rowlands. I'm an associate of Mr Eaton. I've been trying to contact you for several hours now. Apparently you called Mr Carstairs and it sounded pretty urgent.'

'You know Eaton's been injured? Lost an arm.'

'So I understand. Shocking news. I'm on my way up to Cambridge to look into it. I'll be with you nine-ish. Will you be at home or college?'

'If I'm not at one, I'll be at the other. Northgate from Special Branch is up here, too.'

'I know.'

Wilde put the phone down. Time to go next door.

It was Clarissa Lancing who opened the door to his knock, her damp, beautiful eyes peering around the painted edge.

'Professor Wilde – thank God you're here. Come in quickly, come in.'

He hesitated and then stepped forward through the narrow gap, into the hallway. Did she know about the letter Lydia had left for him? Lydia certainly wouldn't have allowed her to read it, couched in those terms. He feigned surprise at her presence here.

Clarissa closed the front door. 'Through there,' she said, nodding towards the sitting room. 'What's going on?'

'Something awful's happened, Wilde. I'm terrified. Lydia's been such a chum, but it's you I need. You're the only one who can help.'

Wilde shrugged and led the way into the sitting room. Lydia was on the sofa. Dexter Flood was by her side, pointing a pistol at her temple.

CHAPTER 39

'Hand out of your pocket, Wilde. Slow and easy. Clarissa – frisk him.'

'My pleasure.' Smiling now as though she had just won a sweepstake, she patted him down for weapons. 'He's clean.'

'OK,' Flood said. 'Now, Wilde, nothing bad need happen. You and Miss Morris here can both get out of this alive. We ask only one thing. We want those goddamn papers you took from the hangar.'

His voice was even, but determined. Wilde had already seen what he and his confederates could do to a man's body; he had no doubt that he would torture and kill him or Lydia or both of them to achieve his ends.

'You look as if you need a drink, Tom,' said Clarissa. 'You've gone as white as a sheet.'

Wilde kept his gaze fixed on the pistol and Lydia's face. 'I don't know what you're talking about, Flood, but I suggest you put that gun down right away.'

Lydia had her hands in her lap. Her face was drawn, but she wasn't shaking, she wasn't pleading or weeping. Seeing her like that, unafraid, defiant, Wilde knew with utter certainty that he loved her.

'You're not listening, Wilde. Goddamn it, we haven't got all day to deal with this! We know you have those papers. Where are they?'

'Why should I tell you anything? You'll kill us anyway.'

Dexter Flood grabbed hold of Lydia's hair, wrenched her head downwards and pushed the muzzle of the pistol hard into her head. She didn't cry out.

'OK, OK,' Wilde said. 'OK, I took the papers, but they meant nothing to me – I tossed them in a bin in the middle of town. I can take you there if you want.'

'Bullshit. They're at your college.'

Clarissa handed Wilde a whisky, then ran her fingers through his hair. He shook her off and put the whisky down, untouched.

She leant over and kissed his cheek. 'You're a bad boy, Tom Wilde. Does Lydia know just how bad you are? Do you think I should tell her?'

Dexter Flood had had enough. He jumped up, grabbed Lydia by the hair and threw her down at his feet. She lay there unflinching, determined not to give them the satisfaction of begging for mercy. He swivelled the pistol from her head to Wilde's chest, then back again to Lydia. 'Last chance, Professor. Last chance.'

Wilde knew he had to give in; it was just a question of timing. Too soon and they would become suspicious; too slow and one or both of them would be hurt. He held up his hands. 'OK, OK, they're still in the saddlebag. They're next door in my house.'

Flood seemed slightly taken aback. Wilde feared he had made his move too soon. But then the colonel shifted his head from side to side, like a man coming to a conclusion. 'OK,' he said. He pulled a second pistol from his pocket and tossed it to Clarissa, who caught it with ease. 'If you hear a shot, shoot her,' Flood said. 'If I'm not back in five minutes, shoot her.'

Flood frogmarched Wilde the twenty steps to his own front door.

'Open it, quietly.'

Wilde did as he was told.

'You go first,' said Flood. 'I'm right behind you with a gun to your back. One bad move, you die – and then your woman dies.'

'Don't worry. I understand.'

Wilde had left the saddlebag in the bootroom, concealed in a cupboard where he kept tools and garden equipment. He pulled it out, opened it up to show Flood the contents. 'There you are. It's all there.'

Flood removed a couple of the sheets, saw the handwriting and the complicated mathematical calculations, then put them back. 'Fine. You carry it.'

Wilde shrugged. 'Tell me one thing, Flood. Why did you pick me? Why did you want *me* close to Milt Hardiman.'

Flood laughed. 'You still don't get it, Wilde, do you? You thought you were keeping an eye on him, but he was keeping an eye on *you*. You were the one with a house full of German physicists and an unhealthy interest in espionage. Keep your friends close, Wilde, your enemies closer.'

They returned to Lydia's house. She was back on the sofa, hands in her lap. Clarissa was drinking whisky, the pistol steady in her right hand. She put down the glass and lit herself a black cigarette. 'Is that it?'

Flood laughed. 'This is it.'

'Are you sure?'

'Don't mean much to me, but this is the stuff. All in the Jew's neat Germanic script.'

'Why, Tom,' Clarissa said. 'I thought you'd make it a lot more difficult for us. I'm disappointed.'

'You promised you wouldn't harm us.'

'Did we? Did we say that, Dexter?'

'Go and get some goddamn rope or cord. Take her,' he thrust the gun in Lydia's direction. 'This is her place – she'll know where to find something. And plenty of it. I want them bound up good.' He waved the pistol at Wilde. 'On the floor, flat.'

Wilde hesitated and received a blow from the butt of the pistol for his pains. The hard metal smacked into his forehead, jerking his neck. He fell to his knees.

'Flat out, goddamn it!'

Wilde lay flat on his face. He felt a slippery skein of blood on his brow where the gun had made contact.

Flood had to get the papers to Germany. Wilde's instinct was that he would want to deliver them personally. He had burnt his bridges in America; what better way to arrive in Hitler's Germany than with a bag full of secrets? Clarissa was another matter. Giving up her career in Hollywood was a hell of a sacrifice – unless you believed the Nazis were going to win the impending onslaught. Either way, if they wanted a smooth departure, Flood and Clarissa would do best to avoid gunshots in the night and the unwelcome attention they could bring. He hoped.

Lydia and Clarissa returned with lengths of cord and baggage straps.

'Where are the Hardimans?' Wilde asked. 'Left you to it, have they?'

'Milt and Peggy have had enough of England,' Clarissa said. 'And who can blame them? This ridiculous little country and its silly empire are done for.'

Wilde had no chance to reply: a bundle of rags was thrust into his mouth. He grunted as Flood knelt on his back and wrenched his arms behind him and began binding his wrists together. By the time he finished, Wilde could not move and could barely breathe. Was this the end? A knife to the throat? He could only see from ground level, and even then his vision was curtailed. But he saw enough to know that Lydia was being bound and gagged, too, before she was rolled across the floor and a long luggage strap was used to bind them together, torso to torso, facing each other. Their eyes were level. How he wished he could communicate his feelings for her or transmit some hope to her. And then he heard the door opening, felt a gust of air cooling his face, and Flood was gone.

Clarissa had not left yet. He heard her out in the hall, dialling a number. Heard her voice . . .

'Geoff, darling,' she said. 'There's something I must talk to you about. Yes, darling, it's very important. Look, can you meet me at Dot's Cafe for a quick coffee at ten past nine? No, no, it won't take long. See you soon then, darling. And don't be late. I mean it – I'm on a tight schedule, so don't be even a minute late. Promise me, darling? Love and kisses.'

The phone was replaced, and he heard Clarissa's heels clicking back into the sitting room. She bent down and patted his cheek. 'Our friends are embarking even now at Southampton if you must know. Lovely stateroom, every luxury a family could wish for.' She patted him again, then kissed his forehead.

Still bent down, she held a bottle in front of their eyes. A translucent medicine bottle but with a clear liquid inside and a device strapped to it with wires protruding. 'Remember this from Paris? I told you it was Remy Martin Louis XIII? A little fib, I'm afraid, but you'll find the bouquet is marvellous nonetheless. Amazing what this one little bottle will do – just think what five of them might achieve.'

She laughed lightly. Straining his neck, he thought he saw her reach up and place the bottle on the top shelf of the bookcase. And then she was gone.

CHAPTER 40

Wilde and Lydia were helpless. They couldn't move, nor could they make a sound. Lydia was struggling, though, using Wilde's shoulder to work at the cords that held the gag in her mouth. It shifted and she was able to push the rag out with her tongue.

For a few moments, she gasped for breath. 'God, Tom,' she said. 'What have we got into?'

He couldn't reply, could barely breathe. But he feared the worst. They were both thinking the same thing: what was in the bloody bottle? Certainly not bloody brandy.

The cords dug into his flesh savagely. Worst, perhaps, was the excruciating pain in his neck and spine. When would Doris turn up?

Lydia seemed to read his thoughts. 'Doris isn't due in until this afternoon. I can shout if you like, but no one is going to hear me. Not unless they're at the door. But if you think differently, then wink your left eye.'

He didn't wink. Perhaps better to let her save her breath until there was some hope of it being heard. What about the MI6 man, Rowlands? Shouldn't he be here soon? Would Northgate come looking for them? Long shots, both of them.

For ten minutes the situation seemed hopeless, but then there was a knock at the door. A second knock, then a pause. Lydia called out. The front door opened. 'Lydia? Tom?'

'In here,' Lydia yelled. Wilde saw two feet approaching – Geoff Lancing's size ten brogues below a pair of grey flannels with rather frayed turn-ups. The most welcome pair of shoes and trouser legs he had ever seen.

'Tom and Lydia – good God!' Lancing got down on his knees and tried to untie the cords. 'This isn't going to work. Stay there, you two.'

'Knives. Kitchen.' Lydia spluttered.

Lancing returned with a large carving knife and a sharpening steel. The rope was tough but after some deft slicing, Wilde and Lydia were shaking off the last of their bindings. Wilde rose to his feet, stretched his body and aching neck. Lydia slumped back on the sofa, panting.

'Thank God you turned up, Geoff,' Wilde said. 'It was your sister and Dexter Flood who did this. Had us at the point of a gun. But first things first – look.' He indicated the shelf.

Lancing reached out for the bottle. There was a small battery, a timer, a detonator, wires. He picked up the kitchen knife from the floor where he had left it.

'Careful! It might be booby-trapped,' said Lydia.

'Simple enough circuit,' Lancing said examining it from all sides. 'Clock's set for nine fifteen by the look of it. I'll just cut the wires.'

'Are you sure?' Wilde said. Then, thinking aloud, he contradicted his doubts. 'No. This thing wasn't left for someone to find; it was left to go off at a certain time. Go ahead, Geoff.'

Lancing slashed through the wires, ripped the strapped detonator and clock from the bottle, and then sighed with relief. 'Looks like I was right.'

'I should hope so – you're the bloody scientist. What made you come here?'

'Clarissa called me, said she wanted to meet me for coffee. I told her I had something on, which was true enough. She was so bloody insistent eventually I caved in. But I knew something wasn't right and I didn't go . . .'

'Well – I have a powerful feeling that she is heading for Boldbourne airfield with Flood.'

'Back to the airfield? Why?'

'To get away from England with a bag full of secrets.'

'Of course. As for the supposed coffee, I began to put two and two together like a good mathematician. I got to thinking about the Winch woman who held little Albert. She's a cleaner at the Cavendish.'

'I thought of that, too.'

'Clarissa said she wanted to meet me at nine ten precisely. Why that time? It's obvious - she was trying to save me.'

'Geoff, I called at the Cavendish before coming here, but Winch had already gone. I asked them to look around, but of course they'd never notice these little bottles - not among all the glassware and other lab equipment. Clarissa mentioned there were five other bottles.'

Lancing was already heading for the phone. He came back less than a minute later. 'Can't make a connection. The exchange seems to think there's a problem at the Cavendish end.'

'Then we'd better make tracks,' said Wilde. 'Lydia, call the police. Get Northgate and Tomlinson on the case. Most importantly, get them to bring the Winch woman along. If anyone knows where these bottles are stashed, it's her. Then call this number.'

He handed her Terence Carstairs's details. 'Tell him to give a message to Rowlands. Go directly to the Cavendish. We'll meet him there. Then follow us.'

Arriving in Free School Lane on the Rudge, it might have been just another day. Cambridge was going about its business, bicycles and workers everywhere. Shops were opening up; clerks were hurrying to their offices; hung-over undergraduates in gowns were dashing to lectures, dizzy with excitement at the thought of the long vacation ahead.

Wilde screeched to a halt outside the Cavendish. Ditching the bike, he and Lancing ran to the porter's lodge.

'The cleaner, Mrs Winch,' Wilde said. 'Where did she work?'

The porter - not the one Wilde had spoken with earlier - looked at him as if he was mad.

'Answer the man,' Lancing ordered.

'Here, sir.'

'Not the Mond?'

'No, sir.'

'New Austin wing?'

'No, sir, never. Not to my knowledge leastwise.'

'OK – well get everyone out,' Lancing ordered. 'Ring the bloody fire alarm – move, man, move!'

The porter hesitated no more than two seconds. He snapped to attention like a sergeant-major, set the fire alarm going, and then he and his assistant plunged into the labs and offices calling out for people to evacuate the building. 'This is not a bloody test! This is real. Get out now. Evacuate! Evacuate!'

Wilde and Lancing followed them into the heart of the building. Wilde looked at his watch.

'How long have we got?'

'Perhaps ten minutes.'

'And you think we're looking for five bottles?'

Wilde shrugged. That's what she said, wasn't it? In his mind he was weighing the leather bag he had carried on the journey back from Paris. Five plus the one left in Lydia's sitting room, that was about right. 'Yes,' he said. 'Five. It has to be five. And don't mess around. If you find one, just cut the bloody wires like you did before. Have you got a blade?'

'Trusty penknife. You know your way around, Tom. Let's split up.'

One tour of a large, complicated building did not mean he knew the way. 'It's six minutes past. Our bottle was timed for nine fifteen. We have a maximum of nine minutes, then we get out.'

'Wait, Tom. Take a few seconds. You were on the floor. They left the bottle above you. The contents of the bottle may be combustible – some sort of incendiary device. Or it might be released as a poisonous gas. In which case the only reason to place the bottle above you is if the gas is heavier than air. That means we should start at the top and work our way down.'

From the small office, Wilde hared up the stone staircase, two steps at a time. A grim corridor with rooms leading off, cigarette ash on the floor. Mrs Winch had obviously not bothered much with cleaning last night. He looked into each room in turn. The air was full of the clanging of a fire alarm bell and the sound of feet on stone floors as the young scientists obeyed the siren and hurried down to the exit.

This exercise had, of course, been drilled into them. No one could work here with all the high-voltage equipment and the potentially catastrophic experiments on radioactive substances without knowing that disaster was always on the cards.

Most of the rooms Wilde looked in were filled with jumbles of wires and untidy tables covered in glass and metal devices: it was impossible to an untrained eye to detect anything out of place. And then, on the second floor, he thought he spotted something amiss: a bottle perched on a shelf among a collection of large bulbs, test tubes, flasks and rubber tubing.

The room was still occupied. A young woman, slim, fair-skinned, peering through spectacles, was just collecting her handbag. Wilde ignored her and picked up the bottle.

He was right. He sliced through the wires then tore the detonator away from the bottle. Carefully, he set it aside beneath the window, where it would not be kicked and would be easily seen. One down. How many to go? Please God no more than four. This was like a hellish treasure hunt.

'What's that?' the woman asked.

'Just don't touch it. Don't break the glass.'

He tried to think. Why this room in particular? It was near a stairwell. If they were hoping the foul contents would seep down through the building it might mean the bottles would all be close to staircases.

'That's the second one of those I've seen today,' the young woman said. 'I saw one in the lecture theatre and wondered what it was . . .'

'Thank you,' said Wilde as he turned to run. 'Now *please*, get out!'

Suddenly the penny dropped. She nodded briskly and left.

He knew where the lecture theatre was. First floor. He ran there, barging his way past stragglers, and found the bottle immediately, right at the top of the high bank of seating. Once again, no ceremony; he simply slashed the wires and tore away the detonator. Two down. He looked at his watch again. Nine eleven. How accurate was the bloody thing?

Coming out of the lecture hall, he almost ran into Lancing. 'How many, Geoff?'

'One. You?'

'Two.'

'Thank God they're not well concealed. Have you tried the Nursery?'

'I don't think so. That's at the top, right?'

'Under the eaves.'

'You go there, Geoff. I'll go down to the ground. Just go up, one look – then down. Christ's sake, Geoff, whatever you do, don't hang around. Last sweep, OK?'

Wilde ran down the stairs. The porter was standing there by the front office. 'One of the research gentlemen found this, sir.' He held up one of the devices, still armed. Wilde carefully removed it from his hands and cut away the wires, clock and detonator. Four disabled. One to go.

He ran from room to room. A quick look in each, among the paperwork, the wires, the incomprehensible mass of equipment. Nothing. He strode back to the porter's office. He had failed. But at least everyone had been evacuated.

Everyone but Geoff Lancing. He couldn't leave the building while Geoff was still upstairs.

'The police are outside, sir,' the porter said. 'Detective Chief Inspector Northgate said he would like a word with you.'

'Advise him and his men to stand well back. Tell them to have the fire brigade and ambulances on standby. Tell him, too, that we don't know what is in these bottles so if they are carrying gasmasks, put them on. Our guess is poison gas, but it could equally be an incendiary device. I'm going up to find Dr Lancing.'

'Yes, sir.'

He came face to face with Geoff at the top of the second flight of steps. Lancing was ashen. He held up one of the devices, disarmed. 'This was in the Nursery.'

Wilde breathed out. 'That's five here, plus the one at *Cornflowers*. That must be it, please God.'

Lancing tapped his watch. 'I found this on the dot of nine sixteen. That's by my watch. The clock on the device said nine fourteen. My watch says nine eighteen now. If there were any more, they should have gone off by now.'

'I pray to God you're right.'

Outside the Cavendish, in the yard beside the Mond building, the physicists and their assistants were milling around, bewildered and somewhat amused by the scare. Tomlinson marched over to Wilde and Lancing.

'Now then, what's this about? IRA bombs, I suppose.'

'Something like that,' Wilde said. He looked past him to the large figure of Northgate, a man he trusted a great deal more than the officious John Tomlinson. He handed the Special Branch officer the bottle Lancing had removed from the Nursery. 'Whatever you do, don't drop that. Don't attempt to open it because it almost certainly contains a poison gas. There are four more in the building, all disarmed. There is also one at Miss Lydia Morris's house. We haven't heard any explosions, so we are assuming that none have gone off, that there are no others and that the building is now safe. But it would be advisable to leave it for at least an hour. Then bring in specialist chemists to take them away for analysis. Is that clear, Mr Northgate?'

Northgate nodded. He wore a grudging smile: *not bad for an amateur, Mr Wilde.*

At his side, the blood had drained from Tomlinson's already pale face.

Wilde walked away, through the arched gateway out onto Free School Lane, Lancing at his shoulder. Wilde was trying to calm his nerves. He looked left and right. A man in a dark grey suit with a regimental tie was walking towards him, cigarette in mouth, yellow silk handkerchief in his breast pocket.

'Ah,' he said. 'Are you Professor Wilde by any chance?'

'Guy Rowlands?'

'The very same.'

'Yes, I'm Wilde. And this is Dr Geoffrey Lancing, a senior man here at the Cavendish.'

'Well, I'm very pleased to meet you both,' Rowlands said briskly. 'Have I missed some sort of show?'

'That's one way of putting it.' Wilde tilted his chin towards the arched gateway. 'Detective Chief Inspector Northgate will fill you in. Just don't let him drop one of those bottles. Some sort of poison gas, we think.'

'You'll be hanging around, yes?'

Wilde looked at Geoff, who turned his gaze towards the Rudge Special.

'We'll be back soon enough. In the meantime, Miss Lydia Morris will be along any moment. She'll help. I'm afraid we have a plane to catch . . .'

CHAPTER 41

Wilde rode at high speed along the familiar roads south. He had picked up the Walther PP on the way out and felt its comforting weight in his pocket as he swerved and leaned through the bends. The Rudge was riding well today. In fine weather on a dry country road she was unbeatable.

He and Geoff had said nothing as they mounted the motorbike. They both knew where they were going. On a narrow lane close to Boldbourne, a farm wagon pulled by a tractor appeared as if from nowhere. Wilde didn't slow down, just left the road, bouncing along the dusty verge before slotting in again ahead of the vehicle. The front wheel rose as he accelerated away from the astonished tractor driver.

And then, at last, they were at the large tarmac area at the front of the airfield. Wilde skidded to a halt and looked around. If the police had ever been here, they were long gone.

'Over there,' Lancing said, pointing towards the grass runway at the other side of the buildings.

The Hornet Moth was taxiing forward. Even three hundred yards away, he could tell that two people were in the cockpit – Clarissa and Flood. And she was at the controls. As he watched, the little plane lined up for take-off, directly into the light wind. The throttle opened and she sped along the dry grass.

'Damn it.'

Could he race across the open airfield and block take-off? No chance. Wouldn't get there. Wouldn't work if they did. They'd all die. Even as his thoughts raced he realised it was too late: the Hornet Moth had become airborne and was gaining altitude. Nothing on God's earth could prevent them escaping.

'Damn.'

More even than his need for retribution, was the knowledge that they were carrying secret papers. Not all of them, because Wilde had secreted the most important portion in Horace Dill's rooms, but perhaps enough to give the Germans an edge. And now they were on their way to Berlin.

Wilde rode the Rudge the short distance to the hangar and looked in. There was no sign of last night's scene. No corpse. Only a dark patch where the body had bled. Lancing's yellow Sopwith was there, but it was out of commission. The engine casing was open, and parts were carefully strewn around.

'They'll have buried the body somewhere nearby. Come on, Geoff, let's go and find it.'

'No, Tom. Duxford.'

'What?'

'Duxford. I told my sister I had something on this morning. I didn't tell her what it was, but in fact it's an appointment with a rather fine little Supermarine Spitfire. I'm a little late – it'll be overheating. The Spits hate being on the ground too long.'

Wilde raised an eyebrow. 'Is this a good idea?'

Lancing threw up his hands. 'Maybe. Maybe not. What do you think, Tom?'

Wilde shrugged helplessly. What was the point in arguing? Leave it to the police to find the body. And the Hornet Moth was long gone. With a range of six hundred miles it could be heading anywhere. If Geoff wanted to go flying, that was his prerogative.

A sunny day in June. Cambridgeshire at its very finest. New green growth everywhere and the morning air fresh and warming up fast. On any other day, Wilde could have found nowhere finer to ride his Rudge Special, his superb and trustworthy 500cc motorbike, a racing champion.

He would have stopped beside a field of young wheat or barley, strolled to the edge of a copse with his binoculars and whiled away a couple of hours watching the larks and the lapwings, the buzzards rising lazily on the warm air, kestrels hovering and hunting for small rodents.

Not today. This morning he saw nothing but the road ahead and a speck in the distant sky. Was that really the Hornet Moth or was it just his imagination?

The Royal Air Force base at Duxford aerodrome was seven miles from Boldbourne. Once again, Wilde threw the Rudge into the bends with abandon. They arrived at their destination in under fifteen minutes. He did a quick calculation. The Hornet Moth cruised at about a hundred miles an hour, so it would already be twenty-five or thirty miles distant.

As he pulled up close to the flight hut, Wilde turned to Lancing, who was already dismounting from the pillion. 'Geoff, this is pointless. You won't stop them.'

'I want to see where they're going.'

'Damn it, Geoff, there's nothing you can do!'

'Nothing ventured, nothing gained, Professor Wilde.'

In the hut, Lancing was greeted by a Flight Lieutenant and a Flying Officer.

'When are you going to give up playing with test tubes and Bunsen burners and do the decent thing?' the Flight Lieutenant asked cheerfully.

'Next month at the latest,' Lancing said. 'I'm off for officer training.'

'Well, you'd better hurry – don't want to miss the war!'

Lancing donned his white flying overalls and helmet with headphones and mic, then strode with Wilde towards the Spitfire. It was attended by two men, the fitter and the rigger, one in shirt-sleeves with cap askew, the other stripped to the waist and streaked with oil.

'Morning, Dr Lancing. She's all ready for you.'

'Full tank, corporal?'

'Yes, sir.'

The engine was turning. The two ground crewmen assisted Lancing up on to the wing.

As he stepped into the cockpit, strapping himself into the parachute and safety harness, he glanced back at Wilde. 'Shame it's not a two-seater, Tom.'

'Don't worry – I've got enough to do down here.'

Lancing did his checks. Oil and coolant temperatures getting towards high, but still within the margins. RPM 1,000, cranking it up to 1,500. Switch mags on and off, thumbs up to the engineer, mask clamped to his face and wave away the chocks. Throttle open. Push stick forward to get the tail up. A blast of smoke belched from the exhaust stacks and the plane began to bounce out along its take-off path, weaving into the breeze.

Wilde watched him accelerate and then he was in the air. As the Spitfire arced into the sky, its undercarriage neatly retracting as Lancing pumped the hydraulic lever, Wilde wished he was going with his friend. The sky looked good today. Blue and clear and free.

He turned to the corporal. 'That thing isn't armed is it?'

'Lord, no, sir. No peas in the pea-shooter today. They're never kept armed. The only time there are any bullets on board is when the pilots have live ammunition exercises, which is rare.'

'Glad to hear it. By the way, what sort of chance would a pilot like Dr Lancing have if he was searching for another small plane?'

'Unless he knew exactly where he was going, none at all sir. Absolutely bloody none.'

Wilde watched the fighter plane until it disappeared, then turned away and walked back to his motorbike. He patted the black fuel tank. She might not be able to fly, but in her own environment there was none better.

Twenty minutes later, he arrived at the gates of the Hawksmere Old Hall estate. Slowly, he turned into the entrance and allowed the Rudge to crawl down the drive. The peacock he had seen on his first visit strode sedately across his path. Apart from that, there was no sign of life. In the forecourt, he stopped, raised the bike onto its stand and looked up at the old Tudor building. It really was magnificent; wasted on a man like Milt Hardiman. For some time it had been in the back of his mind that Albert might be held here. The boy Theo had had a friend – an imaginary friend so it was said – and Wilde had found himself wondering. But that had never been the case; Albert was held prisoner by a woman named Fanny Winch. At least he seemed to have been treated decently enough; that was a small mercy.

Wilde hammered at the front door. There was no response so he tried the handle. Locked. He walked across the forecourt, his shoes crunching the gravel, then onto the grass and around to the back where the marquee had been. It was no longer there. He looked down towards the boathouse and thought about Birbach and Fanny Winch. Had she really needed to play out her role so realistically? She had certainly succeeded in her task of luring poor Birbach into the waiting arms of her confederates. Wilde wanted to laugh at the absurdity of it all, if only the aftermath hadn't been so appalling.

Most of the windows at the back of the house were curtained or shuttered, but the main drawing room's curtains were drawn back so he was able to see inside. Everything was as he had last seen it. No dust sheets. They had left in the night in a hurry. Someone else would close the place up.

What, Wilde wondered, had become of their operatives – the drivers and the servants? Had they been supplied by the German American Bund? Perhaps they had been ordered to melt into anonymity in England and await orders some time in the future? That was something for Special Branch to look into.

He found a half-glazed door around the back of the house that looked as if it led into some sort of kitchen storeroom. It had been locked from the inside, the key still in the keyhole. Turning side on, he cracked his elbow into the glass, shattering it. He leant in and turned the key.

The room was a large larder or pantry with rows of tin cans on shelves, a couple of hams hanging from ceiling hooks and ranks of copper pans and kitchen implements. It led through to the main kitchens and thence into the main part of the house.

Wilde searched the house from top to bottom. When he first came here it had been full of guests and servants, chatter and music. Now it was empty and silent, save for his footsteps and the sound of his breathing. The door to Clarissa's room was closed. He turned the handle and hesitated, suddenly unwilling to face his own dishonour. But in he went, unable to rid his mind of the vivid image of her nakedness.

Her clothes were still in the wardrobes. Though the occupants of this house had been busy during the night they had had too little time to pack everything. Why should Clarissa Lancing care whether she ever saw these gowns and silks again? There were always plenty more to be had.

He searched the rooms one by one, all the time expecting to be disturbed by the arrival of visitors or servants. But no one came. Most of his time was spent in Milt Hardiman's study, hunting for papers. But all that remained were household accounts and shelves full of old books.

The only thing of note he discovered was a handwritten note on a pad by the telephone: *Queen Mary, Southampton.* Would the Hardimans really be welcome back in America? Wilde would call Jim Vanderberg; perhaps he'd be able to organise an FBI or police welcoming party for them. Whether he would manage to provide any evidence to hold them was another matter.

From the house, he rode the Rudge over to the outhouses. He saw signs of digging at the edge of the woods – the dog's grave, perhaps? In the barn, where the lights had been and where he had heard talking, he saw nothing at first. Some old farm equipment. Behind a handcart he found something that Eaton and Northgate had apparently missed – an ancient iron gas canister that looked as though it had been left over from the war. He sniffed at it. It smelt of rust and onions. Was this where they had held and killed Paul Birbach? If the idea had been simply to terrify him, it had worked too well.

There was nothing else for him here. He needed to get back to Cambridge to catch up with Lydia and Guy Rowlands. He wanted to check that the Cavendish had been properly cleared. He also wanted to know what was in the bottles.

As he headed back on the main road, a car came towards him, a battered black Ford Ten: nothing special. As it came nearer he narrowed his eyes. He had seen plenty of Ford Tens, but one particular one emerged from the depths of his memory; at the time it had meant nothing to him, parked in the modest confines of Swaffham Lane in Cambridge.

He studied it now with interest. The woman at the wheel wore heavy framed glasses. She was familiar, though he had not seen her in spectacles before. The three child passengers – one in the front passenger seat, the two smaller ones in the back, their hair slicked back rather than tousled – rang a bell, too. Well, well, Fanny Winch and her brood. He saw them, but they wouldn't have recognised him, not in his riding goggles.

A little way up the road, on a clear stretch, Wilde turned the motorbike around and began to follow them.

Geoff Lancing kept the Spitfire low. No more than five hundred feet. Cruising speed of two hundred and fifty miles per hour on a bearing of south-south-west. The Spit loved it up here. This was her natural element.

He knew his sister would cross the channel at St Margaret's Bay, a mere hundred miles from Duxford, and he knew that she would not be able to cruise at much more than a hundred miles per hour in the de Havilland Hornet Moth and was unlikely to fly at more than three thousand feet. He had flown the little two-seater himself, so he knew its range, its speed and its limitations.

Given that she had a head start of about twenty-five minutes, he reckoned that, if he was right in his deductions, he would catch up with her as she flew over the White Cliffs. If he was wrong, he would never find her.

His eyes scanned the horizon all the way south. He would never see her if she were below him, camouflaged against the Kent countryside with its patchwork of hop fields, orchards and oast houses. And so he kept low, skimming the fields, looking ahead of him and up. And then, suddenly, three miles ahead, and a couple of thousand feet above him, he saw a moving dot. Within half a mile, he knew he had been right.

She wanted to cross the cliffs at the exact spot where she had pushed Nanny Tobin to her death. Just as she had when flying Wilde to Paris. She couldn't resist the scene of her crime.

Lancing throttled back to a hundred and twenty and gained height. She wouldn't see him, of course. Only combat pilots searched the skies behind them. This was slow for the Spit, but Wilde knew her well enough to prevent her stalling. With his right hand on the stick, he pulled back the hood and felt a cool swirl of air on his face. Then he returned his left hand to the stick and took the pistol from his pocket with his right. Fittingly, perhaps, it was a German-made Luger, the weapon Tom Wilde had taken from the guard he overpowered at Boldbourne. A nice accurate weapon – and accuracy was necessary if this was to work. It was fully loaded, eight rounds in a box magazine. He flicked off the safety. He was good with handguns.

He estimated her at two thousand feet. Cutting his speed hard, he climbed as slowly as he could. He would have to be close, very close.

Gripping both the Luger and the stick, he pulled into a gentle climb, all the while throttling back with his left hand. He switched stick hands; it was a complicated manoeuvre, but he was a very good flier. His right index finger was feathering the trigger. He was ready. He let out the throttle a fraction and moved slowly towards the Hornet Moth, no more than thirty feet behind her, no more than twenty feet below.

They were well past the cliffs now, over the sea. In the distance, he saw ferries – one heading for England, one heading for France. He saw tankers and cargo ships, too. Trawlers and yachts. The Channel, as always, was alive with vessels.

The pilot and her passenger would never know he was there. Only at the last moment might they hear him above the din of their own engine and prop, but by then it would be too late. They were at the front of the little cabin, just above the fixed wheels of the undercarriage. The soft underbelly of the beast.

The Spitfire was directly below the Hornet Moth, flying at the same speed. He teased the Spit a fraction higher. He was dangerously close – no more than twelve feet below the cabin where his sister and Dexter Flood sat, blissfully unaware. He stretched his right hand, his gun hand, out straight above him, into the rush of wind above the screen. His breathing was short, his pulse racing. He felt sick at what he was about to do. He aimed a fraction forward, then pulled the trigger.

And again, and again. He emptied the magazine, left and right, varied placement to increase the chances of a hit.

The magazine spent, he let out the throttle hard with his left hand and returned his gun hand to the stick, thrusting it forward and down, away from the Hornet Moth. Once away from the other plane, he pulled back and began to rise steeply, a thousand, two thousand feet and climbing.

For half a minute, the Hornet Moth droned on below him as though nothing had happened, then it wobbled, its nose turned down and it veered sharply to starboard, spinning. There was no smoke, no sign of damage to the aircraft itself. Its nose was vertical by the time it plunged into the sea.

Lancing continued to climb, gazing down all the while at his prey. Was this how Clarissa had felt when she pushed Tobin to her doom? He thought not. He had seen the elation in her eyes that day. He, by contrast, felt only overwhelming sadness. This had broken his heart.

He leant forward and to the side and vomited into the cockpit beside his knee. He took deep breaths, then wiped his sleeve across his mouth and was surprised to see that he still had the Luger in his hand. He threw it out of the cockpit and watched it hurtling down until it hit the water and disappeared. Looking around, he tried to spot any trace of the Hornet Moth or her passengers, but they had vanished, down into the depths beyond the Goodwin Sands.

The black Ford stopped at a little petrol station on the outskirts of Royston. The attendant, in oily blue overalls, slouched towards the car. Wilde had pulled up on the roadside and watched as Fanny Winch wound down her window and told the man what she wanted. He nodded and made his way unhurriedly to the pump.

Wilde hitched the Rudge up on to its stand and walked to her open window. He bent down, raising his goggles onto his forehead.

'Mrs Winch.'

Shock registered momentarily and then she smiled. 'It's Mr Wilde, isn't it?'

'There are three children in your car. I presume they're yours. We don't want them to get hurt, do we?'

She took her hands off the wheel and held them up, palms towards him. 'You're right.'

'Then just step out of the car.'

She nodded. Her hands went down and for a moment he thought she was either reaching for a weapon or was about to drive off with the petrol cap open. His own right hand clutched the Walther in his pocket even tighter, but his grip loosened as she removed the key from the ignition, then pulled down the door handle. She turned to the children. 'You lot stay in the car. Ma's got to talk to this gentleman.'

The elder boy had recognised him. 'That's the one that took Bertie!'

'Just stay there and do as you're told.'

As she climbed nimbly from the car, she removed her spectacles. 'They're plain glass anyway – didn't do a lot of good, did they? Now then, how do we proceed from here? You know you're on the wrong side, don't you, Mr Wilde?'

'You have no idea what side I'm on.'

'Oh, I know a lot about you, sir. By rights, you should be my outrider, escorting me to freedom. But you're not going to do that, are you?'

'You shot Henty O'Gara.'

'He was a traitor. You know, Mr Wilde, they can put me away, like they did my man, but there are thousands more to come after us.'

The pump attendant ignored them. He didn't seem to have any interest in the world. Wilde signalled to him. 'Do you have a telephone? I need to call the police.' He pulled a florin from his pocket. 'Two shillings do you?'

Wilde inclined his head. Fanny Winch shrugged and followed him into the little office at the corner of the covered area. A mechanic was working under a car raised at a precarious angle on a pair of jacks.

She was a small, insignificant woman. Good-looking, but nothing more. Nothing in her appearance to warrant a terrifying name like the Scavenger. But if these past few days had taught him anything, it was that appearances can be deceptive.

'I'd never have hurt the little fellow, you know.'

The irony was not lost on him; or her, perhaps. She had held a child hostage to force Eva Haas to do the dirty work of others; now her own children were held hostage. She wasn't going to pull a gun on Wilde with them so close at hand. Nor was she going to endanger them with a car chase.

'I don't suppose you would have, Mrs Winch,' he said. 'But you'd have killed a great many people at the Cavendish Laboratory.'

'That's war, Mr Wilde.'

'It may be – but yours is over.'

CHAPTER 42

Tom Wilde attended two funerals that June of 1939.

The first was a bleak little affair at a Roman Catholic church in Cambridge, attended only by Wilde, Lydia, a priest and a reporter from the *Cambridge Evening News*. Philip Eaton had said he would have come, but he had not yet risen from his hospital bed.

Henty O'Gara was laid into the ground with a minimum of fuss. No one from MI5 turned up to honour him, even though he had died in its service. And in the next day's paper a short report said only that the IRA bomber responsible for the attack on the Thompson's Lane power station had been buried. It was believed by the security services that he had been killed by one of his own. Wilde had told Detective Chief Inspector Northgate that Fanny Winch had all but confessed to him that she was the killer, but she refused to sign a confession. There was plenty of evidence against her for her other crimes, but not for O'Gara's murder. Case closed.

The second funeral was, in fact, two funerals. Paul Birbach and Torsten Hellquist were laid side by side. Hellquist's body had been found in the woodland, less than a mile from Boldbourne airfield. He hadn't been afforded even a shallow grave by his killers, just dumped and left for the wild animals to pick at.

This double funeral brought out most of the scientists and research assistants from the Cavendish, as well as many dons from both their colleges. Arnold Lindberg was there, too, though he wouldn't be in England for long; word had reached him that he had been found a temporary position at Princeton in New Jersey by his old friend Leo Szilard.

In burying Birbach and Hellquist, Cambridge said goodbye to two of its finest minds. In truth, though, few among the mourners could really say they knew them. Geoff Lancing stood beside Eva, both their heads bowed. She had found her son a place in one of the town's best prep schools and was hoping for a place in the Cavendish. Geoff had confided in Wilde, however, that that wasn't going to happen; she wouldn't be accepted there. For whatever duress she had been under, she had knowingly colluded in torture and murder. Some might be prepared to let her behaviour pass; the Cavendish would not be so forgiving. Her presence among so many young men and women who had known the victims could not be forgotten. Perhaps Oxford or Birmingham or Manchester might be a better option? Wilde got the distinct impression that Geoff Lancing's interest in her was cooling.

Bobby had asked if he could go to the funeral. He had known Dr Birbach as well as anyone.

'Of course you must come,' Wilde said.

'Thank you, sir.'

'No, thank you, Bobby. You have helped me immeasurably in all this. Your head . . .'

Bobby touched the large bruise gingerly. 'Nothing to it, sir. Just like falling off a horse.'

As well as two funerals, Tom Wilde spent some hours at two bedsides.

Horace Dill was somehow defying the prognosis of his doctors. Every day Wilde called on him he expected to find him dead, yet somehow he struggled on. 'You're a shower,' he told Wilde. 'Ridiculous scrapes you get yourself into. Bloody shame you're not fighting for the cause.'

'Bollocks to you, too, Horace.'

Dill laughed until his lungs gave way and he started gasping for breath. He had wanted to visit his protégé Eaton, but Dill's doctor doubted he would survive the journey.

'Give him my love, Tom,' Dill said. 'He's a good man, better than you'll ever know. Bring him here as soon as he's up.'

Philip Eaton, meanwhile, was surprisingly cheerful given that he had lost his left arm and his left leg was in plaster. Both wounds were healing without complications thus far.

'Well, at least the military won't want me when the balloon goes up,' Eaton said to Wilde when the last of his visitors had gone.

'No, I suppose not,' Wilde said.

'Mind you, it'll do bugger all for my golf.'

Wilde managed a smile. So did Eaton. Stoical to the last.

'I did have one question for you, Eaton. How did you know to be in Switzerland waiting for Dr Haas and Dr Lindberg when they escaped across the Alps?'

'That's a good one. Yes, I'm afraid I rather fell for it. An agent I thought was one of ours alerted me. Now I suspect the German secret services were calling the shots.'

'Baumgarten? The man who helped Lydia?'

Eaton raised his right hand in a gesture of uncertainty. 'It's possible there were *two* German agents involved. What is certain is that at least part of our German operation is compromised. But that's my problem, Wilde, not yours.'

'Is that the best you can do?'

'I'm sorry, Wilde, but I *can* tell you that you did some good work in Cambridge.'

'Did I?'

'The attack on the Cavendish was authorised at the very top in Germany. Hitler wants to ensure that if an atom bomb is possible, he'll have it first. We're going to have to beat him to it. This incident has brought the subject to the fore. There may be other attempted attacks, but the big labs in France and the US will be on high alert. We won't be caught off guard again.'

'And what about my poor cousin?'

'Ah, that's something of a mystery. Henty O'Gara was controlled by an MI5 man, name of Captain Hyde, presently missing. It's rather feared the IRA must have got him.' Eaton shrugged. 'That's all I know.'

'I don't like the way Henty's being written out of history,' said Wilde. 'He hated the deal some of the IRA were willing to do with the Nazis. He was trying to stop them launching a major attack in which innocent people would have been slaughtered. Henty was a hero – a flawed hero, maybe, but he put his own life on the line. Many more people are going to have to do that, Eaton. How can we set the record straight? The newspaper report just writes him off as an IRA bomber.'

'*Realpolitik*, old boy,' Eaton said with a weary sigh. 'Just another unknown warrior, joining a pantheon of millions going back to the dawn of civilisation.' He nodded at his bandaged stump. 'And there will be more.'

The rain beat against Lydia's bedroom window. It was mid-afternoon and the sheets were bundled across her floor. They lay naked and spent, their breathing subsiding. Wilde thought he heard her heart beat in time with the pattering of the rain drops. He had asked her to marry him, but she had laughed.

'Let's set a date,' he said.

'War's coming, Tom. Gas bombs are going to rain down on us. What's the point in getting married?'

He chuckled. For as long as he'd known her she had told him she wasn't the marrying kind. But he no longer believed her. 'Well, I'm going to set a date. Middle of August. If you turn up, we'll be married.'

'And if I don't?'

'We can still share a bed. But if we get married, we can go to France on honeymoon. I want to see it properly. Paris . . .'

'Paris is dead in August.'

'The Riviera, Chamonix for some walking, perhaps the Pyrenees and Gascony? We'll make a month of it and travel around. A round tour, hugging the edges.'

'Then you'll have to get a car, because I'm not riding bloody pillion on the Rudge for two thousand miles.'

'Does that mean you agree to it?'

'I agree to the holiday.'

'Honeymoon.'

'You call it what you want; I'll call it what I want.'

The rain was growing heavier. The green of the ash tree outside her window dappled grey light on her walls and its leaves seemed more fresh and intense than he ever remembered. He was not a religious man but a line from school Bible classes would not leave his head. *Hath the rain a father?* A reminder, perhaps, of the smallness and insignificance of man in a time of iron armies and vain leaders? Let the world carry on; he would not be cowed by the gas bombs. Let them all rain down.

They had talked at length about her time in Germany. She was still puzzled by the question of the man she knew as Bloch, but who seemed also to be known as 'Baumgarten'. Who was he? If he was responsible for the abduction of Albert and the blackmailing of Eva, why had he helped Lydia escape Germany?

'Perhaps they just wanted you out of the way without any fuss,' Wilde said. He raised an eyebrow. 'You can be a bloody nuisance, you know . . .'

She elbowed him sharply.

It was a week since the attempted massacre in the Cavendish. Analysis had shown that the bottles contained the liquid form of a new gas that had not been seen in Britain before. From what Lydia had learned in Berlin, it seemed almost certain it was a new weapon devised by chemists at IG Farben. Frank Foley, the MI6 man in Berlin, had confirmed it to Guy Rowlands: the name of the new poison was sarin, named after its inventors, Schrader, Ambros, Ritter and von der Linde. It was designed as a pesticide but now it was in military hands and was about to go into large-scale production.

'Mustard gas was one thing,' Rowlands had said over drinks one evening. 'This is a poison of an altogether different order. Animal tests show it to be pretty devastating. It attacks the nervous system.'

'If only I could have found out more in Berlin,' Lydia said.

'Your information might yet prove invaluable, Miss Morris,' Rowlands continued. 'Through diplomatic channels, we are letting the German regime know two things – one, that we are aware of this gas and two, that if it is used against us we have the technology to respond in kind. They need to know that.'

As for Mrs Fanny Winch, she was languishing in Holloway women's prison awaiting trial for abduction of a child and attempted murder. Although there was suspicion of her involvement in the deaths of Birbach, Hellquist and O'Gara, there was no direct evidence. A pity, but the offences for which there was firm evidence were serious enough. She had been asked about the black car with the two men that supposedly took Paul Birbach from her house. She laughed at that. 'Kept you all busy that, didn't it?'

Her children had already been escorted across the sea to Ireland to be brought up by their father's family. The Hardimans, likewise, had been to sea, crossing the Atlantic aboard the Queen Mary and arriving in New York a few days later. The FBI was waiting for them and they had been taken in for questioning over the deaths of Birbach and Hellquist. There was evidence against them – a mustard gas canister with Hardiman's fingerprints on it, and the testimony of Eva Haas. But Milt Hardiman had expensive lawyers and was out of custody and the couple were back at their large estates in Old Westbury, Long Island, before the sun set.

The university of Cambridge, meanwhile, had closed down for the long vacation. The May Balls were over; picnicking by the Cam was now the preserve of town rather than gown. And in this rain, no one really cared.

The shadow of the recent events still hung over them like a pall. In particular, the fate of Clarissa Lancing. Wilde had not been able to get a straight answer out of Geoff.

'You couldn't have spotted the Hornet Moth, Geoff. What happened? Did you just fly on a bit and then turn back?'

'Think what you like, Tom.'

Wilde had been taken aback by the shortness of the response. He tried prodding him. 'I know bloody well the Spit wasn't armed, Geoff. So Flood and your sister must be in Germany by now, sipping glasses of schnapps with Adolf at his Bavarian mountain retreat. We'll probably spot them applauding him at Nuremberg in the September newsreels.'

'I rather doubt that. I think it's fair to assume that the Nazis have learned nothing from the Cavendish.'

And with that, Geoff Lancing made it clear that the conversation was over.

The following day Wilde had spotted a small paragraph on page 11 of *The Times*. AEROPLANE SPOTTED IN DISTRESS, the headline said. Apparently an elderly couple standing at the rear of the Calais-bound ferry had spotted a biplane falling from the sky in a tailspin, before plunging into the sea. The lifeboat had been sent out, but no sign of the plane was found, nor any debris or bodies. The report, Wilde noted, made no mention of any other aircraft being in the vicinity. Perhaps it was all a coincidence.

That afternoon, he encountered Geoff in Free School Lane, gazing at a snarling Staffordshire bull terrier that a boy was struggling to restrain. At first Lancing hadn't noticed Wilde, but then he looked up.

'Oh, hello, Tom, didn't see you there.'

'That dog looks dangerous.'

'I'd have it put down, wouldn't you?'

Yes, Wilde had thought. Yes I probably would. If I had a gun, I would shoot it. He wondered what had happened to the pistol he gave Lancing. 'That Luger, Geoff. What have you done with it?'

'Oh, I've got it somewhere, I think. Don't need it, do you, Tom?'

Something told him he'd never see the weapon again.

Now here, in this cool bedroom, Wilde's thoughts shifted back to gentler matters. His eyes were on the ceiling, the reflected light of a mirror playing games, weaving patterns that were never still for a moment.

'Who would you have as best man?' she asked, her voice husky and forgiving.

'Jim Vanderberg.'

'Of course.'

'Are we on then?'

She rolled over and stretched her slender body alongside his. Her right hand traced a line down his sternum to his belly. 'What if someone better comes along?'

'Then I'll just have to sack you, won't I?'

She beat her small fist on his chest. 'I meant for me, you swine! Bastard, you *knew* that's what I meant!'

'Come on, Lydia, do you really think there's someone better than me out there?'

She hit him again, then fell across his body and convulsed into gasping sobs. Tears fell like the drip-drip of the rain onto his chest.

'I hated being away from you,' he said softly. It was true. The voyage to America, the book tour, his mother's disappointment at not meeting her, the voyage home, all time wasted without Lydia by his side. And most of all, he had wanted to take her to Charlotte's graveside, to introduce them, for he knew that Charlotte would have approved.

'I love you, Tom,' she sobbed. 'I love you so much. But I had to do something. I just had to. All those poor children . . .'

'I know.' And he knew, too, that there would come a time when every decent man and woman in the world would be called on to do something, to face up to the gas, the trenches, the barbed wire, the tanks and the fission bombs. They couldn't leave it to God, the father of the rain, to bring down the tyrants; this was something mankind had to do for itself.

ACKNOWLEDGEMENTS

I am delighted to thank four remarkable people for the incredible assistance they have given me in my researches for *Nucleus*.

The first is Alan Fry, one of the cleverest people I have ever met, who has helped me understand a little about particle physics. If there are any mistakes in the book, they are mine not his.

The others three are all flying men: Willie Cruickshank and Al Coutts of the Wildcat Aerobatics team – www.wildcataerobatics.com – based at Old Buckenham Airfield, Norfolk, and Squadron Leader Mark 'Disco' Discombe of the Battle of Britain Memorial Flight at RAF Coningsby, Lincolnshire.

Willie and Al took me up in their Pitts S2B planes (which apparently perform and fly very much like Spitfires) and helped me devise a manoeuvre which has special significance for the story – but which I can't divulge here.

Disco Discombe, meanwhile, allowed me to crawl over the BBMF's prized Spitfires and spent hours explaining in wonderful detail how they worked and why they were so important to Britain's survival.

As always, it gives me pleasure to thank my wife, Naomi, and friends for putting up with me when the going gets tough in mid-book and I become difficult to live with. And, of course, my editor, Kate Parkin, and agent Teresa Chris, who do so much to smooth the rough edges of my work.

If you enjoyed *Nucleus* – why not join the
Rory Clements Readers Club by visiting
www.bit.ly/RoryClementsClub?

**Turn over for a message from
Rory Clements . . .**

Dear Reader,

Have you ever wondered what it is like to live on the brink of war? Today's generation has been fortunate thus far, but in the summer of 1939 my parents and their friends must have known that very soon they would have to stand against the Nazis to preserve the freedom of Britain and, ultimately, the world.

It must have been a terrifying experience, for the German war machine looked unstoppable – but how much greater would that fear have been if the young men and women of the free world had been aware that the race for a nuclear bomb had already started and that Germany seemed to be leading the field?

That is the frightening truth at the heart of *Nucleus*. My book is a work of fiction, but in reality Germany *had* achieved fission; they *did* start a nuclear programme in 1939.

However, this book is also about something much more human than war machines: heroism – true, unsung heroism of the old-fashioned kind.

There are my protagonists, of course. Tom Wilde and Lydia Morris are nothing if not brave. But in *Nucleus* there are also two real-life heroes who, in their individual ways, saved many thousands of lives, but whose names are now almost lost to history.

They are Bertha Bracey and Frank Foley. I imagine that if you walked down any street you would be hard-pressed to find a single person who could tell you who these two were or what they did. And that, to my mind, is a crying shame.

Let me tell you a little bit about them.

Bertha Bracey, a devout member of the Society of Friends (the Quakers), was born in 1893. After the First World War, she was a Quaker volunteer involved in feeding a million starving German children.

In November 1938, the terrible events of Kristallnacht made it clear that no Jew was safe in Germany. Bertha was one of those who persuaded an initially reluctant British government to take in 10,000 unaccompanied German Jewish children and provide sanctuary. For the next ten months she worked tirelessly organising the so-called Kindertransports, ensuring that every child was found a home and school in Britain. Those 10,000 children owed their lives to Bertha and her remarkable band of helpers.

Frank Foley also saved the lives of many thousands of Jews. His official role was Britain's Passport Control Officer in Berlin, but he also happened to be MI6 station chief – Britain's top spy in the city.

Jewish people were desperate to get out of Germany – and Foley broke all the rules to make sure they did, handing out visas at the slightest excuse.

He deserves a book in his own right, of course – and there is a brilliant one: *Foley*, by Michael Smith. Novelists, of course, are indebted to such books for their research. Those that have helped me are too numerous to list, but I would recommend *The Years Of Persecution* by Saul Friedlander to anyone interested in those dark days.

Which brings us back to 1939 and the impending war. If you enjoy *Nucleus*, I hope you'll keep an eye out for the third in the series. I haven't settled on a title yet, but it is set later the same year – at the very time the Nazis invaded Poland. Hitler was about to overrun Europe and many eyes were focused across the Atlantic to the USA. Would President Roosevelt step in to help the Allies with weapons and, perhaps, troops? The decision rested on a knife-edge.

If you would like to know more please visit www.bit.ly/RoryClements Club where you can join the Rory Clements Readers' Club. It only takes a moment, there is no catch and new members will automatically receive an exclusive extra chapter that throws more light on the events in *Nucleus*. Your data is private and confidential and will never be passed on to a third party and I promise that I will only be in touch now and then with book news. If you want to unsubscribe, you can do that at any time.

Of course, I would be delighted, too, if you could spread the word about my books. Online reviews are particularly welcome. I always read them!

Anyway, thank you once more for your interest in Tom Wilde and Lydia Morris and the world of 1930s Cambridge. I hope you enjoy reading the books as much as I love writing them.

With my best wishes,

Rory

Want to read
NEW BOOKS
before anyone else?

Like getting
FREE BOOKS?

Enjoy sharing your
OPINIONS?

Discover

READERS FIRST

Read. Love. Share.

Get your first free book just by signing up at
readersfirst.co.uk